PRAISE FOR THE HAN

'Jack Heath's writing grabs you by the t
and washes it all down with a hefty c
violent and oh so good. In Timothy I
one-of-a-kind character. I hope.'—Emma Viskic, internationally
bestselling author of *And Fire Came Down*

'Blake is a brilliant, complex character . . . this quiet and unas-
suming figure might just be the most dangerous man in the room.
Hangman is cinematic and grubby, brimming with pulpy noir.'—
Michael Offer, producer, *How to Get Away with Murder* and
Homeland

'Wild and original, *Hangman* stamps a high and bloodied mark
on this dark genre. Hannibal Lecter will be adding Jack Heath to
his reading list.'—Ben Sanders, internationally bestselling author of
American Blood

'Let's cut to the chase: *Hangman* is a great read! Jack Heath's
boundless imagination and singular voice have produced a truly
unique thriller. By turns psychologically insightful, wonderfully
disturbed and even darkly comedic, *Hangman* will keep you
coursing through the pages at a lightning pace. Brilliant! (Probably
best read with lights on and doors locked. I'm just saying.)'—Jeffery
Deaver, No. 1 international bestselling author

'*Hangman* is ghoulish fun, and fills the Dexter- and Hannibal-
shaped holes in our lives.'—*Books + Publishing*

'A grisly, efficiently written nail-biter packed with riddles and
suspense, *Hangman* has bestseller written all over it. It's a dark
book, but one with plenty of humour, and a twisty plot that keeps
you guessing to the very end.'—*Sydney Morning Herald*

'Compelling . . . Heath keeps the suspense at a high level through to
its stunning conclusion. An addictive and suspenseful thriller that
will keep you reading well into the night.'—*Canberra Weekly*

'Blake is a classic kind of hard-boiled hero, mixing cynicism and honour, brutality and sentimentality ... he's a chivalrous knight of the kind we have never seen before.'—*Weekend Australian Review*

'A cracking read full of well-crafted twists and turns ... Heath manages to bring Blake out from behind the shadow of his predecessors and stand on his own.'—*Australian Crime Fiction*

'Heath has given the crime world an anti-hero for this century. Gifted and flawed, Blake will horrify and entrance readers, quite often at the same time. An exceptionally taut novel both in action and execution, this sledge-hammer story is sure to entice fans of serial crime fiction, taking readers into the dark and dirty recesses of Blake's mind.'—*Good Reading*

'*Hangman* is a pulpy and perverse delight ... Heath makes Blake young, rough, streetwise, and precisely the sort of person Dr Lecter would avoid in the street. This is a gobsmackingly (or lip-smackingly) violent tale, but it is also bizarre, hilarious, and a stealthily astute commentary on post-financial crisis America. Give me more.'—Christopher Richardson

'Richer than Reacher ... *Hangman* literally tingles with tension, and Heath injects a healthy dose of dark humour.'—*Sydney Arts Guide*

'*Hangman* is cheerful in its gore, with a knack for unexpected violence that'll leave even the most jaded crime readers at least a little bit impressed ... It's all the best parts of noir fiction, all the spatter pattern ghoulishness of forensics-focused dramas, and so much fun it might just concern you a little bit.'—Hush Hush Biz

'Fantastic ... an immensely satisfying puzzle box, wrapped up in the unrestrained weirdness that I come to the Timothy Blake books for.' —Shelley Burr, author of *Wake*

'Between the brilliantly twisted mysteries and the biting social commentary, Jack Heath has delivered a self-aware evolution of the Dexter archetype for us to sink our teeth into.' —Shane W. Smith, creator of *Undad*

'Jack Heath writes killer reads.' —Tim Ayliffe, author of *The Enemy Within*

'An irresistible mystery, an insatiable antihero and shock twists galore; with *Headcase*, Jack Heath takes his Timothy Blake series to (literal) new heights, all the while making a puzzle-box plot with multiple strands look easy. Every new book in this gleefully dark saga is a ghoulish treat and this is no exception. Don't miss it.' —Gabriel Bergmoser, author of *The Hitchhiker*

'Thrilling, grisly and inventive: Jack Heath has single-handedly increased my carbon footprint through lights left on.' —Benjamin Stevenson, author of *Either Side of Midnight*

'Made me laugh, and also feel guilty for laughing . . . the growing tension is produced with great expertise.' —Penelope Cottier, *Canberra Times*

'Consistently thrilling. Heath knows how to write an engaging, edge-of-your-seat crime novel that walks the fine line between captivating and all out terrifying.' —novelteacorner.com

'There is something desperate and feral in this character . . . this is an undoubtedly entertaining thriller.' —unseenlibrary.com

'A chilling and sometimes confronting thriller which mines the darkest side of human nature . . . a book which engages the reader from beginning to end.' —Rod McLary, Queensland Reviewers Collective

'There's a level of focus, detail and nuance on offer that firmly placed me in the midst of this unfolding tale and I was riveted.' —Debbish.com

'Despite the darkness there is a nobility to Blake, and some satisfaction to be had in the way he goes after those more despicable than him, often putting his body on the line to do so. *Hideout* is another strong entry in this series.' —Robert Goodman, Pile by the Bed

ABOUT THE AUTHOR

Jack Heath is the award-winning author of forty novels for adults and children. His books have been translated into several languages, adapted for film and optioned for television. He lives on Ngunnawal land in Canberra, Australia.

Headcase contains scenes readers may find disturbing. It is unsuitable for children and some adults.

HEADCASE

JACK HEATH

ALLEN&UNWIN
SYDNEY • MELBOURNE • AUCKLAND • LONDON

First published in 2022

Copyright © Jack Heath 2022

Allen & Unwin
Cammeraygal Country
83 Alexander Street
Crows Nest NSW 2065
Australia
Phone: (61 2) 8425 0100
Email: info@allenandunwin.com
Web: www.allenandunwin.com

*Allen & Unwin acknowledges the Traditional Owners of the Country on which we
live and work. We pay our respects to all Aboriginal and Torres Strait Islander
Elders, past and present.*

 A catalogue record for this
book is available from the
National Library of Australia

ISBN 978 1 76106 523 1

Set in 12.5 on 17.5 pt Sabon by Midland Typesetters, Australia
Printed in Australia by McPherson's Printing Group

10 9 8 7 6 5 4 3 2 1

 The paper in this book is FSC certified.
FSC promotes environmentally responsible,
socially beneficial and economically viable
management of the world's forests.

For Anna and Russell, with gratitude

'If still you think me mad, you will think so no longer when I describe the wise precautions I took for the concealment of the body.'

—*The Tell-Tale Heart*, Edgar Allan Poe

CHAPTER 1

Now

I make your mind broader but your head smaller.
What am I?

'I eat people,' I say.

The psychiatrist doesn't blink. 'Tell me about that.'

Her office is plain. Just two low chairs facing each other, a box of Kleenex perched on a coffee table in between. There's a bookcase, but the shelves are bare. For no reason I can fathom, the only book in the room—a weathered copy of the *Diagnostic and Statistical Manual of Mental Disorders*, fifth edition—is on the carpet, *next* to the empty bookcase. The chairs are the squishy kind you sink way down into.

The room is structured to protect the shrink. If I became violent, I'd have to fight my way out of this chair and then go around or over the table. Plenty of time for her to reach into her open handbag, where there's a tube marked *lipstick* next to her iPhone. Real lipstick doesn't have the word lipstick printed on it, and she's not wearing any. I assume the tube is actually a taser.

Not that I'm much of a threat. A starving, one-armed malcontent.

'There ain't much more to say,' I tell her.

A slight smile. 'I find that hard to believe, Timothy.'

The psychiatrist's name is Renee Diaz. She's in her forties, with cracks around her brown eyes, and long black hair in a loose bun. She wears a double-breasted tan jacket over a black silk shirt, gathered at the neck. Not much meat on the top half of her, but her legs are thick. They'd keep me going for a while.

She doesn't look away, just watches me watching her.

'Why aren't there any books on your bookcase?' I ask.

She glances over, as though she didn't know she had a bookcase. With her head turned, I can see a diamond stud in her ear. 'I'm not sure,' she says. 'I'm not the only one who uses this office.'

'You could put that book on it.'

'Perhaps. But then I wouldn't be able to reach it from here.'

I wonder how often she consults the DSM-V in front of patients. Some might find it alarming, to see their doctor looking for them on a menu of damaged minds.

I remember hearing somewhere that the DSM-V was cobbled together in secret by a small group of doctors, most of whom had ties to drug companies. Many of the 'illnesses' are just commercials for the medications that treat them. I don't think she'll find my brain in there. What's wrong with me can't be fixed by a pill.

'You could move the bookcase,' I suggest. 'Or your chair.'

'I suppose. Is the furniture bothering you, the way it is right now?'

'No.'

A pause.

'I thought it might be a safety issue,' I add. 'Like you were worried patients might throw books at you.'

Again, no blink. This woman has nerves of steel. 'Is that the sort of thing you think about a lot?'

'I guess.'

She reminds me of a profiler I once worked with—a portly white guy named Kennard with a walrus moustache, an imperious manner and an addiction to being described as brilliant. He claimed you could examine the clues at a crime scene, decode the subconscious thoughts of the perpetrator, then catch him. To me, peering into the subconscious seemed like an unnecessary step.

All anyone needs to know about profilers is this: Kennard had a cannibal working alongside him for years, and never suspected a thing.

Diaz is still watching. I turn to the window. It's not barred, but the glass is reinforced by a sheet of sticky plastic, visible at the corners. If I hit it with a hammer or a brick, it might crack but wouldn't break apart. The garden outside is surrounded by a tall brick wall, mostly hidden by dense hedges. Other patients are carrying bags of fertiliser around, or turning soil with implements too short and too blunt to be efficient. Nothing sharp is allowed here.

A trim young man with a stubbly scalp is examining the trowel in his hand, the blade glinting in the sun. After a moment, he seems to sense me looking at him. He lifts his head and meets my gaze with one eye. The other is a dark, hollow socket.

'You mentioned eating people,' Diaz prompts.

I turn back to her. 'You heard that, huh?'

'Where do you think that urge comes from?'

'You're the psychiatrist.'

A wry smile. 'Do you remember the first time you felt it?'

'It's always been there,' I say. 'At the group home they said I was a biter. Mrs Radfield eventually beat it out of me, but that didn't stop me *wanting* to.'

I remember all the other kids waddling around, fat and juicy. After I aged out, I was homeless for a while, begging for change. I'd watch all the pedestrians walk past like a sushi train. When I started consulting for the FBI in my mid-twenties, I sized up every suspect, wondering if they'd fit in my freezer. I'm thirty-two now, and I still can't help seeing everyone as walking, talking meat. It seems unlikely that I'll grow out of it.

'You should keep me here forever,' I say. 'I can't be fixed. If they ever let me out, I'll hurt someone.'

Diaz puts her pen and notepad down, perfectly parallel to the edge of the table and to each other.

'Have you diagnosed me with something already?' I ask. Despite my view that psychiatry is mostly bullshit, I'm curious.

'Let's not worry about diagnoses just yet,' Diaz says. 'Let's just focus on feeling better.'

Imagine any other kind of doctor saying that. *Let's not worry about whether you have cancer or AIDS. Let's just focus on feeling better.*

'Why don't we start with your more recent history?' she says.

'How recent?'

'The events leading up to your stay here.'

Everyone says *stay*. Never *imprisonment*. Never *incarceration*. Like I won't notice all the locked doors, surveillance cameras and armed guards, as long as they keep pretending I'm here on vacation.

'Okay,' I say. 'Let me tell you about the astronaut.'

CHAPTER 2

Two weeks ago

What do you call a zero who goes into space?

It was almost nine am on Wednesday, and I was standing on Mars, looking at a dead astronaut.

He lay on the sandy dirt, legs spread, arms above his head, as though he'd been frozen during a dance routine, mid-leap. His face was mottled purple, like a squid. A mole on his cheek had turned black. Dark blood trickled from his ears, his nose, his lips, his eyes. I'd never seen anything like this.

I crouched next to the body. His helmet was off, but there was no smell of decay. I was starving.

'Remind me who you are,' Detective Jones said. He was a white guy in his fifties whose Houston PD uniform was a size too big. Like a kid playing dress-ups. He had a wedding ring, and his shoes had been recently shined. Clean-shaven, except for a single white hair growing from his Adam's apple. I wondered if he knew it was there.

Cops always made me nervous, even back when I was consulting for the FBI. I could never shake the fear that someone was about to wrestle me to the ground and cuff me.

'Timothy Blake,' I said.

'And you're here why?'

'I'm from ClearHorizon, an outside contractor working for the US Air Force.' I handed him a card. There was a glossy silhouette of a plane on one side and my name embossed on the other. 'We'll be revising the safety protocols so this doesn't happen again.'

I thought this sounded pretty good, but Jones didn't seem convinced. He looked me up and down. My suit and tie were new, but cheap. Ditto for my haircut, and my prosthetic hand. I had chipped teeth, and my accent was the type that an Ivy League college would have scrubbed off, had I attended one.

I didn't look much like a pampered, big-city consultant.

'So *what* doesn't happen again, exactly?' Jones asked.

'I'll leave that for you to determine, detective. I'm just here to observe.'

'I can't have you watching over my shoulder while I decide if this is a crime scene. You'll have to get back behind the tape.'

He had good reason to be territorial. We were at an astronaut training facility in the middle of the Johnson Space Center. This fake Martian landscape was surrounded by buildings owned by the federal government. It was only a matter of time before the FBI or the real air force turned up and tried to take control of the investigation.

'Sure thing,' I said, but didn't move. Agreeable could sometimes pass as obedient. 'Who found the body?'

'Uh, me.' Another man hovered a few feet away. He was in his forties, bald, Black. Thin legs and arms, but with a gut straining the buttons of his business shirt. I imagined his liver would be rich and buttery. Nutritious, too.

A rectangular sticker on his shirt said *Dr Franklin Anders*. He'd written the name in small letters, to make room for *Dr*. He looked sick with worry, the way most people did the first time they saw a corpse. Like they thought the reaper might still be nearby.

'You're one of these NASA poindexters?' I asked.

'I'm an atmospheric composition analyst,' Anders said, which was very much a yes. When he spoke, I saw he had a gold-capped tooth.

'What were you doing out here?'

'Nothing. I mean, I *wasn't* out here—I was at my desk. Sam Garcia spotted something on the sat feed and sent me to take a look.'

'Was the body positioned exactly like this?' I asked.

'Pretty much. I took his helmet off.' Anders gestured helplessly at the helmet, which lay next to a pile of dull red stones.

'Why?'

Anders swallowed. 'To see if he was still alive.'

I'd been told that the astronaut had fallen from the sky. But apparently Anders didn't believe that was what had happened. No point checking the pulse of a guy who hit the ground at terminal velocity.

I wasn't sure I believed it, either.

The dead man's space suit was white with blue nylon webbing and decorated with patches like a boy scout's uniform. The stitching was frayed in places, and the patches had faded, like the guy had fallen not just out of the sky but out of the past. The boots had velcro straps and scuffed, dirty heels. The rest of the body was clean.

Detective Jones hadn't yet noticed I wasn't retreating towards the tape—or he was waiting for the rest of his team to arrive, so there would be someone to haul me away while he stayed with the body. It was strange they weren't here already.

'What language is that?' Jones pointed at the patches.

Anders looked uneasy. 'Japanese, maybe?'

Jones grunted, frowning at the characters like he could read them through sheer willpower.

Anders was wrong. The text on the patches was Mandarin. That was why I was here.

At a data centre in Bluffdale, Utah, giant supercomputers trawl through a vast, ever-changing ocean of information. Emails, text messages, phone calls, photographs, videos, flight records, credit card transactions, 401(k) payments and a thousand other metrics. The web, the dark web, the deep web and whole other continents of cyberspace that don't even have names. Churning through all this are algorithms no human understands because they were created by other algorithms. They connect keywords, people and places via unknowable means and dredge up anything the Central Intelligence Agency might be interested in.

Early that morning, the AI had intercepted a text message about a space launch in Guizhou and an email that mentioned a spy satellite. Both were then linked to a phone call between the Houston Police Department and Sam Garcia, a communications engineer at the Johnson Space Center, reporting that a Chinese astronaut had crash-landed in their Martian training area.

That was bad news, and not just for the astronaut. Officially, there were only nine people in space. Four Americans, three Russians, a Japanese woman and a French man.

All alive and well. This corpse was a mystery—or, as the CIA branch chief put it, 'an intelligence failure'.

I'd been sent to talk to Sam Garcia, because I knew him, and what he'd done. But first I wanted to see the body. For purely professional reasons.

'You're an atmosphere scientist,' I said to Anders. 'Is this what the vacuum of space does to a person?' I gestured to the astronaut's bruised skin.

Anders looked panicked. 'I really couldn't say.'

'Was the helmet attached properly?' I asked.

'I guess? It was hard to take off, at least.'

'It didn't look defective, or damaged?'

'Not in any obvious way.'

I lifted one of the astronaut's arms, feeling the flesh through the fabric. Fat is liquid at ninety-eight degrees, the temperature of a living human. After death, the body cools, and the fat firms up. This guy had a good amount of it, padding the muscle.

'I need you to step back,' Jones snapped. His hand was on his belt, near the pouch that held his handcuffs.

I laid the arm back down. 'Well, the impact didn't kill him.'

'How's that?'

'If he was alive when he hit the ground, he'd have tried to protect his head with his arms. They'd be broken. His legs, too. And he wouldn't have landed face up.'

'He could have bounced. Bodies do that. I've seen it many times.'

I bet he had. Cops spend more time dealing with suicides than murders, and Houston has plenty of high-rise buildings.

'On concrete, sure. Not here.' I prodded the soft dirt with my shoe. 'This surface would have absorbed the force. Is it possible that his suit malfunctioned during a spacewalk, or something? So he asphyxiated and then fell off his spaceship?'

'Everything you're saying is impossible,' Anders said.

We both looked at him.

'Firstly, astronauts are tethered during spacewalks,' Anders said. 'And if one became untethered somehow, they wouldn't "fall". They'd spin off into space. Secondly, no astronauts are missing. There's no way to get astronauts into orbit secretly.'

I thought he might be surprised what the CIA has done in secret, but I said nothing.

'Thirdly, what are the odds he would land here?' Anders continued.

Detective Jones cocked his head. 'Meaning what?'

Anders gestured at the field around us. 'If he was on a ship orbiting Earth, he could have landed anywhere on the planet. The ocean, the Sahara desert, Antarctica, wherever. The Earth's surface is 196 million square miles, but he landed right in the middle of the Johnson Space Center. Doesn't that seem like a hell of a coincidence?'

He was right. A cold wind tugged at the collar of my shirt. I tightened my jacket, thinking.

'Even if you ignore all that, why didn't he burn up on re-entry?' Anders asked. 'Orbital velocity is at least 17,000 miles per hour. Hitting the atmosphere at that speed creates a tremendous amount of friction. That's why shuttles have heat shields.'

'Maybe he got frozen and the heat just thawed him?' Jones said thoughtfully.

That seemed unlikely to me. In a frying pan, frozen human flesh doesn't thaw—it chars. I studied the fabric of the space suit. 'What's this made of?'

'Kevlar,' Anders replied. 'Like a bulletproof vest. It protects the astronaut from micrometeoroids.'

'Could that explain why he didn't burn up?'

'No,' Anders said, looking annoyed.

'What's the visor of the helmet made of? Glass?'

'Polycarbonate, but it's only an eighth of an inch thick, and it's designed to withstand pressure from *inside* the suit, not outside. Even if the visor somehow made it through re-entry intact, it would have cracked when he hit the ground.'

Everything Anders said made sense. But there was something off about the way he spoke. Urgent, worried. Glancing at me and Jones to read our reactions. Like he was keen to convince us.

I'd already established that none of the astronauts who trained here were missing, and no Chinese astronauts had been visiting the complex. The Johnson Space Center was surrounded by a daunting security fence. If this guy hadn't fallen out of orbit, then who was he, how did he get here, and what killed him?

I kneeled next to the corpse's head. I'd never seen a body with bruising like that. Maybe it tenderised the meat. The hunger grew and grew.

Don't, I told myself.

A van pulled into the parking lot in the distance. There was a satellite dish on the roof and a rainbow peacock logo on the side. The door rolled open and a woman climbed out, carefully, so as not to stretch her pencil skirt. She had a microphone and a bouncy mane of red hair. A burly guy wearing a wool cap followed, a huge camera on his shoulder.

'Uh oh,' I said. 'MSNBC is here.'

As Jones and Anders turned to look at the van, I leaned towards the dead man's ear, and opened my jaws wide.

'Did you call them?' Johnson demanded.

'Hell no!' Anders sounded alarmed. 'I haven't talked to anyone!'

I was already standing up again. 'I'll leave you to it,' I mumbled. It was hard to talk with the dead man's earlobe tucked into my cheek.

I had intended to save it for later. But the taste was overwhelming. Unable to resist, I crushed it between my molars as I walked off. It was plump and juicy.

This meat hadn't been frozen, nor burned.

'Mr Blake,' Jones called.

I pretended not to hear.

'Mr Blake!'

I looked back at him and raised an eyebrow.

Jones held up the card I'd given him. 'Don't leave town.'

He was smarter than he looked. I nodded, like that wasn't a problem.

'You're bleeding,' Anders said.

I wiped the trickle of pink drool off my chin and swallowed. 'Sorry. Root canal, this morning.'

The simulated Martian landscape ended a hundred yards away. Soon I was walking across the dead grass that made up the rest of the field. I was headed for the parking lot, but I took the long way around, not wanting to end up on the news.

Partway there I saw a depression in the ground and paused for a closer look. It was a footprint.

There had been no footprints in the Martian soil except for mine, Anders' and Jones'. I realised now that there should have been, if people trained there regularly. Someone had swept the area around the body, obscuring any tracks.

I crouched next to the print. In real life it's usually impossible to identify a shoe from a print outdoors. This print was smudged, incomplete and mostly hidden by flattened grass. But I could tell it had been made by a large shoe. The print was pointed towards the body, and it was recent. A mayfly had been squashed by the sole and hadn't yet been devoured by other insects.

Someone had found the body before Anders had. And instead of telling anyone it was there, they had simply swept the dirt clear.

CHAPTER 3

Where does a space station make a choice between two bits?

'The branch chief is riding my ass,' Zara said. 'He wants to know if there really are Chinese astronauts in orbit, and if so, how long they've been up there. Everyone's losing their shit. What have you got?'

She sounded distracted, like I'd caught her in the middle of something. I couldn't tell what, because the software that encrypted the call also eliminated background noise from her end, and I had the car stereo cranked up on mine. The cheery babble of advertising was supposed to thwart eavesdroppers.

The commercials themselves were fake, running from a hidden app on my phone. They had been recorded in a CIA studio—apparently real commmercials could be filtered out too easily.

From where I was parked, I could see Jones and Anders still arguing in the distance. The body itself was hidden behind a slight rise in the dirt. The media had stayed behind the tape, so far.

'I'm not a rocket scientist,' I said. 'But Franklin Anders, the guy who found the body, thinks it's impossible. And he's one of these NASA nerds. He'd know.'

'Anders? I sent you to talk to Sam Garcia.'

'He's next on my list.'

'You don't have a list,' Zara said. 'I gave you one name. A single item is not a list.'

I kept silent. The radio made a valiant attempt to sell me a tumble dryer.

Zara let it go. 'If the guy didn't fall off a secret space station, where does Anders think he came from?'

'He doesn't know,' I said. 'But if you get me the rest of the body, maybe I can figure it out.'

'"Rest of"?'

'I, uh, only got to see him from the neck up.'

Zara sighed. 'Sorry, Blake. There are too many eyes on this. It's about to turn into an international diplomatic catastrophe.'

She didn't sound scared. Zara was a seasoned CIA agent, well used to catastrophes. We first met three months ago, when she'd been undercover among a group of psychopaths who sold torture porn on the dark web. After I blew the operation, she could easily have disappeared. Instead, she came back to recruit me for special off-the-books jobs. Usually domestic intelligence gathering, which was supposed to be done by the Department of Homeland Security, not us.

She'd promised me food and still hadn't delivered.

I said, 'Someone else found the body before Anders did.'

A squeal broke through the noise suppression on Zara's end of the call. A cat wailing, or car tyres screeching. I heard

16

a thud, like maybe Zara had closed a window, and then she was back: 'How do you know?'

'I found a footprint. From a big shoe.'

There was an unimpressed silence.

'The body was positioned face up,' I added. 'Like someone had rolled him over.'

'You don't work for the FBI anymore. You're an Agency asset. I sent you to talk to Sam Garcia, not to play CSI. Hurry the fuck up.' The line went dead.

This case was personal for her. We'd been in Los Angeles last week, and followed a target into an underground nightclub. While we were there, someone else had tipped a small vial of colourless fluid into Zara's absinthe. I'd stopped her from drinking it just in time, but the perpetrator had escaped into the crowd, and we hadn't been able to identify him. Zara suspected the Ministry of State Security—China's equivalent of the CIA—had been behind the attack.

A few years ago, a key CIA communications channel was compromised, exposing dozens of American assets in China. They were caught by the MSS and executed. Our whole network went dark, all at once. All the CIA agents I'd met talked about this event like it was 9/11— although, to be fair, they also talked about 9/11 like it was 9/11. The old guard were still around, shellshocked and paranoid. They remembered how suddenly an intelligence failure could lead to things like bodies falling from the sky.

Zara only had one asset left in the People's Republic. The identity of that asset was the most closely guarded of all her many secrets.

Emboldened, the Chinese Communist Party cracked down on civil rights in Hong Kong, testing the waters. Washington remained silent, so the CCP started eyeing off Taiwan. It had once been part of China, and the CCP wanted to reunify the country. But the US didn't want to lose such an important ally in Asia. Both sides edged closer and closer to war.

And now a body in a Chinese space suit had been found at NASA. The world might be one step closer to nuclear annihilation if we didn't figure this out. Or even if we did.

It was hard for me to care about any of this. My son was dead. The love of my life had left me. But if we were all going to die, I didn't want to die hungry. Since Zara wouldn't give me this body, I would have to find another.

A car pulled up next to me. I glanced over. The occupants were both men, white, wearing sunglasses and dark blue windbreakers. The FBI had arrived.

One of them clocked me, and I looked away, too quickly. Out of the corner of my eye, I could see he was still staring. I tapped at my phone a few times with my good hand, as though putting an address into the maps app. Then I mounted it on the dash and started the engine. I checked my mirrors as conscientiously as a student driver before I reversed.

I wasn't supposed to be here. Officially, the CIA didn't conduct clandestine operations on US soil. If I got caught, I'd be on my own. Burned, in their parlance.

As I pulled out of the parking lot, I finally glanced back. The FBI men were getting out of their car, neither one looking at me. I told myself they were low-level agents, just here so their field office director could claim there had been interagency cooperation with the Houston PD.

But Zara was right. I needed to hurry the fuck up.

•

The Johnson Space Center was nicknamed Space City, and I could see why. There were at least a hundred buildings, including hangars, warehouses and office blocks. Well-maintained roads, some four lanes wide, connected everything. Cyclists in Spandex pedalled furiously, some almost keeping up with the cars.

The complex was surrounded by a mixture of flat fields and dense woodland. Maybe the radio equipment needed some distance from other built-up areas to work properly. One of the fields had a pair of longhorn cows in it. I wondered if that was part of an experiment. They've sent dogs into space—why not cows?

It had just gone nine-thirty, and gaggles of pedestrians with lanyards and go-cups were everywhere. They must all have been workers, since none glanced up at the decommissioned aircraft that lined the roads, mounted on poles with brass plaques affixed to them.

I could see police cars in the distance, clustered around a giant airliner like remoras around a shark. Detective Jones would be pissed when he realised the rest of his team had gone to the wrong place.

Most Texans drove one-handed, but that didn't mean it was easy, even in an automatic. There were three left turns between me and my destination, each tight enough that I had to slow way down to work the wheel. I parked in a lot outside a sleek monolith of glass and steel, three levels high, where a sign said *Atmospheric Research Unit*. As the crow flies, it wasn't far from the Martian training area, but there was no direct line of sight. Hopefully Jones assumed I'd left the complex.

As I was fumbling with the seatbelt, some more media approached me. A tall Latino guy with a jawline that could cut glass, and a white woman with a clipboard and a headset mic who was probably his producer. Behind them was a cameraman who looked exactly like the one from the first van. Probably grown in the same vat. The camera had the peacock logo on it—I wondered why the same company had sent two teams. Maybe this one was for B-roll footage or something.

'Excuse me, sir?' The guy with the jaw tried to flag me down as I got out of the car.

I wanted to know who'd tipped off the media, but there was no way he'd tell me. 'No, thank you,' I said, heading towards the sliding glass doors at the front of the ARU.

He followed. 'Our colleagues saw you talking to the police earlier.'

The burly camera guy swung the lens to face me.

I kept my head down as I walked.

'Is it true that it's a Chinese astronaut?' Jawline asked.

Apparently the story was well and truly out. Zara wouldn't be happy.

'Shit,' I said, knowing they wouldn't use any footage with coarse language. The sliding doors opened for me, and I escaped through.

The lobby of the ARU was fittingly airy and well lit. Potted plants soaked up the early spring sunshine near the windows. Behind a curved blue desk sat a forty-something receptionist with several earrings, nose rings, eyebrow rings and a tongue ring. He probably spent his whole life avoiding magnets.

'Timothy Blake,' I said. 'Here to see Sam Garcia. He's on level three, right?'

'Yep.' The receptionist pushed a visitors' log across the counter.

I was still getting used to writing with my left hand, and without a thumb. I had to clench the pen like a toddler with a crayon. My signature was a meaningless squiggle.

There had been no other visitors that morning. 'Can I see yesterday's log?' I asked.

'Why?'

'To see who visited.'

'Are you police?'

'Security consultant.'

'Right. Yeah, I'll run that request up the chain,' the receptionist lied. He gave me a swipe card. 'You have visitor-level access privileges across the complex. If a door won't open for you, that's because it's not supposed to.'

I don't like elevators, so I took the stairs. On my way, I dropped the pen into my pocket. I never turned down free stuff. My years of homelessness and starvation were still too fresh in my memory.

Level three had tough grey carpet, the dense weave gripping the soles of my loafers. The doors were maroon-painted wood with silver brackets holding nameplates—the kind you could slide in and out whenever someone got promoted or fired. I passed one that said *Franklin Anders* and paused. Anders had seemed like he was hiding something, and he was still on Mars. Now would be the perfect time to snoop around his office.

I tried the handle. Locked.

'Can I help you?' said a voice from behind me.

I turned. Sam Garcia had huge hands, a heavy brow and a receding hairline. His tie looked like a clip-on. His broad shoulders were straining the seams of his short-sleeve polyester shirt. The faint spiderweb patterns on his arms might have been mistaken for veins, if you'd never seen the inside of a human arm. I was pretty sure they were the remnants of tattoos that had been lasered off.

He'd bulked up a bit since I'd seen him last. It was almost impossible to get fat on prison meals, but candy bars and soda were available from the commissary, and most inmates didn't get much exercise, so they often gained weight.

His eyes widened. 'You.'

'Me,' I said.

He looked around, as though worried someone might see us together. 'What do you want?'

He had a deep voice. That usually meant nice, fatty vocal folds at the back of the throat.

'I want to talk about the body,' I said.

'FBI send you?'

'No.'

He nodded slowly. 'Follow me.' As he turned away, I noticed that one of his socks had two big holes in it, like the very hungry caterpillar had gone through it.

His office was only a few doors further up. He held the door open for me, and I walked in. A big window overlooked the rest of the complex. Most of the buildings were only one or two levels, so I could see a lot of rooftops with satellite dishes and solar panels.

As Garcia entered behind me and closed the door, I took in the rest of the room. Half his desk was taken up by three computer monitors, side by side, and the other half was filled with photos of him and other men in waders, holding giant fish and grinning. I'd never understood why hurting animals for fun was considered an early warning sign of serial killer behaviour, while fishing and hunting were seen as healthy male bonding activities.

I only had a second to note all these details before Garcia's knuckles crashed into my ear.

CHAPTER 4

What do you call it when you lift an armed robber?

I didn't scream. I'd learned that lesson early in life. As I stumbled sideways into the wall, knocking down a whiteboard covered with Greek letters, I was already recalculating. I hadn't expected this reaction. Some of the criminals I'd put away were angry, sure—but most were too shamefaced to actually attack me, particularly in their workplaces.

I couldn't fight Garcia. He was too big. 'Hold up,' I said.

He didn't. He twisted his core like a batter swinging for the stands and drove his other fist into my stomach. The air exploded out of me, along with a good deal of spit and blood. I hit the floor, wheezing.

Garcia aimed a stomp at my chest. I waited for him to lift his leg all the way up, then twisted around and kicked his other ankle. He yelped as he fell ass-backwards onto the carpet. I scrambled over and went to grab his throat, but without a thumb, I couldn't clench it.

He swiped my hand away, and then gripped my other wrist, trying to pin me. The snap fasteners around my

24

shoulder popped and my fake arm came off at the elbow, the loose straps slithering out of my sleeve.

Garcia dropped the prosthesis, alarmed. It wasn't one of the expensive ones that could clench and unclench. The hand was just limp silicone, like I was part sex doll. Still, it was the same colour as my skin, and most people didn't look closely enough to notice that it wasn't real. Apparently it had fooled Garcia.

I could see him deciding whether or not he was the kind of man who would beat up a cripple.

'You finished?' I wheezed.

After a beat, Garcia nudged the prosthesis across the floor towards me with his shoe. 'I haven't done anything wrong.'

'Other than just now? And seven years ago?'

'I served my time. You can't harass me like this.'

I clambered to my feet and picked up my prosthesis. I wasn't about to take my shirt off, so I just pushed the fake wrist back into my sleeve and buttoned the cuff to hold it in place. Buttons were hard without a thumb—I clamped the fabric between my teeth to keep it still.

'There's a body,' I mumbled as I worked. 'You're a felon. You didn't expect a visit?'

'You said you weren't with the FBI anymore.'

'It might have been wise for you to ask some follow-up questions before you—'

Someone knocked on the door. Garcia shot me a look and then said, 'Yeah?'

A woman opened it. Forties, squat, lots of make-up, greying hair cut short. 'Everyone okay in here?'

Garcia forced a smile. 'We're fine.'

The woman looked uncertainly from him to me and back. 'I thought I heard . . .'

'Mr Blake was helping me move my desk, but we bumped the whiteboard.' He gestured to the fallen panel.

She seemed to believe this. 'All right. Holler if you need anything.'

'Thanks, Grace.'

The woman disappeared.

'She's helpful,' I said.

'Amazing Grace, we call her.' His eyes were hard. 'Who are you working for, Blake?'

'I'm a security consultant.'

'Uh-huh.' He looked doubtful.

I wiggled a finger in my sore ear, looking out the window at the matrix of square buildings. 'I don't see a launch pad.'

Garcia rubbed his knuckles. 'We don't do launches here. We train astronauts, design their equipment and run comms for spaceflights. You know, "Houston, we have a problem?" We're Houston.'

'What's your job?'

'Data transmission. I maintain secure connections between satellites and ground systems.'

'I'm amazed NASA hired you, given your background,' I said.

The corner of Garcia's mouth twitched.

'They don't know? How'd you hide it?'

'A friend from college works here.'

'He erased your criminal record?' That was mid-level treason, right there.

'He didn't erase anything. My name was automatically flagged. He unflagged it.'

'So the recruitment officer wouldn't delete your application without reading it?'

'Right.' Garcia sat down on his swivel chair. His bulk made the desk look tiny, like you'd see in an elementary school classroom. 'I was ready to explain everything, but they just hired me, no questions asked. Guess they didn't read past page five.'

'Who was this friend?'

'What do you want, Mr Blake?'

I sat opposite him. 'Firstly, I want to know why you told the 911 dispatcher that the body was Chinese.'

'I just told her what Franklin Anders told me.'

'Anders seemed to think the body was Japanese.'

'Oh.' Garcia shrugged his big shoulders, like the difference didn't matter. 'That would make more sense, I guess, since there *is* a Japanese astronaut in orbit right now—but Mission Control would have heard about it if anything had happened to her. And didn't you say the, uh, body was male?'

I hadn't said that. 'You're not saying you think the corpse actually came from space?'

'I heard his face was swollen and purple, and he was bleeding from both ears. That's what happens if your space suit leaks.'

'Anders told me it was impossible.'

'Did he?' Garcia looked thoughtful.

'He said no one could get an astronaut into orbit in secret, and that the guy would've burned up on re-entry.'

Garcia's chair squeaked as he leaned back. 'Maybe he was aiming to dock with a space station, and he got beyond the atmosphere, but failed to reach orbital velocity? His suit could have been punctured when he bailed out. His rocket's probably at the bottom of the Pacific.'

It still sounded absurd to me. 'And his body landed in the middle of a NASA training field?'

'On a long enough timescale, the unlikely becomes inevitable.' Garcia sounds like he's quoting someone, but I don't know who. 'We've had sixty years of human spaceflight, and plenty of strange things have happened.'

'As strange as this?'

'Look, I'm just a communications engineer. If you want a better theory, you'll have to talk to an actual rocket scientist.'

'I'm told you spotted the corpse on a satellite feed?'

'Actually I saw him out the window, but he was just a tiny speck. Could have been anything. There's a weather satellite that passes right over us, so I checked the feed for a better view.'

I looked back at the window. The Martian training area was visible, but it was a long way off. I wouldn't have noticed a tiny speck out there—and I was very observant. 'What time was this?'

'Um . . .' Garcia tapped on a keyboard and pointed at one of the screens. 'I checked the most recent aerial photograph at seven thirty-one.'

'Are you always here so early?'

Garcia gave me a searching look. Like he was trying to work out if I already knew something.

'My wife served me with papers six months into my sentence,' he said finally. 'So I come in early. No sense hanging around in an empty apartment. My colleagues are my family now.'

This was exactly what you'd expect the boss to say

at a farm, or a restaurant, or an auto shop. In an office environment, it came off as creepy. Office drones were interchangeable. They weren't supposed to care about one another.

I noticed Franklin Anders in one of the fishing photos on Garcia's desk, holding up a tackle box. Grace was in another, and I could see the receptionist from downstairs in the background.

'Six months?' I said. 'That's fast. Was she already seeing someone else when you went away?'

When I looked back at Garcia's face, I was startled to see tears in his eyes. Apparently the wound was still raw.

I wasn't going to waste any sympathy on a man like him. 'Could the body have been here yesterday?'

Garcia took a deep breath, steadying his voice. 'No. I went back and checked yesterday's pictures.'

'Email them to me,' I said.

'No can do. Space City is on an air-gapped network, for security. We can send files from one building to another, but nothing touches the internet.'

'All right. Just show me.'

Garcia used a swipe card to log into his computer, tapped at his keyboard for a minute, then swivelled one of the monitors around. There was the body, lying in the middle of the field. From that height, it didn't even look like a person. More like a tiny white starfish.

'So this is at seven-twenty this morning.' Garcia clicked. 'And this is ninety-five minutes earlier.'

The screen was black.

'Your satellite can't see in the dark?' I asked.

'Correct.'

'Why ninety-five minutes?'

'That's how long it takes to go around the world and take another picture.'

'Pretty limited.'

'Well, if you think you can do better, feel free to design, build and launch your own satellite.' Garcia clicked back a few more times, and the field reappeared. 'Sunset yesterday: no astronaut. So he must have landed during the night.'

'Or he's just some guy who climbed the fence.'

Garcia shook his head. 'The fence is surrounded by cameras that *can* see in the dark. And even if he somehow avoided them, then what? He walks into the middle of the rock yard and suddenly dies of decompression sickness? Now *that's* impossible.'

I thought of the text message about the space launch in Guizhou, and the email about the spy satellite. 'How hard would it be to get something into space in secret?'

'OPIR—Overhead Persistent Infrared surveillance— is designed to detect rocket launches. But if you set off some other explosions nearby to confuse the signal, and if you had total control of the local media, and the capacity to arrest anyone who asked too many questions . . .'

'If Beijing wanted to spy on us, why wouldn't they just use existing satellites, like you?'

'The cameras up there are twenty years old. They can barely tell the difference between a human and a stain on the sidewalk.' Garcia gestured at the starfish on the screen again. 'If Beijing launched a new satellite with up-to-date camera technology, they could use it to read text messages off the screen of your phone as you walked down the street.'

No wonder Zara was concerned. 'So you saw the body this morning. Then what?'

'I didn't know it was a body,' Garcia said quickly. 'I thought it might be someone on drugs, just lying down in the middle of the field.'

'Are you thinking of someone in particular?'

'No, but this place . . .' He moved his mouth in silence for a moment, trying to find the words. 'We spend all day every day talking about unfathomably giant, heavy objects travelling incredible distances at mind-blowing speeds over stupendous timescales. It's a trip, even if you're not on anything. Sometimes you just want to lie down and marvel at it all.'

I found myself a bit jealous—I wished I cared about anything as much as Garcia seemed to care about space. 'Why did you tell Anders to investigate, instead of going yourself?'

'I didn't exactly tell him—I asked him.' Garcia shifted on his chair. 'He got in early. About eight. We were the only two people in the building at that stage, and I was supposed to be preparing some files for the deputy cyber-security chief, who's covering for her boss while he's on leave. I could have asked the guards at the gate, but if drugs were involved, I didn't want to get anyone fired. Whoever it was, I thought Anders might be able to wake them up, and either sober them up or tell them to call in sick.'

'But he found a dead body instead. And called you?'

'Right.'

'At what time?'

Garcia checked his phone and showed me the call log. 'Eight-fourteen am. I told him to wait right there, and then I called the police.'

'After that, you didn't go out to join Anders?'

'The cops told me not to. Didn't want the scene contaminated.'

I could see the outgoing call to 911 on the screen, at eight-fifteen. There were no calls after that, but he could have deleted the records. I hadn't trusted him seven years ago, and I didn't trust him now.

'Show me the CCTV from the fence,' I said.

'I don't have access to that. You'll have to talk to Rob Cho, chief of cybersecurity—but he's on leave this week, like I said. He's visiting his sister in hospital.'

He was avoiding my gaze. I could imagine why he might not want me talking to the cybersecurity chief.

'So who do I talk to?' I said.

'Hazel Cuthbert, I guess. She's the deputy. Her office is in the museum.' Garcia blinked a few times, his breathing shallow. 'You're not going to tell her about . . .'

I stood up. 'I'll be in touch.'

•

Diaz taps her pen on her notebook. 'Was Sam Garcia a good friend of yours?'

Apparently she's only been half-listening. Some therapist. 'No. He was a suspect in a case I investigated.'

Diaz stares, that polite half-smile still fixed on her lips. 'You mentioned several times how big he was.'

'Yeah. Six three, maybe two hundred pounds.'

'Were you attracted to him?'

I think of his thick forearms and his bulging chest. The memory alone put my saliva glands into overdrive. 'Not in the way you're thinking.'

She waits for me to fill the silence.

'Anyway, that wasn't the deal,' I say.

'The deal?'

'When I was at the FBI. The director used to reward me with cadavers after executions. But he only brought me in to consult on kidnappings, and didn't pay me unless the victim was found alive. Kidnapping isn't a capital crime if the victim survives. Therefore, I never got to eat the suspects from my own cases.'

If Diaz is shocked by any of this, she doesn't show it. 'I'd have thought that the substances used in lethal injections couldn't be safely consumed.'

'They used a special chemical, just for me. Suxamethonium chloride.'

Her eyebrow twitches. She writes the name down, maybe so she can google it later. I'm sure a proper doctor would have recognised it.

'Perhaps you can tell me how you and Sam met,' she says.

'You want to hear about the case?'

'Right. The case.'

I look at the clock. Twenty minutes left. Then she'll let me out of this little room, and into the rest of the Behavioural Health Unit, where I'll be surrounded by the other crazies. There's one in particular I have my eye on.

I settle deeper into my chair. 'It started with the guy in the river . . .'

CHAPTER 5

Seven years ago

I take your bike over and over. I melt it
and build it anew. What am I doing?

I found Peter Luzhin behind his desk on the fourth floor
of the FBI field office, still wearing his coat, chewing on a
popsicle stick. According to rumour, he'd injured his jaw
by grinding his teeth, and his doctor had given him the
popsicle sticks to help him relax. He shot me a glare that
implied the treatment wasn't working.

'The guy in Buffalo Bayou was murdered,' I told him,
by way of greeting.

He took the stick out of his mouth and examined the
tooth marks. 'How's that?'

'Put me on the case, and I'll tell you.'

'I choose the cases, not you.'

Luzhin was a bulky man with grey sideburns, a faded
suit and a permanent slouch. He was forty-four, but the
lines around his eyes made him look sixty. When I first met
him, he was a detective in the Houston PD with a cocaine
habit and a fondness for brothels. Now he was sober, and

the director of the FBI's Houston Field Office. It seemed like an impressive turnaround, but I knew him better. He let his agents plant evidence to secure convictions and encouraged violence to encourage confessions. In addition to all that, I knew his darkest secret—the deal he'd struck with me. He was worse now than he'd ever been.

'The dead man had goggles on,' I said. 'Why? No chlorine in the river, and it's not like you'd see anything at night either way. Anyway, who goes swimming in the middle of winter? And his Jeep was parked *downstream.*'

Luzhin went to sip a go-cup of coffee and then, finding it empty, tossed it into the recycling can in the corner. 'You want to tell me how you know that?'

The truth was I'd been walking along the riverbank at dawn yesterday, unable to sleep. I'd found the body tangled in the mangroves. I should have gotten started on it then and there, but I was too greedy. I went to fetch my car so I could take the whole thing. By the time I got back, the police were on the scene, and I had to slink off before they saw me, empty-handed and hollow-bellied.

'Internet,' I said.

Luzhin gave me a look that was equal parts disbelieving and disgusted. 'Whatever. I'll pass the information on to the Houston PD.'

My heart sank. 'You don't want me to interview the family?'

'Let me take a second to explain, *again*, what the FBI does.' Luzhin started counting on his fingers. 'Terrorism, organised crime, counterintelligence, missing persons. This is an accidental death—or, if you're right, a plain old homicide for the county cops.'

'I want my reward,' I said.

'Then you can work the cases I give you.' He slid a file across his desk. 'One for one, Blake. That's the deal.'

I knew what he meant. He would give me a cadaver in exchange for every life I saved, not every case I closed. That was how he could look at himself in the mirror afterwards.

I'd long since given up on looking at myself in the mirror.

I opened the file and found a picture of a girl with a big chin, dark hair parted in the middle and a wry sort of smile. Lilah Parget, almost thirteen years old.

I sighed. 'Where was she last seen?'

•

I was on the second floor of the parking garage, surrounded by oil stains and crumpled burger wrappers, looking at the sliding glass doors that led into the mall.

Special Agent Richmond rested his elbows against the chest-high wall that ringed the lot. 'Are we going in, or what?'

Richmond was perpetually bug-eyed, with a squashed nose and fat hands. He looked like a bulldog stuffed into a suit. As usual, he had a steaming cup of noodles in one paw.

I ignored him, examining the big, square trash cans next to the entrance. One was for recycling, the other garbage. There was a pile of squashed cigarette butts behind them, as though someone had been building a monument to cancer. I wondered why they hadn't been thrown in the trash.

Texas is full of abandoned malls, killed by online shopping. This one looked like it was on its way out. Weeds were pushing up through the asphalt around it, the rain had left streaked stains on the concrete walls, and when I reached into the recycling—

'Gross,' Richmond said.

—it was only half full. I dug out a greasy receipt from three days ago. If there wasn't enough foot traffic to fill the trash faster than that, surely the businesses inside the mall were dying.

I turned and pointed to a parking space. 'Jeb Parget says he didn't get out of his car. He watched Lilah go into the mall through these doors, then he drove off. When he came back to pick her up, she wasn't here, so he called her, no answer, went inside, blah blah blah.'

'No security cameras out here to confirm his story,' Richmond observed. 'Nine times out of ten, the kidnapper is the dad. You know that.'

I did. But in those cases, the parents were usually separated. Jeb lived with Lilah and her mother.

We'd met him two hours earlier. A slight man, with glasses and a button-down shirt. The sort of guy who got away with bad behaviour by looking respectable. There was a coldness behind his green eyes. An anger. His wife, Faith, was Vietnamese, and had let him do all the talking. I noticed that he told her, rather than asked her, to make coffee for everyone. When she poured it, her sleeve rode up, exposing a ring of yellow bruises around her thin wrist.

But that didn't mean Jeb was the kidnapper.

I crushed the receipt in my fist. 'The camera next to the boom gate confirms that Parget's car arrived at four forty-six, like he said, and left five minutes later. Then it came back at a quarter to eight.' I hadn't seen the footage, but a guy named Vasquez had called me from the field office with a brief summary.

'Five minutes is long enough to stuff your daughter into the trunk of a car.' Richmond sipped his noodle soup. 'And three hours is enough to take her fifty miles away, leave her tied up someplace and come back without her.'

He was right.

I approached the dirty glass doors. They slid open with a reluctant squeak, as though they could tell I had no money to spend. Inside was a tiled walkway with shuttered shops on either side, lit by murky skylights above. No people. I took a step, then another, and then the security camera came into view above me—a dark plastic bubble mounted on the ceiling.

I pointed. 'If she'd actually gone into the mall, she would have been visible on that camera. Vasquez said she wasn't.'

'Great. So the dad did it,' Richmond said. 'We'll get a warrant for the cell tower data to trace his movements during the three-hour window. Can we go back to the field office now?'

I walked backwards through the squeaky doors. As they slid shut again, I squinted at the trash cans.

'Come on, Blake,' Richmond said. 'Jeb Parget's alibi for the three hours is clearly bullshit. You said yourself that no one plays golf by themselves, in the rain, and that his clubs weren't even wet. He has a history of violence. Neighbours have called the cops to his house several times. You saw the bruises on the wife. You're making this more complicated than it needs to be.'

'Imagine you're Jeb Parget,' I said. 'You've decided to kidnap your own daughter for some reason. To punish your wife, maybe—domestic abusers often use their kids that way.'

Richmond glanced at his watch.

'You wouldn't do it like this,' I said. 'You'd open her bedroom window and make it look like she ran away in the middle of the night. Why would you put yourself in a position where you'd be the obvious suspect? The last person to see her alive, with the world's least convincing alibi?'

'He's not a Rhodes scholar,' said Richmond, who was himself not a Rhodes scholar. 'Could've been a spur-of-the-moment decision. Maybe he and Lilah had an argument in the car on the way here, and he decided to stuff her in the trunk to teach her a lesson.'

It was possible. But I remembered the look on Jeb Parget's face, and the wobble in his voice. The fear could have been fake, or it could have been fear of getting caught. But his anger was all too real. He thought someone had taken his daughter.

I looked at the mountain of cigarette butts behind the trash cans. Someone had waited here for a long time. They could have thrown their butts in the trash, but they'd stayed hidden behind the trash cans instead and dropped their butts on the ground.

'You stand over there,' I said. 'Where the car was parked.'

Richmond groaned, but obeyed. I followed him about halfway.

'You're Jeb and I'm Lilah, okay?' I walked towards the sliding doors again, stooping to match the height of a twelve-year-old girl. When I was almost at the entrance, I pictured someone leaping out from behind the trash cans and grabbing me. I stumbled sideways, like I was being dragged behind the cans. I opened my mouth to scream, then imagined a strong hand clamping over it.

As I crouched behind the cans, I spotted a plain black hair tie on the ground a few feet away. It didn't look broken. No obvious reason to throw it away.

'Well?' I called. 'Did it look like I went into the mall?'

'What?'

I emerged from behind the cans. Richmond looked startled to see me, which answered my question.

I went over to the chest-high wall and peered down. There was a rusty ladder bolted to the exterior side, probably to meet the fire code. So it was possible to leave on foot without passing any cameras—but not if you were carrying a kid.

Richmond peered at the pile of cigarettes. He took out a Ziploc bag from his pocket and used it like a glove as he picked up a butt, then flipped the bag inside out and sealed it.

'Tell Vasquez I need to see the security video from the boom gate,' I said. 'I don't think Jeb Parget had Lilah in the trunk—but someone did.'

Richmond spent twenty minutes on the phone to the security company, alternating between listening to muzak and arguing with support reps. Eventually they emailed the footage to his phone. Three cars had gone through the boom gate between four forty-six and five o'clock. We checked the licence plates against the DMV registrations. One car was Jeb Parget's. Another belonged to a 61-year-old woman named Victoria Jackson.

The last one belonged to a big, scary-looking guy named Sam Garcia.

CHAPTER 6

Two weeks ago

I am an organ, an instrument and the
source of all music. What am I?

I left Garcia's office at the Atmospheric Research Unit and
stood in the corridor for a moment, surrounded by the
rumble of the air-conditioning. Voices carried from downstairs, too far away to make out any words. My ears rang,
one eardrum still vibrating from the punch.

According to Garcia, the body could have come from
space. According to Franklin Anders, it couldn't have.
Anders was more convincing, but he hadn't offered another
explanation for how the dead man might have ended up in
a restricted area, wearing a space suit and showing obvious
signs of decompression.

The back of my neck prickled. I turned in time to see
a young woman—shaved head, tan skin—peeking out of a
stairwell at the far end of the corridor.

When our eyes met, she quickly shut the door.

'Hey!' I called. I ran down the corridor and shoved
the door open with my good arm. I could hear her shoes

squeaking on the polished concrete steps, but the echo off the cinderblock walls made it hard to tell if she'd gone up or down.

Peering over the painted steel handrail, I saw her tattooed arm a level below, exposed by a rolled-up denim sleeve. Her nails were painted silver.

I hurried down the stairs after her. She didn't wait for me, shoving open a door on the ground level. Light flooded into the stairwell. By the time I reached the doorway, there was no sign of her. Just another empty corridor, lined by offices.

She could have gone left or right. I went left, operating on instinct. One of the doors had a small, square window inset. As I ran past I saw a flash of red through the glass.

I backtracked and peered in, not sure what I was looking at. One wall was lined with racks of vials.

They were filled with blood. All of them.

It didn't make sense. This was a space research facility, not a blood bank. The vials were much smaller than transfusion pouches. Plus, the room wasn't refrigerated. The glass was room temperature. It wasn't until I made this observation that I realised I was pressing my palm against the window, almost hard enough to crack it. I'd forgotten all about the woman with the shaved head.

A voice came from behind me. 'Ah, you must be Henry.' The accent wasn't Texan—Bostonian, maybe.

I turned. A short woman in a lime-green blazer that made her look like a leprechaun was coming down the corridor, towelling off her ash-blonde hair. Her tanned skin was damp and free of make-up. A gym bag hung from her shoulder.

'Pardon me,' she said. 'I was just in the pool. You're a bit early.' She offered me her hand.

I was looking at the leprechaun, not really seeing her. The blood sang to me from behind that thin pane of glass. There must have been gallons of it.

She noticed my prosthesis and quickly lowered her hand. 'How was the drive?'

I cleared my throat. 'Just fine, thank you, Dr Laurie.' Her surname was on the lanyard hanging around her neck.

She didn't offer a first name. 'I've been looking forward to your visit. Shall we go in?'

I didn't know who Henry was or why he was supposed to be visiting, but I needed to get into that room. 'Please,' I said.

Laurie unlocked the door with a keycard. 'I read the paper you co-authored with Dr Singh. It's an intriguing area of study. I'm quite envious—the ethics committee here is squeamish about experimenting on vertebrates. I told them the subjects needed albumins, but they said . . .'

As she talked, I floated in after her. It was a laboratory as well as a storage room, two microscopes and an extractor fan on one side, the shelves of samples on the other. I half-expected the aroma of blood to wash over me, but the room smelled of nothing but disinfectant. I could see a jug of floor cleaner in the corner, next to a mop with reddish-brown stains on the head.

I picked up one of the vials. It was double-walled glass, so I could see the inner workings. A hypodermic needle was recessed within the device, protected by a safety cap. At the other end was a compressed spring. This seemed to be an auto-injector, like an EpiPen. Rather than a blood type, the label had a long list of letters. A serial number.

Laurie hung her gym bag on a hook behind the door, and unzipped it to cram her towel inside. While she was facing the other way, I pocketed the injector. I couldn't help it. By the time she turned around, I had picked up another and was studying that.

'May I?' Laurie held out a hand.

I gave her the injector. She held it up, tilting it to catch the light.

'In your email, you made the comparison to dodeca-fluoropentane emulsion, but this is a significant improvement on that technology,' she said. 'On a plane, they tell you to put your own mask on before assisting other passengers—that's because after just a few seconds without oxygen, you'd be too confused to put on your mask, or even to realise that you were in danger. The higher the altitude, the faster it happens. And we work with *very* high altitudes here—' She breaks off. 'Sorry, I went into autopilot there. You obviously know all this.'

I smiled. 'Obviously. But go on.'

'Well, an oxygen mask tethers you to a tank. In an aircraft, that usually means you're attached to the ceiling. You can't help anybody who's out of arm's reach.' I could tell she was trying not to look at my prosthesis. 'And tanks of compressed gas are of course an explosion risk. Our idea was to eliminate those risks by oxygenating the blood directly via injection. In the event that the O_2 in the air supply gets dangerously low, crew members just uncap a syringe and inject the solution intravenously. They're essentially breathing through their veins, rather than their lungs. They'll remain conscious for about sixteen minutes, which might be long enough to repressurise the cabin.' She shrugged modestly. 'Others have explored the possibility before, but I had the courage to see it through.'

I wasn't a doctor, but I knew what an embolism was. 'Wouldn't having air in their blood cause a heart attack?'

'This isn't air. It's oxygenated perfluorocarbon.'

Oh. I glanced at the shelves, less interested now. The blood was fake. Like the tofu in the supermarket that pretends to be chicken. I wondered if there was a way to casually return the syringe I'd stolen.

'Excuse me a moment, Henry.' Laurie was backing away towards the door. She seemed to have realised that Henry, whoever he was, wouldn't have asked such a dumb question.

'Henry?' I tried to sound puzzled. 'My name's Timothy. Timothy Blake.'

Laurie stared at me. 'What are you doing here, Mr Blake?'

'I'm a security consultant for ClearHorizon. Sam Garcia sent me down here. He didn't tell you?'

'He did not.'

I laughed. 'Well, that explains it! No wonder you were talking to me like I was a scientist. Sorry for the confusion. I'm investigating an incident in the Martian training area.'

'What incident?'

I could have told her it was classified, but that would only have made her curious. 'Some kind of equipment failure—I'm still waiting on the details. But Sam said you could answer some questions about the oxygen-hemoglobin dissociation curve.' I was reading the words off the whiteboard behind her.

'Well, I'm a bit busy right now—I'm expecting a visitor from Yale.'

'Henry, I assume.' I attempted another carefree chuckle. 'What a mix-up! Who is he?'

'He's a professor researching emergency medicine. He wants me to publish my formula so paramedics can use it to prevent brain death after respiratory failure. And he'll be here any minute now, so . . .'

'Don't worry, I'll be quick. You're a medical doctor, right?'

'Yes . . .?' Laurie replied warily, as though I might be about to ask her to examine a rash.

'If someone ran out of oxygen, they'd go blue, wouldn't they?'

'Yes, at the lips and fingernails. Why?'

'They wouldn't go kind of purple all over? Like bruising?'

'No,' Laurie said.

'What would happen to a person if their suit was punctured on a spacewalk?'

'Oh. Well, depressurisation is much more serious than just a loss of oxygen. The astronaut would go into shock more or less immediately. The eardrums would probably burst. In a vacuum, the boiling point of water drops to almost nothing, so their saliva would boil, and their tears, too. Soon all their orifices would be completely dry. Their skin would be scorched by the cold, and the blood vessels close to the surface would rupture. So, in that case, there would be bruising everywhere.'

That was exactly what I'd seen on the body outside. 'Would the cold stop the body from burning up on re-entry?'

Laurie raised an eyebrow. If my earlier question had been dumb, this one was apparently even dumber. 'Have you ever seen a shooting star, Timothy?'

'Sure.'

'Any rock smaller than a stadium gets torn apart when it hits the atmosphere. What do you think those forces would do to a human body?'

So she agreed with Anders. 'Fair enough. Thank you for your time. Say, do you know a woman with a shaved head? Asian or Latina, twenty-something?'

Laurie's eyes narrowed. 'That's Rachel. She's an intern.'

I wondered why an intern would flee from me. 'I just missed her earlier. I'm supposed to interview anyone who was in the complex prior to eight this morning. Perhaps you could ask her to give me a call?'

I held out a business card, and Laurie took it.

Rachel was unlikely to call the number on the card. She'd made it clear she didn't want to talk to me. But she might google 'Timothy Blake, ClearHorizon'. If she did, the CIA would have her location within minutes. And then I could find out what she knew.

I paused with my hand on the doorhandle, looking back at the syringes. 'Would your formula *taste* like blood?'

Laurie frowned. 'I don't really know. There's iron in it, hence the red colour. The flavour might be similar, I suppose—why?'

'Just curious.'

When I opened the door I came face to face with a tall man in a brown suit, rumpled after a long drive. He wore his thinning hair in a comb-over, and his eyes were magnified by frameless glasses. This would be the Yale professor.

He looked me up and down—mostly down, on account of his height. 'Oh. Hello. Well. I'm here to speak with Dr Laurie.' He saw her over my shoulder and gave her the same stare I gave pedestrians when I was a beggar. Hopeful, with a dash of suppressed contempt. He really wanted that formula, and he didn't think she would give it to him.

'I've warmed her up for you,' I said, and slipped past.

CHAPTER 7

I ask you questions and steal your underwear.
What am I?

I'd told Zara I would come straight back to the safe house for a debriefing. Instead I took the exit off the tollway towards Jacinto City, headed for a street I'd only seen pictures of. The dead spaceman was a good riddle, but not good enough. He could only keep my mind busy for so long.

I left the radio on—a real broadcast this time. Over the course of the hour-long drive, news of the Chinese astronaut was reported, exaggerated and then forgotten in favour of a story about the Texas Reaper's latest victim: a middle-aged woman found strangled in her own home. The perfect story to scare listeners and hold their attention long enough to sell them air-conditioners and insurance. *More on this story after the break.* I briefly wondered if the serial killer was a CIA invention, designed to distract the public from a national security crisis. But the public probably didn't need help getting distracted.

A couple of strangers waved at me as I turned onto a broad, leafy street. I didn't wave back. They probably wouldn't have noticed my prosthesis at that distance—but if they had, and if they'd told the occupant of the house at the end that they'd seen a one-armed man hanging around, she'd have known immediately who they meant.

I shouldn't be here, I thought, but I didn't turn back.

It seemed like a nice place, which both pleased and saddened me. Fences were only knee high, and the strip of lawn down the middle had been mown recently. The house itself was painted a cheery yellow to match the daisies planted in the front garden. A clothesline around one side. A tall oak was visible over the roof, which had pristine tiles, as though even the birds thought this was too respectable a place to take a shit.

I'd told myself it wasn't really stalking if I didn't stop the car, though I wouldn't want to test that theory in court. Yet I found myself slowing down, pulling on the park brake and killing the engine. It was safe enough. She wouldn't be here at two o'clock on a Wednesday. She'd be out hunting people like me.

When I lost my arm, the stump took ages to heal, because I couldn't help poking it. I was doing the same thing now. Prolonging the pain by sitting across the street from this house, looking up at the second-floor windows that reflected the blue sky and trying to imagine what it would have been like to live inside. If only I was him, instead of me.

A figure emerged from behind the house. A woman, five foot eight, long hair, dark skin. The air in my lungs evaporated, as though I was an astronaut with a punctured suit. It was her.

Reese Thistle put down a basket of wet laundry under the clothesline. I'd hardly ever seen her in casual clothes. Today she wore mom jeans and a crew-neck sweater, her

50

hair loose around her shoulders, brown eyes focused on the pegs in her hands. Maybe she'd taken a sick day, though she looked healthy. Maybe she'd quit.

Thistle hung up the clothes the same way she did everything. Efficiently, determinedly and optimistically—those clothes wouldn't dry on a cold day like this. She had a faint frown, her lips slightly parted. It looked like she was thinking about something else. I hoped it wasn't me. I hoped she'd forgotten I existed and was living a happy life in my absence.

Just leave, I told myself. But I couldn't.

The clothes were all hers. Her FBI suit pants, a few blouses, some flannelette pyjamas. So she was living in her ex-husband's house but wasn't washing his clothes. The bras and panties were practical rather than sexy. I tried to snuff out the flicker of hope in my chest. Zak was probably a good man who did his own washing and loved her no matter what she wore.

Thistle hung up the last pair of socks and picked up the empty basket—

Then she spotted my car. She paused, looking right at me.

My heart pounding, I waved my good hand in what I hoped was a non-threatening way.

Thistle turned back to the house and went inside. I realised that the sun was reflecting off my windshield. She hadn't seen me at all.

I told myself I'd had a lucky escape. But as I started the engine and drove off, it was hard not to feel like I'd swallowed a bone and it was lodged right next to my heart.

•

The safe house was a half-finished home in a half-finished suburb on the edge of Houston. From the outside it looked complete—a huge house squeezed onto a tiny block, with a facade of dark grey bricks shaded by an overhanging corrugated roof. But inside there were no doors. Halls became bedrooms became walk-in robes with no delineation. No carpet, and the rough pine floors hadn't been lacquered. The whole place smelled of sawdust. No stairs led down to the tiny yard—if anyone walked out the back door, they would fall four feet onto bare dirt. Drills, hammers and crowbars were scattered throughout the house, and there was an abandoned ladder in the yard. It was as though the rapture had happened and the people building the house had simply evaporated. There was running water and electricity, but no heat. No furniture, except the self-inflating foam mattresses Zara had brought.

I'd wanted to take the house next door, which was complete, and furnished. But Zara had said the owners might drive past to check on their belongings, though they wouldn't dare get out of the car. The insulation pumped into the walls of every house on this street had a manufacturing defect that meant it would degrade over time, potentially leading to lung and throat cancer for the occupants. It was scheduled to be removed and replaced by experts with specialised equipment and protective clothing.

That was the official story, anyway. In reality, the insulation was fine. As soon as Zara and I left, the developers would be notified that the faulty insulation had been removed and replaced, so the construction workers could return. The owners would keep the whole thing under wraps to avoid hurting the house prices. Two operatives—or, technically, one operative and one asset—would have had a few days of free accommodation.

The longer I worked for the CIA, the more impressed I was by their ability to manipulate other people into keeping their secrets, and to get things done on a budget. Zara had hired me on nothing more than the promise of the occasional corpse.

When I walked in, she was sitting cross-legged in the corner of the room, between a nail gun and a saw.

'What's the situation?' she asked, without looking up from the phone in her lap.

'Garcia is scared,' I said. 'He'll say whatever we need him to say. But journalists are onto the story.'

She waved that off. 'No one trusts journalists anymore. Did anyone else seem to be taking an unusual interest in the body?'

When I'd first met Zara, she'd had hair as black and shiny as a grand piano, flawless skin, and had worn a cocktail dress and heels at all hours of the day. Now her hair was brown, she had a sprinkling of freckles across her nose, and she wore leggings and a running jacket. Her accent had shifted, too—a little less Texas twang, a little more Valley girl. She had driver's licences from Ohio, Michigan and Wyoming, with various birthdates that put her age between thirty-six and forty-two. Her names included Jasmine, Michaela, Sandra.

People talk about soldiers giving their lives for their country, but to me, that doesn't seem quite right. Soldiers give their deaths for their country. Zara, whose original name, face and voice were long gone, had given her life.

'There's more.' I told her about Rachel, the young Asian woman with the tattoos and the shaved head.

'Interesting. Did you recognise her?'

'Didn't get a good look.'

'How about a last name?'

I shook my head.

Zara turned back to her phone. 'Okay. Can't be many Rachels working at Space City who match that description. We'll find her.'

'I want the body,' I said.

Zara sighed. 'Let's not have this conversation again.'

I threw up my hand. 'Why am I here?'

'Because I knew you'd scare the shit out of Garcia, and hopefully shake something loose.'

'I mean before that,' I said. 'Why did you recruit me, if you didn't need an investigator?'

'I enjoy the company of like-minded individuals.' She stood up and stretched. 'I'm going to have a shower.'

My stomach growled. As Zara strolled away, I went to the kettle and switched it on. The less meat I got, the more I craved coffee—maybe caffeine stimulated the same part of the brain. The way some people only smoke when they drink, or vice versa.

I clamped the jar of instant between my knees so I could open it one-handed, then spooned it into a mug, along with sugar and some salt. I took the long-life cream out of the cooler Zara and I had been using, and added a generous splash. I wanted the coffee fatty, and not too hot. As close as I could get to the taste and texture of human blood.

I poured the water, stirred, and dipped a finger in to

check the temperature. I was about to take a sip when I remembered the syringe I'd stolen from Laurie's lab.

I took it out of my pocket and examined it. It was shrink-wrapped, like a drinking straw attached to a juice box. In this light the fluid inside was vivid red.

I'd forgotten the syringe as soon as Laurie told me it wasn't real blood. But it probably tasted more convincing than salted coffee.

I tore the plastic with my teeth, uncapped the syringe and raised it to my mouth. Plungers were hard without a thumb. I had to use my pinkie, the other three fingers wrapped around the shaft.

Nothing happened. Maybe the auto-injector was like the nail gun on the floor—for safety, it would only fire if the tip was pressed against something.

I wanted to taste the contents, but I didn't want to stab myself in the tongue. I pushed the tip against my teeth instead, my jaw slightly open, so the needle would go between them—

Zara touched my arm from behind.

I yelped and dropped the syringe. It bounced off my foot and skittered across the floor.

'Sorry,' Zara said. 'Didn't mean to sneak up on you.'

I was sure that was a lie. When Zara had been embedded with the dark web group, she'd had a playful, sadistic streak. It had helped her blend in with the other occupants of the house, but I didn't think it was part of her cover. I thought it was what had drawn her to spying in the first place.

I swerved, mentally. It was painful to think about that house, where I'd lost so much. My love. My arm. My son.

Zara was looking at the syringe. 'What's that?'

'EpiPen.' It was the first thing that popped into my head.

She looked at me for a long moment with her big, dark eyes.

'What?' I said.

'I trust you, Blake,' Zara said. 'You can trust me, too. You know that, right?'

I didn't think either of those statements were true.

Zara had sold me on this partnership because she knew what I was. Wouldn't I rather work alongside someone I didn't have to hide from? Someone who wasn't disgusted, or afraid? But it hadn't worked out that way. I didn't trust anyone who would want me for a partner.

'Of course,' I said, but I'd hesitated too long.

Anger flashed across her face. Her stance changed, too—the elongated neck becoming hunched, her pushed-out chest caving in, the raised hip levelling out. A more masculine stance. For a second, the seductress was replaced by a real person, full of messy frustrations. I had time to think: *Zara uses her femininity to hide her humanity.*

But then she transformed back, so fast that I wondered if I'd imagined the change. Her gaze softened, and she was back to standing like a catwalk model.

'That girl you're carrying a torch for,' she said.

'Woman,' I said.

'She's never coming back. You know that, right?'

Her phone vibrated on the laminate benchtop.

Zara gave me a meaningful look before she sashayed over and picked it up. 'You're speaking with Cassandra, hello?'

It had to be those words, in that sequence. If she'd said, 'Hello, you're speaking with Sandra,' that would mean *I've been compromised*. Any other phrase, and the CIA would assume they were talking to an impostor.

Zara listened for a long time. She had the volume turned down too low for me to hear the person at the other end. Eventually she said 'Got it' and hung up.

'What's up?' I said.

'My asset in Shanghai has reported back. The Ministry of State Security has hi-res aerial photographs of Space City. Best guess, they have a secret spy satellite watching it. Come on.' She picked up her keys. 'Wilcox wants to see us.'

CHAPTER 8

I'm an untidy period of time, delivered
to your phone. What am I?

I lounged in the passenger seat of Zara's Prius, watching Houston zip by. Dark clouds were gathering behind the skyscrapers downtown, and everyone seemed to be trying to beat the rain. Zara drove at terrifying speeds, always riding either the brake or the gas. She kept the stereo way up, some commentator shouting over the top of us, confusing anyone who might have planted a listening device in the car.

Her phone beeped. She took her eyes off the road and swiped down to read a message. 'We have a location for the meeting,' she said. 'And OPIR analysis is back. No suspicious infrared disturbances in China for at least three months.'

'Meaning no rocket launches?'

'Right. Whatever's up there, it's been up there a while.' She looked troubled, probably mentally cataloguing all the things the MSS might have seen during three months of covert surveillance.

This also eliminated Garcia's theory that the astronaut had crashed after failing to reach orbit. 'Tell me about your asset in Shanghai,' I said.

'No.'

'Okay, fine,' I said. 'But don't you think it's convenient that your contact didn't tell you about the satellite until *after* we found the body? A body that should have burned up on re-entry, according to the experts at NASA?'

'You mean like there was no point hiding it anymore?'

'I mean like the satellite isn't there at all.' I could still taste that earlobe. Soft and fresh. Neither frozen nor burned.

'Where'd you get the EpiPen?' she asked, changing the subject.

'Found it in Garcia's office. Prison records didn't list any allergies—thought I'd run the serial numbers, see if I can work out whose it is.'

'Uh-huh. You know, they used to chop your hand off for stealing.' Zara glanced at my arm. I've never told her how scared I am of losing my other hand and becoming completely helpless, but she seems to sense it.

'I wonder who got all the hands afterwards,' I said. Did some lucky cannibal work at the jail? Maybe there'd always been someone like me, begging for scraps from the justice system. In the hospital, after I lost my thumb, I'd seen part of a documentary about weird medical practices throughout history. Apparently people used to think that drinking blood was good for you. At beheadings, there would be beggars with cups, lined up to catch some nectar from the condemned.

I thought of Laurie and her room of fake blood. Maybe those beggars had the right idea.

'I get why you want to take risks,' Zara said. 'To put yourself in more and more danger just so you'll feel something. But we've got a good thing going here. Don't fuck it up.'

I wasn't convinced that her profile of me was accurate, and I was even less convinced that we had a good thing going. Our 'thing' seemed to be her gathering intelligence while I went hungry.

'Slow down,' I said. There were police cars up ahead.

It wasn't a roadblock—just a cop in a windbreaker, gesturing for some cars to pull onto the shoulder and waving others on. Random breath testing, maybe. 'Have you been drinking?' I asked. It was three pm, but Zara never seemed constrained by social norms, or even the law, although the freewheeling side of her personality might have been a cover.

Zara gave me a withering look.

The cop checked Zara out through the windshield, then looked at me, and pointed to the side of the road.

Zara pressed the brakes and cruised into the queue. I got the insurance papers out of the glove compartment and gave them to her.

'We're backstopped, right?' I tried to talk without moving my face, in case the cop could lip-read.

It was illegal for the CIA to conduct operations on US soil. This was Homeland's turf. If the police worked out that Zara's ID was fake, we were in deep shit.

'Shut up.' She buzzed the window down and turned off the stereo. The sudden silence was suffocating.

We eased forwards and soon came level with a second cop. Hooded eyes, very short hair, Latina. She didn't look as bored as I would have expected, or hoped.

'Licence and proof of insurance?' she said.

Zara handed over the papers, dug a wallet out of her bag and produced an ID. Today she was Cassandra Holcroft.

I didn't get a false name, because I was an asset, not an agent. This meant I had more to lose.

The cop took the documents but kept her eyes trained on me. 'Sir, I'll need your licence, too.'

'Okay.' I squirmed in the seat and pulled out my wallet with my good arm. 'But I'm not the one driving the car.'

The cop didn't smile. 'I see that.' She looked down at the photo, then back at me. 'Been to California lately?'

We had, but it seemed like a bad idea to say so.

Apparently Zara was thinking along the same lines. 'No,' she said.

'How about you, sir?' the cop asked.

I shook my head. 'Why?'

The cop didn't take her eyes off my face. 'You may be aware of a recent homicide in Los Angeles.'

'One a day, probably.'

She ignored this. 'A man fitting your description was spotted at the scene.'

'Why are you looking for him in Texas?'

'We have evidence that he crossed the border.'

'I'm sitting down,' I said. 'So I take it your description doesn't include height. And the first thing a killer would do is change his hair. So what's your description? White male, thirties, average weight?'

'Can't be many of those around,' Zara said.

In retrospect, it probably wasn't a good idea for either of us to play smart-ass.

'Step out of the vehicle please, sir,' the cop said.

I did, wondering if I was about to get shot. The cop looked me up and down. Perhaps height *was* part of the description.

I couldn't afford to get arrested. My cover story wouldn't withstand much scrutiny. I needed to convince this woman I was innocent, but I didn't even know what I was suspected of.

Zara was quicker on the uptake. 'If you're looking for the Reaper, I think it's safe to assume he has two arms.'

The cop glanced at my prosthesis.

'Pretty hard to strangle someone one-handed,' Zara added. 'I'm not sure it's even possible without thumbs.'

I waved my mutilated hand. 'But I'm happy to discuss my movements down at the precinct, officer. I kept all my receipts for the IRS.'

The cop chewed her lip. Then she said, 'You folks can move along. Sorry for the inconvenience.'

I shrugged. 'No problem.'

She watched me carefully as I got back into the car. Zara pulled off the shoulder. I watched in the side mirror as the cop and her car shrank behind us. She made no move to follow us. Didn't touch her radio. We were okay, for now.

Zara signalled, then merged onto the Interstate 610, which encircles Houston—locals call it the Loop. Soon we were hurtling west at fifty miles an hour. I watched for signs of pursuit. There were none.

'How did you know she was looking for the Reaper?' I asked.

Zara kept her eyes on the road. 'He strangled someone in California last week.'

'How do they know it's the same guy?'

'Are you still looking for cases to solve? Jesus.'

'Just curious.'

'Well, I haven't been following the story closely. Google it.'

I got out my phone. It seemed like the police hadn't released much information, but intrepid crime reporters were serving up the frightening details for a titillated public. The victims were all divorcees, killed in their homes and found just inside the front door. No forced entry. All left to rot for at least a few days before they were discovered. There had been four victims in Houston, one in New Mexico and one in California.

'The killer used a stun gun,' I said. 'And a garrotte.'

Zara grunted, bored.

'So I *could* have murdered those people, as far as that cop knew.'

She patted my knee. 'Of course you could. I believe in you.'

•

We entered the theatre just as the trailers started. Explosions, bass synth and shouted dialogue hit us from all directions via Dolby Atmos. It felt like being in a plane during turbulence, especially with the strip lighting on either side of the aisle.

As instructed, Zara had bought a dainty chocolate ice-cream cone, and I was carrying a bucket of popcorn roughly the size of an oil drum. We found our row and started shuffling along it.

The only other person in the theatre was a prim-looking woman in her forties with shoulder-length chestnut hair, deep-set eyes and a double chin. She wore a purple V-neck sweater with a gold brooch glittering just under her collarbone. She didn't seem to notice us as we sat in front of her. But after a minute, she said, 'Excuse me, what's this picture rated?'

'PG-13,' Zara said. 'They cut the sex to avoid an R-rating.'

The woman dropped the act. 'Okay, what have you got?'

Zara crossed her legs. 'Only two staff saw the body before the cops took it. A communications engineer saw a lo-res photo with no identifying details, and an atmospheric composition analyst saw it in person.'

'The engineer is Sam Garcia?'

'Right. Blake used his criminal record to lean on him.'

Zara phrased this as though it were my criminal record rather than Garcia's, possibly for her own amusement.

'And the other witness?' The woman talked in a cowgirl drawl. I'd been told to call her Ariel Wilcox, though I was sure that wasn't her real name. She was on the CIA black-ops team, like us.

'Franklin Anders, forty-three years old, born and bred in Texas,' Zara said. 'He saw the body up close. According to his healthcare records, he has a sick daughter. Could be a pressure point we can use to keep him quiet. The police will be much harder.'

'I'll handle the police,' Wilcox said. 'You steer clear of them. Understood?'

'Copy that.'

'Who talked to the media?'

'We don't know,' Zara said.

'It was Garcia,' I said.

Zara gave me a sharp look. I heard Wilcox shift in her seat. 'Explain.'

I'd been watching Garcia's body language as he showed me his phone's call log. But I thought Wilcox would want more evidence than that.

'The MSNBC producer asked me if I knew anything about a dead Chinese astronaut,' I said. 'He can't have talked to Anders, because Anders thought the writing on the suit was Japanese.'

'It could have been the dispatcher who took the 911 call,' Zara said. 'Or anyone she talked to.'

'Nope. She mixed up the address. The police went to the wrong place—I saw them hanging around the museum rather than the Martian training area. Whereas the news van went to exactly the right spot.'

A thought distracted me: *What about Detective Jones? How had he found the body so quickly, if the dispatcher got the location wrong?*

'Was there anything unusually high-tech about the space suit?' Wilcox was asking. 'Something that might explain why it didn't burn up on re-entry?'

'No. The suit looked old, if anything. But I can help you figure out why he didn't burn up, if you get me the body.'

Zara rolled her eyes at me.

'I'll arrange for you to meet with the pathologist,' Wilcox said. 'He can tell you anything you need to know about the corpse.'

'I have to examine it myself,' I insisted.

'I'll see what I can do.'

I stuffed some more popcorn into my mouth. It tasted like human sweat.

'I'll need the name of your asset in Shanghai,' Wilcox told Zara.

'I can't give you that,' Zara said.

'Do I need to emphasise the seriousness of this situation? We need to find out if there's a crewed Chinese spacecraft over the continental United States—'

'I'll reach out to confirm. My source only trusts me.'

'What if something happened to you? The Company can't protect your source if we don't know who they are.'

I doubted very much that Zara cared.

'You can pressure headquarters to fire me,' she said. 'But you'll lose your best-placed source of intelligence inside the PRC.'

There was a pause, long enough for the actress on screen to slap the actor playing opposite her. Zara licked her ice-cream while she waited.

'I've heard some troubling gossip,' Wilcox said finally.

'Oh?'

'Rumour has it that the Company has accidentally hired a serial killer.'

My breath hitched, and a piece of popcorn got lodged in my throat. I didn't dare make a sound. Luckily, I have good control over my gag reflex. I just held my breath, waiting for a less suspicious time to cough.

'The Company doesn't do anything by accident,' Zara said. 'Maybe someone decided this killer would be useful.'

'Hmm.' I could feel Wilcox's eyes drilling through the back of my seat. 'Sounds like the kind of mistake that could cost a person her job.'

I wondered if it would help to explain that I wasn't technically a serial killer, just a scavenger. Sure, I'd killed people, but only in self-defence.

I finally coughed, freeing the popcorn from my windpipe.

Then I turned around to look at Wilcox, not wanting her to think she'd rattled me.

'Remind me,' I said. 'Is it our job to gather real intelligence, or will the bigwigs be satisfied with rumours and gossip?'

Wilcox smiled thinly.

'Because if it's the latter, I've got all sorts of stories,' I continued. 'Did you hear the Russian defence minister is actually a lizard?'

'I don't have time for this,' Wilcox said. 'There's a USB modem under your seat. I need you to plug it into one of the terminals at Space City so we can monitor their communications remotely. You'll need to get a staff login to install the spyware—someone with administrator privileges. Either the head of cybersecurity, the deputy, or the sysadmin. Use a well-hidden port. If anyone unplugs it, we'll lose access.'

I remembered Garcia telling me that the Space City network was secure because there was no connection to the internet. Not for much longer, it seemed.

Zara reached under her seat as though scratching her leg. 'Got it.'

'I'll also need you to overwrite all the security footage from yesterday. Use the files from the day before—if anyone notices, they'll think it's a malfunction. Whatever the hell happened, we don't want anyone else figuring it out before we do. Understood?'

'Copy that,' Zara said.

'Afterwards, go to the safe house and wait for instructions. Keep a low profile. The political climate being what it is, I don't want to invite any attention.'

Wilcox wasn't just talking about China. Two years ago, a CIA drone strike in Pakistan had killed fourteen civilians, three of whom were children. It had been hushed up. But just yesterday, details about the strike had surfaced in the French media. The director had been given a dressing-down by the president. Now would be a very bad time for anyone to find out that the CIA was illegally spying on US institutions like NASA.

I bit down on an unpopped corn kernel, which crunched like a small tooth in my mouth.

'Do we know yet what happened last week?' Zara asked.

A team of analysts was trying to identify the person who had spiked her absinthe in LA. I didn't envy them. The description I'd offered—white, twenties, slight build—seemed to describe every male in the club that night.

'We've background-checked everyone who was there at the time,' Wilcox said. 'No flags. Looks like would-be date rape rather than an assassination attempt.'

Zara didn't look convinced. 'Was anyone else targeted?'

'As a matter of fact, a young woman died after her drink was spiked that same night.'

'She died? Doesn't sound like a roofie to me.'

'No one is disputing that you were in real danger, and we commend Mr Blake on his quick thinking.'

Zara clenched her fists and crushed them between her knees. 'Understood.'

On the screen, Chris Somebody—Pine or Pratt, I wasn't sure—tapped his earpiece, growled some tough-guy dialogue and then leapt off a skyscraper in a wingsuit. We watched him soar between buildings for a while, helicopters shooting at him, bullets shattering windows all around. Real-life spying didn't seem to be like that, but then again, I'd only been with the CIA for three months.

'Speaking of poison,' I said, 'will you ask the pathologist not to pump the body full of toxic chemicals? I'm concerned about the evidence being tainted.'

Wilcox said nothing for so long that I thought she was seriously considering this. But when I turned around, she was gone.

CHAPTER 9

What do you call a doorman with hay fever?

From the outside, it looked like an ordinary deli, next to a doughnut store on a quiet road. The windows had so many words painted on them—*Prime Beef, Buffalo, Cajun Stuffed Chicken, Boudin, Deer Processing*—that I couldn't see the interior.

'You sure this is the place?' I tried not to sound desperate.

Unexpectedly, Zara reached over and squeezed my good hand. Her fingers were cool. 'Relax.'

We crossed the threshold and were immediately surrounded by the smell of butchery. Long glass sneeze guards protected every kind of meat imaginable, bar one. The cuts were decorated—ruined, in my opinion—with sprigs of parsley. The floor was chequered red and white. Only half of it would show blood. Maybe that reduced the mopping time.

Zara nodded to the butcher, a hulking man with wide-set eyes and a bulge under his apron that I suspected was a gun.

'Help you?' he asked.

'I'm having a barbecue,' she said. 'Six people—have you got anything that won't taste too gamey?'

He looked around, checking the store was otherwise empty, then unlocked a steel door and rolled it aside, revealing the back room. He didn't follow us in.

Zara and I walked past the pigs hanging from hooks and the bundled-up turkeys, went down some stairs and found ourselves in a room filled with knives, weighing trays and stainless steel drawers. I'd known that the CIA had black-ops sites around the world where they interrogated suspects, but I hadn't known they ran black-ops morgues. In the centre, under a spotlight, was a slab draped in a sheet. I could make out a human shape underneath. A man in scrubs stood next to it, holding one corner of the sheet, like a magician about to make something disappear.

In reality, the trick was already over. The police had loaded the body into a transport van for a post-mortem, but the doctor never received it. Instead she got some paperwork which said that a different doctor would be performing the autopsy, at a different hospital. This doctor had a phone, an email address, and a co-worker who would swear he existed.

I stared at the shape under the sheet. Too much saliva had built up in my mouth, and I had to swallow it.

The pathologist was a gaunt, pale man with dark hollows around his eyes. I wondered how often he got mistaken for one of his charges. He wore a butcher's apron rather than a lab coat. He had no name badge, but Zara had told me to call him Holstein.

He shook her hand, ignoring mine, then pulled back the sheet with a flourish.

Without the space suit, the dead astronaut looked smaller. Sadder. Less heroic. With no blood pressure, his muscles had deflated. His skin had wrinkled too, and his shrunken penis flopped sideways. The mole under his eye, previously black, had faded to brown.

'Male, thirties,' Holstein said. 'Five foot ten, a hundred and eighty pounds.'

I reached for the dead man's thigh, to squeeze some of those pounds. Zara slapped my hand away and peered at the bloated face of the corpse. 'Cause of death?' she asked.

'You want the short version or the long version?' Holstein asked.

'Short,' Zara said.

'Long,' I said at the same moment.

'Alveolar haemorrhage consistent with explosive decompression,' he said, apparently deciding Zara outranked me.

'Like, hypothetically, he went into space without a helmet?' she prompted.

'I've never had the opportunity to examine anyone who died that way. But if I had, this is what I'd have expected to see. The bruising is the clearest indicator. Notice how it covers the whole body, even parts that aren't vulnerable to blunt force trauma.'

I did. There was no focal point for the bruising, and the dead man was purple in all his crevices.

'The other giveaway is his lungs.' Holstein gestured to a tray filled with what looked like raw hamburger. 'As you can see, they're badly ruptured. It's not unlike what happens to divers who surface too quickly—but far more severe.'

'Time of death?' Zara asked.

'Between five and seven pm yesterday. Tuesday.'

'That's very precise,' I said, without taking my eyes off the tray.

Holstein shrugged. 'Bodies that are exposed to the atmosphere get devoured from the outside by insects. Bodies that aren't, get eaten from within by bacteria. I'd already determined that this man was deprived of air for some time, so comparing the outer decomposition with the inner gave me a fairly reliable time of death.'

'Any sign that he'd been burned?' I said. 'Or frozen?'

'Certainly not burned,' Holstein said. 'As for frozen, it's harder to tell, but I examined several tissue samples under the microscope. The cell membranes were largely intact.'

'What does that mean?' I asked.

'Freezing a body doesn't do much damage, but thawing it usually ruptures the walls of the cells. I took the samples at room temperature and saw no such damage.'

'So he can't have been in space.' I exchanged glances with Zara.

'Well, imagine putting a steak in your freezer,' Holstein said. 'It wouldn't freeze right away—the process takes hours. This man *might* have been exposed to the vacuum of space for a few minutes, I suppose. I'm speaking medically, here. I have no expertise in astrophysics.'

It wasn't a steak that I was imagining. Even so, I took his point.

'What would his last moments have been like?' Zara asked. I was surprised. It wasn't like her, to empathise with a victim.

'Awful, I'd imagine,' Holstein said. 'His flesh would have swollen to about one-and-a-half times its normal size, stretching his skin. Bubbles would have formed in his blood, triggering a heart attack. When he tried to hold his breath, the air expanded in his lungs, causing them to explode.' He gestured to the tray again. 'Mercifully, he would have lost consciousness after thirteen to fifteen seconds and died less than two minutes later. Whoever tried to resuscitate him had no hope.'

'Hold up,' I said. 'No one tried to resuscitate him.'

'Are you sure?' Holstein pointed to the chest. 'The ribs are fractured here, and here. I assumed someone adminis-tered CPR.'

'Could the fractures have happened when he hit the ground?' Zara asked.

'Not if the ground was flat. There's no angle he could have landed at that would have cracked those ribs without also breaking his collarbone, or his neck.'

Franklin Anders hadn't mentioned any attempt at CPR. I thought again of that big footprint. Of the area that had been swept clear. 'Where are his clothes?'

Holstein pointed to some trash bags in the corner. I tore them open like a raccoon and started pawing through them. In addition to the space suit, there was a tank top and some underwear with labels that said *Made in China*. They didn't look warm enough for space, but I supposed that was what the suit was for. No damage to the chest of either the suit or the tank top.

I checked inside the backpack of the space suit. Most of it was taken up by a canister of compressed air and a bottle of water, along with a web of tubes and valves.

'Another thing,' Holstein said from behind me. 'One of his ears is damaged. See here? Probably an animal, startled when the corpse was discovered, perhaps. But I thought I'd mention it in case it's relevant to your investigation.'

'Yup,' I said. 'Animals for sure.'

Zara raised an eyebrow at me and then turned to the pathologist. 'Thank you for your time.'

'Of course.' Holstein pulled the sheet back over the corpse.

'What will happen to the body?' I asked.

'Incinerated, I imagine. I'm just waiting on the paperwork.'

What a waste. 'Okay.' I pointed at the tray of exploded meat. 'But we need to take the lungs with us.'

Holstein looked surprised. 'What for?'

'That's need-to-know, I'm afraid.'

Zara sighed heavily.

'Well, all right,' Holstein said. 'Let me put them on ice for you.'

A minute later we were on our way out. The rain had started, cold little drips worming into my hair. I barely felt them. There was a parcel wrapped in butcher's paper under my arm. I was conscious of its weight as we walked towards the car. I wanted to eat now.

To distract myself, I added to my mental case file, trying to sort out who had told me what. The pathologist said the body might have been killed by the vacuum of space. According to Anders, the guy couldn't have fallen from space, because he would have burned up on re-entry. Zara's asset in Shanghai said something was taking pictures from above, but it seemed unlikely to be a satellite big enough for a crew. Garcia had suggested the astronaut might have failed to reach orbital velocity while trying to get to the satellite, perhaps to conduct repairs. But the CIA analysts said there hadn't been any recent rocket launches. On top of all that, Space City was surrounded by a fence, and cameras. If the guy hadn't come from space, then where?

I couldn't think of a theory that explained it all. But it turned out I didn't have to.

Zara's phone rang. She picked up without breaking stride. 'Yeah?'

She listened for a long time. Long enough for us to walk all the way back to the car and climb in. 'Got it,' she said finally, and hung up. 'You need to see this,' she told me, and brought up YouTube.

The video had only fourteen views, and no likes. It was grainy, and the phone had automatically boosted the colours. The ocean was too blue, the spire rising up from the vessel too white, the faces of the fishermen too red. Whoever was holding the camera kept lurching, like maybe they didn't have their sea legs yet.

'Where is this?' I asked.

'Just off Port-de-Paix.' Zara tapped her nail against a dark shape on the horizon that looked like a cloud but might have been land.

At my high school, international geography had been cut from the curriculum. 'Where's that?'

'Haiti.'

It looked like a commercial fishing vessel. Dozens of lean men in coveralls pushed crates across the slick metal deck, while others wrestled with nets.

There was a bang, and a creaking of metal. Someone yelled something. I didn't recognise the language, but I got the gist from the tone: *What the hell was that?* The camera swivelled and jerked, too fast for me to follow, then I saw what looked like a safety rail.

'Who's holding the camera?' I asked.

'A biology student from Cambridge. She was on the vessel

to collect samples from each catch and check the average age of the tuna.'

'Why?'

Zara shrugged. 'Something about climate change? Doesn't matter. Forget her.'

The camera peered over the edge of the ship, down at the choppy water. The creaking grew louder. The grumbling of the engine became a roar. There was more yelling from the workers, panicked now.

'Is that French?'

'Creole,' Zara said. 'Though about half the workers are Dominican.'

'And the ship itself?'

'Owned by a US company.'

The sea looked unremarkable, until the angle changed. There was a shadow beneath the water, tangled in a net. It looked like a giant stingray.

'What is it?' I asked.

'Just watch.'

The panicked workers produced knives and started sawing at ropes. They all seemed to be leaning in the same direction, and I realised the vessel must be tilting.

The last rope snapped before the worker's blade touched it, with a sound like a gunshot. He stumbled, clutching his face. The vessel lurched back to horizontal, sending the crew staggering.

The camera swung back to the object the net had been caught on. The sun emerged from behind the clouds, lighting it up for a split second before it sank out of sight.

Zara tapped the screen, scrubbed back a couple of seconds and paused the video.

It wasn't a stingray.

'That,' Zara said, 'is a Chengdu J-20S. A Chinese stealth fighter aircraft. We got lucky—it landed right in the middle of the trawler's path. If it hadn't, we'd never have found it.'

'How can you tell the model?' To me, all fighter jets look the same, especially underwater.

'IMINT analysed the video to calculate the distance from the nose to the tail, and from wingtip to wingtip. It matches a photo taken late last year.'

IMINT was Imagery Intelligence. I stared at the plane, thinking.

Zara kept talking. 'No sign of external damage. But it sinks slowly, and the front looks lighter than the back, which could mean the fuel tank is empty. Our best guess is that the pilot bailed out, and then the autopilot kept the plane in the air until it ran out of fuel.'

My stomach gurgled. More excitement than hunger. 'Meaning what?'

'Meaning our dead astronaut wasn't an astronaut,' Zara said. 'He was a fighter pilot.'

CHAPTER 10

Seven years ago

I wake you up. When I tickle your
lungs, you let me out. What am I?

I found Garcia chopping wood behind his home in Louetta,
dressed in work boots, a sleeveless shirt and polyester
shorts despite the weather. The axe looked like a toy in
his big hands. He'd been at it a while—his face was red,
the blood deliciously close to the surface. His muscles were
pre-seasoned with sweat.

'No,' he said, as I showed him the photograph. 'Never
seen that girl before.'

'You sure?' I asked.

He nodded.

At the group home, I'd sometimes played Go Fish with
a kid named Ritchie—he was the only kid with a complete
deck. I could always tell when he was cheating. I'd ask, 'Got
any sixes?' And he'd say no right away, without taking a
second to check his hand.

I'd pulled some records on Garcia before I came here.
He'd graduated from Texas A&M with an engineering

degree, and was now a communications engineer for a start-up that was about to be purchased by Lockheed Martin. The deal, if it went ahead, should make him a rich man. He'd been married for eight years but had no kids.

'Can you tell me where you were between four-thirty and eight o'clock yesterday?' I asked him.

An innocent man would ask why we wanted to know.

'At home,' Garcia said, without hesitation. Like he'd known in advance we would be asking about that specific window of time.

Richmond was behind me, holding a coffee cup instead of noodles this time. One hand was tucked into the pocket of his suit jacket. 'Can anyone verify that?'

'My wife. She'll be home soon.'

If this were a homicide case, I would have waited for the wife to get home and see if she supported his story. But for all I knew, Lilah Parget was running out of air in a coffin somewhere. I wouldn't get my reward unless she was found alive. *One for one.*

I pocketed the picture. 'You didn't go to the mall?'

Garcia swallowed. 'Oh, yeah. That's right. I guess I left the mall at about four-thirty, then came home.'

'You drove straight here?'

'Yep.' He balanced the axe on its head next to the woodpile.

'What were you buying at the mall?' I asked.

Another swallow. 'Just some food, you know.'

We had him on camera entering a sporting goods store, but there was no footage from inside. The owner had told us she didn't believe in security cameras. She said they would scare off her privacy-conscious customers, and that no one would be stupid enough to rob a place with so many guns behind the counter.

'You went all the way to the mall for food?' I asked. 'There's a grocery store just around the corner from here. A diner, too.'

'I wanted to drive,' he said. 'I like listening to podcasts.'

Richmond crossed his arms. 'You keep the receipt?'

'From the food court? No.'

I kept the pressure up: 'What podcast did you listen to?'

'Don't know. Something on NPR.'

At the time I didn't own a smartphone and wasn't sure how podcasts worked, so I couldn't tell whether that was a realistic answer.

'What's this about?' Garcia asked, too late. 'Who's the girl?'

His face was a masterclass in fake confusion. If he hadn't already lied about going to the mall and what he bought there, I might have fallen for it.

'Her name is Lilah Parget,' I said. 'She was at the mall too. She disappeared a few minutes before you left. You don't mind if we look in the trunk of your car, do you?'

I could see the moment Garcia realised how much trouble he was in. His cheeks went grey, and his breathing stopped. It was like looking at a corpse.

'Got a warrant?' he asked.

'We can get one,' I said. 'If that's how you want to play it.'

'I'm not playing at anything. I just don't want you going through my stuff.'

'Why? What are you worried we might find?'

'Nothing. It's just, you know, privacy.'

Privacy did seem hard to find these days. I wondered if that was partly because so many of the people advocating for it had been exposed as criminals.

Richmond was already on the phone, requesting the warrant.

That seemed to give Garcia an idea. 'I'm calling my attorney,' he said triumphantly.

He was wealthy, but not the kind of wealthy who could prevent this, attorney or no. 'Fine,' I said.

There was a lot of standing around after that. While both Richmond and Garcia were on the phone, I walked around the house, looking in the windows. It was reasonably tidy. A rental—all the photo frames were on shelves rather than hung on the walls. A wedding photo was visible, but I couldn't tell anything about the bride from this distance. Some books on a coffee table, coats hanging from a rack, a TV switched to a 24-hour news channel.

Garcia and Richmond ended up putting both their phones on speaker so the lawyer and the judge could argue directly. The lawyer said Garcia's visit to the mall didn't constitute probable cause to search his car. The judge seemed to agree. Richmond pointed out that only two other cars had left during the same window and that the other two drivers had alibis, though he left out how shaky Jeb Parget's was. He mentioned the holes in Garcia's shapeshifting story about where he was and why. The judge seemed to agree with all that, too. Everyone's voices were quiet and level, but there were clenched jaws all around, as if we were all being electrocuted by a low-voltage current.

Finally the judge gave us permission to search the car. Garcia sagged, defeated. He led us into his garage. The tyres had left a faint trail of mud on the floor.

Garcia handed Richmond his keys. 'I'm telling you, there's nothing in there.'

Richmond fiddled until he found the button. The trunk popped open.

I knew immediately that Lilah wasn't inside. She had been missing for more than twenty-four hours, and after that long in the trunk of a car, there would have been an odour of piss, and maybe decomposition.

Instead we found a lug wrench, a jack, some wheel chocks and an air compressor. That was it.

'See?' Garcia said.

Richmond sighed. 'Why'd you make such a fuss?'

He went to close the trunk, but I put a hand up to stop him. 'Why indeed?'

Richmond's eyes narrowed.

I lifted the stiff carpeted board that concealed the spare tyre. Something had been stuffed into the hollow where the jack was supposed to be.

I pulled it out and unfolded it. A ski mask. Underneath it was a nylon rope, and underneath that, a handgun.

'Those aren't mine,' Garcia said. Of the many lies he could have chosen, this was probably the dumbest.

'Whose are they?' I asked, still holding the mask.

Garcia opened his mouth and closed it again.

'What were you buying at that sporting goods store, if not this?'

Still Garcia said nothing.

None of the items in the trunk were illegal. In Texas, even the handgun didn't require a permit. But Richmond must have decided we had enough to work with.

'You have the right to remain silent.' He zip-tied Garcia's hands behind his back. 'A piece of advice, though—the sooner you tell us where that little girl is, the less time you'll spend in prison.'

•

I drove through the dark, not quite aimlessly. Letting my subconscious decide the route.

The evidence had been stacking up against Garcia. A packet of cigarettes matching the brand behind the trash cans was found in his home, and the woman in the sporting goods store identified him as the one who'd paid cash for the ski mask, the gun and the rope. She said it hadn't seemed suspicious at the time, because he'd bought some other things, too. Mostly swimming gear, she thought. Garcia's wife, Esmerelda, hadn't supported his claim that he came straight home from the mall. She'd told us he got to the house around seven. But her husband wouldn't have done anything wrong, she'd added quickly. Too quickly.

Garcia was still denying everything. He claimed the cigarettes weren't his, that he'd bought the gun and the rope for hunting, and that the ski mask was for snowboarding, even though he didn't own a snowboard. He'd denied having anything to do with Lilah's disappearance. Which probably meant he had killed her and was hoping we wouldn't find the body.

If she was dead, I wouldn't get my reward.

Garcia couldn't have taken Lilah more than thirty miles from the mall—not if he was home by seven. But that was still a huge search radius. Richmond had pointed out that it got even bigger if you factored in the possibility of an accomplice, though I thought that was unlikely. Garcia and the accomplice would have alibied each other, if he'd had one.

I'd started at the mall and spiralled outwards, always choosing the darkest alleys in the worst neighbourhoods. Potholed roads, graffitied walls, crumbling buildings coated in lead-based paint, dogs with no collars running around. Sleeping bags in doorways. The sort of places I used to live. Places where people might ignore a kid being dragged along, because they knew if the cops were called, things would get worse rather than better.

I didn't look like a cop, so I'd hoped to have more luck than the Houston PD, who'd been doing this all day. But after almost nine hours, I'd found nothing.

Whenever I saw a pedestrian, I slowed down and held Lilah's picture out the window. 'You seen this girl?'

Most people walked faster, pretending not to hear. But some looked, and sadly shook their heads.

When I stopped at one corner, a guy shuffled up to the car. He was white, with a knit cap, a puffy jacket and brows so thin he might have plucked them. 'Hey man, what do you need?'

'I'm looking for this girl.' I held up the picture.

He didn't seem to hear me. 'I got a little bit of shirt and some pants.'

I thought those were probably drugs. 'Seen this kid?'

He finally registered the picture. 'Fuck you, man.' He hurried away.

I kept driving. The sun would rise soon. The world had started to seem unreal because I hadn't slept or eaten. The buildings looked like movie sets. I found myself gazing at the homeless people huddled in corners, sheltering from the wind.

I knew all too well that none of these people would be missed. One could vanish, and their friends would assume they'd found a place in a shelter.

There was plenty of room in my trunk.

Go home, I thought, but I didn't.

When I slowed down at a crosswalk, a woman in fish-nets and a crop top approached me. She saw me looking at all the exposed flesh and flashed me a wicked smile.

I rolled down the window.

'Hello, handsome,' she said, in a British accent that may or may not have been fake. Her smile faded as she saw the picture in my hand. I'd forgotten I was holding it.

'You her dad?' she asked.

'No,' I said, too tired to work out whether I should have lied.

'Try the tents,' she said, then walked away, ass jiggling.

I knew where she meant—a public park which was basi-cally a refugee camp. It expanded and contracted with each housing crisis, like the city's lungs breathing in and out. Soon I was on the outskirts, looking at the wall of card-board signs, scrawled with pleas for help. I parked nearby and wandered into the mass of tents, brandishing Lilah's picture.

No one had searched here. The police assumed the girl was either dead or being held captive somewhere. No one had considered the possibility that she'd escaped from

Garcia. But if she had, why would she hide here instead of going home? The sex worker's tip seemed unlikely. Still I searched, too tired to think of a better plan.

For a place with so many people, it was eerily quiet. Tent flaps rustled and shopping cart wheels squeaked, but there were no voices. A fire crackled from a pile of broken two-by-fours, middle-aged women staring morosely into the flames. One of them had a bundle of blankets that might have been a baby. I made my way through the labyrinth, showing the photo to people who looked fat because they were wearing everything they owned. I tried to let my subconscious guide me again, but someone was cooking meat somewhere. I fought temptation, but the smell kept luring me back. I was circling like a mosquito around a bug zapper.

Eventually a man with a dirty face looked at the picture and wordlessly pointed a gloved finger down a narrow gap between the rows of tents. I trudged through and found myself facing a portable barbecue on which hot dogs were cooking. A few people were standing around it, warming their hands. I should have let my hunger guide me here after all.

A twelve-year-old girl was staring at the hot dogs, crying.

•

'She says she can't remember anything.' Dr Norman peeled off a latex glove and threw it across the examination room. It landed in the trash without touching the rim. She was tall—maybe she played basketball.

'Drugs in her system?' I asked.

'It'll be a while before the blood test comes back, but there are no obvious signs of that.'

'What about the saliva on the cigarette?'

Richmond had found a butt in Sam Garcia's trash.

Norman pulled off her shower cap, freeing her wavy hair. 'It's a DNA match for the smokes you found at the mall.'

Luzhin, the field office director, was hovering nearby, looking relieved. DNA held more sway with a jury than a confession. Garcia was definitely going away.

'Does Lilah have a head injury?' My voice reverberated against the hard surfaces of the laboratory—the tiled floor, resin countertops, a full-length mirror on the back of the door. I felt like singing, and this would be a good room for it. The girl was alive. My luck had never been this good.

'No injuries at all.' Norman signed a form, closed a manila folder and handed it to Luzhin. 'My guess is she's blocking something out.'

'I don't believe in repressed memories,' I said. 'At least not right after the event.'

Norman raised an eyebrow. She always towered over me, but today she seemed especially imperious. 'Remind me—where did you study medicine?'

'*You* work mostly on dead people. Don't pretend psychology is your specialty.'

'Okay, that's enough.' Luzhin stepped between us. 'Do you have anything else we can charge this asshole with? Signs of sexual assault, maybe?'

'Nothing physical,' Norman said.

This was consistent with Garcia's statement. After Lilah was found, he finally broke down and confessed to the kidnapping—but swore he'd never harmed her.

Still, people had varying definitions of 'harm'. When investigators asked him why he'd taken Lilah, he clammed up.

'I'm just saying people often pretend they don't remember something when they're ashamed of it,' I said. 'He could have done all sorts of things to her without touching her, things she might not want to tell us about.'

'How can we make her remember?' Luzhin asked Norman. 'Without her statement, we only have him on the kidnapping charge. He could be paroled in six years.'

'You can't *make* her remember. The brain doesn't work like that. It might come out in therapy twenty years from now, or it might not.'

I thought Lilah could probably be coaxed, since she was only pretending to have forgotten. But I didn't care how long Garcia went to prison for. I'd saved Lilah, so I got my reward. *One for one.*

'A person doesn't just wake up one day and decide to kidnap a stranger,' I said, trying to move things along. 'Garcia will have been building up to this for a while. You'll find child exploitation materials on his computer, or the number of a trafficker in his phone. Or evidence of a previous attempt. Show his picture around. Some kid will recognise him as the guy who claimed to have a puppy in a windowless van. Then you'll be able to put him away for longer.'

Luzhin perked up a bit. 'Yeah, I guess.' He turned to Norman. 'Thanks for coming in at short notice, doc.'

'No problem,' Norman said. 'I wanted to come in anyway—my morgue is missing a body, and I thought it might have been sent here by mistake.'

'Oh?' I said. 'Whose body?'

'A serial rapist they executed in Huntsville. Nasty piece of work. There wasn't going to be a funeral, but some family came out of the woodwork at the last minute.'

My poker face was better than Luzhin's. He was sniffing and fiddling with his watch, like it was suddenly too tight.

'No sign of it, though,' Norman continued. 'Maybe it's already at the funeral home. These mix-ups happen more often than you might think.'

'I'll bet,' I said. 'See you round, doc.'

CHAPTER 11

Two weeks ago

Stay away—I'm sharp and thin.
Send some money, shave your skin.
What am I?

The fence around Space City was chain-link, with razor wire at the top. The kind of thing you see around a minimum-security prison. The security cameras were blocky, weatherproof things, mounted every thirty or forty feet.

'The fence looks new,' I observed, as we rolled towards the checkpoint in Zara's Prius.

'It is,' Zara said. 'Space City was recently identified as a target for cyberattacks, because it's the primary source of visual data about the sky over the United States. The network isn't connected to the internet, which helps with security, but they needed the fence, too. The air gap is pointless if anyone can just walk in and install a virus manually.'

'Like we're about to do?'

'Correct.'

As far as Zara was concerned, the crashed Chinese plane explained everything. It must have been flying over Space City on a reconnaissance mission, taking hi-res photos of the equipment below—the same photos her source in Shanghai had seen. The plane had malfunctioned somehow. The pilot had bailed out. But he'd been too high, and his suit had leaked. Decompression killed him before he hit the ground. The plane had continued on autopilot until it ran out of fuel and crashed into the sea. The pilot's body hadn't burned up on re-entry because it never reached orbital velocity. Everyone else at the CIA was apparently scrambling to work out where the plane had taken off, since it didn't have the range to get from China to here.

I had other questions. 'Why didn't the fighter pilot have a parachute?'

'Parachutes are usually attached to the ejector seat rather than the pilot, at least in the US Air Force. If he wasn't buckled in properly, the seat could have landed in the bay, miles from his body. I don't know much about Chinese aircraft, though. Did it look like there was room for a chute in his backpack? They pack down pretty small.'

'Maybe.' I hadn't thought to look for a chute compartment. The flight suit had looked so much like a space suit that I'd seen only what I expected to see when I opened the backpack. As usual, the meat had distracted me.

We stopped in front of a security guard, who checked our IDs while two others looked inside the trunk and peered under the car with a mirror on a stick.

'Can I walk along the fence-line?' I asked the guard.

A guard peered at me over her sunglasses. She had piercing blue eyes, with crow's-feet around them—she was older than she'd looked. Thin lips, a crucifix on a gold chain around her neck. 'Who are you?'

'Timothy Blake. You just checked my ID. I'm here to update the security protocols.'

'If I get orders from my CO to let you look around, then sure,' the guard said. 'Not that there's any point. Until then, I'll have to ask you to move along.'

Zara started to ease the car forwards, but I yanked the park brake. 'Why isn't there any point?'

'I did a full perimeter this morning,' the guard said. 'I do it every day. There were no gaps in the fence, no holes under it, nothing. Whatever security problems you're here to fix, that fence ain't one of them.'

'Thank you.' Zara released the brake and zoomed forwards before I could ask any more questions.

'I need you to listen carefully,' she said, once the windows were up.

'I'm listening.'

'The investigation is over. Our mission is to plant the USB modem, erase the security footage and leave. That's it.'

'What's the point of trying to cover this up?' I asked. 'The media already ran the story.'

'They ran a story about a dead astronaut. The MSS doesn't know we've figured out what really happened, and we want to keep it that way.'

'We *don't* know what happened,' I said. 'How did the pilot land without breaking his legs or arms? Whose footprint was that in the field? And why would Bluffdale alert us to a space launch that apparently didn't happen?'

Zara huffed. 'Why do you care? You got some meat.'

'Hardly any.' Those exploded lungs weighed three pounds at the most.

'Well, the sooner we move on to our next assignment, the sooner you can get more. So, for once, let's just do our jobs without making things more complicated than they need to be. Okay?'

Years ago I ran a mail-order business solving riddles and puzzles for cash. It was supposed to be a money-laundering scam, but it surprised me by becoming a genuinely profitable side hustle, at least for a while. I liked solving those puzzles because it kept my brain from straying into dark territory.

With my son dead and Thistle out of my life, there were only two things I cared about. Food, and puzzles. The dead fighter pilot was both. I didn't like leaving him unfinished, in either sense of the word.

But I shrugged. 'Fine.'

The museum was two buildings, one low and flat, the other more like a cube. A sign said *Space Center Houston*, which seemed like a confusing name for a museum housed within the Johnson Space Center in Houston. We parked in the shadow of the Space Shuttle *Independence*, which was mounted on top of a giant plane. This was where I'd seen all the police cars yesterday.

Hazel Cuthbert, the deputy cybersecurity chief, worked in this building. With her boss on leave, she was the only one who could give us access to the video footage from Tuesday night.

As we approached the front doors of the museum, I saw that one of the ground-floor windows had been boarded up.

'I saw cop cars parked here yesterday,' I said.

'You mentioned that,' Zara said. 'So?'

'I figured Detective Jones' team had gone to the wrong address. Now I'm thinking they were here to investigate a break-in.' This meant that the 911 dispatcher could have leaked the story about the astronaut to the media after all. But I still liked my theory that Garcia had done it.

'Interesting,' Zara lied, and led the way into the building.

The entrance was filled with exhibits—a Mars rover, a detached cockpit from a rocket, some moon rocks in glass cases. In keeping with NASA's 'for all mankind' ethos, the curators hadn't limited themselves to American achievements. There were flags from several countries next to examples of their contribution to space science. The place had a model UN feel. Tourists in polo shirts wandered around with DSLRs dangling around their necks, oohing at replicas hanging from wires.

'Isn't this better than the Kennedy Space Center?' an old man whispered to his family, who ignored him.

The shatterproof glass had been swept off the floor, but hastily. Some was trapped in the corners of the room. While Zara introduced herself to a receptionist and asked to speak to Cuthbert, I examined the debris.

Most of the glass was transparent and of uniform thickness. But some was thinner, coloured and curved. This window had been rammed by a car, and the car had cracked a headlight. Some of the pieces had flecks of paint on them, too. But the flecks were too small to identify the colour.

I pocketed some glass and wandered over to one of the exhibits—it looked like a giant robotic butterfly. Apparently it was a half-scale replica of a Japanese probe called Hayabusa that had collected dust from an asteroid and returned it to Earth.

I was reading the plaque when Zara approached with a willowy woman in her fifties. She was unexpectedly glamorous, with vivid lipstick, a wraparound dress and dangling earrings shaped like atoms, diamond electrons caught mid-spin around a pearl nucleus. But she had nicotine nails, and looked stressed.

'Sorry I'm late,' she said. 'My boss was scheduled to take some leave next week, but he seems to have decided to go early. I confess I wasn't quite ready. I'm Hazel Cuthbert, by the way.'

'Timothy Blake. We're here to see some security footage so we can prepare a report for the air force.'

'Yes, your authorisation just dropped into my inbox.' She gestured to the butterfly robot. 'You're admiring Hayabusa?'

Actually, I'd been wondering why anyone would bother to collect asteroid dust. 'Yeah.'

'I was in awe of the Japanese when that one came back. Hayabusa2 is in the sky right now. Scheduled to return in 2031.'

'Do the scientists need more dust?'

Cuthbert's laugh was high and nervous. 'Let me put it this way. Valuable metals, such as gold, tend to be heavy. This means that over the last four billion years or so, most of the gold on Earth has settled towards the lower levels of the crust, too deep to mine. But asteroids don't have as much mass as the Earth, and therefore not as much gravity. So the gold is on the surface, just waiting to be scooped up. In fact, most of the gold mined on Earth has come from ancient asteroid impacts. One asteroid between Mars and Jupiter, called 16 Psyche, contains enough gold to make every person on Earth a billionaire.'

That seemed unlikely to me. If that asteroid were ever collected, I figured one rich person would get a whole lot richer and nothing else would change.

'Is gold useful?' I asked. 'Or just expensive?'

'It makes an excellent shield against infrared light in spacecraft and flight suits.'

'So we go into space to find gold so we can keep going into space to find more gold?'

'Ah, you're a cynic.' She sounded amused.

'So, the footage . . .' Zara prompted.

'Right. My office is this way.' Cuthbert led us through the crowd of tourists towards a bank of elevators.

I pointed back at the boarded-up window. 'Looks like you've had a break-in.'

'On Tuesday night. Fortunately, nothing seems to be missing. The culprit was probably a vandal rather than a burglar.'

She held the elevator doors open for Zara and me, then let go. The steel doors slid inwards, trapping us. A thought popped into my head, the same one that appears any time I'm in an elevator with another person: *If we get stuck between floors, how long should I wait before I suggest we draw straws?*

'I know what you're thinking,' Cuthbert said.

I doubted that.

'Why would the deputy head of cybersecurity choose to work in the museum?' she continued. 'You'll understand when you see the view from my office.'

We rode the elevator all the way to the top floor, then walked down a tiled corridor to her door. The office was bigger than Garcia's had been, and devoid of personal touches. Sticky notes surrounded her computer monitor. Her window overlooked the gigantic space shuttle—approaching the glass gave me vertigo. In the far distance, I could see the place where the fighter pilot's body had been found.

'Did you happen to look out your window yesterday morning?' I asked.

'No, why?'

'Because the sunrise was amazing,' Zara interrupted. 'Anyway, can we see the CCTV from Tuesday night?'

'Of course.' Cuthbert swiped her access card to wake up her computer. 'I'm afraid there are no cameras in the rock yard, so you won't be able to see the astronaut landing—'

'There was no astronaut,' Zara said. 'One of the staff had a seizure out there. He was diabetic, apparently. They found him in a comatose state. But the doctors think he'll pull through.'

This part of the cover story was essential. No death meant no gossip.

'Really?' Cuthbert sounded confused. 'Sam Garcia said it was a Chinese astronaut. And it was on the news. Everyone's talking about it.'

'They are?' Zara rolled her eyes. 'More conspiracy theories. God, this is going to be Area 51 all over again.'

Cuthbert clicked on some icons and typed in a password. A series of video files began to fill the screen.

'If it was a diabetic coma,' she asked, 'why do you need to see the surveillance footage?'

Zara waved a hand around. '*Thank* you. That's what *I* said. Now . . .' She peered at the screen. 'Wow, that's a lot of files. This will take us a while. Any chance of a cup of coffee?'

Cuthbert looked a little put out but said, 'Uh, sure. Simone!'

Silence fell. There was no sign of Cuthbert's PA. I wondered if that was just good luck, or if Zara had somehow arranged her absence. Maybe she was in Guantanamo Bay.

Cuthbert sighed. 'How do you take it?'

'Cream, and one-and-a-half sugars, and not too hot, please.' Zara's order would be time-consuming to make, but it wasn't so complicated that Cuthbert would come back early and ask for clarification.

'Cream, sugar and salt,' I said.

'Salt?'

'Right.'

'Oooookay.' Cuthbert left us to it.

As soon as she was gone, Zara inserted the USB modem into the back of the computer. There were no lights on it—the grey plastic was almost invisible among the cables. She wiped it for prints, then leaned over the computer. A dialogue box had appeared. She clicked *run as administrator*. As the spyware installed itself on the computer—on the whole network—she went back to the CCTV files, hit *select all*, and reached for the delete key.

'Wait,' I said.

Zara glared at me. 'We're not here to investigate, Blake.'

'Just hang on.' I'd spotted a file from five pm Tuesday. The time of the pilot's death, according to Holstein. I double-clicked it.

The video included sixteen feeds, all laid out on a grid. I boosted the speed to 32x, my eyeballs flitting from one square to the next. I could see Anders, the guy who'd found the body the following morning. He was in an office, typing, pausing occasionally to adjust the height of his swivel chair. In another square I saw a swimming pool, with a woman doing laps. At one point, Anders left his office and walked to the pool. But, seeing it was occupied, he went right back to his office. The woman got out soon after and disappeared into the showers.

Another square showed the cafeteria, where Garcia was talking on a cell phone. He picked it up and put it back down a lot, like he was making several calls. He went to the bathroom and was off camera for about six minutes.

Garcia's feet were big enough to make the print I'd seen. But was six minutes long enough to get from the cafeteria to the rock yard and back? I didn't think so. He didn't even look out of breath.

'We don't have time for this,' Zara hissed.

There were other staff I didn't recognise. A few clocked out at five-thirty, and a few more at six. By seven there was just a lone janitor, pushing a vacuum cleaner along a corridor. I wasn't sure exactly what I'd hoped to see, but I hadn't seen it.

'Move.' Zara shoved me aside, hit CTRL+A, and then SHIFT+DELETE. All the records from the astronaut's time of death vanished.

As Zara started copying the files from Wednesday into Tuesday's folder, I heard high heels clicking up the corridor towards us. Cuthbert was back already.

'Incoming,' I said.

'Asshole,' Zara muttered, still tapping at the keyboard. 'Stall her.'

I stepped out into the corridor and felt all the blood drain from my face.

It wasn't Cuthbert.

It was Reese Thistle.

CHAPTER 12

Now

I'm severe until a change of character
puts me at peace. What am I?

'Tell me more about Thistle,' says Dr Diaz, with a serene smile. 'How did you meet?'

The clock on the office wall doesn't tick. The second hand glides around in silence, a vulture circling.

'We grew up together.' I rub my knees as though my palms are sticky. 'Same group home. She got adopted out, I didn't. Later, when I was consulting for the FBI, I bumped into her again.' I find myself looking out the window at the walls surrounding the hospital. 'That's pretty much all there is to it.'

'What's she like?'

I don't want to tell Diaz anything about Thistle. It feels like a betrayal. 'I liked her.'

'Was she working for the FBI too?'

'Yeah. She never got the respect that she deserved there. Other agents were always either dismissing her work or taking credit for it. But she stayed, because she believed in the job. Defending victims. Standing up to organised crime. All that.'

'And you became friends?'

That doesn't even begin to cover it. At the group home I survived neglect, starvation and physical violence. I wasn't the only biter there. Add to that the fact that my parents died, violently, in front of me. I'd always told myself that I was doomed to become a monster. I never had a choice.

But Reese Thistle endured exactly the same hardships, and she turned out fine. Better than fine. When I realised that, my whole sense of self crumbled. But that was okay, because she loved me.

Until she didn't.

I don't tell Diaz any of this. 'Friends, yeah.'

Diaz's voice is careful. 'Was this a romantic relationship?'

I nod, still without looking at her.

'Was it your *first* romantic relationship?'

A smaller nod.

'Did it become sexual?'

I say nothing.

Diaz writes something down in her notebook. 'But you stopped seeing each other.'

That's one way of putting it. 'Right.'

'Recently?'

'About four months ago.' Like the exact date isn't burned into my brain.

'Why was that?'

I don't want to talk about the corpse Reese Thistle found in my freezer. The look on her face when she realised what I was. The way I corrupted her—she was too horrified to keep seeing me, but cared about me too much to turn me in.

'She didn't want to date a cannibal,' I say. That seems to cover everything.

'Before the break-up,' Diaz says, 'what do you think Thistle liked about you?'

'She thought I wasn't a cannibal.'

'Presumably she knew lots of men who weren't cannibals. Why did she choose you, specifically?'

I hesitate. 'She thought I was smart, I guess. And tough— she said that once. She didn't realise how messed up I was. And that I was mostly solving cases by committing crimes, rather than by being clever.'

Diaz sighs, like I've disappointed her. Then she stands up. 'Let's swap seats.'

I cock my head. 'Huh?'

'You sit here—I'll sit over there.'

Puzzled, I obey. We circle each other, like dance partners. I sit. Her chair is a little firmer than mine. Warm from her butt—one of the more nutritious parts of the body.

She sinks into my chair. 'Imagine you're the psychiatrist and I'm the patient,' she says.

'Sure.'

'I've just come in, and I've told you that I'm a CIA agent.'

'CIA asset.'

'Okay, asset. What would you assume, after I told you that?'

'I'm not a doctor,' I say.

'Pretend you are. Don't tell my colleagues I said this, but a lot of psychiatry is just common sense.' She smiles, like she's revealing a juicy secret. As though I hadn't already guessed that her whole profession was bullshit.

'I guess I'd think you were lying for attention,' I say. 'Or maybe delusional.'

She lets that hang in the air.

'I'm not, though,' I say. 'It's all real.'

'All right. But now imagine I tell you about my first and only girlfriend, someone who'd known me all my life, who knew me better than anyone else, maybe somebody I'd had a crush on long before we hooked up. I tell you she rejected me about four months ago. Right before I was *recruited by the CIA*.' She doesn't do air quotes, but I can feel them. 'And then I tell you that I met this woman again, shortly before I started therapy. What would your reaction be?'

I think about it. 'I'd assume that the break-up was traumatic, and that it caused the delusions.'

She gives me a patient look.

'But I was eating people before Thistle left,' I say. 'I told you that.'

'It's not uncommon to rewrite the past so it fits with our view of the present. We all do it, to one degree or another.'

'Aren't you supposed to try to build a rapport with me before you tell me I'm crazy?'

She takes this as rhetorical. 'How did you feel, when Thistle rejected you?'

'Not great,' I say.

Diaz waits for me to elaborate.

I don't want Thistle to be blamed for what's wrong with me. 'She did the right thing, though.'

'Tell me what you mean by that.'

'She's better off without me in her life.'

'The break-up made you feel like a bad person?'

'I *am* a bad person.' I hold her gaze now, a bit defiantly.

But she just smiles. 'I think it might be a little more complicated than that, Timothy.' She stands up. 'I'd like you to do some journalling. Each night, write down everything you experienced that day, in as much detail as you can remember. No one else will read your journal, unless you choose to share it. It's just to help you make sense of things. Try to resist the urge to interpret the events. We want just the facts, no theories. Okay?'

'Okay,' I say.

•

I leave Diaz's office and turn left, towards my room. But when she closes her door, I do a one-eighty, heading for the main entrance.

The Behavioural Health Unit at the George Clark Red Memorial Hospital is T-shaped. The doctors' offices and administration are on the east side. There are communal facilities to the west, including a kitchen, an eating area, a TV and another walled-off garden. To the south is a long corridor of patient bedrooms.

Most of the Behavioural Health Unit is tiled with green linoleum, faded from decades of mopping. The walls are plain, with glossy white paint. Vomit and shit wipe right off. But the closer you get to the entrance, the more attractive everything becomes. There's a Persian rug as long as a bus, a miniature palm in a huge ceramic pot and paintings of mountains and lighthouses on the walls. This is the bit outsiders see, and the decor probably makes them feel better about having their loved ones committed.

Dr Diaz would say I'm *interpreting*.

Eventually I reach reception. The counter is protected by a tempered glass screen, like you'd see at a bank, with a two-inch gap between the counter and the screen so you can hear the receptionist's voice. The counter faces the entrance: two doors, one in front of the other, like an airlock. The doors are also made of tempered glass. It looks fragile, but I know it isn't. A resident recently tried to smash her way out with a shovel stolen from the garden. She kept swinging until the head of the shovel snapped off. The glass didn't crack.

There's a keypad next to the inner door, and another next to the outer door. I don't know the code for either one, but the receptionist can open them with a button under the counter.

Today, the person on duty is a woman in her fifties, with friendly brown eyes, curly hair pulled back, and the teeth of a lifelong smoker. I hear her voice through the gap under the glass: 'What are you up to, Timothy?'

'I was expecting a visitor,' I say.

She's not fooled. 'Oh? Who's that?'

'No one in particular.'

'Is this the same no one you were waiting for yesterday?'

'I won't know for sure unless they turn up.'

On the wall behind Smoker Teeth is a pegboard, dozens of keys hanging off it. Metal keys are too sharp to be taken into the building, so all the staff leave theirs here. The keys used inside the building are all made of plastic.

I try to guess which ones belong to Diaz. Not the key ring with the bejewelled love-heart chain. Nor the one with the Kawasaki tag—a motorbike helmet wouldn't agree with her hair. There are a few keys for ambulances, stickered with the licence plate numbers—I rule them out, too. Soon I've narrowed it down to two unadorned sets, one for a Toyota, another for a Nissan.

Smoker Teeth leans over, looking past me and through the doors to the parking lot outside. 'I don't think anyone's coming.'

'Probably not,' I agree.

She smiles. 'Maybe you'll have better luck tomorrow.'

I haven't eaten—properly eaten—in weeks. I'm starving. If there's no way out of the hospital, I might have to make do with the food that's already here.

I smile back at Smoker Teeth, all hundred and sixty pounds of her. 'Maybe I will.'

CHAPTER 13

Two weeks ago

What kind of drink is made with a fist?

Thistle and I stared at each other.

I had convinced myself I was making progress. Some nights she didn't appear in my dreams. Some days I managed to keep myself distracted with thoughts of meat. Now I realised I had accomplished nothing. Seeing her up close, her dark eyes, her soft lips, her thick hair—it all came rushing back. What I'd had, and what I'd lost.

As shocking as this was for me, it was clearly worse for her. She stumbled backwards like she'd taken a punch. Her jaw dropped, and she reached for the gun on her hip.

But she stopped herself and didn't draw. She just stood there.

I spoke first. 'Hi.'

'Hi,' she said warily.

'What are you doing here?'

'Me?' She gave a startled snort. 'I'm an FBI agent. This is a federal facility, and a crime scene. What are *you* doing here?'

It sounded like Detective Jones had been forced to give up his case. 'You think it's a crime scene?'

She still had one hand on the gun. 'I think there's no legal way that guy could have ended up where he did, how he did.'

'You saw the body?'

'No, it was described to me by witnesses. The photos are missing, and for some reason the remains have already been incinerated—'

A look of dread crossed her face as she realised she was talking to a cannibal about a missing body. I wondered if she'd be reassured to learn that I'd only gotten the lungs and part of the ear.

'It's good to see you,' I said. I wanted to reach out and touch her. Make sure she was real. But I could tell she would shrink away. I was lucky she hadn't shot me already.

'Your arm grew back.' She pointed.

I chuckled nervously, waving my silicone hand. 'Pretty convincing, right?'

'I've seen worse, for sure.' She let go of the gun, her arms awkward by her sides. 'How have you been?'

'Fine,' I lied. 'You?'

She looked away. 'Yeah. Fine.'

Zara emerged through the doorway. I'd forgotten she existed. I'd also forgotten that she and Thistle had met before. When Zara was undercover with the dark web psychopaths, Thistle was one of the people they had abducted and held prisoner. But she'd only seen Zara briefly, and Zara had changed her hair and eye colour since then—would Thistle recognise her?

'There you are,' Zara said to me. She turned, and appeared to notice Thistle for the first time—though I was sure she'd been eavesdropping. 'Oh! Sorry, didn't see you there.'

'Who are you?' Thistle asked.

'Sandra Holcroft,' Zara said smoothly. 'Timothy and I work together at ClearHorizon.'

'What's ClearHorizon?'

I needed Thistle to believe the cover story. If there was even a hint that she didn't, Zara would report her as a potential threat. Who knew what the CIA would do then?

'It's a parasite,' I said. 'Another independent contractor soaking up your tax dollars. We send reports to the US Air Force that will be tossed in a filing cabinet and never read.'

Zara laughed. 'Do you need some more coffee, Timothy?'

Thistle still looked suspicious. I'd lied to her so many times that distrust was her default. If I told her the Earth was round, she would expect to fall off the edge. 'What kind of reports?'

'We investigate accidents and rewrite safety procedures,' Zara said. 'Timothy is one of our most capable new hires, cynicism aside. And you must be . . .?'

'Special Agent Reese Thistle, FBI.' Thistle didn't offer a hand to shake.

'My goodness! I've heard so much about you,' Zara lied.

Thistle looked alarmed. 'You have?'

'Of course!' Zara touched my elbow. Tenderly. Protectively.

Thistle noticed this, like she was supposed to. Her gaze went cold.

I needed to get away from her, before she saw through our cover and ended up at a CIA black site. I was trying to work out what to say when Cuthbert reappeared.

'I found someone to make the coffee.' She sounded relieved. 'Now, where—oh, hello.' She'd noticed Thistle.

Zara did the introductions. 'Hazel Cuthbert, this is Agent Reese Thistle.'

Cuthbert's eyebrows shot up. 'FBI? What can I do for you, agent?'

'I'm here to see some surveillance footage,' Thistle said.

Presumably the footage Zara had just overwritten. Ariel Wilcox had said no one would notice that the time stamps were wrong, or would attribute it to a malfunction. But she didn't know Thistle.

'We'll take a raincheck on the coffee,' I said. 'I'm sure Agent Thistle would like to run her own investigation without anyone watching over her shoulder.' I fixed Thistle with a pleading look.

I was a cannibal, but I'd also saved her life. Lost my arm doing it. Would she trust me?

'Yes.' Thistle's expression was unreadable. 'I'm afraid this is a confidential matter.'

'Of course.' Zara smiled pleasantly and passed a business card to Thistle. 'If we can be of any help at all. Good luck.'

Thistle looked down at the card and then tucked it into a pocket.

We walked away down the corridor. I couldn't resist a glance back. Thistle hadn't followed Cuthbert into the office. She was just standing in the corridor, watching me.

Our eyes met. I wished I could say something. Apologise for scaring her. For existing, maybe. But I looked away, and followed Zara around the corner.

•

'The spyware should have already infected the whole network,' Zara said as we drove back towards the safe house. 'I'll get SIGINT to confirm when we're back at the safe house.'

I barely heard her. I was thinking about the look on Thistle's face. I'd been overjoyed to see her, but clearly the feeling wasn't mutual.

In the time we'd spent apart, I'd apparently convinced myself that there were no hard feelings. That she thought of me fondly, and often.

I'd been a fucking fool.

The traffic around us was as thick as tar. The AC didn't quite filter out the gasoline fumes, and they were giving me a headache.

'The program will track keystrokes from every terminal and record audio from all the webcams in Space City,' Zara continued. 'So we can check if people believe the story about the diabetic coma and delete any messages that contradict it. But that's a lot of data, so we don't have the budget to listen in for very long. A week, tops.'

I kept my eyes on the road. I was counting cars, memorising licence plates and mentally rearranging the letters on signs. Trying to crowd out the dark thoughts.

'But things could get more complicated,' Zara said, 'now that your girlfriend is involved.'

I glanced over sharply. 'She's not my girlfriend.'

'Ex-girlfriend, whatever. Having spyware on the Space City network won't help us monitor an FBI investigation.'

'There won't be an investigation,' I said. 'We got rid of the body. Erased the videos. The witnesses will keep their mouths shut.'

'Agent Thistle can be very persistent,' Zara said. 'I seem to remember that you rescued her from the slaughterhouse, and then she came right back.'

The slaughterhouse was an old shed where the dark web psychopaths had kept their prisoners. Zara had let those men torture and kill their captives to maintain her cover. This hadn't seemed to trouble her conscience, then or now. She was mentioning it only to remind me that she was dangerous.

'If the FBI finds out about the crashed fighter jet, they'll draw the same conclusion we did.' Zara signalled and merged onto the freeway. 'And they suck at keeping secrets. We may need you to sabotage their investigation.'

Perhaps this was the real reason Zara had recruited me. She had known a situation like this might come up—that one day she'd need someone both well connected to the FBI and completely expendable.

'I don't have many contacts at the Bureau anymore,' I said.

'There's Thistle. And you might be pleased to hear that Agent Ruciani and Dr Norman still work there. I believe you've met Peter Luzhin's replacement, also. But if you don't think that's enough . . .' She shrugged. 'I suppose I could find another way to cut Thistle's investigation short.'

Something choked me—a mixture of panic and cold fury. I spoke without thinking: 'If anything happens to her, I'll kill you.'

Zara looked amused. 'Is that so?'

'Yes.' It was much too late to pretend Thistle didn't matter to me. My only hope was to make Zara believe the threat. 'I don't even care what happens to me afterwards. I'll kill you, and then I'll eat you.'

Zara took her gaze off the road for a moment and searched my face. Then she said, 'You're sexy when you're possessive. You know that?'

I looked out the window, heart pounding. I told myself Thistle would give up on the case. There was no evidence left that anything at all had happened. I wouldn't need to get involved.

I stared hard into the side mirror, forcing myself to breathe deeply. Counting cars, reading licence plates.

One in particular caught my eye.

'We're being followed,' I said.

Zara was experienced enough not to react. 'Where?'

'Grey Jeep Wrangler. Three cars back.'

She glanced at the side mirror, moving her eyes but not her head. She wouldn't have been able to see much. The sun was bright, glinting off the windshields of all the other cars.

'Is it your girlfriend?' Zara asked.

'She's not my girlfriend. And no.' I couldn't actually see the driver, but I wanted Zara to forget about Thistle.

'How long has it been on us?'

'Just since that last set of lights. But I saw it this morning, too.'

'Common model,' Zara said.

'Same plates.'

'Where did you see it this morning?'

'We picked it up on Katy Freeway,' I said. 'About where the traffic stop was yesterday. It turned off towards Bellaire.'

'You've only seen the one car?' Zara had caught my meaning. If the Jeep had taken the Bellaire exit but found us again here, that probably meant it was working in concert with a second vehicle.

'So far.' I wished I had sunglasses, to make it less obvious that I was examining the other vehicles. But nothing said *spy* like sunglasses, so CIA agents never wore them, except on vacation. None of the cars in our immediate vicinity looked familiar.

'How about a late lunch?' Zara signalled right. We turned, cruising into the mouth of a drive-through.

Rule number one when tailing someone: *Don't get too close*. Rule number two: *No sudden turns*. I expected the Wrangler to roll straight past. But it broke both rules, turning into the drive-through right behind us.

'You got a gun?' I asked Zara.

She raised an eyebrow.

'Just checking,' I said. 'I know you're not from Texas.'

A speaker box crackled to life next to Zara's window. 'Welcome to Jack in the Box. Can I take your order?'

'What do you want?' Zara asked me, without taking her eyes off the mirror.

'Uh . . .' Usually I would quickly order the meatiest thing on the menu. Today, I made a big show of thinking about it first.

'I'll get the Bacon Ultimate Cheeseburger,' I said finally. 'With fries.'

While the box was offering me a Coke, I turned and used my good hand to give an apologetic wave to the car riding our bumper.

No movement from behind the windshield. I still couldn't see a face, but I saw hairy knuckles on the steering wheel. Not Thistle. I was both relieved and disappointed.

'No drink,' I said.

'Will that be all?' the box asked.

'Yeah.'

'If the order on the screen is correct, please drive—'

We were already moving, turning the corner.

I buzzed down my window so I could listen. I heard the box crackle again, asking the driver behind us what he wanted. His voice was low and firm. The kind of voice I associated with military people.

When we reached the cashier's window, a lanky-haired white boy held out a POS terminal. 'Eight-fifty.'

'Quiet,' I said, still listening to the car behind.

'Excuse me?'

I couldn't make out the words, but I got the tone and rhythm of the conversation. The driver had a passenger and was asking if they wanted anything. I couldn't hear the passenger, but I could tell from the brevity of the pause that the answer was no.

Zara handed some bills to the kid. 'Pardon my friend. He's autistic.'

The kid's expression changed from annoyed to uneasy.

'You can, uh, move along to the pick-up window,' he said. 'Have a nice day.'

Zara buzzed the window back up and eased the car further along. 'There's an alley that cuts between Commerce and Franklin,' she said. 'We can lose them there.'

I knew the one. We'd driven past it this morning. A garbage truck had been trundling through, so the alley was likely to be clear now. Even if our pursuers saw us go in, there would be no subtle way to follow us. They would probably let us go.

But if they *did* follow us in, that meant they were ready for a confrontation. I got the feeling that was what Zara wanted.

'Right now, they don't know we're onto them,' I said. 'That changes as soon as you start swerving into alleyways. It's an obvious attempt to lose a tail.'

'We don't have a choice,' Zara said.

'Yes, we do. Just act natural.'

'And then what? Lead them the whole way to the safe house?'

'No, to a motel. Mid-range. The kind of place travelling consultants might stay at.'

Zara chewed her lip.

'I don't have a gun,' I added. 'And my one-two punch is just a one, these days. You think you can take out both people in that car—plus however many are in the other vehicle, the one we haven't identified—by yourself?'

We reached the pick-up window and stopped.

'Because if you can't,' I continued, 'and we both end up dead, we can't complete the operation. Which could mean a nuclear confrontation between China and the USA.'

A girl with tangled bangs appeared at the collection window. 'Sorry, there's a delay on that burger. I'll get you to pull into the waiting bay.' She pointed.

Shit, I thought.

Zara looked at me. 'Do we do it?'

I hesitated. We could just drive off, but the people in the Wrangler would have noticed that we hadn't received any food or drink. They'd realise that we'd gone into the drive-through because we were onto them. But if we pulled over, they'd pass us, and get a clear look—or a clear shot—into our vehicle.

If I'd ordered nuggets, we wouldn't be having this problem.

'Sorry, there's a delay on that burger,' the girl said again, in exactly the same voice, like we'd gone back in time ten seconds. 'I'll get you to pull into the waiting bay.'

'Do it,' I told Zara. Our pursuers would see us—but we'd also see them.

Zara eased the car forwards and pulled over. In the mirror, I saw the driver of the Wrangler reach out and take a cup from the window. It looked like he'd just ordered a soda, maybe to avoid the risk of getting stuck in the waiting bay. Smart.

Zara had drawn her Ruger LCP II, and was keeping it hidden under the handbag on her lap. It was a small gun, with a six-round magazine. I wondered what our pursuers had.

'Don't,' I said.

She ignored me. If the driver of the Wrangler pulled his own gun, she might be able to hit him before he hit her—but the muzzle flash would burn my face off.

The Wrangler caught up to us, and then overtook us. As it passed, I looked at the driver. He had a bent nose, a receding hairline and a suit jacket. He was sitting a bit higher up than me, so I couldn't see past him to the passenger. He met my gaze and held it for a beat. Then the Wrangler eased forwards, and I couldn't see either of them anymore.

It drove back out onto the road, turned right and disappeared.

Zara breathed out and put her gun away. 'You recognise that guy?'

'No. But he didn't look like a Chinese spy.'

'What, because he was white? Most spying is done by locals. Either hired or blackmailed. That guy could easily work for the MSS.'

This was true. But there was something about the way the guy looked at me. Not threatening, but not evasive either. He was suspicious of me and didn't care if I was suspicious of him in return.

Someone tapped on Zara's window. It was the girl with the bangs, holding a paper bag, the grease from the fries already soaking through.

'Bacon Ultimate Cheeseburger,' she said.

I took it. The smell of the meat made me forget all about the driver of the Wrangler.

'Have a terrific day.' The girl was already walking away.

'We still haven't identified the other car,' Zara said. 'They could be watching us right now.'

'So act natural.' I took a bite. Nearly a thousand calories in one burger. I closed my eyes so I could pretend the meat didn't come from a cow. 'Let's go to a motel.'

CHAPTER 14

When does a cut of meat watch your house?

We took a circuitous route, but not suspiciously so. We stopped for gas, even though the hybrid car was nearly full. We parked in a lot for a while, Zara pretending to make a phone call. We went to a diner, ordered coffee, acted natural. No sign that we were being followed. Either our pursuers were very good, or we weren't being pursued at all.

Clouds were creeping in by the time we reached the motel, staining the horizon lurid pink. Zara had picked a small, one-level block of rooms facing the road. If our pursuers wanted to do an overnight stake-out, they'd have to park on the road, or rent a room, either of which would give us a chance to identify them.

The woman in the little office had grey hair that concealed her hearing aids, and a wedding ring with dull, cracked stones. Signs littered her desk, pleading with visitors to rate the motel on Google, Yelp and Tripadvisor. She rattled off the rules—no smoking, breakfast orders complete by midnight, et cetera. I got the impression she thought we were having an affair. Zara encouraged that, standing on my left so she could brush her fingers against mine.

We paid for three nights. The woman got us to write down our licence plate and our fake ClearHorizon email addresses. 'Enjoy your stay,' she said finally, and handed over the keys to room four.

'Can we take room seven instead?' Zara asked. 'Better view.'

The woman looked doubtful. There was nothing worth seeing in any direction. But she gave us a different pair of keys. I followed Zara to room seven, carrying the overnight bag she always kept in the trunk. I couldn't tell if we were being watched—not without looking around in a way that would be suspicious. Zara unlocked the door, and I followed her in.

I used to clean motel rooms, so I knew more or less what to expect. A wall-mounted TV, a desk that doubled as a dining table, a closet with an ironing board and a tiny safe. A bathroom with a shower over the tub.

The room had only one bed, I noticed.

Zara was arranging the kettle and the coffee mugs, making sure all the handles were pointed in certain directions. It looked random, but it wasn't. The kettle was pointed at the door, one of the mugs was perpendicular to the wall, and the other was parallel. Anyone who searched the room thoroughly was likely to check under those objects. If they put them down again even slightly wrong, Zara would know there had been an intruder.

I sat by the window, watching the parking lot through an inch-wide gap in the curtains. I waited for five minutes. Ten. Twenty. Pebbles of rain started to appear on the glass.

Finally Zara switched on the TV, flipped to a news channel and cranked the volume. She kept her own voice low: 'Anything?'

I shook my head. 'Best guess, they parked the second car out on the road and they're waiting to see if we come out.'

'Or there is no second car.'

'That's possible,' I said, though I doubted it. 'Can you call for backup?'

'No.' Zara didn't elaborate.

I stood up and stretched, blinking to moisten my sore eyes. 'So I guess we wait for it to get dark, then go see if anyone's actually out there. If not, we can head back to the safe house.' I sat on the bed, kicked off my shoes and unhooked my prosthesis. If I wear it for too long, sores grow on my stump.

'Okay.' Zara sank down next to me, close enough that our thighs touched. 'What would you like to do while we wait?'

Zara couldn't have been attracted to me, but she wanted me to think she was. Maybe she hoped that would make me easier to manipulate. I wondered how far she'd go to maintain the illusion.

It would be a bad idea to find out. For me, people fell into two categories. There was food, and then there was Thistle. If I ate Zara, I'd be out of a job.

Without looking at her, I turned up the TV even louder.

The news story was about the Reaper: an interview with the daughter of one of the victims, who was clenching her jaw and holding back tears, and the son of another, who didn't hold them back, blubbering helplessly.

Zara looked annoyed. 'Can you change the channel?'

I flipped past *The Simpsons*, *Law & Order* and some drama with a lot of staring. Eventually we settled on another news channel, but it was entertainment news, as though that wasn't a contradiction in terms. There was a floor-length mirror next to the TV, and I could see the time reflected backwards on the bedside radio. I was watching that rather than the screen.

When the clock hit 19:45, Zara unzipped the overnight bag. No spy gadgets in there—just toiletries and quick-dry clothes, the kind travelling consultants might wear. She tossed some clothes to me, and didn't turn her back as she peeled off her shirt and pants, then took her time picking new ones.

She wasn't as muscular as Thistle, and her skin was smooth—no scars.

My stomach growled.

A smile tugged at the corner of Zara's mouth. She seemed flattered.

I averted my eyes as I pulled on the polyester pants, wondering which one of us was crazier.

Soon I was dressed in a puffy jacket with a fur-lined hood. I didn't have a gun—without a thumb, the recoil was likely to break my nose—so I took a cheap knife from the cutlery drawer and zippered it into one of my pockets.

Zara had finally selected a ball cap and a dark UCLA sweater, the Ruger taped to her belly beneath it. 'Good to go?' she asked.

I peeped through the slit between the curtains. It was dark out there now. Still no new cars in the lot. Either our pursuers had decided to stake us out from the road rather than getting a room, or they were gone.

Or maybe they didn't exist. There might be no second vehicle. The Wrangler could have found us some other way. A bug in our car, or spyware in our phones. Or, if it was the Chinese government, a secret spy plane hovering above our heads.

'Good to go,' I said.

The window in the bathroom wasn't designed to open all the way, but Zara got the brackets off with the screwdriver on her Swiss Army knife while I put my prosthesis back on. I dragged a chair across and flung a towel over the window-sill. Zara went out first, as nimbly as a cat. I was clumsier, bruising my chest despite the towel, and knocking over the chair with a flailing leg. Zara wrapped one arm around my torso as I wriggled through, and helped me get to the ground without further injury. She was stronger than she looked.

I pulled up the hood of my jacket to keep the rain off, and looked around. There was a vacant lot behind our room, separated from us by a wire fence. According to a weathered sign, a fire station had been demolished after dangerous chemicals leaked into the soil. Judging by the rips at the bottom of the wire, the sign hadn't deterred people from sneaking in. Maybe it had even encouraged them. People thought this would be a private place to do drugs or have sex, because everyone else would be smart enough to stay away.

We walked along the fence, past the back of a tyre store and the dumpsters behind a greasy spoon. After about two hundred yards we turned right, and soon met the road again. It was a desolate stretch of blacktop. There was no sidewalk on the other side, just an overgrown verge leading to a concrete stormwater channel. Nothing on this side except the motel and a few businesses that had closed for the night, or maybe for good. The rain had eased to a sprinkle, though I could hear thunder to the east.

Three cars were parked nearby. On a road like this, I'd have expected to see one or two, maximum.

'Split up,' Zara murmured. It made sense. If our pursuers were watching for a pair, they might not recognise us individually.

I crossed to the other side and started walking along the street, as close to the kerb as I could get without stepping in the puddles. I could hear water churning in the channel, but couldn't see it from here.

The first car I came to was a taxi with a dented bumper. A taxi is a great surveillance vehicle, because they all look pretty much the same, and they're often parked in strange places between fares. I walked past it, keeping a distance of about five yards.

The driver had her seat tilted back, wireless earbuds in. She was looking down at her phone. Not surveilling us, or at least, not well. And the dented bumper made the cab distinctive—not the sort a spy would use.

On the other side of the street, Zara was approaching the second car—a midnight-blue Mitsubishi with tinted windows. She'd opted for the riskier direct approach. She tapped on the window. It rolled down, but from this angle, I couldn't see the driver.

Zara smiled and leaned in, so the driver could see down her shirt. 'Are you my Uber?'

I couldn't hear the reply.

'Okay, sorry,' Zara said, and kept walking down the street, frowning at her phone as though confused by an app. With her other hand, she tucked her hair behind her ear, which meant *no contact*. Whoever she'd seen in the car, she didn't think they'd been following us.

That left one more car—a white Ford sedan on my side of the street, opposite the motel. Texas plates. I didn't recognise the numbers, but the car might have kept well back while following us. The tyres looked over-inflated. The car had been cleaned recently, but had driven through mud even more recently. Possibly a rental, though any signage had been removed.

I walked past, this time only three feet away. As casually as I could, I leaned forwards, trying to snatch a glance at the driver.

The car was empty. Perfect. I dug a month-old cigarette from my pocket and stuck it in my mouth, like this was my rental and I'd gotten out for a smoke. I held a lighter in my hand, even though I couldn't operate it without a thumb, and leaned sideways against the car, peering in the window.

The binoculars in the passenger-side footwell made it pretty obvious this was the car that had been following us. There were also packets of nuts, empty coffee cups and those massage toys you use when your legs cramp up. There was a bottle to drink from, but I didn't see one to piss in, which could mean the occupant was female, and also explain where she'd gone.

I scratched the back of my neck, which meant *confirmed*. Then I shifted sideways and wiped the rain off the glass with my palm so I could see more of the interior.

A manila folder on the seat caught my eye. It was closed, and face down, but one of the papers inside had slid far enough that I could see the bottom edge. In a tiny font, the footer read: *Order through law, justice with mercy.*

I knew that motto. We were being pursued by the Houston Police Department.

I tried the handle. Locked. My mind was racing. Chinese spies might have made sense, but why would the local cops be following us?

'Hey!' a voice shouted.

My gaze snapped up. A woman stood on the other side of the street, maybe fifteen feet away. She was short, forties, with dark hair, wearing a jacket over a V-neck shirt, jeans and boots. I guessed she was the driver. Once she was convinced Zara and I weren't coming out of our room, she must have gone in to question the owner.

As she crossed the street, I recognised her. She was the cop who had pulled us over on our way to the meeting with Ariel Wilcox in the theatre. The cop who'd thought I was the Reaper, until she saw my prosthesis.

Behind her, Zara had flattened herself against the exterior wall of the motel, like a lizard. The woman hadn't spotted her.

'What do you think you're doing?' she demanded. Maybe she didn't recognise me through the rain, in the dark, under the hood of my jacket—or maybe she was pretending not to, so I wouldn't realise she'd been following me.

'This your car?' I mumbled around my cigarette.

'Yes sir.' She used *sir* as a period, rather than a mark of respect.

'How much did it cost? I'm thinking of buying one.' I lifted one of the wipers and peered into the gap between the windshield and the hood.

She didn't look convinced. 'I'll need you to step back.'

'Okay, okay. Have a nice night.'

As I backed away, I went to put my hands in my pockets. She must have thought I was reaching for a weapon—in an instant she had a Glock 22 pointed at my chest.

So she did recognise me. My heart rate kicked up a notch.

'Hands where I can see them,' she said.

'Whoa, take it easy.'

The woman didn't take it easy. Tendons bulged in her neck. Her eyes were wide with fear. Whatever she'd been told about me, it was bad.

'Turn around,' she said. 'Right now.'

'I don't know who you think I am—' I began.

'Do it!'

Out of the corner of my eye I saw Zara peel herself off the wall. She crossed the street towards us, fast, silent, wraith-like. As she closed in, she reached under her sweatshirt for her weapon.

'There's no need for this,' I said, talking to both of them.

The Glock trembled in the cop's grip. 'Turn around. Interlace your fingers behind your head.'

'Okay, okay.' I couldn't actually do that, since the silicone fingers were attached to each other, but I put both hands on the back of my skull. As I turned away, I saw Zara drawing her gun. Lining up the sights on the woman's back.

I spent half a second churning through options and outcomes.

Then I ran.

'Hey!' the cop yelled. There was no cover, so she could easily have shot me in the back. But police are trained not to open fire unless they've seen a weapon, and this officer, at least, remembered her training. She didn't shoot me, and Zara didn't shoot her. Instead, the cop ran after me, her heavy shoes pounding the mud as I sprinted towards the stormwater channel that cut through the field. My hood blew off, and the rain speckled my face.

The closer I got, the longer and wider the channel seemed—a deep concrete groove with angled walls, stretching to the horizon in both directions. When I reached it, I realised I'd made a mistake. I'd expected to be able to leap over, but the torrent was ten feet wide and moving fast. I'd heard that floodwater five inches deep could sweep a person away. Ten inches could carry off a car.

I wasn't weighed down by a gun, a radio or a pair of handcuffs. Maybe the cop wouldn't try to make the jump. That was more or less my only hope.

I took a run-up and then threw myself over the channel. The dark water rushed past beneath me. My legs pedalled the air as I soared through the rain. Halfway across, I could already tell I wasn't going to make it.

I splashed down a foot from the far edge. The flow was only knee-deep but seemed to have incredible power—it knocked my legs out from beneath me and suddenly I was under. The cold blasted my face and my hand first, then penetrated my clothes a second later and flash-froze the rest of my body. The water wasn't deep enough to swim in, even if I'd been capable of swimming with only one arm. Instead it dragged me along the concrete bed of the channel, scraping the skin off my palm and the flesh off one of my cheeks. My nose flooded, then my sinuses. My heart hammered.

If I didn't get out of this, I'd end up in the Rio Grande. I couldn't swim, so I rolled, as if a gator had me in its jaws. This didn't take me any closer to the side of the channel, but it slowed me down, enough that I finally got some grip with my shoes. Fighting the current, I dragged myself sideways out of the flow, bleeding and shivering.

Gunshots popped in the air. The cop must have decided it didn't matter whether she'd seen a weapon—she'd rather face a tribunal than let me get away. The first bullet hit nothing. The second ricocheted off the concrete to my right with a twang like a bowstring, sending fragments of lead and concrete upwards. I wasn't hit. I scrambled up the angled wall of the channel and kept running, arms covering my head.

The cop didn't try again. 'Dispatch, I'm in pursuit of a homicide suspect, white male, five foot eight, wearing a brown jacket with a hood, suspect is on foot, halfway between—'

That was all I heard before I was out of earshot, still running through the weeds.

Soon I reached another road and ran across. No cars. There was a fast-food place and a strip club ahead—I ducked through the alley in between. Broken glass, worn down to grits, crunched under my cheap shoes. I took a left turn towards the lights of the city. Other police would arrive to search the area before too long. My best hope was to find a crowd and disappear into it. A dripping-wet one-armed man didn't attract as much attention in Houston as you might think.

I made it two hundred yards before Zara's car screeched to a halt next to me.

I wrenched open the passenger door and threw myself into the seat. Water quickly saturated the fabric. The AC chilled me to the bone.

Zara floored the accelerator. The car hurtled towards the Loop, which was the fastest way out of any potential police cordon. She looked like she was buzzing with energy.

Plenty of tangy adrenaline in her blood. Mine, too.

'What the hell was that?' she said, by way of greeting.

'That was the cop who pulled us over yesterday.'

'You sure?'

'Very sure.'

'Detective Jones was supposed to let the FBI take over the case,' Zara said. 'Maybe he slow-walked it. The local cops don't always trust the feds.'

'This has nothing to do with the body at Space City. She thinks I'm the Reaper.'

Zara glanced at me. 'Why would she think that?'

'I don't know.' I watched the mirrors. I couldn't see any signs of pursuit, but I could hear them. Sirens on the wind.

I caught sight of my own reflection. My hair was slicked to my skull, and blood trickled down my cheek where the concrete had scraped it.

Zara took an exit, headed for the safe house. The car zipped through the dark, quiet suburbs, headlights catching the rain.

'I saw you go under,' she said. 'I thought you were drowning.'

'So did I.'

'What did it feel like?'

I squinted at her. 'Drowning?'

'Thinking you were about to die.'

Water was still tickling my lungs. I coughed into my elbow. 'It wasn't my first time.'

Zara left this alone. The wipers carved overlapping semicircles through the rain. Finally she said, 'I'll go to the Houston PD tomorrow and find out why they're after you.'

'Won't they recognise you, from when they pulled us over?'

Zara gave me some side-eye.

'Sorry,' I said. 'Forgot who I was talking to. What about me?'

'*You* go to the FBI field office. Talk to your old colleagues. The sooner we can kill their investigation into Space City, the sooner we can get you out of Houston.'

I doubted she was concerned for my safety. She probably just didn't want to expose an illegal CIA operation.

'Okay,' I said.

Zara was looking at my hands. 'Oh my God. You're hit.'

The cop's first shot hadn't missed after all. It had punched a hole through my right palm. As I looked at it, the pain hit me, a hot throb surging up my arm. But it was imaginary, like the tingles you feel when you see someone else getting a scalp massage.

I held up the hand and peered at Zara through the hole in the silicone. 'No, I'm not.'

Her laugh came with a little gasp. It sounded like genuine relief, which surprised me. I hadn't really thought Zara cared whether I lived or died, except my body would be hard to dispose of, with no cannibal available.

I found myself laughing, too. A dark chuckle that became helpless giggles. Mad laughter at a mad world.

Soon we were at the safe house. As we entered, Zara did her usual sweep, checking the sawdust on the floor and the alignment of the furniture. No one had been here in our absence.

I was freezing. 'I'm gonna take a shower.'

'No, you're not.' Zara sat me down on a milk crate in the corner of the living room, surrounded by power tools. She got a first-aid kit and a flashlight from the cupboard.

'I can patch myself up.'

'You need stitches.' Zara brought back the kit and pulled out a bottle of Elastoplast wound spray.

'I've given myself stitches before.' Though I'd had two hands at the time.

'So have I. Trust me, it's much, much better to let someone else do it.'

She squirted a stinging mist on my face. I hoped it was as painful for the bacteria as it was for me. She unwrapped a sterilised cloth and dabbed my cheekbone. It came back pink with blood.

Once the wound was clean, Zara picked up a needle and threaded it. She held my chin with one hand. The tip of the needle hovered dangerously close to my eyeball.

'Stay still, okay?' she said.

I thought back to the motel room, where I'd watched her undress. Her unblemished skin. 'Where did you give yourself stitches?'

'Pakistan.'

'I meant where on your body.'

She hesitated. I'd caught her in a lie.

'I really can do this,' she said.

'All right,' I said. I closed my eyes and breathed deeply.

The needle hurt. I focused on her other hand, cool on my chin. Not holding me still, just resting there.

It seemed like a long time since anyone had touched me like that. Gently, carefully, no judgement. Even people who didn't know I was a cannibal avoided getting too close, sensing something was wrong with me. I remembered hearing somewhere that babies died without regular skin-to-skin contact. Maybe it was true for adults, too.

We perished but kept walking around, for fear that someone would realise we were dead. That we were so repulsive no one had been willing to touch us with their bare hands.

It felt like I'd been dead since Thistle left. But Zara had chosen to bring me back, even though—or perhaps because—she knew the truth.

I tried to talk without moving my face: 'How'd you find me, after I got out of the water?'

'I don't know. I ran back to the car and started driving, and I just . . . guessed which way you'd go.'

'It's probably a bad sign that I'm so predictable.'

'Only to me—we have a lot in common.'

'Thank you,' I said. 'For saving me.'

'Any time. All better?'

I realised it was over already. I opened my eyes. My cheek was stiff, and even sorer than before. I nodded.

Zara went to put the first-aid box away, but hesitated. She reached in and unwrapped a bandaid. Then, smiling, she carefully stuck it over the bullet hole in my prosthesis.

CHAPTER 15

Now

I keep waiting, waiting, waiting for this
sickness to leave me be. What am I?

Dr Diaz snaps her notebook shut. 'I think that will do for
today.'

I look at the clock. It feels like I've been talking for years,
but only the usual ninety minutes have passed. The hands
sweep silently past eleven-thirty.

'Your call, doc,' I say, and stand up. It takes effort. I feel
simultaneously drained and energised. Precisely once in my
life I went jogging, and I felt this same way afterwards.

Diaz stands up, too. 'Have you prepared something for
group this afternoon?' she asks.

'No.'

'Are you going to?'

I shrug.

'I think you should,' she says. 'Remember, speaking up
isn't just about feeling better. I think the other patients
could learn quite a lot by listening to you.'

Stoking my ego. Maybe she thinks I'm a psychopath—they like that sort of thing.

'See you Friday?' she says. 'Ten o'clock?'

She says it like I have a choice. Like I might find somewhere else to be.

'Right,' I say. 'See you then.'

She holds the door open. I walk out, feeling her gaze on my back, and head west towards the communal facilities.

This part of the Behavioural Health Unit reminds me of a high school. There's a drinking fountain, a brick wall with patchy paintwork and a fern in a glazed ceramic pot. Its fronds wave gently in the air-conditioning.

The only indication I'm in a hospital is the row of wheelchairs, parked like shopping carts near the windows. As with a high school, there are no obvious means of escape.

I'm about to enter the southern corridor, where the patients' bedrooms are—every day I check if the exterior door at the far end is unlocked—when I notice Nurse Kelly leaning against the wall. He's short and wide, with bushy brows and a beard like steel wool. He has pecs that imply push-ups, and quads that imply squats. An uninspired snake tattoo coils around one bicep. He looks like Santa's jailbird cousin.

Down the corridor, someone is screaming wordlessly. It's a hoarse voice, regularly interrupted by heavy breathing. They've been going for a while. Kelly doesn't look concerned, staring at me with his arms crossed over his broad chest.

'You all right, Timothy?' he asks. He talks like he has a cold. Diseases spread like wildfire in this place.

I keep my voice casual. 'Who's that screaming?'

'You don't need to worry about that.'

'I wasn't worried. Just curious. Is it Seamus?'

'You don't need to worry about that,' Kelly says again. 'You always take your medication, don't you, Timothy?'

'I don't have any medication,' I say. 'Just talk therapy for me.'

He nods slowly. 'Right.'

The staff here aren't well paid. The job therefore attracts a mixed bag of noble people who want to support the sick, and less noble people who enjoy having power over them. Too soon to be sure which camp Kelly falls into, though I have my suspicions.

There's a pause while we each wait to see if the other is going to say anything else. My gaze creeps down to Kelly's thick forearms. Seamus's screams fill the silence.

Kelly dismisses me. 'Have a nice day.'

My gaze snaps back up. I give a cautious nod and amble towards the communal areas.

The lunch hall is pleasant enough, with a lot of natural light and a few more potted plants. A rainforest mural covers one wall. It's like they've filled the place with vegetables just to mock me. The windows are tempered glass, but they aren't barred. Some patients are at a table playing Uno. A woman with a pen behind her ear is reading an old magazine with Sarah Jessica Parker on the cover. Being imprisoned in the Behavioural Health Unit sometimes feels like visiting the late nineties, not least because no phones are allowed here.

I stand in front of the lunch counter, waiting for the dented shutter to roll up. I can hear activity behind it, other patients helping to prepare the food. I've volunteered for kitchen duty but haven't been accepted yet. The staff don't yet trust me enough to let me near the knives.

'Timothy. Timothy.'

I turn around. A patient hovers behind me. She's short, twenties, with huge eyes that leave only a little room for her tiny mouth. Too thin to be of much interest.

'Hi, Dasha,' I say.

'How'd you go with Dr Diaz, Timothy?'

'Fine.'

'I think she'll be really good for you.' Dasha squeezes my arm. 'You're such a thoughtful person, and you deserve someone who listens to you.'

I've overheard Dasha doing this to other patients. She warms them with the spotlight of her attention so they feel special, valued, connected. Then, once she senses that they're on the hook, she starts telling outrageous lies.

'Not like Dr Kobald,' she adds. 'You know he used to bring his dog into our sessions—this big German shepherd. He told me that I should try to be more like the dog. He said dogs lived in the moment and were more social animals and so on. Sounds good, right? But then he wanted me to crawl on all fours around his office. He asked me to practise barking. He even wanted me to sniff the dog's butt.' She lowers her voice. 'I think it's a sex thing for him.'

As usual, she's pitched this story perfectly. Outrageous enough to get attention, but still plausible, and told with enough earnestness and detail that even though everything else she's ever told me has turned out to be false, I'm almost convinced.

'Wow,' I say. 'That sounds awful. What was the dog's name?'

She's good. It only takes her a split second. 'Razzle. Anyway, I wouldn't do it—sniff the dog, I mean. I told him that enough was enough, and that he had to respect me and my boundaries.' She takes a deep breath. 'That's the thing with these doctors. You have to let them know you'll stand up for yourself, and that they work for you, not the other way around.'

They work for the hospital, but I don't argue. 'Thanks for the advice.'

'What did you and Dr Diaz talk about?' Dasha acts like this is a normal thing to ask after a private therapy session.

'I told her I eat people, but I don't think she believed me.'

Dasha watches me for a moment and then laughs— a short, jagged sound, like a cat coughing. 'You're hilarious, Timothy.'

'So I've been told.'

'You know who *would* believe you?' Dasha turns.

I follow her gaze. The woman in the corner is scribbling in her magazine, maybe doing one of the quizzes. She's in her forties, Asian, with freckles, glasses and hair pulled back in a way that looks painful.

'Harmony,' Dasha whispers. 'Since her family stopped visiting, she's really gone off the deep end. There's no story too ridiculous for her.'

'Does anyone else visit her?' I ask.

'I don't think so. She's got no one.'

I've noticed that Harmony doesn't seem to socialise very much, either. She's isolated. Vulnerable.

The shutter unlocks and rattles upwards. Behind it, another patient—a guy named Bennett—is standing over a tray of sushi rolls. He's a balding white guy with a sad, Paul Giamatti stare. Two hundred pounds, mostly fat.

'First in line again, Timothy?' he says.

'Yup. Any bacon today?'

'Sorry. I got chicken or vegetarian.'

A few years ago, Bennett was in a shopping mall parking lot, loading Christmas presents into the trunk of his car, and he got distracted by his phone. While he was checking Twitter, his two-year-old daughter walked behind another car, which reversed over her.

Bennett spent two years in prison on a charge of negligence causing death. When he was released, he still didn't feel like he'd paid the full price, so he slashed his wrists. Now he's here. I get the feeling that he'll try again, when he's eventually discharged.

I'm not convinced that he's crazy. Despair seems like a sane reaction to his circumstances—but I'm not a doctor.

'I'll take the chicken,' I say.

'Okey doke.' Bennett drops two sushi rolls onto a plate and hands it over.

Other patients file in. I take an empty table and stare gloomily at my sushi roll. The chicken is grey. Not only does it not look human—it doesn't even look like meat.

I tell myself that I won't be here much longer.

A man sits opposite me. He's bulky, but with sharp edges—a square nose, square jaw, square knuckles. Like a background character in an animated movie, not rendered properly. His hands, clenching plastic cutlery, are still dirty from gardening.

'Eli,' I say.

'Timothy.' He leers at me. 'How was therapy?'

'Fine.'

'What was Dr Diaz wearing?'

Eli is obsessive. He won't let me get away with silence,

or changing the subject. And if I lie to him and he finds out, I don't know what he'll do.

'Tan jacket, black shirt,' I say.

He smiles. 'Nice.'

Most of the people in the Behavioural Health Unit aren't dangerous. If they were rich, they'd be described as eccentric rather than mentally ill. Eli and I are the only exceptions.

As a teenager he had blue eyes, but the right was flecked with brown. Eli hated those flecks. He spent hours glaring into the mirror and was often late to school because of it. He wore sunglasses all the time. He googled laser eye surgery and was disgusted to learn that while it could cure blindness, it couldn't do anything about eye colour.

When he was nineteen, Eli sterilised a fork in boiling water. He downed a bottle of his father's whisky and stabbed himself in the hated eye. He managed to wrench it out of its socket before he blacked out.

In the hospital, he claimed the injury was accidental. He said he'd had a seizure while he was eating in front of the TV. This story might have seemed implausible, except he'd researched epilepsy ahead of time and knew exactly how to describe his invented symptoms. The overworked doctors accepted his explanation, since he was cheerier than any of their self-harming patients. If his parents suspected what he'd done, they didn't admit it.

Eli's happiness didn't last. When the bandages were removed, he found the lack of symmetry in his new face off-putting. He started to wonder if maybe, just maybe, the empty eye socket was even worse than the brown flecks had been. He got an ocular implant and attached various prosthetic eyes to it, but none was a good match. In some the colour was too flat, in others there appeared to be too much texture. He became angry.

One day he was on a bus to college. His driver's licence had been revoked, not because of his monocular vision, but because of the fake epilepsy. Another passenger got on—a woman with two beautiful blue eyes, exactly like Eli's remaining one. He was mesmerised.

Later, Eli told the police that he wasn't crazy. *Obviously* he knew that he wouldn't be able to see through the eye he'd stolen, and *obviously* he knew that it would decompose after a while. But how could he let an opportunity like that slip past? 'Those eyes,' he kept saying. 'They were two in a million.' This was why, he insisted, he should be released. It was incredibly unlikely that he should ever see such perfect eyes again. Therefore he wasn't a danger to the community.

The judge didn't buy this logic, but to be fair, Eli has been at the Behavioural Health Unit for almost a decade and hasn't attacked anyone in all that time. Nor has he managed to convince any of the psychiatrists that he's sane, though. He's stuck here until a sufficiently gullible doctor comes along.

When I got here, the other patients all assumed that Eli and I would get on, because I had one arm and he had one eye. Apparently, that's enough basis for a friendship. Eli seemed to make the same assumption—he sits near me every day. Right now, he has a prosthesis in. An acrylic blue eyeball, too white around the edges. He keeps self-consciously touching it.

'I told Dr Diaz that she should wear warmer colours,' he's saying. 'I have a good eye for that sort of thing.'

This might not be a joke, so I don't laugh. I just chew

my sushi roll, looking for patterns in the scratch marks on my tray.

Eli doesn't start eating. 'Hey, did you hear what happened with Seamus?'

I shake my head, my mouth still full.

'He wouldn't take his antipsychotics. They had to sedate him.'

'Ah.' This is what passes for gossip in a madhouse.

'Thank God someone realised. He could have snapped. Killed us all.'

The way Eli says this makes me wonder if it was him who told the nurses that Seamus hadn't taken his meds.

Seamus has schizophrenia. He tells stories that don't seem to go anywhere, and when you ask him a question, he typically answers a different one. But, like every other schizophrenic I've ever met, he's never shown any sign of violence.

'Yeah, lucky.' I point at Eli's untouched sushi roll. 'You gonna eat that?'

'Yes,' he says, but doesn't move. Just clenches his fork like a mad king, meeting my gaze—or perhaps examining my eyes. They're blue, like his.

'Enjoy it, then.' I get up and walk away, slowly enough that I don't appear to be fleeing in terror.

•

'Milla still hasn't written to me,' Casey says.

For group therapy, we sit in a circle on chairs with worn-through rubber feet and popped stitching in the cushions. The circle is deformed, because the people who are reluctant to speak have shifted their chairs back a little, and those who are eager have scooched forwards. I've moved back. So has Harmony, who's to my left, and Eli, who took the seat to my right. We all have handwritten name labels stuck to our shirts. A few people have written their full names in tiny handwriting, like Dr Franklin Anders did. Mine just says *Timothy*.

In the corner of the room, there's a chair with a missing leg. Possibly vandalised—it's hard to see how the damage could have happened accidentally. I feel oddly sympathetic towards the chair. Missing something, unstable, pushed aside, soon to be replaced.

Casey, a forty-something woman with wispy chestnut hair trapped under a headband, has her own chair pushed way back, so naturally Dr Kobald has asked her to speak first. He can sense that she's on the verge of a breakthrough.

'At first I assumed that her publicist was intercepting her letters, or maybe her husband.' Casey takes a deep breath. 'But I've been considering other possibilities, like we talked about on Monday.'

Casey used to work in a senator's office. She turned up on time, wore appropriate clothes and bantered pleasantly with her co-workers. For years, there was no outward sign that anything was wrong with her mind.

One day, the senator noticed Casey writing a letter in the break room. He took note, because she seemed to be doing it secretively. Perhaps she was leaking information to a journalist. But when he confronted her, Casey confessed that she had a secret friendship with actress Milla Jovovich, star of *Resident Evil* and *The Fifth Element*.

This was surprising, but the senator assumed it was true, until he pressed for more detail. Apparently, Casey had never met Jovovich. Nor had Jovovich ever responded to any of

Casey's letters. But, Casey said, the actress included hidden messages in her Instagram posts—hand signals and code words, designed for Casey and only Casey to understand.

Casey lost her job. It was a tough time, made bearable only by Jovovich's covert messages of support. Now she's here.

None of these people *seem* crazy. We could be anywhere— a classroom, a town hall meeting, a Walmart staffroom. Nothing the patients say or do would be out of place in any of those settings. For a while after I was admitted, I wondered if the doctors had some kind of scam going, filling the psychiatric ward with healthy people for government kickbacks or something.

Now I know better—and it makes me wonder how many people on the outside are deeply, truly mad.

Dr Kobald crosses his legs. 'What other possibilities have you considered?'

Casey looks uncomfortable. 'Well, maybe she's been too busy to write to me. Or she might not even know I'm in here.'

'Or maybe she doesn't know you exist,' mutters Seamus, the schizophrenic.

Dr Kobald raises a hand to silence him, but it's too late.

'Or maybe the moon landings were a hoax,' Casey snaps, 'or maybe vaccines cause autism, or maybe Lee Harvey Oswald was a stooge for the Mafia. Anything's *possible.*'

'Vaccines *do* cause autism,' someone says, apparently offended that their beliefs are being lumped in with conspiracy theories.

Dr Kobald ignores this and tries to take charge of the discussion again. 'Casey's right. There are many different explanations for everything that happens to us, and almost all of them are possible. So how do we decide what to believe?'

There's silence for a moment.

Dr Kobald is Black, fifties, with a trace of a moustache close to his lip. Like always, he's wearing jeans, running shoes and a polo shirt. In his casual attire he looks more like a patient than a doctor, but he has enough authority in his voice that he can usually keep these discussions from turning into a fight.

'Question everything,' Seamus says softly. He's a compact man in his twenties, with neatly parted hair and green eyes that are usually turned to the floor.

'That may not be practical,' Kobald says. 'When I go to work each day, I need to believe that my keys will unlock my car, that my car will slow down when I touch the brakes, and that I haven't been fired without my knowledge during the night. If I question all those things, it becomes impossible to live my life.'

'So we choose to believe people who seem trustworthy?' someone suggests.

'That's one option,' Kobald says carefully.

'Some liars are very convincing,' Dasha puts in. 'I once met a man who—'

I don't want to hear another one of her fabricated stories, so I interrupt. 'We choose to believe whatever seems most likely.'

Kobald smiles. 'Very good, Timothy,' he says, not because I've been particularly insightful, but because it's the first time I've spoken up today, and he wants to encourage me. Sometimes he sounds like he's teaching kindergarten.

'Unlikely things do happen, though,' Eli says thoughtfully, with no idea that he's sitting right next to a former FBI cannibal consultant turned CIA asset.

'They do,' Dr Kobald says. 'But as human beings, we need to make sure we're not giving unlikely possibilities more consideration than they deserve. If I wake up one day with a stiff neck, there's a ninety-five per cent chance that I just slept badly and a massage will fix it—'

Dasha shoots a delighted and triumphant look at me, like the fact that Dr Kobald gets massages is proof that he's also a pervert with a dog-sniffing fetish.

'And there might be a four per cent chance that it's something more serious, like meningitis or osteoarthritis,' Kobald continues. 'So I'll consider those possibilities. But I'm not going to spend an equal amount of brain power ruminating on things that are possible but vastly improbable, like . . .' He trails off, realising that he doesn't want to put any crazy ideas in our already crazy heads.

'Ants have infested your spinal column,' someone suggests.

'You're turning into a giraffe,' someone else puts in.

'Right,' Kobald says, and quickly changes the subject. 'So how do we decide what's likely?'

'Someone might have injected you with poison while you slept,' Seamus says, still thinking about Kobald's neck.

'One technique you might try,' Kobald says, undeterred, 'is to pretend that someone else is describing your situation to you. Ask yourself how likely it would seem. Sometimes we have more clarity when we're thinking about *other* people than when we're thinking about *ourselves*.' He has his kindergarten voice on again.

Casey squirms in her chair. She's smart enough to know that if someone else claimed to have a secret celebrity friend sending coded messages, she would think they were crazy.

'Thank you for sharing, Casey,' Kobald says. 'I think we're making real progress. Harmony?'

The woman next to me stiffens in her seat.

'Would you like to share what you've been working on?' Kobald asks. 'Or something you've struggled with, that we could unpack as a group?'

Harmony swallows. 'No, I'm doing okay.'

Kobald claps his hands together, but gently, so they hardly make a sound. 'Great! Tell us all about it.'

Harmony looks around. 'Well,' she says, 'my delusions are decreasing in frequency and intensity.'

Everyone nods, even though she's clearly parroting a textbook. Kobald remains silent, letting her fill the space.

'I haven't had any hallucinations lately,' Harmony adds. 'Auditory or visual.'

'Now, you know there's no judgement in this room.' Kobald gestures at the group. 'We're all here to support each other. But it's important that we're honest about what we're going through.'

'I'm being honest,' Harmony says stubbornly.

'Well, that's good news,' Kobald says. 'Can you tell us a little about the techniques you've been using?'

'Just, uh, deep breathing, and mindfulness.'

'So, when a troubling thought enters your head . . .'

Harmony shoots him a suspicious glare. She's complained in the past that someone is monitoring her thoughts. She said she woke up one morning and found a tiny transmitter on her pillow, which had apparently fallen out of her ear during the night. When she brought a nurse to look at it, the object had vanished, leading her to believe that other patients—or perhaps even hospital staff—were part of the conspiracy.

'. . . how do you deal with that?' Kobald finishes.

Harmony clears her throat. 'I acknowledge the thought, then let it go.'

Kobald smiles. 'You let it go. That's very good, Harmony.' He turns to the rest of the group. 'Remember, thoughts are funny things. If we try to push them away, often they bounce back, with more force. But if we accept that the thoughts are there, they lose their power over us. We can decide what, if anything, to do with them.'

'No one is spying on me,' Harmony says. 'It's safe to go outside.'

It's unclear whether she's trying to convince Kobald or herself. Either way, it doesn't seem to be working.

'Thanks, Harmony,' Kobald says. 'Seamus, how are you feeling today?'

As the discussion moves on, I shift my chair a little closer to Harmony's. She pretends not to notice.

'Hey,' I whisper.

She looks over. The woman whose family has stopped visiting. The woman no one will miss.

I speak so quietly it's little more than mouthing the words: 'I believe you.'

'About what?' she asks warily.

'It's not safe to talk here,' I say, and look up, as though there are cameras in the ceiling, which there aren't. But she follows my gaze. It's the beginning of a rapport.

I sit back in my chair and pretend to focus on the discussion, feeling Harmony's thoughtful eyes on me.

Soon she'll come to me.

CHAPTER 16

Two weeks ago

What kind of punch works best on a fish?

I woke up with blood in my mouth and a fork in my hand—the long, two-pronged kind you use on a barbecue.

I sat up, disoriented. A shaft of sunlight cut through a gap in the cardboard that covered the bedroom window. I was in the safe house, on a sleeping mat that was slowly deflating through twin punctures near my hip.

The house was half-built. There were no kitchen utensils. Zara and I had been living off granola bars and drinking straight from the faucet. Where had I gotten a barbecue fork?

I quickly ran through the previous night in my head. That cop had chased me, and I'd nearly drowned in a stormwater channel, then Zara had taken me here and stitched me up, touching my face with her soft hands, and after that—

What? It wasn't coming to me.

Whose blood was I tasting?

And where was Zara?

I scrambled off the mat and hurried into the hall. I didn't dare shout her name in case she didn't respond. My feet left

150

smudges of mud on the floor. I passed a balled-up towel—that's right, I remembered showering before bed, to warm up after nearly drowning. So why was I dirty?

I entered Zara's bedroom. There was a lump under the blankets. A dark blob at one end that might have been her hair. Heart pounding, I peeled the blankets back.

Zara lay there, motionless.

'Zara,' I whispered.

She didn't move. She was curled on her side, her body like the hook of a question mark, her shins making the tail, one ankle tucked behind the other. A tank top and loose cotton pants hid most of her skin, but I couldn't see any stab wounds or bite marks.

I crouched over her. Her chest rose and fell. The blood in my mouth must have been my own, leaking from the inside of my cheek.

I was a sleepwalker, and I sometimes woke up holding strange objects. But this was a new record. To get this fork, I must have used the abandoned ladder in the yard to get over the fence and started rummaging through the neighbours' stuff, all without waking up. Either that or I went to the store and purchased it.

Sleepwalking I could live with. Sleep-stealing or sleep-shopping could get me in trouble. And what if it kept escalating? What other things might my body do while unsupervised?

I watched Zara for a moment, her hair fanned out across the thin pillow, the curve of her neck, her bare arms. They looked soft. Juicy.

I quickly backed away. My foot caught one of the straps of her backpack, and it scraped loudly across the floorboards.

Zara opened her eyes. They focused on me. 'Hey, you,' she said sleepily.

'Hey.'

'You okay?'

'Yeah.'

'What are you doing?'

I kept the fork behind my back. 'Just checking on you.'

She yawned. 'Are we late?'

The sun was up. I needed to get to the FBI field office, and she needed to visit the Houston PD. 'Probably.'

'All right.' She stretched like a lioness. Then she seemed to wake up properly and remember we weren't a couple. She quickly gathered the blankets around herself. 'Give me a minute to get ready.'

'Right.' I went back to my own bedroom and dressed quickly. When I found the syringe, I saw what looked like saliva residue around the tip. Maybe I'd been sucking on it during the night like a baby with a bottle. Didn't look like I'd managed to get any out, but I wondered if there was a casual way I could ask Laurie about side effects.

Soon a woman I didn't recognise emerged from Zara's room. She had streaks of grey in her hair, horn-rimmed glasses and a string of pearls around her neck. Her cheeks were rounded, her posture stooped.

The stranger held out a hand. 'Jean Barnes. Mayor's liaison.' She sounded like a New Yorker, the vowels slightly drawn out.

'What's in your mouth?' I asked.

She opened wide. Dull pink circles sat between her teeth and her cheeks, padding her face. 'You think they'll buy it?'

She knew they would. She just wanted a compliment.

'If your documents are convincing,' I said. 'Did you bring a disguise for me?'

She smiled, then looked away. 'You're fine as you are.'

•

The FBI's Houston Field Office hadn't changed much—a slab of glass surrounded by flags and dry grass, just off the Northwest Freeway. Even the cars in the lot were the same. FBI agents don't upgrade often. Thistle was probably still requesting her favourite Crown Vic from the motor pool.

Zara dropped me off and sped away towards the police precinct. She wanted to find out why the cops thought I was the Reaper. I was here to see what the feds had figured out about the fighter pilot and stop them working out anything more.

A security guard looked me up and down but said nothing as I entered the lobby. The bureau's motto was carved into the wall—*Fidelity, Bravery, Integrity*—over the photos of the last ten presidents, at least five of whom had been investigated by the FBI.

The receptionist had a broad grin and caked-on make-up that made her look like a child's doll from a horror movie. 'Mr Blake!'

'Good memory,' I said. I'd only ever been a visitor, without a cubicle of my own.

She noted the stitches on my face. 'Oh dear.' Then she saw my missing hand. 'Oh dear!'

'Shark attack,' I said. 'Can you sign me in?'

'Of course. Gosh.' She slid a tablet across the counter towards me. 'So, I hear you're in the private sector now?'

I tapped in my name and the ClearHorizon phone number. 'Who told you that?'

She avoided the question. 'Must be nice. Do you get dental?'

Best guess, Thistle had been asking around, trying to poke holes in my cover. 'You bet. I need my winning smile.'

A tinkle of laughter. 'You still got your old pass?'

'Nope.'

'Glad to hear it.' Her nails clacked on the keyboard for a while, and a small printer spat out a sticker. 'Keep this on you while you're in the building.'

I smoothed it across the lapel of my polo shirt. 'Will do.'

She gave me a sympathetic smile. 'Head on up. Thistle knows you're coming.'

My heart beat a little faster.

I took the stairs up. The cubicles had been replaced by an open-plan layout, with computer monitors exposed and confidential papers clearly visible on desks. Wall monitors displayed faces from the Most Wanted list. None of this seemed very secure, but to be fair, management didn't know a cannibal spy was roaming the building.

While I was looking for Thistle, I was sidetracked by the smell of bacon coming from a conference room. The door was ajar, and I could hear voices from inside. I guessed it was a breakfast meeting that had run overtime, all the agents chomping down drive-through while they discussed some case or other. Through the gap in the door I could see a whiteboard with a list of addresses next to a list of dates and times. The addresses spanned four states—Houston and Katy in Texas, Sugartown in Louisiana, Las Cruces in New Mexico and Santa Monica in California. Something about that list unsettled me, but before I could work out what, an agent saw me peering in.

'Help you?' she said.

'Sorry, wrong meeting,' I replied, and pulled the door shut.

'Blake.' Thistle was behind me, arms folded, keeping a safe distance. I wondered if the sight of her would ever stop feeling like a punch to the chest.

'Oh my God.' Her eyes widened. 'What happened to your face?'

'I'm okay,' I said.

She stared at me.

I sighed. 'I fell in a stormwater channel and got swept along.'

'You *fell in*?'

'I was trying to jump over. Didn't make it.'

'Why were you—'

'That's not what I'm here about. Can we talk in your office?'

Thistle hadn't told the FBI about my crimes, which made her complicit. The agents around here were a threat to us both.

'I don't have an office,' she said. 'Come on.'

She led me to the cafeteria, which was close to deserted at this time of day. At the machine, she made me a coffee with sugar and salt, and one for herself with just sugar.

I sat at a formica table. 'How come you still don't have an office?'

'Offices go to superstars.' Thistle removed her cup from the machine and stirred the liquid. 'And my two biggest cases both exposed corruption within the FBI. You may recall them.'

I did.

'Not the sort of cases the new director wants to call attention to.' She didn't sound bitter. Just tired. 'Plus, there was the whole thing with Bucetti.'

Bucetti had been Thistle's old partner, before he was shot by a domestic abuser. Bucetti tried to sue her, arguing that Thistle could have prevented his injury by opening fire sooner.

I'd lost my old partner in almost the same way. Richmond had been wounded in front of me; shot by a suspect I had goaded on. That was how Thistle had become my partner. She and I seemed to have led parallel lives, from birth onwards. She was the Earth, damaged but beautiful, while I was the Moon, cold and lifeless. We were on the same trajectory around the sun but couldn't have been more different.

'Management doesn't want to give me too much of a profile,' Thistle was saying. 'Which means I end up with all the work the superstars never get around to doing. I'm very busy, so . . .' she sat down in front of me '. . . you've got fifteen minutes.'

Zara had given me straightforward instructions. Find out what Thistle knows, then feed her some misinformation to stop her getting any further.

But I was all done lying to Thistle.

'The dead man at Space City wasn't an astronaut,' I said.

'No shit. Who was he?'

'Our working theory is that he was a Chinese fighter pilot on a recon mission. His stealth jet malfunctioned, he bailed out, and then he asphyxiated on the way down. This is classified, by the way.'

Thistle looked intrigued. 'You got any evidence of this?'

'We found his plane in the Pacific Ocean. Again, classified.'

'*We* being ClearHorizon?'

I said nothing, letting her fill in the blanks.

'Hmm.' Thistle drummed her nails on the tabletop. 'Okay, you said recon mission. What was he trying to get a look at?'

'Unknown. There are several technologies in development at the JSC. But I'm not sure anything useful would be visible from the air. And just because he bailed out over Space City doesn't mean that was the target.'

'Did you recover any photos from inside the plane?'

'*I* didn't. The people who pulled the wreckage out of the ocean may have. I don't know.'

'You're sure this plane exists?'

It hadn't occurred to me to doubt the authenticity of the video until now. 'Pretty sure. But no one's told me what was inside.'

'Why would anyone tell you? You're just a consultant from the private sector.' Thistle watched me closely.

I swallowed. It was one thing to risk getting tried for treason by telling her about the plane. But if I told her who I was working for, and the CIA found out, they might consider her a threat. So I stayed silent.

'Well.' Thistle sipped her coffee. 'It's a good story. But it doesn't hold together. If the pilot ejected, where did his ejector seat land? Where was his parachute?'

Zara had covered this. 'If he wasn't buckled in properly, the seat and the chute might have landed someplace else. Like the bay.'

'Someone would have noticed that, surely?'

'Okay, maybe it landed in the woods around Space City. They're fenced off. No foot traffic to find the debris.'

'Let me get this straight.' Thistle held up one finger. 'You think the pilot's jet malfunctioned, in some as-yet-unknown way, so he bailed out.' She held up a second finger. 'You also think he didn't know how to work a seatbelt, so he fell out of his ejector seat halfway down.' A third finger. 'And you think his seat and chute happened to land within the fence, but far enough away from the buildings that no one has found them, days later. Have I got that right?'

When she summed it all up like that, it did sound unlikely. But as Garcia had said, on a long enough timescale, the unlikely becomes inevitable.

'It could have happened,' I said.

'It could have, but I'll bet you a million bucks it didn't.' Thistle's phone buzzed in her pocket. She checked the screen, cursed, and drained the last of her coffee. 'I gotta go. Let me know if you hear anything else. Nice to see you, Blake.'

I doubted she meant it. Once I'd been a brilliant investigator, and she'd trusted me. Now I was a crank, not worth even ten of the fifteen minutes she'd promised. She probably wanted to sweep away all memory of me, erase the dirty footprints I'd left all over her life—

'Wait,' I said.

She paused on her way to the door. 'Yes?'

'What about the partial footprint? In the field, near the Martian training area. When I saw it, I thought someone might have found the body before Anders did, then swept the dirt to hide their tracks.'

Thistle folded her arms. 'Wait. You think someone found the body and then took away the ejector seat and the chute?'

'No.' She hadn't seen the dead man in the flesh. Face up. Legs wide. Heels scuffed. Arms above his head. Like he'd been dragged by the wrists. 'I think the body landed in the woods and then someone moved it. Someone who knew him, and cared about him—otherwise they would have pulled him by the ankles.'

'Why would they move the body?'

'Imagine you're a Chinese fighter pilot.' I talked quickly, urgently. 'You've been sent on a recon mission over the southern United States. But something goes wrong with your stealth plane. You and your copilot are forced to bail out.'

Thistle's eyebrows shot up. 'Copilot?'

'Right. You survive the landing in the woods. But when you check on your copilot, he's dead. His flight suit is old, and it wasn't airtight. He asphyxiated, because you both bailed out so high.'

Thistle opened her mouth to object. I talked faster, needing to get this all out.

'Now what do you do?' I continued. 'You're trapped in Space City, surrounded by a razor-wire fence patrolled by armed guards. Your plane is on its way to the Pacific Ocean. Your government doesn't know where you landed, because it was a stealth plane—untraceable. And any beacon you set off, the Americans will see the signal before the Chinese do. They can't send anyone to rescue you. Finally you have an idea.'

Thistle's eyes widened as she realised where I was going with this. 'You're kidding.'

'You drag your copilot's body to an obvious place,' I said. 'Right in the middle of the Martian training area. His flight suit looks a lot like a space suit. When the Americans see it, they'll have no idea what it means. They'll scratch their heads, wondering how a Chinese astronaut landed there without burning up on re-entry. Word will get out, because Americans suck at keeping secrets. And when Beijing hears that *just one body* has been found, they'll realise that you survived, and that you must be nearby. They'll send someone to rescue you.'

'You think the pilot is still hiding at Space City?' Thistle asked.

I nodded. 'And Chinese agents are coming for them.'

CHAPTER 17

I cut away the fat, tilting sideways.
What am I doing?

Zara picked up straight away. 'What's the status of the FBI investigation?'

I cupped the phone to shelter it from the wind. I was leaning against the side of the FBI building, which provided the only shade for miles around. It was early spring, but my skin burned easily.

'Thistle doesn't think the dead guy was an astronaut, but without a body to examine, she's hit a dead end,' I said. 'Neither Anders nor Garcia has given her anything beyond what they told us, and the case files Detective Jones sent over are worse than useless. We have nothing to worry about.'

The lie sounded natural, but without seeing Zara's face, it was hard to guess if she'd bought it.

'How did you go at the precinct?' I added.

She didn't let me change the subject. 'Did you feed Thistle the cover?'

'Yeah.' I kept my voice neutral. 'Diabetic coma. I think she believed me, but she's likely to check the hospital admission records, just to be sure.'

'Not a problem. On paper, there was a patient admitted and then discharged.' Zara didn't sound suspicious. But she knew how much I cared about Thistle, and that I would lie to protect her.

'Okay. What's going on with the Houston PD?' I asked.

'Apparently they've got a description of the Texas Reaper. White male, five foot nine, a hundred and seventy pounds. Short reddish-brown hair, freckles.'

I was five eight and one-sixty, but otherwise that sounded a lot like me. Just the same, I would have guessed there were thousands of people in Texas fitting that description. 'Two arms?'

'I assume.'

'Is that an eyewitness description?'

Zara hesitated. Then she said, 'No, it came from a photo.'

'They have a photo of the guy? Why isn't it all over the news?'

'Maybe they don't have enough evidence for an arrest, maybe they don't want to bias the jury pool, I don't know— this is your world, not mine. Either way, that cop thought you were behaving suspiciously after she pulled us over, so she and some colleagues tailed us. Then, when you ran, they assumed you were guilty and passed the information on to the FBI task force.'

She meant the task force working out of the building right behind me. My skin crawled. 'What information?'

'Not your name. Just the plates for the car that we've been driving, and the fact that you fled when confronted yesterday. I've ditched the Prius, but we still have to get you out of Texas, pronto. I'm ten minutes away.'

I didn't want to leave Texas. If I did, I might never see Thistle again.

But wasn't that what I'd promised myself? To get out of her life, before I put her in any more danger?

An FBI agent emerged from the building with a pack of cigarettes in one hand. I recognised him—Ruciani.

'Gotta go,' I said, and ended the call.

Ruciani gave me one of those upside-down nods, chin jerked upward, as he sidled up to me and shook a cigarette free. I got the feeling I was in his usual spot.

'Hey, Pope,' I said.

Ruciani blinked, recognising me. 'Blake? Shit. How are you?'

Ruciani had a leather jacket, crumpled ears from years of boxing and skin that always seemed stretched, like he'd gone through the tumble dryer and it had shrunk around his skeleton. He'd never liked me, but now that he was here in the only patch of shade, he seemed too lazy to move away.

'Been worse,' I said. 'You?'

'Been better.' He craned his neck and cupped his hands around the fragile flame from his lighter. 'Reaper case is killing me. Director's breathing down my neck.'

My heart pounded. I tilted my head a bit away, hoping he wouldn't notice any resemblance to the photo. 'They'll screw up sometime,' I said. 'Serial killers usually do.'

'*Usually* is my problem. *Usually* serial killers have a small hunting ground, but this guy goes all over. *Usually* they leave prints or hair or saliva or semen at the scene, but this guy tasers and strangles each woman as soon as she opens the door, and leaves straight after. *Usually* we can tell how they choose their victims, but not here.'

163

This last part made me curious. 'Could it be random?'

'No. He's clearly stalked them for a while. He knows they live alone, and that they're frail. He knows they have—' He broke off, glancing down at his cigarette. I couldn't read his expression. 'Anyway, they're not all on Facebook, so that's not how he's finding them.'

The sooner the FBI caught the real Reaper, the sooner they'd stop chasing me. Maybe I could lend a hand. 'Sounds like your killer works for the IRS,' I said.

'How's that?'

'If the victims are from all over, the killer is unlikely to be stalking them in person. But like you said, he or she knows they live alone. Tax records would show that.'

I wished I'd given this insight to Thistle rather than Ruciani, but it wasn't her case. I wondered if he was one of the 'superstars' dumping extra work on her.

'Or a health insurance company,' Ruciani said thoughtfully.

That was an interesting guess. Clearly Ruciani knew something I didn't. I was about to probe some more when a shiny blue pick-up—a Ford F-150—pulled into the lot with Zara behind the wheel. She'd changed out of her mayor's liaison garb and was back in an enigmatic suit, her cheekbones high without the padding. The headlights flashed.

Ruciani squinted at her. 'Who's this fine piece of ass?'

The expression grated. It reminded me how hungry I was, and anyway, he couldn't even see her ass while she was sitting in the car. 'She's nobody,' I said.

He held up both hands, and chortled. 'Whoa, okay. Just asking.'

'So long, Pope.' I jogged over to Zara's car and climbed in.

'Why is that guy staring?' she asked, looking at Ruciani.

'He thinks you're hot.'

'Oh?'

'He used some very disrespectful language,' I said. 'Can I eat him?'

Zara leaned over and kissed me on the cheek, tenderly, one hand splayed on my chest.

Her breath was cool on my ear: 'Does he look jealous?'

I glanced at Ruciani. 'More like suspicious.' He could probably tell the kiss had shocked me. Zara should know better than to get so close. I was dangerous. Didn't she get that?

'I didn't defend your honour,' I said.

Zara laughed. 'I can take care of myself.' She shifted the stick into drive, but kept her foot on the brake. 'Where are we going?'

'Back to Space City. I want to look for that ejector seat.'

•

The woods at the edge of the Johnson Space Center were denser than they had looked from a distance. Twigs scratched my face and neck. Dogwood trees cast tangled shadows, fungi growing around the roots. Vines crept along the forest floor. A rich, earthy smell filled the air. Birds shrieked above, more of them than I'd ever heard all at once. I guessed the fence kept out cats and other predators, so the birds bred like crazy in here.

Zara trudged along behind me. 'It would take weeks to search these woods thoroughly,' she whispered. We'd already been walking for an hour.

'We don't have to search everywhere,' I replied. 'Just this little bit.'

'How's that?'

I hadn't wanted to tell her my theory yet. It had felt too fragile to share with anyone except Thistle. But Zara was the expert at spotting foreign spies. If MSS agents really were on their way, looking for their stranded pilot, then I'd need her help identifying them.

'Dogwoods aren't hard to climb,' I said. 'I've done it before. If you crashed here, the first thing you'd do is try to get the lay of the land.'

'Maybe not if you're injured,' Zara pointed out.

'If you're too wounded to climb a tree, you're too wounded to carry a corpse,' I said. 'No, they climbed up, looked around and then decided to dump the body in the nearest obvious place. So we only have to search the area near the rock yard.'

'Wouldn't they have wanted to leave it a long way away from themselves?'

'They might have wanted to, but it wouldn't have been possible. Dead people are heavier than you'd think.'

'Have you forgotten who you're talking to again?'

I ignored this, scanning the area around me. I didn't see any sign of an ejector seat, or a parachute. And there had been no footprints anywhere around.

We kept walking, spiralling outwards from our starting point, seeing nothing.

'Sorry. I think your theory's a bust,' Zara said finally.

'Just wait.' I'd seen something. A patch of white on one of the trees.

'What's that?'

'Don't know.' I trudged closer. It was a rectangular

sticker, like a label, slapped against a tree trunk. Nothing written on it. Meaningless to me, but not random.

I turned to Zara. 'Spies sometimes do that, right? Put stickers on things to send a message to their colleagues?'

'So do teenagers.' Zara thumbed the corner of the sticker. 'School groups come here all the time.'

I kept my voice low. 'What if the MSS is already here?'

A bird fluttered over our heads and landed somewhere unseen. The undergrowth rustled.

'Now even *I* think you're paranoid,' Zara said. But I couldn't shake the feeling that the whole time I'd been at Space City, someone was watching. Matching me, move for move.

I grabbed the bough of a tall tree and tried to heave myself up onto it.

'Blake, don't.' Zara sounded genuinely concerned. She needn't have worried—I barely got a foot off the ground before I fell back down.

'Can you climb that tree?' I asked, puffing.

'I *can*,' Zara said, 'but I'd rather not. Why?'

'I want to know what the pilot might have seen from the top.'

Zara sighed, hiked up her skirt and started clambering towards the canopy. She made it look easy—having two hands probably helped. Soon she was perched on a branch high above my head, scanning the horizon.

'Well?'

'I can see the whole complex, basically,' she said. 'Are you looking for something in particular?'

'Can you see Mars?'

'Yep. Front and centre.'

I tried to visualise what it might look like up there. I imagined myself as the pilot, examining the hostile landscape. Alone. Desperate. Scared, maybe—or maybe not, as a soldier in the Chinese air force. But smart, and ruthless. Ruthless enough to use their dead comrade as a message. Like a single dot of Morse code.

And hungry.

'Do fighter pilots have emergency rations?' I called up to Zara.

'In China? No idea. You're thinking he might have snuck into one of the buildings looking for supplies?'

I was looking at the nearest building. It was the Atmospheric Research Unit, where I'd seen the young Asian woman with the shaved head. The woman who fled when she saw me outside Garcia's office.

'He or she, yeah,' I said. 'Did you ever get around to checking all the Rachels at the Space Center?'

•

By the time we'd hiked back to the building, Zara had files for every Rachel on staff. It was alarming how quickly she could access information like that without having to get a warrant or explain herself to anyone.

I suspected the woman with the shaved head was the pilot of the crashed plane, who had snuck into the building for food or water, and fled when I spotted her. Laurie, the blood scientist, had said the woman was an intern named Rachel—but I hadn't given her much of a description. My theory was that Laurie had been talking about someone different. Zara was trying to get a picture of Rachel the intern, so I could confirm it wasn't the woman I'd seen.

'You said she had tattoos.' Zara didn't look up from her phone as the automatic doors slid open for us. 'That's uncommon in China, especially in the military.'

'How long since you've been there? She was young. Maybe it's a trend.'

'How young?'

'Twenties was my guess,' I said.

We walked past the reception desk. The guy with all the piercings ignored us, perhaps because we'd signed in yesterday. It was hard to imagine he'd ignore a Chinese fighter pilot, though. She'd obviously found a change of clothes somewhere—she hadn't been in a flight suit when I saw her—but it seemed unlikely that she'd been able to talk her way past him. Maybe there was another way into the building.

'She could be Rachel Cochran,' Zara said. 'Born in 2002, according to DMV records.'

'You got a picture?'

'Not yet.' Zara frowned as she scrolled. 'There's something weird about her file.'

'Oh?'

'Yeah. On paper, she doesn't exist until about two years ago.'

My spine tingled. 'Go on.'

'Her bank accounts, her social media profiles and her IRS file are all new. And there's no birth certificate for Rachel Cochran.'

'What does *that* mean?' I wondered aloud. This wasn't what I'd expected Zara to find.

'Not sure yet. SIGINT will keep digging.'

We made our way through the corridors towards Laurie's lab. I was hoping she could describe her intern in more detail and confirm my suspicions—and I wanted to see all that blood again, even knowing it was fake. I felt like a mosquito, drawn inwards.

Finally we reached the door and knocked.

Laurie, the leprechaun blood scientist, opened up. She raised an eyebrow when she saw me—surprised, annoyed and a bit impressed. An *I-thought-I-got-rid-of-you* look. 'Mr Blake! And . . .'

'Sandra,' Zara said. 'I work at ClearHorizon with Timothy. Can we come in?'

Laurie hesitated. I could hear a machine keening some-where behind her. 'We're about to get the results of a test,' she said. 'What's this about?'

'We had some questions about Rachel,' I said.

Laurie sighed and turned her head. 'Rach? Someone's here for you.'

The woman with the shaved head and the tattooed arms stepped out from behind a 3D-printer. I was shocked to see that she *was* the woman who had fled from me outside Garcia's office, which blew up my whole theory. The fighter pilot wouldn't have an internship here.

She was even more shocked to see me. Her eyes widened behind her safety goggles, and she dropped the test tube she was holding, but she recovered quickly, catching it before it hit the ground. She glanced around for an escape route. But there was only one way out of the lab, and Zara and I were blocking it.

The printer whined like a trapped animal.

'Rachel Cochran?' Zara asked.

The woman hesitated, then gave a tight nod.

But she was lying. Because I recognised her now. The shaved head and the tattoos had thrown me, but those were the same sad eyes I'd seen in among the tents in that park, seven years ago.

'No, you're not,' I said. 'You're Lilah Parget.'

CHAPTER 18

I tell you what to write, then put you to death.
What am I?

We all stared at each other for a long moment.

Laurie looked baffled, and a bit annoyed. She probably wasn't used to being the least well-informed person in the room. 'This is Rachel,' she said, as though she could restart the whole conversation. 'She works for me.'

'We've met,' I said.

Zara's posture had shifted. I imagined she had no idea why the girl Sam Garcia had kidnapped was now working as an intern one floor beneath his office, and the uncertainty had manifested itself physically. It wasn't quite an attack stance, but if Lilah ran, Zara was ready to grab her.

'What is this?' Laurie gave Parget a suspicious look.

'Mr Blake works for the FBI.' Parget's voice was soft, but there was more steel in it than I remembered. She was no longer a scared little girl.

'The FBI . . .?' Laurie looked at all of us, perplexed.

'That was a long time ago,' I said, and turned to Lilah. 'We need to talk to you. In private.'

She hesitated. But whatever her explanation was for being here, I was sure she didn't want her boss to hear it.

She slotted the test tube she'd been holding into a rack. A fine grey powder settled inside.

'I'll be back in twenty minutes,' she said.

Laurie glared at her. 'Make it fifteen. I'll need you as soon as the sample tray cools down.'

Parget rubbed some sanitiser on her hands, like an Olympic weightlifter preparing to grip the bar, and followed us out the door.

'There's a rec room on level two,' she said. 'Private, at this time of day.'

I stayed close to her as she climbed the stairs, in case she tried to run from me again. She didn't.

The rec room had a beer fridge, a pinball machine, a pool table, some beanbags and no people. It was the kind of place management showed to prospective employees to lure them in but then fired them if they ever used it.

Parget picked up a pool cue. 'You play?'

'No,' Zara said.

I indicated to my prosthesis. Parget did a double take, then shrugged and chalked the tip of the cue, avoiding our gaze.

'Almost everyone here plays,' she said. 'They spend all their work time calculating trajectories and collisions, then spend their breaks doing basically the same thing. They're good at it, but they take forever lining up their shots. They all suck at pinball, because the machine doesn't wait for them to be ready.'

The way she said this implied that she was good at pinball—and at thinking on her feet. I got the feeling she was deliberately running down the clock. Using up the fifteen minutes her boss gave us.

'You changed your name,' I said.

She nodded.

'Why?'

'You try being the girl who got kidnapped. It was all anyone wanted to talk about.' Parget gathered the balls into a frame up one end of the table. 'I figured it would die down, but it never did. Every time I met someone new they'd google me, and the whole mess would drop into my lap again. Everyone was so goddamn *sorry* for me. I needed a fresh start. New friends.'

'New family?' I added.

She glanced sharply at me, then turned back to the table. 'My dad was already controlling,' she admitted. 'After the kidnapping, he got a million times worse. He put a lock on my door, location tracking on my phone, cameras all around the house. Said it was for my safety. He wanted regular urine samples to test for drugs. He said that was for my safety, too. I left when I turned eighteen.'

I remembered Jeb Parget. The coldness in his eyes, the rage in his voice when he asked me: *Who took my daughter?*

'So he doesn't know about your new name,' I said.

'He's probably figured out that I have one. But he doesn't know what it is.' She took a shot. The cue ball shattered the triangle, colours rolling in all directions.

'What about your mom?'

Parget said nothing in a way that said everything.

'Why did you run when you saw me?' I asked.

'I recognised you. I thought you might have told Garcia who I was. It didn't seem smart to stick around.'

'Garcia doesn't recognise you?'

'We never met.' She hesitated. 'Except when he kidnapped me, but that was just a few frantic seconds, and it was seven years ago. I don't think he'd remember.'

'He would have seen pictures,' Zara put in.

Parget gestured at her shaved scalp. 'I don't look much like my picture these days.'

'Do you remember the kidnapping?' I asked.

She shook her head. I still didn't believe her.

After I got my reward, I didn't follow Parget's case closely. But I had heard from Luzhin that she had written a letter to the judge, saying she'd forgiven Garcia, and begging for leniency. She'd sent a similar letter to the parole board. It was thanks to her that he'd been released so early. Luzhin had been disgusted.

Victims sometimes became sympathetic to their kidnappers during long periods of captivity. Stockholm syndrome. But not after 'a few frantic seconds'.

Zara was looking around the rec room. 'You ended up working in the same building as your kidnapper.'

'Dr Laurie is a genius.' Parget made a shot, pocketing a ball. 'She was on the team that invented lab-grown meat. Since then she's made several important breakthroughs. Scientists all over the world have been working on intravenous oxygenation. She's miles ahead of all of them.'

'Don't pretend that's why you're here, though,' I said.

I could see Parget wanting to pretend exactly that. 'No,' she admitted finally.

'So how'd it happen?'

'I got a scholarship to study at the University of Texas in Austin. The application essay was supposed to be about hardship—I guess none of the other candidates had a story as good as mine.'

I wondered how it had felt, running away to college to escape from a trauma, only to need that same trauma to get accepted.

'I was studying pre-med when I heard Garcia worked here, at Space City,' Parget went on. 'So I went for an internship. That was actually much harder than the scholarship. You wouldn't think there'd be much competition for an unpaid position, but actually it was a long time before my application was accepted.'

I leaned on the edge of the pool table. 'And NASA never found out that you weren't who you said you were?'

Parget glared at me. 'The name change is legal. I *am* Rachel Cochran now. NASA found out about my past, but I explained my situation to Rob Cho, who's in charge of vetting candidates, and he cleared me to work.'

'Did you tell him about the kidnapping?' Zara said. 'Or just about your father?'

Parget bounced the cue on the toe of her shoe, not speaking. I could guess the answer. Cho wouldn't have let a victim work right downstairs from her kidnapper.

'Why would you want to work anywhere near Garcia?' I asked.

'I wanted to find out why he did it.'

'And have you?' Luzhin had never found any child exploitation materials on Garcia's computer, or any links to human traffickers. The motive for the kidnapping had remained a mystery.

'No.' Parget pocketed one last shot and then checked her watch. 'And that's our fifteen minutes.'

We walked back downstairs. Something seemed off about the whole conversation, but it wasn't until after Parget disappeared into the lab that I realised what it was. She'd never thanked me for rescuing her.

●

'Well,' Zara said, 'all that had nothing to do with anything.'

I wasn't so sure. I stared out the car window, looking at the distant forest as we drove towards the museum. Still no sign of a parachute, or an ejector seat, or a fugitive.

I turned to my phone and quickly searched for Faith Parget, Lilah's mom. Based on Lilah's reaction, I expected to find she'd been murdered by Jeb. But there was nothing on the crime sites. A broader search turned up an obit. Apparently she'd died of a stroke. She was survived by her 'loving husband and treasured daughter'.

'A body shows up in the middle of the night right next to the office of a kidnapper *and* his victim,' I said, mostly to myself. 'That can't be a coincidence.'

'How could a dead Chinese fighter pilot have anything to do with an American kidnapping that happened seven years ago?'

I had no answer for that.

'I'm sorry, Blake,' Zara said. 'Your copilot theory didn't pan out. Now it's our job to make sure everyone believes the cover story about the diabetic coma.'

I'd been so sure. The footprint, the swept dirt, the way the body had been posed—everything suggested the dead man had been dragged to the rock yard by someone who knew him. But without evidence of a second Chinese pilot,

I couldn't make the story add up. It was infuriating to be back to square one.

I sighed. 'Run me through the details again.'

Zara turned the wheel, taking us towards the parking lot. At the front of the museum, a pair of workers in hi-vis were installing a new window, while a third looked on with a clipboard.

'The body was a technician named Brian Jane,' Zara said. 'He went for a run wearing the flight suit to test it out and then lapsed into a diabetic coma. He's in the hospital, recuperating. He has a birth certificate, a social security number, employment records and a Facebook profile. No one remembers him because he wasn't here very long, and no one will ever see him again because he's about to get transferred to DC.'

'Why was he wearing a Chinese flight suit?'

'He wasn't. He was wearing a backpack with a Cantonese slogan printed on it, and witnesses got confused.'

It was a pretty good cover. 'But the news already ran stories about a Chinese astronaut. Won't Beijing realise we found their pilot?'

'I'm just telling you what our orders are.' Zara eased the car into a bay and shut off the engine. 'We need to seed that rumour at the ground level of the organisation. It's like toppling a dictator—you don't replace someone at the top and hope that the country as a whole starts behaving the way you want. That never works. Instead, you speak with the people at the bottom and get them talking among themselves. By the time anyone starts listening to what they're saying, it's too late. There's too much momentum.'

She said this as though it was an everyday analogy.

We got out of the car and headed into the museum. After signing in at the front desk—I stole another free pen—we went walking. Last time we had gone around to the right, exploring the building counterclockwise. This time we went left, looking for people we hadn't already met and deceived.

I slowed down as we walked past something that looked a bit like a giant shipping crate. The door had fat hinges and a circular window cut into it. The hinges opened outwards—I could see faint scratches in the concrete floor where the door had dragged across it.

I peered through the window. It was dark inside, but I could tell the glass was thick, as though the shipping container was soundproof, and airtight. Two mechanical claws dangled in the shadows, like in an arcade machine. There were two buttons next to the door. One was marked DECOMPRESS. The other said RECOMPRESS.

Zara noticed I wasn't following. 'Weren't you in a hurry, like, five seconds ago?'

I tapped my knuckles on the side of the crate. 'What do you think this is?'

'Are you sure you used to be an investigator?' She pointed to a sign: *Hypobaric Chamber*.

'Yeah,' I said, 'but what does that mean?'

'Can I help you?'

We turned around and saw Hazel Cuthbert, the glamorous deputy cybersecurity chief. She was carrying a laptop under one arm and holding a croissant in her other hand. On her way to eat breakfast at her desk, I guessed. Still trying to catch up after her boss's premature departure.

Cuthbert looked puzzled as she recognised us. 'Oh! You're back.'

'Just finalising our report.' Zara tucked a pen behind her ear. 'Thanks for your help yesterday. Do you know Brian Jane?'

Cuthbert frowned. 'Maybe?'

'Well, he was the technician who had the seizure outside yesterday,' Zara said. 'You can tell his other friends that he's been discharged from the hospital and he's going to be fine.'

'What a relief,' Cuthbert said, with enough conviction that I would have believed Brian was a friend of hers, had he existed.

I jerked a non-existent thumb at the hypobaric chamber. 'What's that?'

'It's a hypobaric chamber.' Cuthbert tapped the sign.

Zara gave me a smug look.

'I see that,' I said. 'What's it for?'

'Oh. We use it to demonstrate how objects behave in a vacuum. The chamber was out of order a couple of days ago, but someone must have fixed it. I think a school group is coming through later today—one of the curators is going to show them how a bowling ball and a feather descend at the same rate when there's no air in the chamber to slow the feather down.'

'No air in the chamber,' I repeated.

'That's what I said.'

I got the tingles then—the fluttering feeling in my gut that meant I was close to a breakthrough.

If Thistle had been there, she would've been getting the tingles too. But when I glanced at Zara, her face was flat, affectless.

'Anyway,' she said. 'We should get going.'

'Hey.' I tapped the thick glass. 'If someone got stuck in

the hypobaric chamber and it got switched on by mistake, what would happen?'

Cuthbert's eyebrows went up. 'That would depend on whether they were wearing a spacesuit.'

'Because if they weren't, they'd die, right?'

'Horribly. There was an accident like that on a drilling rig in eighty-three. Five people died in a decompression chamber when the lock failed and the door burst open. A sudden shift from nine atmospheres of pressure to one.' She parted her hands in a *boom* gesture.

Zara's eyes were wide. 'Sounds awful.'

'I'm told it rained blood,' Cuthbert agreed.

I took a moment to imagine that, then said, 'A person stuck in this chamber wouldn't explode, would they?'

'No, but they'd suffocate very quickly.'

I nodded. The first piece of the puzzle fit. 'The break-in on Tuesday night.'

Cuthbert looked thrown by the change of topic. 'What about it?'

'Have you worked out what was stolen?'

'I'm in cybersecurity, but I haven't heard about anything missing—sorry, who do you work for again?'

'ClearHorizon,' Zara said. She was watching me the way you might look at a rattlesnake in the corner of your dining room. 'A consulting firm hired by NASA to improve your security protocols.'

'I'd like to examine some of the exhibits,' I said.

'All right,' Cuthbert said slowly. 'I'll get Simone to escort you. Simone?'

Silence. There was still no sign of her PA.

'You could take us?' Zara suggested.

Cuthbert looked forlornly down at the croissant she'd been planning to eat at her desk.

'All right,' she said finally, then led us back the way she'd come.

Soon we were in a gigantic hall, surrounded by glass cases and plaques. Cuthbert gestured at the various space-faring objects around us. 'Like I said, nothing's missing. What would you like to look at?'

'Do you have spacesuits from a bunch of different countries?' I asked.

'Yes, but they're not on display right now.'

'Why not?'

Cuthbert shrugged. 'It's a museum. The curators rotate the exhibits so people keep coming back. At any given time, roughly thirty per cent of our stuff is in storage.' She frowned. 'You think someone stole an exhibit that wasn't even on display?'

'Can we see the storage area?'

'Sure.' Cuthbert ushered us to a door marked *Staff Only*. She swiped her card to let us through, then led us down a dark corridor to a cavernous storage room filled with giant plastic crates, arranged in a neat grid with narrow corridors between them. Each one was labelled and barcoded. Some crates were transparent, but the contents were hidden by bubble wrap. A huge dehumidifier roared above our heads.

Cuthbert was looking around for the crate of spacesuits, but I was pretty sure I'd already spotted it. The lid was slightly crooked, as though it had been replaced in a hurry.

The second piece of the puzzle fit.

I nudged Zara and pointed to the unsealed crate of flight suits. Her eyes widened.

'I assume there'll be a stocktake,' Cuthbert is saying. 'But I doubt the thieves could have gotten in here. Even if they did, how would they sell what they stole? What's the street value of Neil Armstrong's toupée?'

I wondered if that was an actual exhibit. 'Okay. Thanks for showing us.'

Looking relieved, Cuthbert led Zara and I back out of the storage area.

'It must be a pain in the ass,' I said casually as we walked back towards the reception area. 'Having a break-in exactly when Rob Cho goes on vacation. What are the odds?'

'It's not really a vacation—he's visiting his sister in hospital. And like I said, he was supposed to go next week.'

'Did he tell you he was leaving early?'

'I haven't heard anything at all, actually.' Her voice had an undercurrent of frustration.

'Say, is he an Asian guy?' I asked. 'Five foot ten, a hundred and eighty pounds? A mole just below his right eye?'

'Oh, you met him?'

I glanced over my shoulder in time to see Zara's expression as she realised that piece number three was a perfect fit.

She mouthed a single word: *Motherfucker.*

CHAPTER 19

Breathe me before I fool you and cool you.
What am I?

'Explain to me what you think is happening,' Zara said. 'Because I'm pretty sure you're about to realise that your theory makes no sense.'

'Challenge accepted.' I slurped my coffee and some ran down my chin. Cream, two sugars and a dash of salt. The barista at 'Grounds Control' hadn't even blinked when I ordered it.

We were in the Starport Cafe, under some retro-futuristic lights that reminded me of UFOs. There were lots of people around—babbling tourists, grumbling staff on a coffee break, and a group of screaming schoolkids, probably the ones who'd be visiting the hypobaric chamber for the demonstration with the feather and the bowling ball. The air-con rumbled under everything. Contrary to popular belief, a private place is the worst place to have a private conversation. Private places are easy to bug. What you want is somewhere loud, full of confusing echoes.

'On Tuesday evening, around five pm, Rob Cho goes into the hypobaric chamber,' I began. 'Someone else switches it on by mistake. Cho suffocates. The killer realises what they've done. They don't want to go to prison, so they quickly come up with a plan. They're going to hide the body in plain sight, disguising Cho as a Chinese astronaut who's fallen out of the sky.'

'How do you know it was a mistake?'

'If they'd wanted to murder him, they would have waited until right before he was supposed to go on leave. Instead, they killed him a week early, which made his absence suspicious. They didn't even close the lid of the box full of space suits properly. This person was panicking.'

Zara apparently couldn't think of a hole to poke in that, so she took a sip of her peppermint tea instead.

'The killer runs through to storage and grabs a Chinese spacesuit. They put it on Cho's body, then put him in the trunk of their car, drive it to the edge of the field and drag his body to where we found it. They sweep away their tracks in the Martian dirt, but they miss a footprint or two on the field around it.' I took a victory sip of my coffee. 'This has nothing to do with China. This is a good old-fashioned Texas manslaughter. It all fits.'

Zara put her elbows on the table, leaning in. 'It does,' she said. 'Except that the whole thing is fucking ridiculous. Here's your first problem: if the dead guy was Cho, why didn't Anders recognise him?'

I hesitated. 'Maybe they didn't know each other? Or maybe because of the bruising from the decompression?'

'Okay, how did the killer *know* that Anders—or whoever found the body—wouldn't recognise him?'

'Well, a lot of people work here. The chances are . . .'

Zara didn't dignify this with a response. 'Second problem. If the killer was already in the museum, why did they need to ram the window to steal the suit?'

'Uh—'

'Third problem. Imagine you've accidentally suffocated someone in a hypobaric chamber. You have a car. You presumably also have the victim's car, and the keys to their house. How would you get rid of the body?'

I opened my mouth to answer, but she quickly cut me off.

'Okay, imagine *I'm* the killer, not you,' she said. 'How would *I* get rid of the body?'

'You'd just ask one of your goons at the Company to do it.'

Zara ignored this. 'I would put Cho in the trunk of his own car and drive him home. I'd pack some of his stuff into an overnight bag—'

'The guards at the gate search all the trunks.'

'On the way *into* the complex,' Zara said. 'Not out. Right?'

I nodded reluctantly. The guards hadn't searched our car when we left yesterday.

'Once I had the overnight bag, I'd unlock Cho's phone with his fingerprint or his face,' Zara continued. 'I'd use it and his credit card to book a hotel room somewhere in California. I'd drive him and the bag halfway there, to a deserted spot along the Santa Ana River. I'd use a plastic bottle to pump his lungs full of river water. Then I'd put him in the driver's seat and send his car over the edge. When he didn't turn up for work the next day, everyone would assume he was sick. When the police were eventually called, they'd think he'd skipped town. And by the time his body was found, no one would be able to tell that he was dead before he went in the water. His death might seem suspicious, but it wouldn't lead anyone back to the hypobaric chamber, and definitely not to me.'

She leaned back again and took her own victory sip. It occurred to me that Zara would be a very capable murderer.

'So tell me,' she said. 'Why the hell would the killer decide to disguise Cho's death as a space accident? An international incident that would lure in the police, the FBI and us?'

I thought hard. 'Because the killer is an employee here,' I tried. 'They have to be—no one else was on campus at the time. Space is their whole thing. This might have been the first idea they had.'

'The fact that they work here might be the only thing *you* know about them, but that doesn't mean they don't also have a personal life,' Zara pointed out. 'You don't think they watch *Law & Order*? You don't think they read Agatha Christie? There are a million better ways to cover up an accidental death, and even if the killer was Buzz Aldrin, he'd still think of every single one of them before he thought of framing it as a spacewalk-gone-wrong. Besides, a NASA employee would understand that it's impossible for an astronaut to fall off a space station and then land on the ground, intact. The killer must have known their colleagues wouldn't believe this for a second.'

'We did, though,' I said thoughtfully. 'The Company, I mean.'

Zara's eyes narrowed. 'So I'm not a rocket scientist. Sue me.'

'No, I mean, what if the killer *wanted* us to be involved?'

'Why?'

'They couldn't risk transporting the body anywhere, in case they got pulled over by the cops, or in case the guards recognised that the driver of the car wasn't the owner. But the killer couldn't leave the body in the chamber, since they were known to be operating it at the time of death. So they used us. They made the death look like an international incident, knowing that the CIA would arrive to sweep everything under the rug. We erased all the CCTV, cooked up a story about a diabetic coma, and even destroyed the body for them.'

'That's even more ridiculous,' Zara said. 'You remember that the spy plane actually exists, right?'

I had forgotten that. 'The YouTube video could be fake.'

Zara's voice was firm. 'It's not. IMINT says the metadata confirms the time, date and location of the recording, and there's no sign the images or sounds have been doctored. In addition to that, SIGINT has been tracking the communications of everyone who was on board the fishing trawler. Not all of them saw the plane, but all of them confirm that the net got tangled on something.'

I went to chew a fingernail, but it turned out to be made of silicone.

Zara said, 'Do you think a Chengdu J-20S flew overhead and then crashed into the ocean on the same night that a killer just happened to disguise their dead co-worker as a Chinese pilot?'

I countered: 'Do *you* think a dead Chinese pilot fell out of the sky and just so happened to land right next to a museum where a Chinese spacesuit had been stolen?'

We glared at each other for a moment. Then a smile tugged at the edge of Zara's mouth. She was enjoying this.

So was I. This kind of puzzle was the only thing that took my mind off meat. But I wished I was solving it with Thistle, not Zara. At the thought, my good mood faded, like a light bulb slowly going cold after the power is shut off.

'Let me look into Rob Cho,' I said. 'I'm sure I can prove the body was his. Remember, we're here to kill the rumour about a Chinese astronaut. If the people here find out that the body in the field was one of their co-workers, that rumour is dead. You have to admit, my theory is more compelling than your Brian Jane diabetic coma story.'

Zara probed the inside of her cheek with her tongue, thinking it over.

'And if I'm wrong,' I said, 'you shouldn't have any trouble proving it. Just show me Cho, alive and well.'

'Fine.' Zara cracked her knuckles and stood up. 'We'll follow the Rob Cho lead. But I want to be on our way back to Virginia within twenty-four hours. You may have fooled your girlfriend, but not the rest of the FBI. Someone could be pulling apart our cover as we speak.'

I was pretty sure I only needed twenty-four minutes. 'We're looking for someone who works here, who knew the victim, who's big enough to carry the body and has a good reason not to tell the cops what really happened,' I said. 'How about we go talk to Sam Garcia?'

CHAPTER 20

I was an instrument, but my eye was moved.
Aha, there it is! What am I?

We found Garcia at a wall-mounted terminal on the ground floor of his building running some kind of scan and arguing with a co-worker—the middle-aged woman he'd called Amazing Grace. There were a lot of numbers on the screen, changing too fast for me to read them, and a rectangle of blackness, dotted with stars. A photo, or a video.

'The latency is the problem,' Garcia was saying. 'This thing is geostationary, going at 7000 miles per hour. The frame rate of the telescope isn't fast enough to catch it.'

'If it's geostationary, then it's not moving at all, relative to us,' Grace said. 'That's what geostationary means. Why would the frame rate matter?'

'The telescope isn't on the ground, it's in Low Earth Orbit.'

Grace gasped. 'You're siphoning bandwidth from Hubble to pursue this crackpot theory of yours?'

I cleared my throat. They both whirled around, as though we'd caught them looking at porn. Maybe we had. They seemed to like space a whole lot.

'Tell me about lab-grown meat,' I said.

Grace frowned. 'I beg your pardon?'

'Will you give us a minute?' Garcia asked her.

Grace looked uneasily from me to Zara, and then said, 'Sure.'

When Grace was gone, Garcia turned to Zara. 'Who are you?'

'Cassandra Holcroft. I work with Timothy at ClearHorizon.'

'She knows,' I added.

'Ah.' Garcia's face fell. He was affable enough—people probably liked him until they found out he was an ex-con.

'Apparently lab-grown meat was invented here,' I said. 'How does it work? You just plug in the DNA of the animal you want, and out comes a steak?'

I could see that Zara didn't think now was the time to ask this question. But I wanted to throw Garcia off-balance. Wrong-foot him before we got to the hard questions. And anyway, if he was about to be whisked off to a CIA black site, then I wasn't sure there would be another chance.

'Well . . .' Garcia blinked a few times, redirecting his brain from what he was doing towards what I was asking. 'Not exactly. The Advanced Food Tech research team remove some muscle cells from the animal—a cow, a chicken, whatever—and put the cells in a bioreactor. It's a bit like microbrewing, if you've ever done that?'

He looked me up and down and seemed to quickly decide that no, I'd never done that.

'The bath of nutrients helps the sample grow,' he continued, 'into a shape determined by a mould. Then you cook it and eat it. Voilà—space steak. But it can be done on Earth, too. It's more ethical and environmentally friendly. Meat without the slaughterhouse.'

Zara grimaced. 'So it's like eating a tumour.'

'It's not *unlike* that,' Garcia conceded.

My stomach grumbled. 'Does it taste like real meat?'

'It *is* real meat. So yes, the taste is basically the same.'

'Could it work with humans?'

'Yes, it's perfectly safe for human consumption.'

'I mean could you grow meat from human cells?'

'What?' Garcia looked taken aback. 'I mean, you *could* . . . but why?'

'Just curious,' I said.

Zara pointed at the screen. 'What are you up to?'

'Oh.' Garcia waved a big hand at the terminal. 'Scanning the sky.'

I looked at the patch of darkness. 'What for?'

'You know. The, uh . . .' He lowered his voice and looked from me to Zara and back again. '. . . the Chinese spacecraft?'

I was surprised that he was running his own investigation, and even more surprised that he was doing it here, where anyone could see. But maybe that was the point. No use acting innocent in private.

'Why can't you do that on the computer in your office?' I asked.

'Is it not connected to the telescope?' Zara guessed.

'The telescope is in orbit. All the computers are connected to it. But . . .' Garcia looked around and saw no one else nearby. 'I'm six foot five. You know how long the mattresses are in Huntsville?'

I did. Six feet, three inches.

'So I have lumbago.' Garcia turned back to the screen. 'Can't sit down all day.'

The terminal on the wall was indeed a better height for him. But if he really was looking for a top-secret satellite, it was idiocy to do it here, where anyone walking past— like us—might see. Zara looked appalled at his lack of tradecraft.

'I thought you said this facility was air-gapped, for security.' I watched his hands as I spoke. They were fidgety, nervous. 'How can you communicate with a telescope in orbit?'

'I said nothing touches the internet.' Garcia glanced at the screen. 'We can communicate with objects in space. It's objects on Earth that are a security risk. That's what we've blocked off.' He tapped at his keyboard. 'I suspect the vessel is about 22,000 miles above Ecuador. But it might only be the size of a school bus. And if you do some basic trigonometry—'

I wondered if there was such a thing.

'You'll realise that while Ecuador is big, the sky above it is much, much bigger. The higher up you go, the bigger it gets. Even with the best telescopes in the world, it's like looking for a needle in a haystack. The computer is working on it, but it's going to take a while.'

'Was Rob Cho the friend who erased your criminal record?' I asked.

He hesitated a moment too long. 'He didn't erase it,' he said. 'He just unflagged my application, like I told you before.'

This fit with what Lilah Parget had told us. 'When did you last see him?'

'We had beers after work on Monday night. Why?'

'Beers on a Monday?' Zara said.

'We'd been working hard.' Garcia didn't meet her gaze. Today was Thursday, and I thought I could smell alcohol on his breath now, too.

'He didn't show up on Tuesday?' I asked.

'Yeah, I think so. Just in the morning, maybe.'

'Why did you tell me he was on leave? He wasn't due to go for another week.'

'Because that's what Hazel Cuthbert told me.' Garcia was beginning to look uneasy. 'What's this about?'

'We think that might have been his body out in the field.' I could have kept this to myself, but I wanted to see his reaction.

Garcia's eyes went wide. 'Rob?'

'You haven't seen him since, I take it,' I said.

'That can't be right.' Garcia shook his head vigorously. 'No. That was a Chinese astronaut. You said so yourself. That's why . . .' He gestured helplessly at the screen, running pointless calculations.

'We think someone wanted us to think so.'

'No, you're wrong. I'll prove it.' Garcia sounded slightly mad now. 'You'll see. When the computer finishes, the scan will show the space station. I know it's there.'

I could feel Zara looking at me, wondering what I thought about this. In truth, I wasn't sure. Garcia seemed guilty as hell. But he also seemed to genuinely believe there was a secret space station, which the killer wouldn't, because they would know the body had been planted.

Franklin Anders, the atmospheric composition analyst who found the body, had said there was no space station. He'd immediately dismissed it as impossible. Why did Garcia still believe it?

'Did Lilah Parget ever write to you?' I asked.

Garcia's eyes narrowed. 'I'm sorry?'

'I know she wrote to the judge,' I said. 'And the parole board. Victims sometimes do, requesting harsher sentences. But she actually asked for leniency. She seemed to be on your side.'

Garcia's nostril twitched, like a fish hook had caught it. His cheeks bulged, jaw clenching. I was suddenly conscious of just how big he was, and how easily he could throw me across the room.

'On my side,' he repeated slowly.

'I just wondered if she wrote to you during your sentence. Or called you, maybe.'

Garcia looked from me to Zara and back again. He seemed angry, though I couldn't fathom why.

'What does *that*,' he asked, 'have to do with *this*?' He jabbed a finger at the screen, still scanning for a space station that wasn't there.

I stepped closer, not giving him room to think up a lie. 'What did she say?'

Garcia bunched his fist, like he was preparing to put it through my face. Then he got a hold of himself, rubbing his forehead with his palm. 'It's nothing to do with this,' he insisted.

'Tell me anyway.'

'She said . . .' He sighed. 'She said she was sorry.'

'About what?'

'Sorry I had to go to jail,' he said. 'Now will you get lost? I'm busy here.'

He turned back to the screen. A chill ran down my spine. Why would Lilah be *sorry* that her kidnapper had been jailed? What had happened between the two of them, during the brief period she was missing?

'Last question,' I said. 'Did Franklin Anders know Rob Cho?'

Garcia shot me a puzzled look. 'Sure. Why?'

Anders was the only Space City employee who'd seen the body up close. If the dead man was Cho, why didn't Anders say so?

'Just wondering,' I said. 'You know where we can find him?'

CHAPTER 21

At what town event does everyone get the same treatment?

The East Houston Children's Hospital wasn't far from Space City, and it wasn't as sad as I'd expected. Adults in superhero costumes roamed the wards, waving foam weapons and talking in gruff voices. Jaunty music bubbled from hidden speakers. Laughter echoed through the corridors. Every surface gleamed. Many American hospitals had a war-zone feel, exhausted nurses running from one bed to another as the backlog of moaning patients grew and grew—but here, everyone seemed to be keeping it together.

Except Franklin Anders. We found him by his daughter's bedside, reading *Charlotte's Web* to her, voice cracking as the pig in the story won some kind of award at the town fair.

His daughter seemed unmoved. I'm not great at estimating the age of children, partly because all the hungry kids I'd grown up with in the group home looked forty. But I guessed this girl was between six and nine. Other than the twin tubes up her nose, she didn't look sick, just bored, her mouth a flat line, her eyes roaming the panels of the drop ceiling.

Anders recognised me, and stopped mid-sentence. 'Oh! Blake, right? What are you doing here?'

Zara stepped in. 'Sorry to bother you—I'm Sandra, a colleague of Timothy's. We wanted to ask about Rob Cho's car.'

She spoke briskly, keen to demolish my theory and get to Virginia.

Anders had every right to be angry about the intrusion, but he just looked baffled. 'Rob's car?'

'Right,' I said. 'What kind is it?'

'I'm with my daughter.' He gestured to the girl.

'Hello there,' Zara said.

I just waved. I did it quickly, but the girl saw my missing digit anyway.

'What happened to your thumb?' she asked, in that blunt way kids do.

'It fell off,' I said. 'I didn't eat my vegetables.'

She didn't laugh. 'I'm only allowed to eat soup. I died on Monday night.'

I wasn't sure I'd heard her right. 'You died?'

'Yeah. But the doctors made me better.' She pointed to the book. 'I've read this already. They're not going to eat the pig at the end.'

'Why not?'

'Because it's famous.'

'Wouldn't people be *more* keen to eat a famous pig? They'd probably pay extra.' I was good with kids.

Zara pursed her lips. Probably jealous.

'Why do you need to know what kind of car Rob has?' Anders said.

Because it was an indirect way of finding out how well

they knew each other. I leaned on the windowsill, the glass cold against my back. 'Mostly we were wondering where it is.'

'I suppose he used it when he went to visit his sister in hospital—not this hospital,' Anders added quickly.

'Are you two astronauts?' the little girl interrupted.

Zara's smile didn't reach her eyes. 'No, sweetheart.'

'Oh.' The girl looked disappointed. 'I'm going to be an astronaut when I grow up.'

Her father's lip trembled.

'Maybe we could talk somewhere private,' Zara suggested.

This seemed unnecessary to me. The kid was already facing death. It seemed unlikely that we'd scare her. But Anders nodded.

'You want a juice, baby girl?' he asked.

'Can I have a Coke?' She looked hopeful.

'Anything.' He patted her hand, stood up and followed us out into the corridor.

'Whatever you want,' he said, 'can't it wait until I'm back in the office?'

'What's wrong with her?' I asked.

Zara looked exasperated by my lack of tact. I thought I'd done well, waiting until we were out of the kid's earshot.

'Lou Gehrig's disease,' Anders said shortly. As I'd predicted, there was no need to be gentle with him. Life hadn't been.

'Can kids have that?' I asked.

He glared at me. It was a dumb question.

'Will she recover?'

'With treatment, she might last ten years. That might be long enough to find a cure, if we're lucky.'

I looked around. 'Nice hospital. Must be expensive.'

'There's nothing I wouldn't do for my daughter,' he said.

The memory hit me before I could dodge it. My own teenage son, dying in my arms, just days after I first met him. I imagined watching my child die for ten years instead of ten minutes and felt a rush of sympathy for Anders.

Then again, he was kidding himself. If the kid had nearly died on Monday, there was no way she'd last another decade.

I breathed out, expelling the grief. 'Who told you Cho was visiting his sister?'

'Dr Laurie. Why?'

'The fake blood lady?' I asked.

'Brenda Laurie, the famous respiratory engineer, yes.' Anders led us past a hand-sanitiser station and into a waiting area with a vending machine. 'The supposed genius.'

I caught that. 'Supposed?'

He winced. 'I shouldn't have said that.'

'You don't think she's a genius.'

'That's not what I—she's belligerent, that's all. Always complaining about ethics committees, refusing scrutiny of her work, and acting like the rest of us aren't as smart as her. Just this morning she tried to explain to me what hypoxia was. I went to Harvard, okay? She made an incredible breakthrough, I'm not disputing that. Every one of her predictions about what would happen in animal studies turned out to be correct. But . . .' Anders gestured back towards his daughter's ward. 'Her invention might someday save the life of a single astronaut, perhaps. If she'd turned her apparently gigantic brain to the task of inventing better drugs to treat ALS—Lou Gehrig's disease . . .' He sighed. 'Anyway, she might have been wrong about Rob.

Rumours fly around all the time at the office. Just this morning someone told me that the dead guy on Mars was alive, and recovering from a diabetic coma.'

I was about to tell him that was true, to reinforce the cover story, and then remembered he was the one who'd found the body.

Found it, and apparently not recognised it as his co-worker.

Zara raised an eyebrow. 'Did you set them straight?'

'No. I didn't want to interfere with the police investigation, and nor should you. You're just consultants, right?'

'We're assisting the police,' Zara lied, 'and we have some bad news. It's possible that the body you found was Rob Cho.'

She was willing to say this because she didn't believe it. The CIA credo: *Hear only truths, speak only lies.*

Anders' mouth fell open. 'Rob? Are you sure?'

'Pretty sure.' I asked the million-dollar question: 'How come you didn't recognise him?'

He didn't give me a million-dollar answer. 'I don't know. He was all . . . puffy.'

This was true, but I still found it hard to believe. If it had been a colleague of mine, I would have recognised him instantly. It was deeply suspicious that Anders hadn't.

But he had an alibi—he'd been sitting at his desk at the time of Cho's death. I'd seen him on the CCTV feed. Also, the killer had wanted us to believe that Cho was an astronaut, and Anders had been the first person to poke holes in that theory.

Anders was frozen next to the vending machine, holding some quarters. 'If it was Rob, how . . . why . . .?'

'We think it was an accident in the hypobaric chamber,' I said. 'He suffocated.'

'Oh God.' Anders looked like he might be sick.

I shuffled sideways, out of the line of fire. 'Can you think how something like that might happen?'

'No. It doesn't make sense—there are safety features. Sam was supposed to do an inspection earlier this week. But he wouldn't know much about the chamber—he just drew the short straw because the regular safety officer is in Maui. Uh . . .' He looked down at the change in his hand as though it held the answer. 'You should talk to Hazel Cuthbert. She works in the museum, so she might know more about the hypobaric chamber than me.'

'You're the atmosphere scientist.'

'Yeah, but I've never used that chamber. It's a museum exhibit.'

'Can it be switched on from inside?' Zara asked.

'No.' Anders swallowed. 'The controls are on the outside. You have to turn the key to switch it on, lift the lid and then push a big red button. There's a warning siren. Then, thirty seconds later, the chamber decompresses. Plenty of time for someone inside to hit the emergency shutdown button—*that's* on the inside.'

It was hard to imagine how Cho might have been trapped in there by accident.

'The door opens outwards.' I remembered the scratches on the floor outside the chamber. 'While the air's getting sucked out, wouldn't the reverse pressure—'

'Negative pressure,' Anders corrected.

'Right. Wouldn't that hold the door closed?'

'It does. That's a safety feature. If the door opened

inwards, and the magnetic lock failed, it would burst open fast enough to damage equipment. Fast enough to kill a person, if they were standing in the way.'

For a guy who'd never used the chamber, he seemed to know a lot about it. 'But it also means that you can't open the door while it's decompressed,' I said.

'Well, not after the first thirty seconds or so. I guess that's right.' Anders took a Coke out of the machine. 'If Rob died in the chamber, how did his body end up in the rock yard?'

'We're working on that,' I replied. 'But in the meantime, we need to know what kind of car he drove, so we can find it in the parking lot and search it for evidence.'

'Uh . . .' Anders thought for a while. Finally he said, 'A Ford Explorer. Blue.'

'You know the licence plate?'

Anders frowned. 'Why would I know Rob's licence plate off by heart?'

'Good point.' Zara nudged me. 'What kind of weirdo memorises licence plates?'

I ignored this. 'What about his address?'

'I've never been to Rob's place. Somewhere in Friendswood, I think?'

'It's all good. We can get that information. Who has access to the hypobaric chamber?'

Anders looked from me to Zara and back to me. 'Well, everyone. There's a security guard posted nearby, but only from ten to four, when the museum is open to the public. Outside of those hours, anyone who can get into the building could get to the chamber.'

'What about the key to switch it on?'

'The key is left in it.'

I'd been afraid he would say that. 'Is it soundproof?'

'Yup. Even when there's atmosphere inside it, there's still a vacuum within the walls. Like a thermos, or double-glazed windows. Sound can't travel through it.'

'And the warning siren . . .'

Anders got the implication. 'It's on the inside. No one would hear it from outside.'

'In space, no one can hear you scream,' Zara said.

The pathologist had told us the victim held his breath until his lungs exploded. I imagined Cho standing at the window, screaming silently, pushing on a door that wouldn't budge, as his skin inflated and his blood boiled.

By the look on Anders' face, I could tell that he was picturing the same thing.

'If you find any clues about who's responsible for this,' Anders said, 'call me.'

'We don't want anyone taking the law into their own hands,' Zara said.

'Of course not.' Anders swallowed. 'I just meant so I can help you understand the evidence.'

I wondered if Zara believed him. I didn't.

CHAPTER 22

I have six sisters—two older, four younger.
All our names end in Y—but I alone
have wed. What am I?

On the inside, the hypobaric chamber was cramped. It was only about ten feet long and six wide. Wall-mounted gauges and pipes crowded in from all sides. The floor was a steel grid, the kind they use to make catwalks. I felt less like I was on a spaceship and more like I was in a submarine. The two mechanical claws I'd seen before were hanging from the centre of the low ceiling, at about eye level for me. One held a long, white feather. The other held a purple bowling ball. I liked bowling. It was one of very few sports you can do with only three fingers.

Zara hadn't talked at all on the drive back to the museum. She'd been happy earlier today, when she was pulling apart my theory, but now she had a sullenness I couldn't explain. It was as if being happy had made her angry, like she wasn't used to it. Maybe she was bored. Or pissed off that my theory was starting to seem plausible—she hated being wrong.

Finally she spoke. 'What are we looking for, exactly?'

'Blood,' I said. The same thing I was always looking for, pretty much.

'If you're right, and if Cho suffocated in here, why would there be blood?'

'His eardrums burst, and he was coughing up bits of his lungs. You'd think there would be something.'

But looking around the chamber, there was no sign or smell of blood. Maybe Cho's death hadn't been as grisly as I'd been fantasising. Or maybe . . .

'The killer came back,' I said.

'What do you mean?'

'They dumped his body on Mars, and then they came back the next day to mop up his juices.'

'Juices,' Zara repeated, looking amused. 'Why the following day?'

'It just makes more sense. If you're caught scrubbing the inside of the chamber during the day, you could say you dropped a vial of Laurie's fake blood or something. If you're caught cleaning the chamber at night, that's much harder to explain. Which means we're looking for someone who left late on Tuesday and came to work early on Wednesday—they wouldn't have wanted to risk anyone else finding the mess. They're going to be hard to find, though, since you erased the security videos.'

'All right, all right,' Zara said. 'Let's not play the blame game.'

There was a red emergency button next to the door, surrounded by yellow and black tape. It was marked CANCEL DECOMPRESSION. I pointed at it.

'Why didn't Cho push the button?' I asked.

Zara frowned. 'Maybe he didn't hear the siren. Ear plugs, or something.'

'It would be deafening, surely?'

Silence fell. The chamber deadened all sound from the rest of the building.

'Let's find out,' Zara said finally, and walked out. Before I could work out what she meant, she was already closing the door.

'Hey!' I tried to push the door open, but it was too heavy, with too much momentum. It would have cut off my four remaining fingers if I hadn't snatched them out of the way in time.

The door slammed shut with a boom that made the whole chamber vibrate.

'Don't,' I told Zara.

She said something back to me, but I couldn't hear it. The chamber was completely soundproof. All I could hear was my own frantic breaths.

'Zara!' I shouted. 'Let me out!'

She reached sideways, out of view.

A siren screamed inside the chamber. The warning sound Anders had told us about. There was also a low, dark hum, making the metal floor tremble under my feet.

I tried to push the door open, but Zara must have braced her foot against the bottom of it. I was bigger than Zara, but that didn't seem to matter. The door wouldn't budge.

I turned to the CANCEL DECOMPRESSION button and pushed it. The siren kept screaming. The door didn't open. Zara watched me thoughtfully through the thick glass.

I kept stabbing the button, with no result. My heart was pounding. I thought of Rob Cho, with his exploded lungs.

'The button doesn't work!' I shouted. 'Let me out!'

She just kept watching, like I was a fish in an aquarium. No emotion in her face. She'd flirted with me at the motel, bandaged me up, kissed me in front of Ruciani—I'd started to think she really cared about me, but it had all been a trick. Now she was going to kill me as a test.

The humming got louder. The machinery was warming up.

I curled my fingers around the lip of the cancel button and twisted. It unscrewed easily, exposing the mechanism underneath. But I wasn't really sure what I was looking at. There was a spring, and a black plastic cylinder, but no obvious trigger. The siren was making it hard to think. Zara was still watching.

I got out my phone. My first thought was to call Zara and try to talk some sense into her. My second thought was to call Reese Thistle, just so I'd get to hear her voice one last time before I suffocated. I didn't make it to a third thought, because a notification flashed up on my phone screen: *No service*.

Then the siren stopped. The humming ceased. There was a faint hiss as the door opened.

I ran out so fast that I nearly bowled Zara over.

'Was that necessary?' I snapped.

'It was a test,' she said.

'Of *what?*'

She took a breath. 'I couldn't hear any warning siren from out here. Was there one?'

I just glared at her, trembling. She gestured to the phone in my hand. 'No service in there, I take it. I saw you disassembling the emergency shutdown button—could you tell what was wrong with it?'

I took a deep breath, trying to get the rage under control. Why had she done that to me?

'I'm not an electrical engineer,' I said.

Zara walked into the chamber to examine the pieces of the button. She must have known it would be easy for me to close the door and trap her inside. But she didn't seem concerned.

It was like she was punishing me for something. But what?

I imagined myself closing the door, bracing my foot against it, watching her panic. As I looked down at my shoe, I saw again the scratch marks on the concrete. Earlier I had assumed they were from the door, opening outwards. But I hadn't heard any scraping sounds just now.

'There are supposed to be two little . . .' Zara waved her hands around '. . . I don't know what they're called. Small springs with square heads. The button won't work without them.'

'Clearly Garcia never did that safety check.' I was still looking at the scratch marks. 'Someone took the springs, and they dragged something heavy in front of the door, so it couldn't be pushed open. See here?'

I remembered what Cuthbert had said: *The chamber was out of order a couple of days ago.* I don't think it was. I think the killer hung an out-of-order sign over the window. Anyone walking past would have had no idea Cho was suffocating right next to them.

This wasn't an accident. Whoever put Rob Cho in this chamber had wanted him to die.

•

I normally hate the sun, but today I was grateful to be outside. Air. I couldn't get enough of it. I walked slowly through the parking lot, breathing deep, turning my head from right to left and back, like an automated sprinkler. There were hundreds of vehicles to examine. Lots of electric cars, lots of bike racks.

Soon Zara emerged from the museum and jogged over. She held up the USB modem she'd plugged into Cuthbert's computer yesterday.

'We were never here,' she said.

Wilcox had told us to remove the modem before we came back to Virginia. SIGINT had already cloned the Space City database, and the branch chief had decided that any further eavesdropping was too risky. If Cuthbert had found the USB modem she would have immediately realised that someone had been stealing data, and suspected us.

Intelligence work wasn't just about knowing things—it was about making sure no one else knew you knew them.

'Got that licence plate yet?' I asked.

Zara checked her phone. 'No. But how many blue Ford Explorers can there be?'

'Five.' I pointed them out. 'And that's assuming Anders was right about the model. He didn't strike me as a car person.'

'What, you don't think nerds like cars?'

'None of them are damaged,' I said, looking around. 'Not just the Explorers—any of the vehicles.'

'So NASA scientists are careful drivers.' Zara shrugged. 'Makes sense. Imagine trying to land on the moon. Reverse parallel parking is hard enough.'

I reached into my pocket and dug out the broken shard

of headlight. 'But where's the car that rammed the museum window?'

Zara squinted into the sunshine. 'Fixed already, maybe?'

I shook my head. 'Even if you could find a body shop to fix your car that fast, it would be a dumb move. You don't take your damaged car to the shop right after a ram raid. You wait for the heat to die down first. Leave it in your garage, take the bus for a week or two.'

'Okay, so that's what the killer is doing,' Zara said. 'If you're right, and there *is* a killer. So what?'

'We can identify them. The car that *isn't* here must belong to the perp.'

'Great. You gonna memorise a few hundred licence plates?'

I could, but it would take hours. 'Let's check the log at the gate.'

We got in Zara's pick-up and drove towards the exit. I kept the window down, despite the cold. Still needing air, after the terror of the chamber.

Zara's phone dinged. She glanced at the screen. 'Cho drives a blue Ford Explorer, registration TCC-4GH.'

'Drove.' I drummed my fingers on my thigh, thinking of the five Explorers in the parking lot. None of them had matching plates. So where was Cho's car?

When we reached the gate, Zara asked for the log. The guard with the crow's-feet gave it to us without complaint.

'I've been instructed to assist you in any way I can,' she said, giving us a suspicious look.

Zara didn't offer an explanation. 'Thank you, sergeant.'

I was already scanning the sheets. There were licence plates next to names, addresses and phone numbers. I wasn't interested in them. I wanted the vehicle that was missing.

My gaze fell on a name. Someone who had arrived without a car every day since Cho's death. My breath caught in my throat. I'd gotten this all wrong.

'Well?' Zara said.

'Cho wasn't the target,' I said.

'What do you mean?'

'Sam Garcia was supposed to check the decompression chamber,' I said. 'But he delegated the job to Cho at the last minute. Someone tried to kill Garcia, but got Cho instead.'

'Who?'

I pointed at the name, and the address next to it. 'Let's go.'

CHAPTER 23

One of me reveals the future.
Two of me obscures the present.
What am I?

Lilah Parget walked in the front door carrying two bags of groceries and nudged it closed with her hip. The lock clicked behind her. The apartment had a galley kitchen, both benches covered in dirty chopping boards and oven trays. There was a stale toast smell in the air. She left the blinds closed, knowing her way around the semi-darkness, and dumped the bags on top of the mess. She opened the fridge, which was already close to overflowing, and searched for somewhere to squeeze in her groceries.

She frowned, perhaps looking for the leftover ham she'd wrapped in foil.

'Hi,' I said.

She whirled around and saw me lounging on a dining chair, my feet on her glass-topped table. 'What the hell?'

'Didn't mean to startle you,' I said, though that was exactly what I'd intended. She'd been so controlled when I last spoke to her. I would only get the truth by rattling her. 'Just wanted to ask you some follow-up questions.'

One of Parget's carving knives was on the coffee table next to my shoe. Not far from my good hand. Her eyes widened as she noticed it.

'How did you get in here?' She kept her distance, her butt pressed against the kitchen bench.

I took another bite of the ham. 'Door was unlocked.'

'It wasn't.'

'You sure?'

'Get out,' she said. 'Before I call the police.'

'Go ahead. That's what an innocent woman would do.'

As expected, she didn't reach for her phone. 'I told Dr Laurie I thought it was too risky to begin human trials, and she blew up at me. My internship has been cut short. So whatever you want from Space City, I can't get it for you.'

'I've been wondering why you would write those letters,' I said. 'To the judge, and the parole board. Begging them for leniency.'

I recognised the emotion on her face. I'd felt it many times: fear of getting caught. The longer you got away with it—whatever *it* was—the worse the fear became.

'Garcia kidnapped you,' I continued. 'Why would you want him released early? Surely you'd want him to be put away for as long as possible. So you felt safe. And on top of that, why would you seek out an internship in the same building as him?'

She was edging sideways along the bench. 'I have a gun.'

'Obviously. This is Texas.'

'I'm asking you to leave.'

'Or you'll shoot me?' I chewed some more ham. 'That's a nice, straightforward way of killing someone. Sure beats a hypobaric chamber. At least you'll know you got the right guy.'

My stomach growled, unsatisfied with pig meat. Parget was thin, but she was available. By changing her name, she'd cut herself off from everyone she knew. That had been the point. But she hadn't been Rachel long enough to put down strong roots. Would anyone come looking if she disappeared?

First, prove she's the killer, I told myself.

She looked at me for a long moment. I returned her stare. My theory fit all the facts, but I didn't have any hard evidence. I needed her to confess. Loud enough so the phone in my pocket could hear.

'You didn't want Garcia in prison,' I said. 'You wouldn't feel safe until he was dead. You've been at Space City for months, waiting for your chance. Finally it came—he was scheduled to visit the museum and do a safety check on the communications systems for the hypobaric chamber. It was perfect. Not just a death, but an agonising one. So you go into the chamber and disconnect the emergency shutdown button. Then you hang around nearby, keeping out of sight, until you hear him arrive. When he goes inside you drag something heavy in front of the door, so it can't be opened, and hang an out-of-order sign over the window. That way if anyone interrupts you, they won't see him through the glass. The chamber is soundproof. He can scream all he likes, and no one will come. You push the button to decompress the chamber and wait. But when you finally take the sign down and look through the window, you realise you've made a mistake. Garcia delegated the job to Rob Cho at the last minute. You've suffocated the wrong guy.'

Parget's eyes narrowed when she heard Rob Cho's name, but she admitted nothing.

'So now what do you do?' I went on. 'The police will have a limited suspect pool. They'll only be looking at people who were in the building at the time. It won't take them long to find you—unless you make it look like the accident happened somewhere else. You're already in the museum, where there are spacesuits available. You grab one and put it on Cho's corpse. You use his car to take him to the rock yard, then drag him to Mars. You use a blanket to obscure any tracks, but you've pulled some big shoes over your own in case you missed any. Where'd you get them, by the way?'

Parget still said nothing. Maybe she suspected I was recording the conversation.

I shrugged, as though it was of no consequence. 'Whatever. You use Cho's car again to ram the museum window. That way, if the cops realise the suit was stolen or work out where Cho died, they'll assume the killer is someone who hadn't used their swipe card to access the building. You come back early the following day, by bus, to clean up the mess.' I leaned back in my chair. 'Obviously you know the ruse won't hold up for long. But you've created just enough confusion to slip away. Here's my question, though: why didn't you?'

She just stared.

'You stayed,' I said. 'Even after the cops showed up. Even after you recognised me, a former FBI guy, outside Sam Garcia's office. You're an unpaid intern—you could easily have vanished into thin air. Changed your name again. No one would have found you.'

Parget released her grip on the kitchen bench and started walking towards me.

'Why didn't you run, Lilah?' I asked.

She whirled and slammed her fist into the side of my head. A bomb went off inside my skull, and I toppled off the chair. As I hit the floor face-first, the ham flew from my mouth.

'I would never hurt Sam!' Lilah screamed.

My ears were ringing. I wasn't sure I'd heard her right.

'He's *everything* to me!' She kicked my chest, the toe of her boot sinking deep into my diaphragm, crushing all the air out of my lungs.

Parget kept shouting, but I couldn't decode the words. I was outside myself, watching Timothy Blake take a beating on a dirty laminate floor. I got the feeling this wasn't going how he'd expected.

Soon I couldn't see him anymore. He was replaced by a vision—Jeb Parget, driving out of the shopping mall parking lot seven years ago. The boom gate camera watched him go. Lilah Parget was hiding behind the trash cans, twelve years old, smoking a cigarette from the packet an older man had given her. Nervous. Excited. When it burned down to the filter, she stubbed it out and lit another.

Finally a car pulled up, Sam Garcia behind the wheel. Lilah leapt to her feet, tossed one last cigarette onto the pile and ran over. She got in the passenger seat, not the trunk. She was smiling.

Was I seeing the past, or only imagining it? Had Lilah known Garcia already? Had she gone with him willingly, to escape from her father? Garcia might have taken her somewhere and promised to pick her up later. But he never came back, because Richmond and I arrested him. No wonder Lilah hadn't gone home. No wonder she'd been crying when I found her, abandoned in the homeless camp. No wonder she'd never thanked me for rescuing her.

Now, as twenty-year-old Parget pounded me into the floorboards, I wanted to tell her that Garcia was a bad man. He'd had rope, a ski mask and a gun in his trunk. If he'd come back for her, she'd be dead now, or enslaved. But I couldn't breathe, much less speak, and a tidal wave of darkness was rushing in.

·

When I regained consciousness, there was something cold and hard pressed against my skull. I squirmed, trying to push it off.

'Hold still.' Zara's voice. I was surprised how relieved I was to hear it. I let her adjust the icepack against my scalp.

I had double vision, and the world was still spinning, but at least it was slowing down. I was in the stairwell outside Lilah's apartment. Concrete beneath me, an Edison light flickering above.

Edison campaigned to have people executed using direct current, I thought. *Because he owned the patent on it.*

'You're talking nonsense,' Zara said, and I realised I must have been speaking aloud. 'You know your name?'

My mouth was dry. 'What happened?' I asked.

'You got KO'd by a hundred-pound girl, that's what.'

'Where the hell were you?'

'Hey, I got to you five seconds after the first punch.'

Unease prickled down my neck. 'What did you do to Lilah?'

'Nothing,' Zara said. 'When I burst in, she fled to another room. So I dragged you out here and shut the door.'

'You didn't chase her?' I was oddly touched. I would have expected Zara to step right over my body and pursue her target.

Zara avoided my gaze. 'Come on. We have to go.'

She was right. For all we knew, neighbours had overheard the yelling and called the police.

Zara held my good arm as I staggered down the stairs towards the car. On the way down, I saw an electric bicycle. Presumably the one Lilah used to get to work instead of a car. I should have checked the logs for the week before. I'd been rushing, because of the hunger.

I stumbled. Zara wrapped her arm around my waist, pulling me closer to her. Our hips bumped as we walked.

'Sounds like you were wrong,' she said.

She would have heard the whole conversation, thanks to the phone in my pocket. I squeezed my eyes shut, trying to clear my head. I thought of the disassembled shutdown button, the out-of-order sign, Cho's car missing from the lot.

'I'm right about what happened,' I said. 'I was wrong about who did it, that's all.'

Zara opened the passenger door of her pick-up and helped me clamber in, like I was an old man.

'Where are we going?' I asked.

'Virginia.'

I shook my head and regretted it. My vision swam, and there was a sharp pain behind my eyeballs. 'I'm *this* close to figuring the whole thing out.' I tried to hold my thumb and forefinger a quarter inch apart, but the thumb wasn't there. 'I need more time.'

'We don't have more time. The Houston PD thinks you're the Reaper, remember? We have to get you out of Houston. Otherwise you'll end up on death row.'

'But I didn't do it.'

'No one gives a shit. This is Texas,' Zara said.

I closed my eyes. There was heat at the base of my skull where it had hit the floor. A bruise was forming—but so was an idea.

'Fine. Take me to Hedwig Village. 251 Wendover Lane,' I said. It was one of the addresses I'd seen on the FBI whiteboard.

Zara glanced sharply at me. 'Why?'

'We're going to catch the Reaper.'

CHAPTER 24

Where do ravens go to drink?

The front porch had a wicker chair, some wind chimes and fig ivy creeping up the walls. The plant looked like it had only recently started to wilt, probably when the person who used to water it got strangled. Crime scene tape was still crisscrossed over the front door, which bore a dent where somebody had used a crowbar to get it open. Someone else had patched up the damage, but not well enough to hide it. There was an old-fashioned bell on a hook in lieu of a button, and a big brass knocker for those who preferred percussion to melody. A peephole above it. I turned around to face the neighbours opposite, but hedges screened their windows from view.

Zara kicked a scuffed corner of the welcome mat. 'Are we going in, or what?'

It was late afternoon. We'd made two stops on our way— one to drop the USB modem in a trash can, then another to mark a traffic pole, letting Wilcox know the modem was ready to be picked up. Zara had scraped a Rolaid across the pole, because Rolaids were less suspicious in a handbag than chalk. Why we couldn't just take the modem on the plane, I didn't know.

'Imagine you're the Texas Reaper,' I said.

Zara sighed. 'Do I have to?'

'You know a middle-aged woman lives here on her own. You know her name from IRS records—Ethel Braidwyn. You've clearly scoped the place out. You know there are no cameras, but you also know she has a peephole, and she'll see you when you knock. How do you get her to open the door?'

'I don't know. You tell her someone's after you, and you need help?'

Zara had made the same assumption as me—that the killer was a featherweight. A big guy like Garcia would have just barged the door open. But this killer used a taser and a garrotte rather than their hands. We were looking for a woman, a teenager or a small man.

'Or you'd dress as a delivery driver,' I said. 'Hold up a package and say you need her to sign for it.'

'Okay, sure. So what?'

I stepped back. 'Open the door.'

Zara didn't. 'I'm not leaving my prints and DNA all over a crime scene.'

'Forensics have been and gone,' I said. 'And we won't touch anything.'

Zara sighed and produced her lock-release gun. There was a whir, a click and a creak as the door opened, revealing a dark hallway.

I stepped across the threshold, looking around. The walls were mint green. A big photo of two young men had been printed on canvas, stretched across a frame and mounted on one wall. Braidwyn's two sons, I guessed. The ones who hadn't visited until her corpse had been rotting for a week. A little Jesus statue stood on a shelf between two candles. A shrine like that typically went on the east wall, but this was on the south. This could have meant the victim belonged to a denomination I didn't know much about, or was more iconoclastic than ecclesiastic. Maybe it meant nothing.

There was a dark stain just inside the doorway. I crouched. Blood had seeped into the floorboards before the trauma cleaners wiped it away. But it hadn't pooled—it made a ring shape, the kind left behind by a coffee mug.

'The killer held her down,' I said. 'To watch her die, face to face.'

'How do you know?'

I wasn't sure—I could just picture it so vividly. I walked deeper into the house, turning a corner to a kitchen. There was a large wall calendar. Nothing on it except for birthdays and the letter C, written in red, every Wednesday. No—not every Wednesday. I turned the page, using my silicone hand so as not to leave prints. Three weeks on, three weeks off, going back to January.

'If the murder happened right here, you don't need to search the whole house,' Zara objected from the hallway.

I was examining a can of herbal tea bags, which claimed to have 'immuno-boosting' properties. 'I'm not looking for the killer, I'm trying to understand the victim.'

'Why?' Zara sounded honestly confused, and I didn't blame her. It seemed unlikely that a cannibal would have much respect for the dead. But this was why I'd bristled in that theatre when Ariel Wilcox implied that I was a serial killer. Sure, I didn't like to see someone's body go to waste after they were done with it, but that didn't mean I was indifferent to the person they had been.

From here, I could see into a living area, where floor-to-ceiling bookshelves were filled with a mixture of science fiction and science fact. Braidwyn had been interested in a variety of things, from the recent past to the distant future. All the paperbacks had broken spines. She'd read all these books, and probably had interesting opinions about them, opinions that were now lost beyond the event horizon of death.

I made my way counterclockwise around the living area. There was an old sofa, a coffee table and an art desk. On the desk were a vase of dead flowers and a half-finished watercolour depicting them.

I made my way back to the kitchen. From this angle I could see a pill organiser half-hidden behind the kettle. The medications were labelled like seedlings. I read the labels through the transparent plastic. Various painkillers, plus Nolvadex and Evista. Estrogen modulators.

'She had breast cancer,' I said.

'Oh?' Zara didn't sound impressed, or even surprised.

I thought about what Ruciani had said before glancing down at his cigarette. *They all had . . .*

'*All* the victims had cancer,' I realised. 'But the feds are keeping it quiet.'

'Maybe they haven't made the connection.'

'They have—Ruciani suspected the killer worked for a health insurance company, or at least had access to the records of one.'

'Does he?' Zara looked interested now. 'They might be hushing it up to hold on to media interest. The public wouldn't care so much if they knew these women had been dying anyway.'

I doubted that—the media loves a tragedy. 'Braidwyn thought her own life was worth fighting for,' I said, looking at the chemo calendar, the estrogen modulators, the immuno-boosting teas.

Zara stuck her hands in the pockets of her silk jacket. 'Are you done?'

'Yeah.' I hadn't spotted the smoking gun I was hoping for—the only deduction I'd made, the FBI already knew. But it made me wonder what I might learn by visiting Rob Cho's house. 'Let's go to Friendswood.'

Zara checked her watch. 'We fly to Dulles Airport in three hours.'

'Great. We have time.'

She threw up her hands. 'Fine.'

As she followed me to the front door, Zara spotted something on the floor. She crouched next to a skirting board.

'What's that?' I said.

'A hair. But don't get excited.' She scraped it up with a nail. 'It's mine.' She held it up next to her own hair, showing me that the colour was a similar maple brown.

'This is why I didn't want us visiting crime scenes,' she said. 'You might have left something behind as well.'

I wasn't sure the hair was Zara's—it was hard to imagine how it could have landed in that spot. 'Can I keep it?'

She smirked. 'Sure, weirdo.'

CHAPTER 25

I parked my car in Georgia,
then got mad. What am I?

It was late afternoon by the time we reached Rob Cho's
house, a two-storey blond brick thing, with arched
windows and a yard full of crabgrass. It was in Pearland,
not Friendswood, so Anders had been wrong, but only by
four miles. The driveway was blacktop, covered by a shade
sail. No car on it.

'Maybe he keeps it in the garage,' Zara suggested.

This seemed unlikely. Most Texans keep only junk
locked in the garage and leave their thirty-thousand-dollar
cars out in the driveway. Strange, but true.

'Maybe the killer still has it,' I said. 'If they used it for the
ram raid at the museum.'

Zara opened her mouth, then closed it again.

The front door was on the second level—I had to limp
up some stone steps to get to it. My ribs still felt tight after
the beating I'd taken. Zara knocked instead of ringing the
bell, just in case the bell was wired to activate a hidden
security camera. Common these days.

'Are we going in?' I asked, after a minute of silence.

Zara looked around. It was more exposed than Braidwyn's house had been. Risky. But I knew she loved risky.

'Yeah,' she said, and dug the lock-release gun out of her purse.

There was a mesh security door and then a regular door. Ironically, the security door was unlocked. Zara's lock-release gun made short work of the regular door.

Once it was open, I poked my head in, looking for signs of an alarm. There was no keypad near the door, and no motion sensor in the corner of the room. It looked like we were okay. We entered, and Zara locked the door behind us.

The living room had a Samsung TV mounted on the wall, a leather couch opposite and a tall mirror that made the space feel bigger than it was. Built-in shelves were stocked with recipe books and country CDs. The adjacent kitchen had a bowl of fruit on the island bench, black spots spreading across the bananas like melanoma. But the apples weren't withering yet, and the tomatoes were still firm. If I had to guess, I'd say the fruit had been here about four days.

There was a dirty bowl in the sink. The gunk on it was solid, but not yet mouldy. Two to three days. I opened the dishwasher. It was full, but the plates inside were clean, beads of water still clinging to the rims. The moisture had been sealed in for too long, and smelled off.

'What do you think?' Zara was looking at a framed photo on the wall. A man at some kind of celebratory dinner, maybe a family reunion. His arms were wrapped around a woman with a cautious smile. A candid shot.

I closed my eyes, thinking of the dead body. Then I opened them and examined the man's face. 'That's him.'

Zara peered closer. 'How can you be sure?'

It was difficult to explain. The man's face was partly hidden by the woman's hair, so the mole under his eye wasn't visible. There were no other distinctive features I could point to, like a scar, a tattoo or a bent nose. The hair in the picture was longer, the skin less purple, the eyes darker without the milky haze of death. But my subconscious must have noted hundreds of more subtle details, like the width of the chin, the shape of the teeth, the distance between the nostrils, the height of the widow's peak.

'I just am,' I said.

'Who's the woman? Wife, girlfriend?'

'Sister.' They had similar faces, and the embrace looked familial rather than romantic. Anyway, this was the house of a lone person—small portions in the fridge, only one genre of music and one kind of book on the shelves, only men's shoes on the rack by the door. It was possible that Cho had a girlfriend who didn't live with him, but if so, she would have reported him missing by now.

A masters degree in computer science from Texas A&M hung near the photo. Same college as Garcia—same year, too. That was probably where they'd met. It still seemed incredible that Cho had unflagged Garcia's application to work at NASA, knowing what he'd done.

I walked into the bathroom to check how many tooth-brushes were on the vanity. None. That was interesting.

'Why hasn't the sister reported him missing?' Zara asked.

'Garcia said she was in hospital. Can you find out which one?'

'Of course.' She sounded offended.

Some stairs led down to the garage. There was a ping-pong table, and a bicycle. No car, and nothing else of interest.

I went back up the stairs and moved towards the bedroom. There was an external door in the hallway, leading to a small backyard surrounded by hedges. The house was built on a slope, so even though we'd climbed stairs to get in, the back rooms were at ground level. I passed the door and entered the master bedroom. The closet held only men's clothes, and not many of them. One suit and two casual outfits. The rest was office wear—polo shirts and chinos.

Zara spoke from right behind me, making me jump. 'Maybe Cho himself is a Chinese spy,' she said. 'Would that fit?'

'Unlikely. He was Korean,' I said.

'How do you know?'

'Kimchi in the fridge. Plus . . .' I pointed to a framed photo on the wall. A wedding, full of shoulder pads and eighties hairstyles. Cho's parents. The groom was giving the bride a piggyback. 'That's a Korean tradition.'

I could see Zara was wondering where I'd heard this, but wasn't willing to ask three questions in a row. She hated admitting ignorance. I didn't know if that was a CIA thing, or just a Zara thing.

'There aren't many clothes here,' she said instead.

I shrugged. 'Men don't care about clothes.'

'Or . . .' Zara pointed to an empty space at the top of the closet. It was exactly where you would expect a suitcase to be.

I peered under the bed. Nothing, not even dust. 'We were both right.'

'Explain.'

'When we were talking about the best way to dispose of a body. I said the killer stole a spacesuit and dragged the body into the middle of a field. You said they would

have taken the victim's car to his home and packed a suitcase to make it look like he left town. We were both right.
The killer did both—'

I stopped.

'What?' Zara said.

I shushed her, and then she heard it, too.

The security door creaking open.

CHAPTER 26

I'm quick, then I'm big. I'm bright,
then I'm loud. What am I?

Zara and I looked at each other for a second.

There was a soft click as someone tried the handle of the front door. Zara had locked it behind her, so it rattled but didn't open.

It couldn't be a coincidence that the visitor had arrived so soon after us. My best guess was that the Houston PD or the FBI had staked out Braidwyn's home, and had followed us here. They must have decided this was their best chance to make a play. I wondered if they'd try to catch me alive.

I pointed silently, through the open bedroom door to the hallway, where the sliding glass door led to the yard.

We crept to the door, but it was locked. Zara fumbled for her lock-release gun. 'Wait,' I whispered. I could hear keys in the front door. If the new arrivals had keys, they would reach us long before Zara could get us out the back.

I grabbed Zara's arm and pulled her into the kitchen. We both ducked down behind the island bench as my brain went into overdrive. The police or the FBI wouldn't have a key to Cho's house. There had been no keys on his body. But his killer would.

The hinges creaked. Cautious footsteps shuffled in.

I leaned slowly sideways, so I could see the living room mirror, and a reflection of the front door.

Two men entered. Both wore white T-shirts and cargo shorts. One had a running jacket and looked like he was in his late twenties. The other wore a baseball cap and seemed to be early forties. Despite the casual clothes, they moved like soldiers. Walking in a combat crouch, checking corners, keeping their heads low.

Both were Asian, and both carried compact semi-automatic pistols.

Zara's eyes were wide. She mouthed 'MSS' at me, like I hadn't already worked that out.

Except it didn't make any sense for the MSS to be here. There had never been any Chinese fighter pilot—it was just Rob Cho, in a space suit stolen from a museum. So who the hell were these guys?

The guy with the cap made some complicated hand signals at the guy with the jacket, who nodded and started to creep deeper into the house, towards the bedroom. Ball Cap softly closed the door behind him as he swept his gaze across the living room. I shifted back behind the bench before he could see my reflection in the mirror.

If he followed Jacket down the hall, Zara and I could sneak around the other side of the kitchen bench and go down the steps to the garage. Presumably we could open the garage door from inside. It would be loud, but we'd be able to escape under it before the two men came running down the stairs. Even if they were willing to shoot, there were plenty of parked cars out there. Lots of cover. We'd be able to get to Zara's pick-up.

I tried to indicate all of this to Zara, but with only four fingers, I wasn't as good at hand signals as Ball Cap was. And anyway, Zara had her own plan.

She stood up and shot Ball Cap in the head.

The crack of the gunshot was loud enough to make my head spin. I scrambled sideways in time to see Ball Cap hit the floor, twitching, a hole where his nose was supposed to be. A puddle of blood grew under him.

Zara had already swivelled to face the hall. Jacket would either try to escape out the back door or return to support his buddy. If he returned, she was ready to shoot.

I reached up and wrapped my fingers around the handle of a carving knife, wedged into a bamboo block on the bench. I wrestled it free. The knife was a single piece of steel, moulded into a handle shape at one end, with a gooseflesh texture for better grip. My heart hammered. The propellant from Zara's gunshot hung in the air, scorching my nostrils.

Footsteps thudded towards us. Jacket was coming back.

Zara stood still, waiting for him to come into view. Ball Cap's blood was going to waste as it leaked out onto the floor. All that muscle and fat was getting colder and less tasty by the second. I found myself crawling towards it.

Something bounced into the kitchen—a black cylinder with a yellow band around it. Jacket had been smart enough not to walk into Zara's trap and had thrown a flashbang instead.

I dropped the knife, plugged my ears and turned my head away, just as there was a tremendous *blam!* For a split second, I saw my shadow in colour on the far wall, while the rest of the world turned white. My left eardrum whined. From my right ear, which I'd plugged with a silicone finger, I could hear nothing at all.

I tried to pick up the knife again, but my clumsy fingers just knocked it sideways, the blade spinning. The noise had made me dizzy. It felt like the floor was at an angle under me. I collapsed, narrowly avoiding the blade.

The front door opened again, revealing a third guy, taller than the other two, with sunglasses and a short beard. He must have been guarding the door. He saw me and raised his gun.

I managed to grip the handle of the knife and lifted it as though it could deflect a bullet. As though it wouldn't fall out of my thumbless hand as soon as I tried to stab anything. 'Get back,' I yelled, but I couldn't hear my own voice. Sunglasses looked like he was shouting, too, but I couldn't tell what. Probably something like *Put down the knife*. His gun was pointed right at my head.

I kept waving the blade around like a crazy person, wondering where Zara and Jacket were, or if they'd killed each other. Sunglasses approached, holding the gun one-handed, like he intended to grab me with the other.

Without a thumb, it was hard for me to hold the blade. If he put enough pressure on the tendons in my wrist, I'd drop it. I slashed the air, still yelling at him to stay back.

With his eyes on me, Sunglasses stepped into the blood puddle. His foot slipped backwards like he was on ice skates, and he accidentally fired the gun. I felt the bullet whiz past my ear like a hornet. It left a ricochet scar on the fridge behind me. Sunglasses tried to regain his balance but overcorrected, tumbling forwards now, arms windmilling. He crashed down on top of me, knocking all the air out of my lungs—and impaling his chest on the knife.

Sunglasses screamed, thrashing around above me. Blood rained down, hot and sticky, drenching my shirt and my neck. It was like someone had up-ended a saucepan of passata onto me. The sunglasses fell off the man's face and I saw his terrified brown eyes. His cheeks went grey. He retched, like he was vomiting up his soul. I tried to get out from under him but couldn't.

A moment later the guy sagged, which somehow made him feel even heavier. I squirmed until he toppled off me, hitting the ground like a sack of flour.

I looked around. Two dead men. No sign of Zara or Jacket. The door was open. I should have run, but instead I started sawing at the guy's armpit with the knife. I knew I couldn't take both bodies, but at least I could take part of one.

Sweat poured down my face as I worked. It was a carving knife, not a hacksaw, so getting through the shoulder joint would be tough. The arm kept flopping around. I pinned it down with one foot and kept going.

Someone grabbed the back of my shirt collar.

I screamed and twisted, trying to slash with the knife, but it was only Zara. She grabbed my wrist, just like Sunglasses had tried to, and dug her thumb in so my fingers jerked apart. The blade clattered to the floor.

'We have to go,' she shouted, her voice muffled, distant.

I could see Jacket on the floor in the hall, his back a mess of exit wounds. I hadn't even heard the shots.

'Not yet,' I said, reaching for the knife again.

She ignored me, grabbing my arm and dragging me towards the door, away from the bodies.

'No!' I screamed. But she was too strong, and I was still dizzy from the flash grenade.

She pulled me out onto the front porch. I tried to get back up the stairs as Zara hauled me down them, my shoes leaving bloody prints all over the place. My shirt was glued to me by sweat and gore.

Curtains twitched in the neighbour's house.

I hadn't gotten a single bite. If only I'd just started eating, instead of getting greedy and trying to take the arm with me. It was the same mistake I'd made with the dead man in the river, the one Luzhin hadn't let me investigate seven years ago, the day Parget disappeared. The confusion crawled in, like I was coming unstuck from time.

The pick-up was twenty yards away. I couldn't hear any sirens, but I could tell from the urgency of Zara's gait that she could.

She threw me into the car. I tried to climb right out again, but she activated the child locks. She started the engine and swerved out onto the road. The air-conditioning blasted my wet shirt and pants, making me shiver.

We made a right turn out of the street just as a police car made a right turn into it. The cop in the passenger seat looked at me but didn't seem to register anything suspicious. Perhaps, driving fast in the twilight, he mistook the blood on my face for a beard.

Zara kept her eyes on the rear-view mirror as we drove, looking for signs of pursuit. I stared at the road ahead without seeing it. I'd read somewhere that the brain of an addict is chemically different to that of a sober person.

Addicts want what they want so badly—whether it is drugs, alcohol, slot machines or social media—that dopamine threatens to overwhelm the brain. To protect itself, the brain kills off some of its dopamine receptors. This is why addicts get so little pleasure from anything else in life. They don't care about fresh fruit, or music, or the beauty of nature. And it's why they need more and more of the addictive substance to get the same fix.

This process somehow weakens the prefrontal cortex, the part of the brain responsible for high-level thinking. The part that tells you it's better not to eat people. Maybe that's why I just sat there for half an hour or so, the blood on my shirt slowly going crusty, the ringing in my ears fading to a distant whine.

When I came back to reality, Zara was talking.

'. . . trying to save your life,' she said. 'Don't you get that?'

'I don't want saving. I want food.'

'They don't serve the food you like in prison. If we'd stayed for three more seconds—'

'I don't care.' I knew I sounded like a petulant teenager, but I couldn't help it. That meat had been so fresh. Alive only seconds earlier.

Zara exhaled through her teeth. 'I have to call Wilcox.'

While she dialled, I leaned forwards, pressing my face against the dashboard. Trying to think about something, anything, other than the hunger raging in my guts.

I found myself thinking about Cho's keys.

The Chinese spies had had them. Therefore, they had killed Cho. But why, then, would they try to make it look like Cho had been the pilot of one of their own top-secret stealth jets?

'I'd like to place an order for pick-up,' Zara said into her phone. 'Three burgers. No fries, maybe one soda.'

That meant three bodies, none were civilians, one possible witness. The code would have made sense a decade ago, but people these days mostly seemed to summon food via apps on their phones. I wondered if anyone still called in orders anymore, or if it was all just CIA agents requesting cover-ups.

'Delivered to 580 Old Oaks Boulevard, Pearland,' she continued. 'As soon as it's ready. What?' She listened for a while. 'What kind of worm?'

She listened a while longer, then ended the call without saying goodbye.

'You know the malware we installed on Cuthbert's computer?' she asked.

'Yeah.'

'Well, someone else beat us to it. There was already a worm inside the network.'

That was unexpected. My legs trembled, probably from the fading adrenaline. 'Someone else was stealing data?'

'No. The worm wasn't copying, or transmitting. The analysts say it looked like it was designed to *delete* something, but they can't figure out what. It was just sitting there, like a tripwire waiting to be crossed—are you sucking your shirt?'

I let the fabric fall out of my mouth. 'Who made the worm?'

'There were Russian words in the code, but SIGINT thinks they were planted to fool us. They think it's the Chinese. Which makes sense, since the MSS just tried to kill us.'

But it *didn't* make sense. The body was definitely Rob Cho's—why would China be involved at all?

I closed my eyes, circling the problem, as though it was a couch and I was trying to work out how to lift it. Streetlights strobed across my eyelids.

'We're not going to Virginia anymore,' Zara went on. 'The op has been escalated. The Company is sending us some supplies, including a disguise kit. Remember, the FBI has a picture of a guy who looks a lot like you—'

I opened my eyes. 'Rob Cho found the worm.'

'He what?'

'He was head of cybersecurity. He found malware on the network. But the MSS killed him before he could tell anybody.'

Zara considered this for a moment. 'But if Beijing is responsible, why would they dress him in a Chinese space-suit? Wouldn't they want to point the finger at some other country?'

She was right. I chewed my lip for a minute, and said: 'Your asset in Shanghai.'

'What about them?'

'After we found the body, you told them to look for evidence of a secret space launch in China.'

'So?'

'So, have you heard from them lately?'

There was a pause, and then Zara said, 'Oh, fuck.' She pulled over and got out her phone again.

The first call she made went unanswered. Her source might have already been in a Chinese prison with their feet in a tub of acid, telling the interrogators everything they'd ever told Zara.

It was a clever plan. The MSS hadn't just killed Cho—they had used him to expose a CIA mole in the Chinese Communist Party. As soon as Zara's source started asking around about a secret spacecraft, the MSS had identified the leak and plugged it.

Zara made a second call. This time, it sounded like she was organising a funeral. She described the kind of flowers she wanted, and the casket, and the order of ceremonies. I wasn't familiar with any of this code, but I could guess that she was trying to get her source out of China before he got captured. Or, knowing Zara, to have him killed before he could reveal too much.

Soon she ended the call and swerved back onto the road, her jaw set, her knuckles white around the steering wheel. I sucked on my bloody shirt some more, looking out the window. We hadn't discussed where we were going, but it looked like she was taking a roundabout way to the safe house.

'I'm sorry about your friend,' I said.

Zara gripped the wheel like she was trying to strangle it. 'He wasn't my friend.'

'I'm sorry anyway.'

She grunted.

'So we know how Cho was killed, and now we know why. We just don't know who. But we can narrow it down to the people who were in the complex at the time of his murder. One of those people is working for the MSS.' I licked the blood off my lips. 'They took out your spy. How would you like to take out theirs?'

•

Back at the unfinished house, I showered, watching the blood splash around my feet and swirl down the drain. Zara said she was going out. She wouldn't tell me where. Maybe she wanted to talk to Wilcox out of earshot. Or maybe she needed to blow off some steam after her near-death experience. I wondered how she did that. Laser tag?

After my shower, I sat on the patio, thinking. Three thousand employees at Space City. Fewer than a hundred there on the night Cho was killed and dragged out into that field. I'd already ruled out several of those. The suspect pool was shrinking.

In my head, I watched the deleted video feeds, over and over. But soon it became hard to tell whether I was noticing new details or inventing them. The memory was like an old videotape, degrading slightly with each viewing.

Zara came back with a new air mattress, a bag of groceries and several documents. There was a list of people who were in the complex at the time of Cho's death. A list of vehicles that had entered and left. A list of swipe cards that had been used to access various areas.

She and I read through these documents side by side on the mattress, like a couple who had been married for decades. Zara wore a black nightdress and frameless reading glasses. I kept sneaking glances across at her. She really was beautiful. But she was also manipulative. Competitive. Cruel.

Then again, I didn't deserve kindness. I was a monster. Maybe we belonged together.

Zara's phone beeped. She checked the screen, harrumphed, and tucked the phone back beneath her pillow.

I recognised that sound. 'I was right about something,' I said. 'And you were wrong.'

She licked her finger, then used it to turn a page. Finally she said, 'The video from the fishing trawler isn't fake.'

'But?'

'But it was staged. The woman who recorded it has ties to China. It looks like the MSS took a Chengdu J-20S and dumped it in the ocean, right in the ship's path. Then they put a spy on board and told her to record some video.'

I frowned. 'So they killed Rob Cho, dressed him in a Chinese flight suit and dragged his body outside. Then, to make the ruse seem more authentic, they abandoned a perfectly good plane in the ocean and organised for us to see it?'

'Seems so. And that's a multi-million-dollar plane. They're desperate to keep the identity of this spy under wraps.' She pointed to an item on the list. 'What about Hadrian Holm?'

'The receptionist with all the piercings?' I asked. I'd seen his name tag.

'Right. According to his swipe card data, he was on the ground floor of the museum at the time of the murder.'

'So were a lot of people,' I said. 'Anything else?'

'He seemed like kind of a dick.'

If anything, that made him less likely to work for the MSS. Spies tend to be charming.

'Let's put him in the maybe category,' I said, humouring Zara. 'Who else was in the complex?'

'Hey.' She pointed again. 'What about Hazel Cuthbert, the deputy cybersecurity chief?'

'What about her?'

'She was there. And she was also one of the first people to enter the museum the following day. Just after seven am.'

'You think she snuck into the building early to clean the blood off the inside of the hypobaric chamber before anybody else saw it?'

'Cho was the cybersecurity chief,' Zara said. 'Who do you think gets that job now that he's dead?'

I nodded slowly. 'His deputy.'

'If I was in the MSS,' Zara said, 'and I had an asset placed inside the Johnson Space Center, and I needed her to rise through the ranks quickly . . .'

There was a knock on the door. I flinched.

'It's just a delivery,' Zara said. 'Relax.'

I didn't relax. 'Who delivers to a half-finished house?'

'The Company. I requested some supplies. Bring them in, will you?'

It wasn't a question. She didn't look up from her list, fully expecting me to obey. Like I was her dog.

I got up and padded, barefoot, out into the living room. A flash of headlights crossed the window, and I heard an engine start. The house had no insulation, so I could still hear the vehicle as it made turn after turn, gradually fading into the distance. Then silence.

I opened the door. There was a small cardboard box on the doorstep. I was probably expected to drag it inside before opening it, for privacy.

But I didn't. At the FBI, I'd studied letter bombs. I knew that if you had to open one, it was safest to do it outside.

Very carefully, I unfolded the flaps. Inside there was a satchel containing a wig and a false moustache, which were more convincing than you'd get at a Halloween store, but not by much. Underneath the satchel was a padded plastic bag, the kind they use to deliver refrigerated food. I listened for ticking and then unzipped it.

The bag was filled with human hands. Six of them, neatly severed at the wrists. All stacked on top of one another, like raw soft-shell crabs.

I stared at them.

'I told my bosses we might need them,' Zara said from behind me. 'To plant fingerprints at other crime scenes. Make it seem like the MSS agents are still alive.'

I kept staring into the bag. Three left hands, three right. Thirty fingers in total. There wasn't much meat on a hand, but I was salivating just the same.

'We don't actually need them for that,' Zara added. 'I got them as a present. For you.'

I turned to face Zara. She smoothed her nightdress, looking bashful. I couldn't tell what was going on behind her gold-flecked brown eyes. Was this an apology? A bribe? A convoluted threat?

It didn't matter. In that moment, I loved her.

'Thank you,' I said.

She leaned forward and kissed me. Her lips were soft and full. The smell of her skin, warm and clean, filled my nose. I wrapped my arm around her waist. Her tongue slipped into my mouth, and I realised just how much she trusted me.

CHAPTER 27

Now

What kind of eye can see, but is never seen?

'How often do you see Zara?' Diaz asks.

I look up. 'Huh?' For a minute I'd forgotten I was here, in her office. My body may be a mess, but my mind's eye is pretty good. I can imagine myself into just about anywhere.

'Zara. How often do you see her?'

'Not at all since I got here.' I haven't had a single visitor, which Diaz should know.

'Have you heard her voice?'

Now I get it. 'Zara's not imaginary.'

Diaz speaks carefully. 'There's a myth that it's masculine to be attracted to vulnerability. But it's very common for men to fantasise about having a partner who's sexually uninhibited, mysterious, even dangerous—'

'My life is dangerous enough. I don't need to fantasise about that.'

'Is there someone else you fantasise about?'

I keep my mouth shut and try not to picture Thistle, as though the psychiatrist can read my mind.

'Some people are aroused by thoughts of being punished by their partner.' Diaz seems to think that this topic won't seem personal if she says everything matter-of-factly. 'It can be confusing, if you don't think of yourself as the kind of person who—'

'You think I imagined getting locked in that hypobaric chamber? You think that was a wet dream?'

Diaz rides the silence.

'It wasn't,' I say. 'Zara's real.'

'Okay.' She nods understandingly. 'What does she look like?'

'Maybe thirty. Five foot six. A hundred and twenty pounds. Dark hair, dark eyes, slightly tan skin.' I hoped all this detail would make Zara seem like a real person, but as the words come out, she sounds more imaginary than ever.

'Does she look anything like your mother?' Diaz asked.

'Jesus.' I rub my face. 'I'm a fucking cannibal. Isn't that enough? Do I have to have mommy issues as well?'

'You mentioned that you worked on a case . . .' Diaz flips backwards a few pages. 'For the FBI. You investigated a boy who may have been molested by his mother. Cameron.'

I don't remember bringing that up. Apparently I've been running my mouth. 'That was a real case.'

'Did Cameron remind you of yourself?'

I think of the handsome, well-liked teenager, and his luxurious house in the gated community. 'Not even a little bit.'

Another silence. This time I refuse to break it, but I'm aware that I seem stubborn, secretive. I've been more honest with Diaz than with anyone else I've ever met, revealing everything to her, but she still thinks I'm lying.

'I'd like to prescribe something that I think will help you,' Diaz says finally.

'What is it?'

'It's quite mild, and it often helps people in your situation.'

She hasn't named the drug, or even categorised it. Does she think I need antidepressants? Stimulants? Antipsychotics?

Whatever it is, it's bound to be wrong, because she still doesn't get that all this is real.

'I'd rather not,' I say.

She looks like she expected this. 'Can you tell me why?'

It's because I'm not delusional. But if I tell her that, she'll be even more determined to medicate me.

'Because I feel like we're getting somewhere with the talk therapy,' I say.

She's not fooled. 'Don't worry, this isn't a replacement for our sessions. We'll keep making progress in here—hopefully faster.'

If I keep pushing back, she'll tell the nurses to force-feed me the pills, instead of just trusting me to take them.

'Okay,' I say.

Diaz checks her little gold watch. 'That's our time,' she says. 'Thanks for coming in, Timothy. I'll see you tomorrow.'

•

Visiting families never get to see the back door, so there's no pretence here. It's thick wood instead of glass and has two enormous locks. A camera stares at me from a small cage in the corner of the ceiling. I doubt anyone is watching the feed right now. Just the same, I won't linger long. I try the handle, just in case someone left it unlocked. It doesn't turn, same as yesterday, and the day before.

The door doesn't have a steel core—I know that from rapping my knuckles on it the first day I was here. But I don't have a hope in hell of kicking it down. It opens inwards, and the hinges are huge. I'd need a battering ram, the kind used by SWAT teams. Even if I had one, and two hands to hold it, the noise would alert everyone in the building. With the hospital security team after me, I wouldn't make it halfway to the road.

'How are we doing today, Timothy?'

I turn to see Kelly, the big nurse with the snake tattoo. 'Hungry.'

'We'll get you to lunch in a minute,' he says, and rattles a little plastic cup in one gloved hand. 'Dr Diaz has prescribed something for you.'

I've only just finished my session. No way could Diaz have contacted Kelly so quickly. She must have talked to him beforehand. She'd decided to drug me before I even walked into her office.

Betrayal is a familiar emotion. I barely feel the sting of it.

'She discussed that as a future possibility,' I say. 'But I got the impression we would keep going with the talk therapy for now?'

Kelly doesn't buy it. He hands me the cup. 'Show it to me on your tongue before you swallow.'

The plastic cup contains a little white pill, broken in half—or maybe halves of two separate pills. 'What is it?' I asked.

'Medication,' he says.

'What kind?'

'Come on, Timothy. I don't have all day.'

I tip the cup into my mouth, then show him the two pills on my tongue. I can feel them there, the broken edges powdery against my tastebuds.

'Great. Down the hatch,' he says.

I think about hiding the pills in my cheeks. But if Kelly notices, he'll never trust me again. I've seen what happens to patients he doesn't trust. Held down, tied up, force fed, injected, sedated.

I swallow the pills.

'Okey doke. Open wide.'

Kelly probes around the inside of my mouth, like a vet examining a dog's teeth. His fingers are warm and fat. I haven't eaten—really eaten—since I got here.

Just bite down, says a voice in my head. *It'll be worth the punishment.*

I don't.

Kelly finishes his inspection. 'Good boy,' he says, and takes the empty cup. 'Enjoy your lunch.' But he doesn't go anywhere. He watches me walk up the corridor towards the lunch hall. I can feel the pills slowly dissolving in my gut, unknown chemicals making their way towards my brain.

I get to the shutter just as it rattles upwards, revealing bread rolls, salad and slices of roast beef. It's Eli behind the counter this time. He fixes me with his real eye and stares just over my shoulder with the acrylic one.

'Timothy,' he says. 'Beef or vegetables?' He snaps the tongs in his hand, like a gator's jaws.

'Beef,' I say, gloomily. It's not going to stay in my stomach for long.

'Damn right.' He gestures at some lettuce. '*That's* not food, is it? It's what food eats.'

I wonder if Dasha has told him I'm a cannibal. 'Right. Beef, please.'

'There are two kinds of animals.' Eli leans over the food. 'Predators and prey. Now why the *fuck* would a predator act like prey? Can you imagine anything more pathetic?'

The line is growing behind me. 'Nice talking to you, Eli.'

'You too.' He winks, like we understand each other, then drops some sliced beef onto a bread roll. I shuffle sideways to make room for the next person and squirt some ketchup on the meat, largely for the colour. I grab four packets of salt, too.

Kelly is still watching me. Acting like I haven't noticed, I sit at one of the tables and start munching on my roll. I close my eyes as I chew, dreaming of a more satisfying meal.

A chair squeaks. I open my eyes to find Harmony sitting opposite me.

'Hey,' she says.

'Hey,' I say, my mouth full.

'I want you to explain what you meant yesterday,' she says. Remarkably straightforward. It makes me feel guilty about what I'm going to do to her.

'Yesterday?' I ask, acting confused.

'At group. When you—' Harmony stops, biting her lip.

I lower my voice and bow my head, talking to my food. 'Don't turn around. Kelly's watching us both.'

This is only half true. I'm the one he's watching.

'You can see his reflection,' I say, and point towards the window. Harmony sneaks a glance, and her eyes widen. She turns back to me.

'Why?' she asks.

'Why do you think?' I say this like it's rhetorical. I don't know the exact nature of Harmony's delusions, so I'm not quite sure what I'm playing along with.

'He's one of them?' Harmony whispers.

'I haven't ruled him out yet,' I say, with no idea who *they* are. 'I'm also suspicious of Dasha. She seems a little too eager to talk, you know?'

Harmony starts to nod, and then catches herself. Still wary.

I tear open all the salt sachets and stir them into my water. 'I want to put my cards on the table. But I don't know if I can trust you.'

'How do I know *I* can trust *you*?' she asks.

'You don't,' I say. 'If I were you, I wouldn't trust anybody. Laugh, like I just made a joke.'

She chuckles. It's very convincing.

I use the beef roll to hide my mouth as I talk. 'Meet me in my room in thirty minutes. Make sure you're not followed.' I down the salt water in three sickening gulps.

'I can't come today,' she says.

'Why not?'

'There's a fly,' she says. 'It buzzes around the corridor every Wednesday. You haven't noticed it?'

'No.'

'There's a condenser microphone strapped to its belly,' she says, utterly serious. 'We can't talk in front of it. But it'll be gone tomorrow—that's when they recharge it.'

This may be harder than I thought. My stomach growls. 'Okay, tomorrow morning.'

'I'm delivering the mail tomorrow morning.' That's the job Harmony volunteers for. 'How about after lunch?'

I take a deep breath. 'Okay. But right after lunch.'

'Which room is yours?'

'Three nineteen. See you.' I stand up and take my empty tray over to the trash. Kelly is distracted, talking to Dr Kobald. I duck into the bathroom.

After checking that all the cubicles are empty, I slip into the one furthest from the entrance. I lock the door, hunch over the toilet bowl and jam my fingers down my throat.

The combination of fingers and salt water does the trick. There's an internal lurch as my digestive system shifts into reverse gear. I dry-retch a few times before my abs clench inwards, my core shudders and everything comes back up. Shredded beef, mushed-up bread and two little white pills, only slightly dissolved. Stomach acid scorches the inside of my throat.

I spit out the last of the vomit. I'm tempted to scoop the meat out of the bowl, but that would only lead to more vomiting. I flush it away, tear off a square of toilet paper with a trembling hand and wipe my mouth.

When I open the door, Eli is standing there.

I'm too slow to hide a flinch. He stares at me with his good eye. The acrylic one is looking over my shoulder again.

'Didn't like the food?' he asks.

'Lunch was fine. I've been feeling a bit off since break-fast.' I thump my chest for effect.

'Since breakfast, huh?'

'Yeah. You might want to keep your distance. Could be stomach flu or something.'

Eli grabs me by the throat and pushes me back into the stall, slamming me sideways against the wall. My skull hits the wood so hard it shakes. He grabs my wrist and crushes it. I claw at my neck with my other hand—but nothing happens. That hand is long gone, and I'm not wearing my prosthesis today.

'Eli,' I croak. 'Don't.'

'You puked up your meds,' Eli says. 'You're going to snap on us. Kill us all in our sleep.'

'I'm non-violent,' I lie, through a windpipe only a quarter inch wide. 'I never hurt anyone.'

Eli looks from one of my eyes to the other and back again, the way people do when they're trying to work out if you're telling the truth. But soon I realise he's just deciding which one to take.

He pulls a fork out of his back pocket.

'No!' I squeal and squirm, but his hand is like a band of iron around my neck. He's released my hand to get to the fork, so I take a swing, but my fist just bounces off his bald head. He doesn't seem to notice, concentrating as he lines up the tines of the fork.

I knee him in the groin, his soft flesh crumpling. He gasps, and his grip on my throat loosens just enough for me to lunge at him, slamming my forehead into his nose. There's a wet crunch. His fake eye pops out and splashes into the toilet.

Eli gives a horrified screech, either because of what I did to his eye, or his nose, or his balls, or all of the above. He swipes at me with the fork, but it's more of a stabbing weapon than a slashing one. The tines scrape harmlessly against my chest as I shove him backwards. He stumbles sideways and falls, one arm disappearing into the toilet. I turn and run, out of the stall and out of the bathroom, and find myself back in the lunch hall, puffing.

Harmony is gone. Kelly is still talking to Dr Kobald. Everyone else is eating. No one seems to have noticed the commotion from the bathroom. Occasional shrieks of terror are just background noise in this place.

I can't hear Eli following. He's probably still fishing his eye out of the toilet, and then he'll want to wash it. I have a minute to decide how to play this.

If I tell Kelly and Kobald that Eli attacked me in the bathroom, they might not believe me. Eli has never displayed any violent behaviour while he's been here, and I'm known to be delusional. And when they ask Eli for his side of the story, he'll tell them I vomited up my pills. Just like he ratted out Seamus, who ended up restrained and forcibly injected.

I hesitate a second longer. Then I take a breath, steady my nerves, and go over to the coffee machine.

By the time Eli storms out of the bathroom, his arm dripping wet and his acrylic eyeball back in, I'm sitting at my usual table with a steaming cup of joe, acting like nothing happened.

He glares at me, then looks at Kobald and Kelly, then at me again. Calculating. I return his stare, challenging him. He's the one in a tough position now. Is he going to walk up to them and say he saw me barfing up my pills? He may not be believed, since he made the same accusation about Seamus earlier this week. And then I would tell them Eli attacked me in the bathroom with a fork. Eli might claim he didn't do it, but he'd have to explain the toilet water on his arm, and the fork he presumably still has on his person.

I watch him think all this through. It takes him a while. Then he sits down at one of the other tables without saying anything. For a while I think he's still glaring at me, then

I realise it's the fake eye. It just happens to be pointed in my direction.

I take a sip of my coffee. Blake one, Eli zero—though I have a feeling the game's not over. When I've finished my drink, I throw the paper cup in the trash and amble back to my room.

It's nicer than a prison cell. There's an empty dresser beside the bed, and carpet—albeit the stiff waterproof kind they use in homewares stores. The window has no bars across it. There are plastic hooks on the walls, but I haven't hung any pictures. Just my prosthesis, the straps trailing like vines. The door has a lock, but I don't have a key. I can secure it from the inside, so no other patients can sneak in while I'm asleep—only nurses, who have keys. But whenever I'm outside this room, it's unlocked, and any other patient could just walk in and start going through my stuff. The simplest solution is not to have any stuff.

I sit on the bed. I try to plan for my talk with Harmony tomorrow, drawing a mental map of all the routes the conversation might take, checking that each path leads to the destination I want.

But the pills are affecting me, even though I only absorbed a little of them. My thoughts are as slippery as octopus tentacles, slithering out of my grip.

CHAPTER 28
Two weeks ago

What do you get when you
reach into a blender?

A grey van with tinted windows and fake plates was parked in a loading zone next to the Atmospheric Research Unit. Zara and I strolled towards the building alongside the crowd of engineers and technicians, pretending the van was invisible. But as we passed it, I saw two men out of the corner of my eye, motionless behind the windshield. One to drive, and another to shoot, if that became necessary. So far, so good.

There should be two more agents in the back. One would grab Hazel Cuthbert and hold her down while the other injected her with something to keep her compliant for the rest of the journey. A crime boss I'd once worked for had a similar system. At the highest levels, the government and the Mob are indistinguishable—wealthy people who eat in Michelin-starred restaurants, reward loyalty over ability, and pride themselves on how untouchable they are. Sometimes the overlap reaches the lower levels, too.

Zara held my hand as we walked. She was wearing a shawl that covered the faint bite mark on her shoulder.

I was tired. That morning I'd woken up in the front yard, no shirt on, spider webs all over my hand. Following my footprints, I realised I'd been fiddling with the mailbox. Apparently my subconscious mind was expecting a package. But there had been nothing in the mailbox except a spider, patiently repairing the web I'd destroyed.

I'd used some of the Company's supplies to make Zara breakfast while she slept. Sliced banana and honey on toast, with a cup of peppermint tea, to repay her for the gift of all the hands. But she hadn't appreciated the gesture. She'd taken one mouthful and thrown the rest in the trash. I couldn't work out what was up with her. I didn't think it was the bite—she'd enjoyed that at the time. Whatever it was, she seemed to have forgiven me now. Her hand was cool in mine.

Wilcox had sent through a dossier—apparently Cuthbert had visited China on a student visa in 2004 and applied for a role at Space City as soon as she returned. Once she got it, she'd risen quickly through the ranks. Now that Rob Cho was dead, she would soon be the cybersecurity chief for the campus.

According to the swipe card logs, she'd been in the museum until late on Tuesday night. When Cho discovered the worm, his deputy was probably the first person he told, giving her the chance to kill him and cover it up. It all fit.

But I had questions. Had Cuthbert worked alone? Was it a coincidence that Cho had found the malware just as the MSS was trying flush out a CIA mole? And what was the malware actually for? I hoped we would be able to take Cuthbert alive.

The doors slid open, admitting us to the Atmospheric Research Unit, where Cuthbert had swiped in this morning. The receptionist, Holm, recognised us—I wasn't wearing the wig, or the phoney moustache. They'd actually looked pretty good, but they were for travelling to and from the safe house. Here at Space City, people already knew me.

Holm was signing someone else in—a wizened man in a yarmulke. The receptionist's piercings jingled as he nodded good morning to us. 'Heard the news?'

I kept my face neutral. 'What news?'

'Another victim. Last night. Not ten miles from here.'

I was alarmed, thinking he was talking about the killer at Space City.

Zara was quicker on the uptake. 'The Reaper? Holy shit.'

'I know.' Holm nodded again. Like he'd needed us to affirm that this was shocking. 'This time they killed an FBI agent.'

My heart skipped a beat. *No.*

'Who?' I demanded.

'The Reaper,' Holm said. 'Keep up.'

'Who was the *agent*?' I realised I was yelling. Didn't care. It couldn't be her. I was already making deals in my head. *I'll give up my other arm. I'll never eat another person. I'll do anything. Just don't let Thistle be dead.*

Holm looked at me like I was nuts. 'What, like the guy's name? I don't remember, man.'

'But it was a guy? A man, I mean?'

Zara squeezed my elbow, and showed me her phone screen. She'd already brought up a news article: *FBI agent found strangled.* There was a photo. A man in a golf cap, smiling, his arm around someone else who had been cropped out of the picture.

The man was Ruciani.

Maybe I should have been shocked, or saddened. Ruciani and I had worked dozens of cases together. But the relief washed every other emotion away. It wasn't Thistle. Nothing else mattered.

Zara was still holding me. 'It's okay,' she told me quietly. 'You're okay.'

I took a breath. I couldn't think of any excuse for my outburst other than the truth. 'I knew him,' I told Holm, who still looked perplexed.

His eyes widened. 'Holy shit. I'm sorry. I didn't—'

'Yeah.'

We signed in without saying anything else. As we walked away, I took Zara's phone and read the story. There wasn't much information. Ruciani had been tasered and strangled at his home, like the other victims. Unlike them, his body hadn't been left to rot—a neighbour saw someone visiting late at night and got suspicious. Rang the doorbell, no answer, called the cops.

'I saw him just yesterday,' I said.

'I know,' Zara said. 'I was there, remember?'

'Why would the killer switch from targeting empty nesters to FBI agents?'

'Maybe Ruciani was getting too close for comfort. Didn't you say he was on the task force?'

The hairs on my arm stood up. I was the one who'd suggested Ruciani start looking at who had access to IRS records. Now he was dead.

Maybe I'd gotten him killed.

'Did he touch you?' Zara asked.

'What do you mean?'

Her voice was low. 'Will the police find your DNA on his body?'

I thought back. Had we shaken hands? 'No. No contact.'

I hoped no one had seen me talking to him. Zara was the only person who could vouch for my whereabouts last night. She couldn't even alibi me for the whole period, since she'd gone out to meet Wilcox.

I told Zara, 'I want to know about the Reaper's other victims.'

Zara looked annoyed. 'What for?'

'It just feels like it's not a coincidence, that murder happening so close to Space City.'

'The victims were just middle-aged women no one would miss,' Zara said. 'None of them were employed here, or knew anyone who was.'

'You don't know that for sure.' She couldn't have researched it already.

She sighed. 'Fine, I'll look into it. But later—we're busy right now.'

We could have asked the receptionist where in the building Cuthbert was. But he would almost certainly have called ahead. And our plan depended on arriving unannounced.

We hurried up the stairs to Rob Cho's office. Since Cuthbert wasn't at the museum, it seemed likely that she was here. Preparing to take over his position.

When we found Cuthbert, Zara was supposed to start with some innocuous questions. Then she would produce a cigarette and ask if we could keep talking outside. Once we were behind the building, the van would pull up and take Cuthbert. We would meet them at the black site later.

I wasn't sure an MSS asset would fall for that, but Zara seemed confident.

She knocked on the door.

No answer.

Zara knocked again. 'Dr Cuthbert? It's Sandra. They told me downstairs that you were here.'

This was a bluff, and either Cuthbert was calling it or she genuinely wasn't in.

'You want to break down the door?' I sipped from my go-cup, which contained what looked like a raspberry smoothie. Zara had told me—affectionately but firmly— that I couldn't just walk around Space City chewing on a severed hand. So I'd gotten creative.

'Let's ask around first,' Zara said. 'A broken door might raise questions later.'

We went back downstairs, where we saw Dr Laurie. The one Anders had called a 'supposed genius'. She must have just arrived—she had sunglasses tucked into her shirt collar, and a coat draped over one arm. As she walked, she was reading something aloud off the screen of her phone, while a man following behind her scribbled frantically in a notebook.

'Oh!' She almost crashed into us. 'You.'

'Us,' I confirmed.

The man was young, with bulging eyes and a long nose. He looked like an intern—Parget's replacement, I guessed. He said nothing, pen trembling over the page.

'Have you seen Hazel Cuthbert around?' Zara asked.

'The deputy cybersecurity chief?' Worry crept onto Laurie's face.

If Zara thought that was a strange question, she didn't say so. 'That's who I meant, yes.'

Laurie took a breath and seemed to recover. 'Last time I saw her, she was in the pool. Why do you want to talk to her?'

'Just a follow-up from earlier this week,' Zara said, which sounded like an answer but wasn't. Laurie tongued one incisor in a way that made me think she didn't quite buy it.

'Which way is the pool?' I asked, before she could think about it too hard.

She pointed. 'Just follow the signs to the Weightless Environment Training Facility.'

'Thanks for your time.' Zara turned away.

I hesitated—something told me we should try harder to put Laurie's mind at ease before we moved on. But Zara was already halfway up the corridor, so I attempted a reassuring smile and followed.

When we got to the pool, it was empty except for a lone woman carving through the water, leaving hardly a ripple behind. The pool was smaller than it had looked on the CCTV; maybe thirty feet wide and eighty feet long, though it was still deep enough to give me vertigo when I peered in. At the other end stood a giant cylinder with a crank, the pool cover rolled around it. Chlorine filled the air, making my eyes itch.

With her swim cap and goggles, the woman was hard to identify at first. But no two people have the same fat deposits in the same places, and I always take note of where the good stuff is. Under the midnight blue one-piece, those were Cuthbert's shoulders, Cuthbert's buttocks.

Zara crouched by the end of the pool and waited. When Cuthbert finished a lap and came up for air, she startled.

'Hazel?' Zara said, smiling sweetly.

Cuthbert pulled off a nose-clip. Her skin was pale in the indentations left behind. 'Sandra. Timothy.'

'So sorry to interrupt you.'

'It's fine. Give me a second to towel off.'

'Take your time.'

She swam over to the ladder. Unlike most pools, the rungs went all the way down. I counted twenty-five rungs, meaning the pool was about twenty-five feet deep.

'You're a bit late to work today,' Zara said.

Cuthbert raised an eyebrow. 'I'm not scheduled to start until nine-thirty.'

'Dropping kids off at school?' Zara sounded sympathetic, but I could tell what she was thinking. Kids were an easy pressure point to lean on. Intelligence agencies sometimes offered to pay for private schools as a bribe—or they went the other way and threatened to kidnap the children.

Cuthbert laughed. 'My kids are in their twenties.' She picked up a microfibre towel from a rail near the edge and pressed it to her face.

'My mistake,' Zara said. 'It's just that you were here much earlier than this on Wednesday morning.'

'Was I?' Cuthbert's voice was muffled by the towel. 'Oh, yes—my husband had a cold and didn't go to work, which meant I didn't have to make his lunch or drop him off on the way. So I was early.' She dropped the towel, and the subject. 'You know they wanted to close this place when they built the NBL.'

'The basketball league?'

'The Neutral Buoyancy Laboratory. The pool there is twice as long and twice as deep. Big enough to hold most of the International Space Station. But I fought them on it.' She peeled off her swim cap, red hair spilling out. 'I said they'd lose some of their best people. Onsite pool is a hell of a perk.'

'And you're much closer to it, with your new office,' Zara observed.

'Not my office,' Cuthbert said smoothly. 'Rob will be back in two weeks.'

'Hmm.' Zara reached for the cigarettes, already keen to end the conversation.

I looked Cuthbert up and down, already waiting for the CIA to be done with her so I could take the body. The hand-shake hadn't quenched my hunger.

But talking about office locations had loosened something in my brain.

'Earlier this week, you told us you requested to work out of the museum,' I said.

'Right,' she replied. 'It has a great view.'

It did. But that wouldn't matter to an MSS asset. Why had she chosen to be so far away from any groundbreaking research?

'It must be much easier,' I said. 'Working out of Rob's office, closer to the action.'

'No.' She pulled a sweater over her swimsuit, apparently forgoing a shower for now. 'All the systems are centralised. I can access everything from any computer in the JSC.'

'You mean like documentation?'

'I mean like equipment. I can log in and start remotely driving forklifts. I could change the temperature of my colleagues' AC as a prank.' She pointed at the water. 'If I wanted to drain the pool, I could do it with one click. It's happened before, by accident.'

This explained why an asset might choose that office. But it also opened up another possibility.

My stomach was screaming at me to shut up. I ignored it. 'What about the hypobaric chamber? Can that be operated remotely?'

'If the key was in, I suppose . . .' She tapped the air with one finger, as though counting something. 'Actually, I'm not sure. Let's find out.'

She pulled on some pants and shoes, no socks. As we followed her upstairs, Zara shot me some meaningful looks, which I ignored.

When we got to Cho's office, Cuthbert sat down in his chair and logged in with a swipe card.

'Is that Rob's card?' I asked.

'No, mine.'

'Then how come it got you into his computer?'

'I told you, everything is centralised. When I'm logged into it, it's my computer, not his.' She tapped at the keyboard for a while, then said, 'Yup. I can do anything I want to the hypobaric chamber. Turn the pressure up and down, flick the lights on and off, whatever.'

'Asshole,' Zara mouthed at me, like it was my fault that our suspect pool had just opened up again. The killer could have been anywhere in Space City when Cho died, not just the museum.

'Can employees operate these systems from home?' I asked.

'No, no, no—our system is air-gapped. Not connected to the internet at all. Can you imagine the chaos if a hacker got in?'

There was a pause as we all imagined pools draining, AC going haywire and rockets blasting off when they weren't supposed to.

'Well,' Zara said gloomily, 'thank you for your time, Ms Cuthbert.'

'Wait,' I said. 'Do you have a record of who logs in where?'

'Sure. I'm the deputy cybersecurity chief.'

'Does it tell you what they did while they were logged in?'

'Up to a point. Why?'

'We need to know who activated the hypobaric chamber between five and seven pm on Wednesday.'

If Cuthbert was surprised by this request, she didn't show it. Her fingers clacked on the keys, and then she swivelled the monitor around.

I knew what I'd see before I saw it. I was remembering the look on Laurie's face when we said we were looking for the deputy cybersecurity chief.

'It says here that Dr Laurie depressurised the chamber at five-forty-one,' Cuthbert said, pointing. 'Why do you ask?'

CHAPTER 29

What kind of stars do you drink from?

Laurie had a huge head start. She'd had it since we first saw the body, and it had only grown over the course of the last few days. Surely she was gone.

But I ran anyway, down the stairs, into the lobby, and out the front into the sunshine, because if I didn't, Zara would blame me for letting the killer get away. Even though if it wasn't for me, the wrong woman would already be drugged in the back of a van.

I looked around the parking lot. The van was missing— by now it would be waiting around the back of the building for us to lure Cuthbert out for a cigarette.

Zara arrived, breathing heavily. 'You see her?'

I squinted at all the shiny vehicles in the lot, and the empty field beyond. 'No.'

'What kind of car does she drive?'

I didn't know—the entry logs I'd been studying only recorded licence plates, not makes and models. As I opened my mouth to say so, I spotted a small Audi, two hundred yards away, getting waved through an open gate. At this distance I could only tell that the driver was someone with short blonde hair. But I could also see something dark on top of her head, maybe the chunky sunglasses that had been tucked into Laurie's collar. It was an expensive car, and Garcia had told us that employees here weren't well paid. MSS assets, on the other hand, could potentially make a fortune.

'That kind,' I said, and took off again. Something must have delayed Laurie on her way off campus. We wouldn't be so lucky twice. If we lost sight of her, she'd soon disappear into a fog of false passports and cash transactions. Or vanish into the Chinese embassy, where we couldn't touch her.

I pounded the asphalt, heart racing, lungs burning. But I couldn't outrun a car.

Zara overtook me easily, running like a terminator towards the gates. Her hunger for revenge was greater than my literal hunger—or she was just in better shape. Either way, she quickly had a lead I couldn't match. The Audi was at the second gate now, the driver flashing a security pass at the guards.

I slowed down so I could breathe and shouted, 'Hey! Stop her!'

The guards didn't seem to hear. I was too far away. 'Hey!' I bellowed.

The gates started to roll aside.

Zara was yelling, too. 'Police!' she yelled. 'Stop that woman!'

We weren't police, and she had no documentation suggesting we were. In her panic, she was telling lies she couldn't back up.

The guard was the same woman I'd talked to two days ago, with the blue eyes and the crow's-feet. She saw us running towards her, then turned to look back at Laurie's vehicle in time to see it zoom through the open gate, much faster than she was probably used to. 'Wait,' she commanded, but it was too late. The Audi was speeding away.

Zara and I reached the gates, out of breath.

'What's the situation?' the security guard asked. Her name tag read *Spence*.

'No situation,' Zara wheezed, bent over, her hands on her thighs.

'She forgot her phone,' I said, holding up my own phone.

The guard's eyes narrowed. 'Didn't you just say you were police?'

Zara shook her head.

'She said *please*,' I put in.

The guard just looked at us, almost certainly not believing our story, but also not sure what to do about us. We weren't stealing anything, damaging property, or breaking in.

Zara didn't give her time to decide, turning on her heel and jogging back towards the parking lot. I followed.

'She'll be headed for George Bush,' I muttered, once we were out of Spence's earshot.

'No. She'll go for one of the smaller airports to avoid us. She'll get out of the state before she tries to get out of the country.'

Zara was right, but the information wasn't helpful. There were hundreds of small airports in Texas.

'She'll have to go to LAX to get to China, though,' I said.

'No. She'll use a buffer country. Fly from Denver to Canada, or O'Hare to Mexico, or Orlando to Japan. Yeah, it's Cassandra.' I realised Zara was on the phone. 'I need something circulated.'

I tuned out her half of the conversation. I'd recovered enough from the sprint to think more clearly. We'd wasted fifteen minutes talking to Cuthbert but still made it outside in time to see Laurie driving away. What had slowed her down?

'She stole something,' I said.

Zara muted her end of the call. 'Huh?'

'She knew she'd been rumbled, so she went back to her lab.' I said. 'Or to *someone's* lab, anyway. She stole something that Beijing wants—or doesn't want us to have.'

I thought of the malware, waiting to be triggered. Not designed to copy—designed to delete.

I started running again, back towards the ARU. I hated running.

'Like what?' Zara yelled after me.

'I don't know,' I called over my shoulder. 'But she didn't have much time to clean up. I'm thinking it'll be obvious.'

•

I'd underestimated just how obvious it would be.

Zara had caught up to me. She stared through the little window into the lab. 'Holy *shit*.'

The shelves were empty. At first, I thought Laurie had taken all the vials of fake blood with her, perhaps in five or six rolling suitcases. Then I got closer to the window and saw the floor. Or rather, the red lake where the floor was supposed to be.

I pulled the door open and floated in. The blood had trickled into the gaps between the tiles, creating a crimson grid around the puddle in the centre. I crouched and rubbed some between my fingers. It was beautiful, but it was wrong.

Too cold, too thin. It was methadone, not heroin. Porn, not sex. Decaf. Stevia. Fake, no matter how much I wanted to pretend.

I put my fingers in my mouth. The fluid was acrid, and gritty with broken glass. Years ago I'd been begging for change on a street corner and had seen a street magician eat a broken bottle. It had seemed odd that passers-by were giving him money to hurt himself but wouldn't give me money to stay alive.

Some plastic coveralls were piled in the middle of the lab, dripping red. A wrench lay nearby. To the police, this crime scene would be incomprehensible, but it made perfect sense to me. I could picture Laurie striding through the room, dragging the wrench along the shelves to shatter the vials, then stripping in the doorway and throwing the coveralls over her shoulder like a lit match.

'Why would she destroy all this?' Zara asked from a few feet away. She'd jumped back quickly enough to keep her shoes dry.

'She wants to give her formula to the Chinese.' I walked across the puddle, ripples spreading outwards from my shoes. 'It's worth more if the US doesn't have it.'

'But we *do* have it.' Zara gestured at the mess all over the floor. 'Even if she triggered the worm and deleted every record of the formula, we could easily scoop some of that up and put it under a microscope.' She eyed my bloody lips. 'Assuming some lunatic doesn't drink it all first.'

'This is way more fluid than she was storing in the vials,' I said. 'She's thinned it. Mixed it with something. Tastes like bleach.'

My suspicions were confirmed when I turned around and saw an empty jug of hydrogen peroxide on its side in the corner.

Zara leaned forwards, taking a whiff. 'You think that will change the composition enough that it can't be reverse-engineered?'

'I think *she* thinks that.' I still had the auto-injector. It was back at the safe house, in the breast pocket of one of my shirts. But I didn't mention that. Fake or not, I wasn't willing to give it up. 'Let's go to her house.'

'She'll be halfway to the airport by now, Blake.'

'I know. And if you take me to her house, I might be able to figure out which one.'

•

Brenda Laurie lived on a property north of Houston that might have once been a plantation. The grounds were grassy now, but it was the sort of land that could support corn or sugar cane. The house certainly had the look. Two storeys, with white weatherboard, big pillars and a wrap-around balcony so some rich asshole could watch his slaves making him even richer.

I'd read that some plantation owners rationalised their crimes using rumours of cannibalism in Africa. Better to be enslaved than consumed, they told themselves—and each other.

Zara parked the car at the end of a long gravel driveway. We got out and looked up at the house. The cold wind cut through my cheap clothes. In case the Houston PD spotted us, I was wearing the moustache and the wig, a tangled black mop that made me look like an ageing porn star.

'I thought all these places got turned into museums,' Zara said. 'After people stopped using them as wedding venues.'

'Even museums go bankrupt,' I said. 'Maybe Laurie got it on the cheap.' It was also possible that the land had been in her family for hundreds of years, but her Boston accent suggested that it hadn't. And she didn't dress like she came from money.

Zara trudged up the gravel towards the house. 'I wonder who gets it now that she's gone? If we can find her family, we can lean on them to get her to come back.'

'That's assuming her family aren't already getting leaned on in China.' I crouched next to the car. There were fresh tyre tracks in the mud next to the driveway. Like someone had driven off-road so they could park around the back.

I pointed out the tracks to Zara. She looked at them for a second, then silently drew her handgun.

'Wait,' I whispered. 'She couldn't manage all this land by herself. Not if she's working full-time at the Space Center as well.'

'You're thinking a gardener?' Zara didn't look like she bought it.

'I don't know. I just don't think we should go in guns blazing—'

Just then, we both heard a shot.

I ducked behind the car, but there was no need. The sound had been muffled—a dull *pop* from somewhere deep within the building. Whoever was shooting, they weren't shooting at us.

I looked at Zara. She made some hand signals that were incomprehensible to me, then started advancing towards the house.

'Zara!' I whispered, but she ignored me, like she had a death wish.

I hovered, torn between driving away and following Zara into the house. Anyone could have been in there: an MSS clean-up crew, a team of FBI spy hunters, or maybe both, hence the gunshot. I didn't want to get shot. But I didn't want Zara to get shot, either.

'Shit,' I muttered, and followed her up the painted wooden stairs.

The front door was unlocked. Zara went in first, checking the corners to her left, apparently expecting me to do the ones to the right. I did. No one was waiting in the shadows to jump us.

The foyer had a vaulted ceiling and a polished wooden floor, so dark that it was almost black. Paintings of the landscape around the house hung on the walls, in case the owner felt like looking at a smudged version of what was already visible out their window. They were originals, not prints. I could see the texture of the paint on the canvas.

There were arched doorways to the left and right, and a hallway ahead. A staircase led up to the second level. Whichever way we went, we risked being ambushed from behind. I shifted my weight, and the old floorboards creaked beneath me.

Another gunshot rang out. I ducked instinctively, and unnecessarily. The shooter was somewhere else in the house. I heard what sounded like wordless yelling, but then my brain kicked in and decoded the sound: dogs barking. Somewhere *inside*.

Zara lowered her gun about ten degrees, just enough that

she'd have a chance if an angry rottweiler came running around the corner. None did.

It was hard to tell exactly where the shot had come from, but I didn't think it was upstairs. Zara didn't think so, either. She made eye contact, jerked her head towards the hall, and then disappeared through the archway to the left.

I crept up the hall, wondering what the hell she expected me to do if I bumped into a crew of MSS agents, or the FBI. When they saw what was apparently a one-armed porn star, sleeve still stained with fake blood and bleach, they might be too confused to shoot—but then what?

Soon I'd reached the back of the house. The windows overlooked a backyard with a picnic area, an archway covered with ivy, and a well-tended vegetable patch. No movement in the woods beyond.

Another shot. It seemed to come from beneath my feet. But I hadn't seen any stairs leading down.

I turned around, went back and scanned the walls, looking for seams. Eventually I found them—two faint lines about three feet apart. I gently pushed against the wall, and the hidden door creaked open, revealing a set of stairs, leading down into the dark.

I hated basements, and this one seemed unlikely to change my view. But whoever was down there would have heard me open the secret door and seen the light fall through, so they knew I was up here. My best chance was to go downstairs before they had time to think.

'I'm not armed,' I shouted, as I walked down the stairs.

It wasn't a basement—it was a home laboratory. There was a computer, a workbench and a bulky machine that might have been a centrifuge, all gleaming under the yellow glow of a heat lamp. In one corner was a miniature version of the hypobaric chamber from the museum, about the size of a chest freezer. Four cages were lined up in the middle of the room. Each of them contained a dog—two black labradors, a pit bull and a golden retriever. The pit bull was barking wildly. The other three dogs were dead.

Dr Laurie stood over the cages, wearing earmuffs and holding a rifle. The pit bull snarled and snapped at her.

She pulled the trigger. At this distance, the shot practically deafened me. The dog crumpled instantly.

Laurie turned to look at me. I'd never been so confused.

She clicked the safety back on, then took off the earmuffs and tossed them onto the workbench. 'I suppose you'll want to take me in now,' she said.

CHAPTER 30

What kind of computer would you lick as it spins?

I paced around the unfinished house until long after the sun went down. I told myself I couldn't sleep because I was desperate to know what Laurie was telling the CIA interrogators. This was kinder than the other two possible explanations—

One: I couldn't sleep because the hands in the fridge were cold, and thin, while Laurie was warm, and plump, and the CIA would soon be done with her.

Two: I couldn't sleep because Zara wasn't in bed beside me.

The second idea made me more uneasy than the first. While I waited, I did research on Zara's laptop. There was no wi-fi router in the house, so the laptop was getting signal via cell towers, and the data was encrypted, which slowed it down even more. But after a few hours of one-handed typing and bleary scrolling, I had learned a little bit of astrophysics.

First, no country could launch a crewed space station in secret. There was a network of six geostationary satellites designed to detect intercontinental ballistic missile launches, and while they weren't unbeatable—China had recently tested a nuclear-capable supersonic missile without the satellites picking it up—any vessel capable of getting humans into orbit had to be much, much bigger. The network would detect it.

We'd already known the space station was fictitious. But now I knew it was *impossible*, even though Sam Garcia, the department head, had told us it wasn't. It seemed unlikely that a NASA scientist would get that wrong. Were these websites incorrect, or had Garcia lied? If he had, why?

I gave up on the space forums and started researching xenotransfusion—the science of taking blood from one species and injecting it into another. I wanted to know what Laurie had been doing in that basement.

I was surprised to learn that the practice of using animal blood in transfusions dated back to the 1600s, though it usually hadn't worked. More recently it became possible with pigs, though no one seemed to be doing it. Apparently it's unethical to raise pigs for their blood, though most people are happy to eat one.

There was nothing about xenotransfusion with dogs. But the research led me to an article which argued that the Laboratory Animal Welfare Act of 1966 had slowed the progress of medical science. I found many other articles that disputed this, but I felt sure Laurie would agree. I remembered that while everyone else described her as brilliant, she herself had only said she had 'courage'.

Zara still wasn't back. Thinking of Anders and his daughter, I did some research into Lou Gehrig's disease. Yes, kids could get it, but it was rare—so rare that it was hard to find doctors with any experience treating it, or medicines that had been approved by the FDA. I couldn't find any examples of kids with the disease entering respiratory depression and then recovering, like Anders' daughter supposedly had—maybe she had more than one illness.

The moon crawled up the sky, filtering though the dirty glass of the windows. I scratched mosquito bites, waiting, waiting.

It was almost midnight when Zara finally opened the door. She looked exhausted, and frustrated. There was blood on her knuckles.

'I want you to talk to her,' she said. 'See if you can work out if she's telling the truth.'

•

The warehouse had no heating, cooling or plumbing. It was off the grid in every sense. To get there, Zara and I had to take a road that wasn't even on Google maps, bumping across a rough dirt track between towering trees, and then unlock a gate in some hurricane fencing.

On paper, the building was abandoned. Unofficially it was run by the police, who sometimes took suspects there and interrogated them before they'd been formally arrested, at which point the suspects acquired certain inconvenient rights, like the right to an attorney and the right to remain silent. The CIA used the facility even more unofficially whenever it was vacant.

On the way, Zara told me what Laurie had told her. Some parts made sense, given what I'd learned in my online research. Others didn't. I was starting to worry that we hadn't caught Rob Cho's killer.

The interview room had no one-way mirror, no table, no chair for Laurie to sit on. Instead it was a bare concrete cell, and she was shackled to a ringbolt in the floor. There were bags under her eyes, and bruises around her throat, as though she'd been choked.

She looked up. 'You,' she spat.

'Me,' I confirmed.

'I should have guessed you were one of them, as soon as you lied your way into my lab. But I like to think the best of people—it's a flaw of mine.'

It sounded like she suspected the CIA had been watching her from day one, which could only mean she was the MSS spy. Practically a confession, and I'd only uttered one syllable. Zara would be impressed.

I kept my expression neutral. 'Why did you kill the dogs?'

'You wouldn't understand,' Laurie said.

'Try me.'

'No. These ridiculous stunts may feel righteous, but they just expose you as thugs. If you can't see that, you have no hope of comprehending my breakthrough.' Laurie rattled her chain. 'You people have gone too far this time.'

'You people?'

'PETA should be listed as a goddamn terrorist organisation.'

I said, 'You think I work for PETA?'

'You goddamn vegans have no idea how much you depend on people like me. If not for us, you'd still be in the stone age.'

I examined the bulging veins of her neck for a moment. 'I'm not vegan.'

She gave me a look that was equal parts disbelieving and imperious.

'You were testing your formula on the dogs,' I said. 'Why kill them afterwards? It's not like they were going to tell us what you were up to. Not unless you were working on some kind of dog-translator prototype.' I paused. 'Were you? Because that's a billion-dollar idea, right there.'

'You won't get away with this.' Laurie rattled her chain again for emphasis. 'I have rights.'

'So did the dogs. I've just been reading about that.'

Zara, listening outside the door, was probably wondering when I'd get to the point.

'They all had burst eardrums,' Laurie said. 'It would have been cruel to keep them alive. I'd expect *you* to understand that.'

'Ah.'

I didn't think this sounded judgemental. I had, after all, done far worse things. But Laurie scowled.

'Do you have a phone?' she asked.

'We're not the police. You don't get a phone call, a lawyer or anything else.'

She dismissed this with a wave of her hand. 'You ever heard of Laika? A stray mutt, picked up off the streets of Moscow. The Soviets figured she could handle cold, and hunger. They put her on Sputnik 2 and launched her into space.'

I leaned against the wall. 'Rings a bell.'

'It turned out that cold wasn't the main problem,' Laurie went on. 'Laika died when the cabin overheated, although the Soviets claimed at the time that she'd been euthanised with poisoned food. Either way, they learned from the experiment. When they launched Vostok 1 with Yuri Gagarin on board, it had better temperature control, and he survived.

If he hadn't, the space race would have ended right there. Instead, it ramped up. We launched more satellites, and got GPS. We got better laptops, thanks to the Shuttle Portable Onboard Computer. We improved smoke alarms, water purification systems, freeze-dried food, robotic artificial limbs.' She pointed to my prosthesis. It had no robotic components, but she probably thought I'd be grateful for this advance in principle. 'And now you have a cell phone. Immediate access to almost anyone, almost anywhere, plus the sum of all human knowledge. All for the low, low price of one dead dog.'

'Well, you killed *four* dogs,' I said. 'I hope you invented something pretty amazing.'

She said nothing.

I winced. 'There are more, aren't there?'

'Do you have any idea what I've accomplished?' she says. 'No, you don't. You'd need at least a masters degree to understand the significance of my breakthrough, let alone replicate it.'

'Why dogs? Shouldn't you have used an animal more closely related to humans, like chimpanzees?'

'You know how hard it is to buy a chimpanzee in Texas?'

Not as hard as it should be, probably. People bought tigers here. Anacondas. Giant jellyfish. I'd met one guy who had a shark in a tank.

'Let me make sure I understand,' I said. 'Your competitors couldn't make intravenous oxygen work—'

'Contemporaries,' Laurie said. 'I have no competitors.'

'Whatever. You leap ahead of them using illegal animal testing. You inject dogs with different versions of your formula and then suffocate them, over and over, until you find a recipe that keeps them alive. You offer to sell it to China, but—'

'What is it with you people and China?' she demanded. 'I've never been there. I don't know anyone who lives there.'

Zara had warned me about this. All night, Laurie had denied any accusations of a connection to China. She'd also denied using a worm to delete all records of her formula off the Space City network. She said she'd done it manually, without any malware. It seemed odd that she would be so open about the illegal experiments but lie about the spying. Then again, animal cruelty wasn't a capital crime, unlike treason.

'Okay,' I said. 'So who *were* you selling your formula to?'

'No one,' Laurie said. 'Science doesn't work that way. I work for NASA, so they own it. They'll use it to benefit all of humanity. I don't care about money.'

She said this with the sort of superiority that only rich people could afford. She would probably take a Nobel over an extra million dollars.

'If you wanted to benefit humanity, then why did you destroy the formula?'

'I didn't.' She tapped her temple.

'You have it memorised?'

'Right.' She looks smug. 'The animal testing might have been technically illegal—but it doesn't matter if you expose it. I won't share what I know without a guarantee of immunity from prosecution.'

'Humanity' seemed to have shrunk to just one human. 'Good luck with that,' I said.

'There are no other samples of the formula. My invention could someday be used by paramedics to keep patients alive on the way to hospital. It could save thousands of lives every year. You think the government will give that up over a few dead dogs? That would be barbaric.'

I didn't tell her I had a stolen sample at the safe house. 'Okay, you destroyed the samples to blackmail the US government—why now?'

'Because of *you*. You asked where the security chief was. You clearly knew about the animals—I had to make my move before I got arrested.' Laurie looked around at her filthy interrogation cell. 'I have to admit, I wasn't expecting this.'

'She's the *cyber*security chief. And she's only the deputy.'

Laurie frowned. 'Really?' It seemed like she only had the vaguest idea what her colleagues did for a living.

'Your plan only works if no one else knows the formula. Did Rob Cho figure it out? Is that why you killed him?'

She scoffs. 'No one could just *figure it out*. Rob Cho wasn't even a doctor.'

'Was it a human test that went wrong, then? You locked him in the hypobaric chamber to see if—'

'I didn't do anything to him,' she snarled. 'I didn't even know he was dead until your psycho girlfriend accused me of killing him.'

I kept pushing. 'All right, he found out about the dogs. You thought he was going to tell someone.'

'I didn't kill Rob! We were friends.'

'I *know* it was you. You switched on the hypobaric chamber with your swipe card.'

Laurie looked flummoxed, but not for long. 'Someone must have stolen it.'

'The card? You had it when we arrested you.'

'Arrested' probably wasn't the legal term for what we'd done, but she let that go. 'So someone took it and then put it back.' She smirked. 'You have nothing on me.'

'The security cameras caught you using the computer at the time the chamber was activated,' I lied.

'Bullshit,' she said, without hesitation.

'You expect us to believe someone stole your swipe card, used it to kill Cho and then put it back, all without you noticing?'

'It's not my problem what you do or don't believe.'

Her version of events didn't sound credible. It was either a very stupid lie, or the truth. And whatever else Laurie was, she wasn't stupid.

'When was Cho's birthday?' I said.

'February nine.'

'What was his wife's name?'

'He wasn't married.'

'How long had he lived in Cloverleaf?'

'He lived in Pearland. Why do you care about any of this?'

Either she really was his friend, or she'd been stalking him. I suddenly wondered if she might have murdered him for fun. Most serial killers start with animals.

But why the ruse with the spacesuit, if she really wasn't connected to China?

'Who were Cho's other friends?'

'Everyone,' Laurie said. 'He was a popular guy.'

'If you want me to think you didn't kill him, you should give me another suspect.'

'I'm not doing your job for you,' Laurie snapped. 'Talk to his other co-workers. Talk to his parents. Talk to his crazy sister.'

My ears pricked up. 'Crazy?'

'Mentally ill, whatever. She's been in a psych ward for two years.' Laurie looked exasperated. 'You didn't know that? What kind of investigation are you running here?'

•

'Was she telling the truth?' Zara asked as we walked back to the car. Zara put a great deal of faith in my ability to tell whether someone was lying. More than she should have—I've been wrong before.

The wind picked up, and the leaves rustled in the trees around us. The moon shone down, a cold blue glow.

'Yes,' I said. 'She has no connection to China and knows nothing about Cho's death. She's just a scientist who thought we were after her for animal cruelty. Also, she thinks we work for PETA.'

'I'm glad you didn't correct her—it's not a bad cover. What about having destroyed all her research? Was she telling the truth about that?'

'Yeah, why?'

Zara got into the driver's seat and slammed the door. 'I got a call while you were in there. My report hasn't been well received up top. Headquarters wants the USA and no one else to have that formula.'

'You're not telling me she might actually get immunity?'

Zara grunted.

I could have told Zara about the auto-injector. It would have made her happy. Laurie would have gone to jail. There would have been justice for all those dogs. But even knowing that it wasn't real blood, I still wanted to drink it—and its rarity made it even more precious.

'If someone else used Laurie's swipe card to activate the hypobaric chamber,' I said, 'can we work out which terminal they did it from?'

Zara cocked her head. 'Why? We erased the CCTV. We don't know who was using which terminal.'

'Sure we do.' I tapped my temple, like Laurie had.

'You think if I can find out where the terminal was, you can remember who was swiped in to it?'

'For sure.'

'Okay. I'll see what I can do.' Zara looked pleased. I felt a funny glow, like a dog who had impressed his master.

We zoomed through the shadows between the street-lights, the roads empty of traffic other than the odd Uber driver. We seemed to be headed for the safe house. It was still a few hours before dawn—apparently Zara thought we had time for some sleep.

Or for something else. My heart rate went up a bit. We hadn't talked about last night, not even in the moment. We had explored each other's bodies in darkness and silence. But I'd been thinking about it all day. The way she'd touched me with no trace of disgust. Let me kiss her all over, without fear. In fact, the danger seemed to be part of the thrill, for her. I'd let myself wonder if this could work, long term.

In the morning, she'd seemed angry at me, though I couldn't work out what I'd done wrong. Maybe it was because she knew she'd always be my second choice—I loved Thistle, even though Thistle had made it clear she wanted nothing to do with me. I'd let myself off the leash with Zara precisely because she wasn't the woman I really cared about.

I tried to banish the thought. 'There's a Chinese spy at Space City,' I said instead. 'We've established this. Yes?'

'Right. And they disguised Cho as a fallen astronaut so we'd go looking for a secret space station that doesn't exist, exposing our best-placed asset in China.'

'That was a secondary objective. Their main goal was to get rid of Cho, because he'd discovered something they wanted to conceal. We know that because they killed him in a hurry, not laying any groundwork ahead of time. Right?'

Zara nodded. 'They killed him because he discovered the worm.'

'Maybe,' I said. 'Or maybe he discovered the identity of the spy themselves.'

Zara was accelerating again, pushing the Ford towards its limit. Houston hurtled past outside, streetlights strobing. 'How does the crashed plane fit into this?' she asked.

'I'm still working on that,' I said, because I knew she wouldn't like my theory. 'But think about this. Cho wasn't shot, or stabbed, or beaten to death. He was suffocated in a hypobaric chamber. It would have taken the killer at least a couple of hours to organise that.'

'Meaning that for at least the last few hours of his life, Cho may have known who the spy was?'

'Right.'

'So why didn't he tell anyone?' Zara asked.

'I think he did,' I said. 'I'm just trying to work out who.'

CHAPTER 31

If I'm out, you're relaxed. If I'm up,
you're done talking. If I'm on my
own, you're dead. What am I?

Sam Garcia's house had changed radically. It was painted
yellow rather than white. The cobwebs had been swept
away from the corners of the windows. A neat path of stepping stones led through a manicured lawn to a front porch
that hadn't been built when I saw it last. I was starting to
think he didn't live here anymore.

I sat in the driver's seat of the Silverado, parked across
the street. Zara was meeting Wilcox, gathering as much
intel about Rob Cho's communications as she could. Every
email, every call, every text message. I'd decided to stake
out Garcia's house in the meantime, because he was the
only person who'd seemed to entertain the possibility of a
secret Chinese spacecraft. I thought that meant Cho might
have told him about the spy.

Esmerelda, Garcia's ex-wife, walked out the front door
carrying a folding chair, a rubber band around one wrist.
She'd dressed up a bit, her dark hair blow-dried, big
sunglasses hiding her eyes, a gold necklace hanging in the

deep V of her black dress. She took quick, dainty little steps along the path, pausing to pick some flowers. Once she had a few, she bound them together with the rubber band and climbed into the Nissan Pathfinder in the driveway.

Evidently Esmerelda had got the house in the divorce. Garcia wasn't here. But I was curious. Why the chair? Who was she going to meet?

The Pathfinder pulled out of the driveway and cruised towards the corner of the street. I turned the key and started the Silverado.

Esmerelda led me through the streets of Houston, always signalling, making no sudden turns, never doubling back. Whenever I could see her through the back window, her head was swaying to music.

Eventually she turned into the gravel parking lot of an old church, with large doors shaped like upright canoes and a stained-glass window like a huge red eye. The only modern touch was a cross made from solar panels on its steep roof. I rolled past without turning. Churches had pews. Why had Esmerelda brought a single folding chair?

Esmerelda got out of the car, pulled the chair out of the trunk and walked towards the church—then went around the back of it, rather than going inside.

I pulled over and thought for a moment. Then I unstrapped my prosthesis and chucked it on the passenger seat before I got out of the car and followed her.

Around the back of the church was a shady little glade filled with headstones. Some were crumbling, dating back to the 1800s. Most were newer, the granite polished, gold paint inside the carved letters. No one was there except Esmerelda, sitting on her folding chair. She had laid her flowers on a grave and seemed to be talking to it, though she stopped when she heard me behind her. She didn't turn around.

'Sorry to interrupt,' I said.

Esmerelda glanced back. 'It's fine.' Her smile didn't reach her eyes. We'd briefly met seven years ago, but she showed no sign that she recognised me, perhaps because the guy she'd met had two arms.

I picked a headstone at random, kneeled in front of it and patted the dirt affectionately. The inscription read *Alex Grayning, Beloved, 1961–2016.* Not much information. Most engravers charged per letter.

'I should have brought one of those.' I gestured to her folding chair. 'You must be a regular.'

She grunted.

'I don't visit my Uncle Alex as often as I should,' I said. 'I live in Dallas. You from around here?'

Esmerelda looked amused. 'I didn't know Alex had family in Dallas.'

'I only moved there recently.' I hadn't guessed she'd know the guy. I gestured at the grave she was sitting at. 'I'm sorry for your loss.'

'Are you?' She kept her gaze on me.

A beat.

'I guess not,' I admitted. 'It was just something to say.'

A bird tittered in the awkward silence that followed. This was a waste of time. I shouldn't have come here.

The name on the headstone in front of her was *Harold Broughton.* It looked more expensive than the others, with gold trim and the day and date of death, not just the year. 'Who was he?'

'A good man.' Esmerelda stared down at the dirt, as though X-raying it to see the coffin beneath. 'Not perfect. But good.'

'Family?'

'A friend. He drowned.' She stood up and closed her chair with a decisive *snap*. 'The pain doesn't fade, Mr Blake. It just becomes a different kind of pain. You'll realise that, when your *Aunt* Alex has been gone a while.'

She strutted back towards her car. So she had recognised me after all. I cursed the engraver who had charged by the letter. I should have guessed that Alex might be Alexandra.

Enough wasted time. Too much. I turned to leave, but then turned back. Because I recognised the date on Harold Broughton's headstone.

He had died seven years ago, on the same day that Lilah Parget was kidnapped.

•

Back in the car, I dialled Special Agent Richmond's number from memory. His rumbling voice kicked in after a few rings: 'You've called Doug at SOS Security. Leave a message.'

My old partner had taken medical leave after he was shot six months ago. The bullet had broken a rib even through his vest. Seemed like he was in the private sector now.

'Richmond, it's Blake. Call me back, will you?'

He called back a few seconds later, apparently not having listened to the message. 'Who is this?'

'It's Timothy Blake,' I said.

There was an uneasy pause. 'Hangman,' Richmond said finally. 'Long time.'

'Yep. How's the chest?'

'Not too bad, most days.' He sounded annoyed, possibly remembering that I'd been there at the time, antagonising the shooter. 'How are you?'

'I'm good. I was hoping you could help me with something.' There was a receipt in the cup holder. I flicked the corner of it a couple of times, trying to sound like I was going through notes. 'Do you remember Sam Garcia?'

It took him a minute. 'Kidnapper, right?' he said. 'Took some little girl from a mall?'

'That's him.'

'You got her back, right?'

'I did. But the guy's out now, and there's been a suspicious death at his place of business.'

'Shit.' Richmond didn't sound too concerned. 'I'm not with the Bureau anymore, pal. I can't help you.'

'I think maybe you can. I remember you found a cigarette butt at his house. The DNA matched with the smokes I found at the mall, where Lilah was taken.'

Richmond didn't reply. I wished I was there, so I could see his face.

'You planted it, didn't you?' I said. 'Don't sweat it—we already knew he was guilty. You did the right thing. The evidence kept him off the streets for seven years. I just need to know.'

There was another pause as Richmond decided how much to admit. Then he said, 'Nope. Sorry, man. If someone planted that, it wasn't me.'

'Huh,' I said. 'Guess it's a mystery. Thanks anyway. Before I let you go, do you remember what brand Jeb Parget smoked? The victim's father?'

'Jesus, Blake, it was years ago. Look, I have to get back to work.'

He hung up, and I sat for a while, testing the weight of my new theory. It felt right. But there were only two people who could confirm it for sure. One of them was sure to lie.

And the other might knock me out again.

•

I found Lilah Parget in a below-ground sports bar on 14th Street, giant TVs blasting ESPN all around her. The lunch crowd had only just started to trickle in, staring slack-jawed at the menu behind the bar like it was a UFO. Parget was drinking a club soda at an otherwise empty table, her face lit by the ghoulish glow of her phone.

I sat opposite her, and she looked up. Her smile faded as she recognised me. I was used to that.

'I'm meeting someone,' she said.

'Yep. Me.'

She wasn't amused. 'You don't look much like your profile picture.'

The photo she'd swiped right on was a composite of all the other pictures she'd swiped right on over the years. The description had been Frankensteined together in a similar way. Terrifyingly, it had taken Zara less than ten minutes to organise this.

'The camera adds ten pounds,' I said.

'Are you after another beating?'

I held up my hands. 'Hell, no. Once was enough.'

'In that case, I'm leaving.' She stood up.

I let her get a few steps away, then I called out, 'Like you left when you were twelve?'

She stopped.

The zombies near the bar glanced uneasily at me, then her, then me again.

'That's what really happened, right?' I said. 'You weren't kidnapped. You ran away.'

Parget came back to the table. 'Keep your voice down,' she hissed. 'I don't know what you think you know, but—'

'I'll tell you.' I took her soda and sipped it. 'Your dad was a violent asshole. The kind who liked having power over people, particularly women. He'd been hitting your mom, and then one day he hit you. Right?'

A shadow crossed her face.

'So one day you got him to drop you off at the mall, but instead of going in, you hid behind some trash cans. You waited until it was safe, smoking some cigarettes you'd stolen from him, and then you climbed down the ladder to the street and ran.'

'This is all bullshit,' Parget said.

'But you were twelve,' I said. 'And you hadn't thought it through. You didn't have enough money for a Greyhound out of town. You didn't know where the shelters were. So you wandered around until you found the homeless camp, hoping to disappear in there somewhere. And I found you.'

I remembered the look on the girl's face. Not happy to be rescued. Devastated. Terrified.

'You thought your father would kill you for running away,' I went on. 'But then—a miracle. He didn't know. He thought you'd been kidnapped. And, even more incredibly, *someone else had confessed to the kidnapping.*'

Parget stared at me. She was angry, but there was a sense of wonderment, too. Like she still couldn't believe her luck.

'So you stay quiet,' I continued. 'You pretend you can't remember anything. The police go along with that, because they already have all the evidence they need to put Sam Garcia away. They've even taken one of your cigarettes and planted it at Garcia's house to make sure the conviction sticks. No one punishes you—maybe your father is even nice to you, for a while. And your saviour goes to prison, even though you wrote to the judge, begging for a lesser sentence. You write to Garcia himself while he's inside, thanking him, and saying you're sorry. But he never writes back, does he?'

I let that hang in the air. Parget didn't reply.

'Five years later, you escape from your father again. This time you're better prepared. You get help from friends. Soon you have a new name, a new place to live, and a bank account he can't touch. You're finally free—but the lie still haunts you. When Sam Garcia gets out of prison, you keep tabs on him. That's not hard—victims can request regular updates on the movements of perpetrators. Soon you find out that he got a job at the Space Center. So you apply for an internship. To watch him. Because you want to know *why*. Why would a man confess to a kidnapping he had nothing to do with?'

I could see from the look on Parget's face that I'd finally reached the truth. Garcia hadn't kidnapped her. His confession had been bullshit.

That was all I needed to know. I drained the last of Parget's drink and stood up.

'Well?' she demanded.

'Well what?'

'Why did he do it?'

I could have told her. But it would have broken her heart. *I would never hurt Sam. He's everything to me.*

'No idea,' I lied, and turned away.

'Why?' she shouted, heedless of the stares from the others in the bar. But I was already on the stairs, on my way back up to the street.

CHAPTER 32

One of me contains victory, two of
me contain flesh, three or more
contain drinks. What am I?

Zara's meeting with Wilcox should have been over, but she
wasn't at the safe house. She hadn't left a note—spies don't
do that. I could tell she'd left the house willingly, though.
She'd sprinkled some sawdust near the exits to show any
footprints, and arranged her cups in the usual way, ensuring
the place couldn't be searched without her knowledge.

I hung around for a while, gnawing on metacarpals.
I thought about sleeping, but didn't know where I'd wake
up if I did. The sleepwalking got worse when I was stressed.
To keep myself awake I ran through the last few days in my
head over and over, wondering if I'd missed something or
drawn the wrong conclusion somewhere. I felt like I knew
what had happened, mostly, but I hadn't seen much of it
with my own eyes, and that made me nervous.

After a few hours there was still no sign of Zara, and she
wasn't answering her phone. I paced. What if the MSS agents
had gotten her? What if they were on their way to get *me*?

I used the ladder to climb the fence again and broke

into the house next door. That way, if anyone came to the safe house, I'd see them, and they wouldn't see me. The next house was just like ours, but with a mirror-image layout, and furnished—I sank into a creamy leather sofa and listened to the ticking of a wall clock.

There was no sign that this house had been occupied recently. No one had been spying on us, at least not from here. This thought made me want to check the house on the other side of ours. I climbed two more fences and broke another lock. Another mirror-image house. Empty. No one had been here—or someone had been and was very good at cleaning up after themselves.

Skin crawling, I walked around a few blocks, making turns that would be hard for an observer to predict. I followed the Fibonacci sequence, turning left for odd numbers and right for even ones. I didn't see many people, and saw no one more than once. No one seemed to be following me, but it was hard to shake the sense that this was because my pursuers were highly skilled.

Maybe spy work did this to everyone, eventually. You stopped wondering if some people might be enemy agents and started assuming everyone is.

A middle-aged man with a brown hat was watering his front lawn. At ten-thirty am, on a weekday, when it had rained less than two days earlier? Suspicious. He raised a hand in greeting, then saw my missing arm. He looked alarmed and stuffed his hand back into his pocket, as though I might be planning to steal it.

I felt too exposed, out in the open. I shouldn't have left the safe house. I made my way back, resisting the urge to look over my shoulder. I climbed over the fence and entered via the back door, then hid in a closet. Nothing happened, for hours, but my heart was racing the whole time. Enemy observers must know I was in here. They were waiting for me to make the first move.

Eventually I heard the front door open. Footsteps crept through the house. I shrank into the corner, cursing myself for choosing such an obvious hiding place, with no escape routes.

Someone wrenched the door open, and I squealed.

It was Zara. She lowered her gun when she saw me, hugging my knees at the back of the closet.

'Christ, Blake,' she said. 'What's happening?'

'Nothing.' My voice came out too loud. 'Where were you?'

'Meeting with Wilcox—we have a plan.'

'A plan for what?'

'To find out what Cho's sister knows. I want to check you into a mental hospital.'

●

Zara took me to a nearby cafe. She must have figured some food would fix whatever was going on in my head.

She was right. After a bacon sandwich with bright red ketchup, I felt much better.

The cafe owner seemed desperate for business. I guessed she'd scheduled her grand opening to line up with the date all the new residents were moving in. She hadn't factored in a delay caused by toxic insulation. Anyway, she gave us plenty of privacy.

'Laurie's card was used at a terminal not covered by CCTV,' Zara said. 'So that's a bust. But we've recovered the spy plane.'

This wasn't what I'd expected. 'From the ocean?'

'Right. The fuel tank was dry, and the ejector seat and the pilot were missing.'

I chewed a torn fingernail until it bled. 'Any sign of why the pilot bailed out?'

'I suspect there never was a pilot. We found slip lines within the fuselage and one of the canard wings,' Zara said. 'It looked like a manufacturing defect. It would have broken apart on the landing strip. The engineer we got to look at it said she was surprised it had even been able to take off.'

'That explains why they were willing to dump it in the ocean.'

'It does. Anyway, that's not what I wanted to talk to you about.'

Zara watched me carefully as she explained the plan. I would voluntarily admit myself to the hospital where Harmony Cho was staying. The Company would prepare a fake referral from a psychiatrist and pay for my stay via an insurance company. Inside, I would get close to Harmony. Once I knew if her brother had told her anything, I would stick a piece of paper to the window of my bedroom. That was the signal for Zara to come and sign me out, posing as a doctor. The whole operation was expected to take two weeks.

'Why am I the one going into the hospital?' I asked. 'Why not you? Harmony might be more likely to trust another woman.' The thought of getting locked up, however briefly, made me nervous.

Zara sipped her tea. 'You can pull off crazy better than I can.'

I supposed she had a point. 'What's my cover?'

'You're Timothy Blake. Your parents died violently in front of you, you were abused in foster care, and you spent a few years homeless when you aged out. Now you have fantasies of violence and self-harm.'

I paused with the bacon sandwich halfway to my mouth. 'What?' she asked.

'You want me to go in as *myself*?'

'Why not? They can check it from any angle, and it will hold up.'

'But what about after you get me out? They might come looking for me.'

Zara raised an eyebrow. 'You think hospitals chase escaped patients who haven't committed any crime and paid their bills in full? That's an optimistic world-view.'

'But it will be on my record forever.'

'It will be on your record for precisely three months, at which point no one will notice when the Company has it wiped. Why are you being so difficult about this?'

I put the sandwich down, wondering if a direct accusation was the best tactic. Probably not. 'You need me to identify the spy at Space City.'

'No shit. Why do you think I want you to talk to Harmony Cho?'

'If I get killed in the nuthouse, I can't help you.'

Zara laughed so hard she choked on her croissant, showering me with pastry crumbs. When she recovered, she said, 'You're worried that someone at the hospital will be even more crazy and violent than you are?'

It did seem unlikely, when she put it like that.

'I can't take any weapons there,' I said. 'I'm guessing I won't even have a phone.'

'Listen.' Zara reached over and squeezed my hand. She hesitated, as though about to confess a painful secret. Then she said, 'I won't let anything happen to you. Okay?'

I could see the woman who had switched on the hypobaric chamber while I was inside. But I could also see a woman who genuinely cared about me. Which one was real? I found myself leaning back so I could see the whole picture.

She let go of my hand, suddenly uncomfortable. 'Anyway, it would be very difficult for an MSS agent to get to you inside this hospital, even if they somehow worked out you were there. Like you said, no weapons inside. Trust me—you'll be safer in there than out here.'

CHAPTER 33

Now

This mucus is heavy when it flows
backwards. What am I?

Dr Diaz has had a rough night. She comes in late, though only by a minute. Her eyes are slightly pink. Her slacks are a different shade of brown to her jacket, the contrast large enough to notice but too small to be deliberate, as though she grabbed them while thinking about other things. There's a trace of powdered sugar on her collar and a smear of snot on her shoulder. She never wears much make-up, but today she has even less, and what little there is has been crudely applied.

'Good morning, Timothy.' Her smile seems forced.

I don't return it. 'You okay?'

'Fine,' she lies. 'How are you?'

'I haven't been sleeping well.' I squirm in my chair. 'I'm not sure the new meds agree with me.' If I can't convince her to get me off the meds, someone will eventually notice I'm not taking them. Last time I felt drowsy for hours, even after vomiting them up. I struggled to see my own thoughts through the mist.

Diaz doesn't take my concerns seriously enough to write them in her notebook. 'Stick with it,' she says. 'Sometimes things have to get worse before they get better.'

'I'm a broke, one-armed cannibal trapped in a nuthouse,' I say. 'How much worse could things get?'

'You reach for humour often,' Diaz observes. 'Particularly when a topic might be uncomfortable.'

'I wasn't joking.'

Diaz sighs, like I'm frustrating her. It's the sort of reaction she normally hides better. Soon the fake smile is back.

'Maybe we could talk more about your parents,' she suggests.

'Why?' I ask. It comes out sounding more defensive than I'd like.

'Is there some reason you don't want to?'

'It just doesn't seem relevant. They died when I was small. I don't remember them.'

'You don't think the early loss of your parents might affect your mental state?' Her tone is neutral, but I don't think I'm imagining the sarcasm.

'We could talk about Mrs Radfield instead,' I say. 'She ran the group home where I grew up.'

'Sure.' She makes a note. 'What was she like?'

'She didn't tolerate disobedience. She was sometimes violent. She seemed keen to be rid of me, the whole time I was in her care. Which was a long time.'

Diaz scribbles frantically to keep up with me.

'See?' I say. 'You say the *absence* of my parents is significant, but obviously Mrs Radfield's *presence* mattered more.'

Diaz's eyes narrow. 'Why do—' She cuts herself off. She likes to phrase her statements as questions, and her questions as statements, and this time she forgot to do the switch.

'You seem . . . reluctant to be helped,' she says.

I'm annoyed with her. Maybe because she doesn't believe anything I say. Maybe because it's off-putting, seeing your psychiatrist in a bad mood. How can she be qualified to fix other people if her own life isn't perfect?

'What do you expect to happen?' I ask. 'I'm supposed to describe my childhood, so you can point out that it was traumatic, and then I'm somehow cured? I don't need you to tell me how fucked up my life is. I'm not an idiot.'

Diaz's jaw is set, her shoulders square. I'm only now realising how relaxed her posture usually is. 'You've decided that I can't help you without giving me the opportunity.'

'Some people can't be fixed,' I snap. 'No matter how soothing your voice is, or how much thoughtful nodding you do. Some people are just bad, deep down.'

'That's true,' Diaz says. 'But you're not bad, you're just lazy.'

This is so far from what I expected her to say that it shuts me right up.

'You want to believe you were doomed from the start,' Diaz continues. 'Dead parents, abusive foster home, boo hoo. It clears you of any responsibility—'

'I take full responsibility,' I object. It sounds phoney, like a soldier in a bad movie. But it's my one redeeming feature, and I won't let Diaz take it away.

'No, you don't,' she says. 'You hate yourself, but that's not the same thing.'

I open my mouth for a counterargument that doesn't come.

'You tell yourself you're a monster,' she continues. 'Because if you're not, if you're a regular human being with human faults, then you might feel obligated to improve. And that sounds like a lot of work, doesn't it?'

I can feel my face twisting into a snarl.

'I've met people who are too stupid or too sick to do the right thing, but that's not you. You have *decided* you can't change.' Diaz points at the wall, towards the rest of the hospital. Where the sane patients are. 'There are people over there dying of cancer. Heart disease. Alzheimer's. You know what they'd give for a choice about whether to stay sick?'

'You don't know anything,' I say, because it's clear she knows everything.

'I'm paid by the hour. You think I care if you get better?' She folds her arms. 'But I'm not going to lie to you just so you don't have to feel guilty.'

This is ridiculous. I'm undercover. I'm not here for real therapy.

I stand up.

'You can't think of a joke to put between yourself and the truth,' Diaz says. 'So instead, you're trying to leave. But you need to stay in that chair for another forty-five minutes.'

I remain upright. 'You drank too much last night. This morning, you gave up on your diet and ate a donut. One of your kids is sick, but you sent them to day care anyway. Who are you to tell me what to do?'

She doesn't ask how I know any of this. 'And now, because I won't let you go, you're deflecting. It's uncomfortable, isn't it? The idea that change is possible.'

'Fuck you.' I can't think of anything else to say.

'You're angry with me,' she observes. 'An understand-able reaction. But I'm surprised—the medication should be levelling everything out.' She writes a note in her journal. 'I'm upping your dose.'

'Don't.' I sit back down. 'I'll behave.'

'This isn't a threat, or a punishment. I'm trying to help you.'

'How can you help me when you don't believe me? You're trying to treat me for a disease I don't have.'

'The belief that you aren't sick is a symptom of the illness.'

'Is this a goddamn witch trial? It's also a symptom of being healthy.'

'Healthy people don't believe they are cannibals who work for the CIA.'

No matter what I say, she'll use it against me. So I clamp my mouth shut.

She watches, waiting for the silence to become intoler-able. It's a tactic I've often used on suspects. It won't work for her. I don't even break eye contact, just staring at her. The clock doesn't tick, but I count the seconds in my head.

Two thousand, three hundred and twelve seconds later, Diaz stands up and opens the door.

'I'll see you tomorrow, Timothy,' she says.

•

Harmony Cho doesn't knock. She darts into my bedroom and closes the door behind her, turning the handle so as not to make an audible click. She's wearing slippers, loose linen pants and a blue long-sleeved shirt with rolled-up sleeves.

Perched on her head is the small-brimmed hat she only wears when she's delivering mail to the doctor's offices. I don't think anyone official told her to do that. It's not a uniform, but she wears it like one.

I stay on the bed, not making any sudden moves. 'Hi, Harmony.'

'Mail for you,' she says loudly, holding out an envelope.

I take it. On one side she's written *Are you alone?*

I nod. We *are* alone. No one could stop me from—

I squeeze my eyes shut, banishing the thought.

When I open them again, Harmony is listening at the door. Finally she seems to relax.

'We're good,' she says. 'But I have to get back to my mail route in five minutes, tops, or they'll know something's up.'

'Is there anybody in particular you're concerned about?' I ask. 'Someone who seems to have been watching you especially closely?'

'The doctors pay more attention than the patients,' Harmony says. 'But I can't narrow it down more than that.'

'Who's your doctor?'

She looks suspicious. I hold up my hands in surrender. 'You're right, don't tell me. It might be safest if I don't know.'

'Out with it,' Harmony says. 'Who are you? Who do you work for?'

This is the risky part. I can't just pretend to be a concerned citizen, or a friend of her brother's. She's already suspicious of me and is likely to see through either story. I can't think of anything that will be more convincing than the truth.

'I work for the CIA,' I say.

She tilts her head back slightly—the first half of a nod. Gives me an *I-knew-it* sort of look. 'What are you doing here?'

'I have some bad news. You brother is dead.'

Another *I-knew-it* look—this time less triumphant. 'He used to visit me every week,' she says. 'As soon as he stopped, I knew they'd gotten to him. What happened?'

'He was suffocated.' I'm not great at bad news. 'Someone put his body in a spacesuit and dumped him in the middle of a field at the Johnson Space Center. To make it look like he'd fallen out of orbit.'

'Jesus.' Harmony blinks away tears. 'Robbie.'

'I'm sorry,' I say. It's easy to forget the meat once had a life, a nickname, a family who cared about him.

She takes a deep breath. 'Who did it?'

'We think someone at the Johnson Space Center is working for the Chinese Ministry of State Security. Rob was killed because he knew something. Something the MSS didn't want America to know.' I leave that hanging for a second.

'Probably lots of things,' Harmony says darkly.

'Probably,' I agree. 'But we think there was something quite specific. There are signs that they killed him in a hurry.' I take another risk. 'Whatever it was, we're hoping he told you before they got to him.'

'Me?' Harmony frowns. 'Why would he tell me?'

'That obviously depends on what the information is. But I was thinking he might have told you to keep you safe.'

Harmony is silent for a long moment. Then she says, 'Rob didn't tell me anything.'

She watches me carefully to see if I believe her.

I squeeze my real fingers around my silicone ones. 'Listen. Whatever it is, the only way to keep you safe is to expose it. Make it very public. If there are only a couple of loose ends, the MSS will try to tie them up. But if the whole world knows—'

'I mean it,' Harmony says. 'Robbie never talked about his job. He would tell me about his neighbours, and our cousins. He'd sometimes talk about his friends from work, but never the work itself.'

'Whatever he told you, it may have seemed innocuous at the time,' I press. 'Who were his work friends?'

'He mentioned a Maia, a Chris, a Sam, a Paul, a Ryan, a Jack . . . but it was just normal office gossip.' Her eyes narrow. 'Unless he was speaking in code.'

I can't think of a reason for Rob to do that. 'We think he saw or heard something that identified the MSS agent. Anything at all he said—'

Harmony clamps her palms against the sides of her head. 'I'm telling you, there's nothing.'

Her voice and body language suggest she's telling the truth. And why wouldn't she be? Sure, it made sense for Cho to warn her, but he may not have gotten the chance.

I was optimistic coming here. Foolish even. I got myself institutionalised for nothing. I'll have to put the paper in the window tonight, so Zara will see it and get me out.

'Wait,' Harmony says. 'Why would an MSS spy put Robbie in a spacesuit?'

I rub my face. 'It's hard to explain.'

'Try.'

This is probably all classified, but I'm past caring. 'The Chinese government wanted us to think they have

311

a crewed space station in a geostationary orbit right over our heads.'

'But they do.'

'No, they don't. They made it look like they did, so we'd tell our last asset in China to start digging. That helped them identify and eliminate the asset.'

'But they *do*,' Harmony said again.

I hesitate. 'Did Robbie tell you that?'

'No, I told *him*. He said it was ridiculous. Impossible. But I know it's true, because of the TV.'

'The TV?'

'Yeah. The one in the common room. It picks up certain frequencies—secret transmissions, bouncing off satellites. Sometimes you can see a slight flicker at the corner of the screen. The others haven't noticed it, or they're pretending not to, but I have. And it always, always happens whenever there's a story about China on the news. Flicker, flicker. They have a space station, manipulating the signal. Replacing the story with one that's more positive. Think about it—how could they do that if they didn't have people up there all the time, filming their own news stories? Look at the news anchor's hair. The way it stays up like that. You can tell he's in zero gravity.'

I look at Harmony for a long time.

'What?' she says.

'Nothing,' I say. 'Good work, Harmony.'

She nods seriously. 'I notice things. I have good eyesight.'

It's close to what I told Thistle, when we first started working together. I wonder if Thistle was thinking what I'm thinking—*I'm stuck with a crazy person.*

'We have to get out of here,' Harmony says. 'To spread

the word, like you said. You can talk to your CIA person—your handler. They can have us released, right?'

'I'll get on that,' I say gloomily.

'Great.' Harmony rubs her hands together. 'I'll come back after lunch tomorrow, see how it's going.'

The thought of lunch makes my stomach gurgle. I look Harmony up and down, weighing her in my head.

'You should leave,' I say.

'I'm gone,' she replies, and slips out the door.

I peel the *Timothy* name label off my shirt and slap it against the window.

Zara visits the main hospital every day, and my window is just visible from the parking lot on top of the hill. When she sees the sticker through her binoculars, she'll bring some dummy paperwork and get me out. And I'll have to confess that I've found nothing. Whatever Cho knew, it died with him.

•

I can't think when I'm eating—maybe that's why I like it so much. The process of cutting and chewing and swallowing wipes my mind clean. I regain consciousness to find myself seated at a table in the lunch hall, staring down at an empty tray. Where the chicken nuggets were, there are only crumbs and a smudge of ketchup. No one is sitting opposite me. But Nurse Kelly is approaching, the armpits of his white shirt dark with sweat.

'Must have been tasty,' he says.

I grunt.

Kelly holds out a plastic cup. 'Hope you saved room for these.'

I take it. Five half-pills rattle around the bottom, not just two.

'That's too much,' I say.

Kelly's expression doesn't change. 'I think that's up to the doctor to decide, don't you?'

Eli is on a chair in the corner, long legs crossed at the ankles. His cargo shorts leave his meaty calves exposed. He's holding the TV remote, but his good eye isn't pointed at the screen—it's aimed squarely at me.

'She said she was doubling my dose,' I tell Kelly. Diaz said no such thing, but it was worth a try. 'There should be four, not five.'

Kelly checks a clipboard. 'Nope,' he said. 'Fifteen milligrams.'

'Can you ask her?'

He's starting to look suspicious now. 'It's the right dose, Timothy. Are you going to be a good boy?'

'Of course.' I tip the cup onto my tongue, show him the pills and then swallow. I think again of the magician who ate the broken glass. He also swallowed five razor blades—or made it look like he had. I wish I'd watched him more closely and learned his method.

I open my mouth again, and Kelly probes around my gums with his fingers. Over his shoulder, I look for Eli, but he's gone. Maybe someone told him TV gives you square eyes.

Kelly peels off his gloves. 'Have a nice day, Timothy.'

I can already feel the pills dissolving in my stomach, doing who-knows-what to my brain chemistry. 'You too.'

He goes over to the bathroom, but doesn't go in. Just stands next to the door, watching me. I start walking back to my room, like he expects me to. As soon as I'm out of sight around the corner, I break into a run.

There's no toilet in my room. But there is a drain under the carpet. I can vomit into that. But I have to work fast. The amount I absorbed last time filled my brain with fog, and that was a much smaller dose.

I open the door to my room and rush in, my eyes already focused on the corner of the carpet. So I don't see Eli stepping out from behind the door. I only feel the movement, something rushing towards me. I turn my head in time to see the missing chair leg swing inwards. I duck, but too slowly. The steel bar comes crashing down on my skull, and everything goes black.

CHAPTER 34

I took aim at the fog, but didn't hit it. What did I do?

The world comes back slowly. Everything is blurry, but I can make out a drop ceiling, a fluorescent light, and a curtain. I can smell disinfectant, and feel thin sheets. I'm in a hospital bed.

Three facts hit me at the same time—

One: Eli was in my room.

Two: I was unconscious for some time.

Three: I can't see out of my left eye.

I let out a moan and reach for my face. Where my eyeball should be, there's something wet and spongy. The fear spikes. I blink my other eye frantically, trying to clear the blurriness away.

'Whoa, he's awake.' The voice comes from my right. Through the mist I can make out a woman in scrubs holding a thin tube.

Someone I can't see pins down my arm. 'Don't touch it. Okay, Timothy?'

'Where's my eye?' I scream.

'Your eye will be fine,' the voice says. 'The cornea has

been scratched. Your vision will be blurry for a while. But it will heal, as long as you don't touch it. Okay?'

I can't just take his word for it that my eyeball is still there. But if I touch it and he's telling the truth, then I might lose my vision. It's another one of those lose–lose witch trial situations. But he hasn't released my wrist, so the choice is made for me.

I recognise the voice now. 'Dr Kobald?'

'Right. How's your head?'

Now that I'm not so focused on my eye, I notice a pounding headache. My neck and shoulder are stiff, probably from hitting the ground.

'Sore.'

'I'm sorry to hear that. Harmony got you pretty good. I'll prescribe some stronger painkillers.'

'Harmony?' I say.

'She attacked you in your room. If Eli hadn't found you when he did, I don't know what would have happened. Don't worry, we'll be keeping a very close eye on her from now on.'

'You've got it the wrong way around,' I say. 'Eli attacked me. He wants my eye. Harmony must have interrupted him before he could finish the job.'

Kobald doesn't respond, and when I turn to face him, I see that he isn't there. The woman has gone as well, though there is a structure—a bit like a coat rack—with the tube dangling off it.

'Hello?' I call out. As my voice echoes through the shadows, I realise the overhead lights are off. The only glow is from wall-mounted LEDs near the floor. But it was daytime a second ago.

I'm wearing a hospital gown. I sit up, trying to ignore my throbbing brain, and look around for some clothes. I'm not in the Behavioural Health Unit anymore. They must have taken me across to the main part of the hospital, where all the non-crazy people with gunshot wounds and cancer and pregnancies are. This place won't be as well guarded as the psych ward. This is my chance to escape.

Escape isn't supposed to be my plan. I haven't completed the message—I mean, the mission. But I feel a powerful need to get out, *just get out.*

'Probably because you have a head injury,' a voice says, and I realise that Kobald is back. It's daytime again.

'What?' I say.

'You're very lucky that you were already in a hospital when this happened.' He reaches for my eye.

I shrink back, but he's just peeling off a soft, damp bandage. 'Bacteria thrives in the darkness,' he explains. 'It never stops eating. Never stops. Eating. Eating.'

I still can't open my eye. It's been scotch-taped closed. 'Eli attacked me, not Harmony.'

He nods reassuringly. He doesn't believe me.

'He had a chair leg. He wants my eyes.'

'You have a few different medications in your blood-stream right now,' he says. 'Try to relax.'

If you have a mental illness, people don't trust you. And if you take drugs to fix the illness, they trust you even less.

I realise I'm holding a spoon. I look down at my distorted reflection in the curved metal. I try to speak, then realise there's food in my mouth. I choke.

'Easy, now.' Kobald pats my back.

I let the sludge dribble out of my mouth, onto the plate.

'It's not the head injury. It's the meds Diaz prescribed for me. They're messing with my head.'

'They shouldn't be. I started you off with a small dose in case you had a bad reaction, and you were fine.'

'I haven't been taking them. This was my first dose.'

Silence. I look over at Kobald in case he's vanished again, and realise I'm talking to Dr Diaz herself.

'I see,' she says, expressionless.

'Please help me. I'm losing time. Seeing things. I need—'

I'm talking to no one. Diaz is gone. Was she ever there?

I haul myself off the hospital bed and stagger barefoot across the ward. I only make it a few steps before there's a painful tug from my forearm. I'm connected to an IV drip. I wrench the needle out and let it fall to the floor. I head for the door, dripping blood.

The corridor is dark, but I can hear the soft shuffle of footsteps somewhere. Nurses, I guess. Do they patrol regularly, or wait for a machine to beep before they check on their patients? I don't know. Don't want to stick around to find out.

I keep moving until I find a stairwell door and push it open. An alarm screams—

Suddenly I'm at a bus stop, the concrete cold and gritty beneath my feet. No sign of a bus. There's trash in the gutter. Clouds peel back, like the moon is opening its eye. The wind blows at my hospital gown, and I fight to keep it closed.

'You okay, man?' Dr Diaz says. But when I look, it's not her. It's a guy in a Cougars jersey. He's a big guy. Meaty. Coming closer.

I bare my teeth. He backs off.

'Come closer,' I say.

Someone is screaming. The noise is a power drill, burrowing right into my eardrum. The man is gone, and Reese Thistle is standing there instead, clad in the tan uniform of a sheriff's deputy, her gloved hands outstretched. A copperish tang fills my mouth.

'Let's just take it easy,' she says, her dark eyes wary.

The blood spills from my lips and down the front of my gown as I try to speak: 'This isn't what it looks like.'

'He's a zombie!' the screamer says, from behind me.

I look down. The puncture wound from the IV has been replaced by a bite mark on my forearm. My prosthesis is nowhere to be seen.

'Interlace your fingers behind your head,' says the love of my life.

'Thistle, please help me.'

Thistle doesn't react to her name. She can't understand me—or it's not her. Thistle is FBI, not a beat cop, and this woman has lighter hair, and a softer jawline. But those are Thistle's eyes. Has this cop stolen them?

'I'll kill you!' I screech and lunge at her.

'Stand clear,' the cop tells the screamer. There's a sharp pop, and suddenly the skin all over my body is burning, my hair standing up so straight that it hurts. As the cop moves in, the crackling wires connecting me to her go slack, and I find myself falling. I try to raise my hands to break my fall, but one arm won't move, and the other isn't there. The concrete rushes up to meet me. Meat me. Me meat.

CHAPTER 35

I hold doors open, but clothes
closed. What am I?

I wake up in my room, as though the whole thing never happened. Like Eli never attacked me, like Harmony never saved me, like I wasn't rushed across to the main building of the hospital where the sane patients are. I'm dressed in the same clothes as I was after lunch, my prosthesis back on, the buttons on my shirt done up all the way to my throat.

Except my vision is still blurry in my left eye, my forearm is bandaged, and my chest stings where the two needles from the taser punched holes in my skin.

I try to sit up but can't. Groaning, I slump back down. There doesn't seem to be a reason to try again. I have nowhere to be.

After a while, someone knocks at the door.

'Come in,' I say. If they mean me harm, they will, either way.

Dr Diaz opens the door and slips in. She looks taller in here than in her office. Maybe my ceiling is lower. She's also dressed more casually. A sweatshirt and jeans, like she's visiting a friend rather than a patient. Maybe she's come in on her day off.

She quickly scans my room with a practised gaze. Looking for what, I don't know.

'How are you feeling?' she asks.

My voice comes out in a rasp. 'Not great.'

She glances around for somewhere to sit and, seeing nothing, leans against the wall instead. 'Do you know what day it is?'

'No. Friday, maybe?'

'That's correct. Do you know who I am?'

'Sure,' I say. 'Michelle Obama.'

She hesitates.

'Sorry,' I say. 'Reaching for humour as a deflection, again. You're Dr Diaz.'

She smiles, relieved, and asks me a few more questions. It's like a history test, with a bit of math mixed in, and some spelling. My brain seems to be working fine. Then again, how would I know? It occurs to me now that only someone else can tell you your brain isn't working properly. But Diaz looks satisfied.

'I owe you an apology,' she says, when the questions are done.

I clear my throat. 'It's not your fault. I never warned you about Eli.'

She raises an eyebrow. 'Eli? I was told it was . . . someone else.'

'No.' My head is a little clearer now. 'Eli attacked me a few days ago, in the bathroom. I didn't tell anyone, because I thought he'd snitch on me for puking up my medication.

But then he was waiting for me in my room, with a chair leg. He wants my eyes.'

Diaz keeps a poker face through all of this.

'But Harmony got to him before he could do more than scratch my cornea. I assume—I don't remember what happened after he hit me.'

'I see.' Her voice is neutral.

'I get why you wouldn't believe me,' I say. 'I'm crazy, and I'm guessing Harmony's keeping quiet because she thinks it's all a big conspiracy or whatever. But—'

'I believe you,' Diaz says.

The relief is like a physical thing. My head sinks back into the pillow.

'I'll keep Eli away from you,' Diaz says. 'But that's not what I was going to apologise for. I wasn't honest with you in our session on Wednesday.'

I run through the conversation in my head. *You're not bad, you're just lazy. It's uncomfortable, isn't it? The idea that change is possible.*

'You were a little too honest, if anything,' I say.

The corner of her mouth twitches. 'I said I got paid by the hour, and I didn't care whether you got better. That's not true. You got under my skin, so I reacted defensively, which was unprofessional. I do care, Timothy. I mean that.'

She seems genuine. But maybe she just feels guilty because her meds nearly killed me.

'I'm sorry I didn't take the pills.'

'I get it,' she says. 'You didn't think you were sick, so you thought the medication might harm you.'

'I still don't want to take them.'

'And I won't make you. I do think you need medication of some kind. But not *those* pills, which clearly didn't agree with you. Can we revisit the subject in about a week?'

I hesitate, and then nod.

'Whatever we try next,' Diaz says, 'we'll start with a small dose, so we can identify any side effects before they get too severe. That is, assuming you actually take the small dose.' She holds my gaze.

'I will,' I say.

'Good.' She clears her throat. 'I need to tell you that your circumstances have changed.'

'Oh?' I doubt they've improved.

'When you were admitted, you were told you could leave as soon as you felt ready. But after yesterday's episode . . .'

My heart sinks. 'You're keeping me here.'

'That's the protocol after any incident of self-harm.' Diaz's gaze flicks to my chewed forearm.

I tell myself it doesn't matter. Zara's wizardry with paperwork will get me out of here, regardless of my legal status. I'll be gone long before Diaz tries to medicate me again.

'Don't worry,' Diaz says. 'You're making progress. You won't be here forever.'

'If you . . .' I trail off, remembering that I'm not really here for therapy. I'm here on a mission.

'Go on,' she says.

'You gave me something to stop the delusions,' I say. 'But it made things worse.'

Diaz is watching me carefully. 'You think that's proof you're not delusional.'

'That's not what I was getting at. Well, kind of. But I was wondering . . .' I turn my head on the pillow, unable to look at her face. 'If I wasn't delusional, if it was all real—could you help me?'

'You're asking if I could cure a cannibal? A real one?' Diaz sounds faintly amused.

'Hypothetically,' I say.

'Yes,' Diaz says. 'To be clear, that's not what I think is happening. But I would treat a person like that with a combination of talk therapy and medication. Just like you.'

'You wouldn't just throw them in jail?'

'I'm a doctor, not a judge. But I don't think jails are the best place for sick people.'

My former colleagues at the FBI would argue that it's not about what's best for the perpetrators, it's about justice for the victims. But I'm touched that she thinks I'm—hypothetically—worth helping.

Maybe she's the crazy one.

'Did anyone come to visit me?' I ask. 'While I was unconscious?'

'Not that I'm aware of,' Diaz says. 'Are you expecting someone?'

'Zara.'

'Ah.' Diaz doesn't push this.

Zara was supposed to come when she saw the paper in the window. To find out what Harmony had told me, and get me out of here. It's been two days. What's taking so long?

I know what's going through Diaz's head. She thinks Zara isn't real, so of course she hasn't visited. But Zara *is* real.

Isn't she?

•

'In one of our sessions, you mentioned a sun,' Diaz says.

My head is feeling better today. Clearer. I'm telling myself it's because the drugs are out of my system and the concussion from the chair leg has worn off.

I don't want to believe that it's because therapy is working.

We're not in Diaz's office. We're alone in the garden, sitting on hard metal benches. Her notebook is on a wrought-iron table between us, and she hasn't touched it so far. This morning, Diaz could see that I was gloomy and suggested that being out in the sunshine might help. I hate sunshine, and we're sitting facing the brick wall that imprisons me here, which isn't exactly perking me up. But I let her think she's helping.

'Sun?' I say.

She nods. 'From a sperm donation. You said his name was Kyle.'

Oh. *Son.* I don't remember telling her that. But this place is playing tricks on my memory. I no longer know how long I've been here. Whether Zara is a day overdue, or two, or a week.

'He died,' I say.

'What was he like?' she asks.

'A lot like me,' I said. 'Five eight. Scruffy. Kind of an asshole.'

Diaz laughs gently. We look at the flowers in front of the wall for a while. A lone bee buzzes around them. Perhaps the swarm has moved on, and no one told her.

'How did you find Kyle?' Diaz says. 'After the donation.'

When I infiltrated the house of dark web criminals and met Zara, Kyle was there too. A teenage boy, just as lost as I'd been at his age. He was cruel, and stupid. He might have grown out of it, except he was murdered right in front of me. I was too slow to save him.

I give Diaz the shortest, least painful version of this story: 'I just walked into a house, and there he was.'

'You recognised him?'

'Yeah, he looked like me.'

Diaz pauses just long enough for me to feel how unlikely she thinks this is.

'He looked like me,' I say again.

'Before you arrived at this house,' Diaz asks, 'how were you feeling?'

'Bad.'

'Just bad?'

It was significantly worse than that, and she knows it. I drove to that house with the intention of killing myself after one last meal. 'What's your point?'

'With seven billion people on Earth, what are the chances that you would bump into your long-lost child at—'

'With seven billion people on Earth, some weird things are gonna happen. In the seventies, a seventeen-year-old kid in Hamilton, Bermuda, was run over by the same taxi that had killed his brother on the same day the previous year, and it was carrying the same passenger.'

'I've heard that story before. Do you know how small Hamilton, Bermuda, is? Not many cabs. Especially not in the seventies—' She breaks off. 'You're very good at that.'

'At what?'

'Changing the subject. Are you willing to hear a different theory?'

She's asked the question in such a way that it's difficult to say no. So I say nothing.

'The mind is a funny thing,' she says. 'If I have the time-line right, you arrived at that house just after a traumatic break-up with your first love.'

'Thistle found a human head in my freezer,' I say.

Diaz pretends to believe this. 'You might have felt like you didn't have much left. So, when you walked into that house, your mind *gave* you something to live for. You saw a kid who looked a bit like you, and—'

'I lost Kyle once,' I say. My voice cracks. 'Now you're trying to take him away from me again. Saying he wasn't my son.'

'No,' she says. 'I'm saying he *became* your son, because that's who you needed him to be.'

My throat is closing up. I don't trust myself to speak.

'I have a daughter,' Diaz said. 'We decided my wife would be the one to carry her, since her job didn't pay as well as mine. So my daughter has some DNA from my wife, some from a male friend, and none from me.'

As an orphan who never got adopted, I've always hated couples who insist on having their own biological children. I take a shaky breath. 'Do you feel left out?'

'No. She's my daughter because I love her.'

'I don't know if I loved Kyle.' My voice falters. 'I didn't know him very long.'

'How did you feel when he died?'

Just like that, I'm in the back of the van again. Cradling his broken body, howling.

'I think you loved him enough for it to count,' Diaz says.

'He never knew.' I can't meet her gaze. 'I never told him.'

'I'm sorry. That will probably always be painful.'

I can't hold back the tears anymore, but I manage to

keep them quiet. She knows I'm crying, but I can pretend she doesn't, as long as I don't make a sound.

When I'm done, I find myself watching that solitary bee humming around for a while.

'You said you don't remember your own parents,' Diaz says finally.

I clear my throat. 'Right.'

'So you don't remember them telling you they loved you, either.'

It's like she's *trying* to hurt me. 'Are you sure you're a real therapist?'

She ignores this. 'I bet they did, though. Love you, I mean. They would be glad to see that you turned out all right.'

I snort, but she doesn't seem to be joking.

'You think I turned out all right?' I intended to sound incredulous, but it comes out like a plea.

'I do,' she says. 'All things considered.'

'They're not watching me. I don't believe in heaven,' I say.

'Nor do I,' Diaz says. 'I said they *would* be glad, not they *are* glad. But still.'

We sit in silence for the rest of the session. But it's not a hostile silence, like when she called me lazy. It's comfortable.

Just as we're getting up, Nurse Kelly approaches. He's been watching me more warily since my near-escape. I wonder if he was told that I'd been vomiting up the pills. Maybe he got in trouble for not monitoring me closely enough. He might be angry at me.

Or possibly not. It might be par for the course. Like Diaz said, people with mental illnesses don't believe they are sick. They probably all try to avoid taking their meds.

'Timothy,' Kelly says. 'You have a visitor.'

Zara. She's finally here for me. On the one hand, I'm desperate to leave. But on the other, I feel like I was just starting to make progress.

Diaz asks me, 'Do you feel well enough for a visit?'

'Yes,' I say. 'Thank you, doctor.'

She gives me an odd look. She doesn't know that this is the last time I'll ever see her.

'You're welcome, Timothy,' she says.

Kelly leads me through the corridors to a locked door. He unlocks it and takes me into a room filled with tables and chairs, plus a vending machine. I've never seen the room before, because I've never had a visitor before. A window looks out onto a small aviary, filled with tiny, sickly-looking birds. I sit at one of the tables and wait. Kelly takes a seat in one corner, scrolling through his phone.

I'm there a long time. Long enough for me to wonder if Zara has breached protocol somehow and been sent away. It's very peaceful here, watching the birds hop from one withered branch to another.

Then my visitor walks in, and it's not Zara.

It's Thistle.

CHAPTER 36

What's black and white, but red all over?

My shock must show on my face, because she mirrors it. Thistle has always been empathetic. Good at consoling victims by sharing their pain, celebrating someone else's victory when they solve a case, catching killers by sensing their rage. It's like she takes some of my surprise and wears it on her own face, to spare me.

'Thistle?' I say, a bit stupidly.

'Blake.' She generously pretends I was just greeting her.

She's wearing dangly gold earrings and a leather jacket over a cream turtleneck. She smells good. I want to slide my arm around her, underneath that jacket, and pull her chest against mine.

This isn't a prison. Hugs are allowed. Just the same, I don't touch her. I take a seat opposite her, my elbow on the laminate tabletop. 'What are you doing here?'

Immediately, I wish I'd said *It's good to see you.*

'You weren't hard to find,' she says. 'Medical files are confidential only up to a point.'

This is true. Zara uses them all the time.

Thistle looks around at the vending machine, the little stack of newspapers on a table, the aviary outside the window, taking it all in.

'How are you?' she asks finally.

'Embarrassed.' I don't know where the worst place to bump into your ex is, but I'm sure a mental hospital is in the top five.

'About being here?'

I nod.

'You shouldn't be,' she says. 'I'm told you admitted yourself.'

'Is that less embarrassing than being committed against my will?'

'Much less. It takes guts, to admit that you need help. And to check yourself into a place like this . . .'

'I didn't really have a choice,' I say.

What I mean is, if there had been another way to investigate Cho's murder, I would have taken it. But Thistle gives me such a sad look that my throat closes up, and I can't say any more.

'Are you allowed to leave?' she asks.

'Not till I'm better.'

She doesn't ask how long that will take. Maybe she knows the answer.

'So . . .' she begins. But I don't want her to get to the purpose of her visit. I want to keep talking to her forever.

'How's your husband?' I ask.

'Ex-husband,' she corrects me.

'Right.' I knew they were divorced, but assumed they were back together, since she was living with him again.

She seems to choose her words carefully. 'He seemed

glad to have me back. But I don't think it was because he'd missed me. I think it was just pride. Me coming back proved there was nothing wrong with him.'

'I'm sorry.' And I am. She deserves to be happy with someone.

'It's okay. I realised I hadn't missed him, either. Anyway, that's not why I'm here.' She taps her long nails on the tabletop. I want to reach for her hand. It always surprised me how soft her palms were, given how tough the rest of her is. But I don't move.

She glances at Kelly in the corner. He's not watching and doesn't seem to be listening. She lowers her voice. 'I hate having to ask you this. But I'm hoping you'll understand.'

I force a smile. 'I don't think you can offend me.'

'It's about the Texas Reaper,' she begins.

Okay, I'm a *little* offended. On the one hand, Thistle is the only person at the FBI who knows I'm a cannibal. But somehow I also expected her to be the one person who would know I didn't strangle a bunch of innocent women.

'It's not me,' I say.

'The killings started pretty soon after you and I escaped from the dark web house.' She takes a folder from her bag and places it on the table but doesn't open it. 'I checked hotel records and phone tower data. You were here in Houston when the first two bodies turned up. Then you drove to California. You stopped overnight at Las Cruces, New Mexico, where victim number three was found.'

Remembering the list of addresses on the FBI whiteboard, I realise it wasn't the locations that bothered me. It was the dates.

'When you got to LA, another woman was killed,' Thistle continues. 'Since you got back to Houston, there have been two more.'

My heart is pounding. 'I didn't do it.'

'You were seen talking to Ruciani on the day he died. Forensics searched some crime scenes a second time. There was a partial print on Ethyl Braidwyn's doorhandle, and another on one of her pill organisers. They match yours.'

I thought I'd been careful not to touch anything. Apparently not.

'I broke into her house,' I say. 'I wanted to help solve the case.'

Thistle stares at me for a long moment. 'That's a very dumb lie.'

'It's true.'

'If so, that would be even dumber. Look, I'm not going to turn you in. What would be the point? You're already institutionalised.'

Hopefully she's trying to trick me. I don't want to think I've compromised her so badly. Before we fell in love, she never would have agreed to conceal evidence to protect a serial killer. The betrayal—mine, not hers—is like a shard of broken glass wedged through my heart.

'I didn't strangle anybody,' I say. 'Why would I hide something like that? You already know I've done far worse.'

Thistle's gaze hardens, and I realise I've said the wrong thing. Eating dead bodies is more disgusting than strangling innocent women—but it's not 'worse'.

'You know what I mean,' I say. 'I already know I don't have a chance . . .' *With you.* 'A chance of convincing you that I'm a decent guy. Why would I deny some murders but not others?'

'I want to believe you, Blake,' she says. 'But you've lied to me before.'

'I know. I'm sorry.'

I have no way to prove my innocence. If I want Thistle to believe I didn't do this, I need to confess to something else.

'I slept with Zara,' I hear myself say.

She flinches. 'What's your point?'

'I betrayed you.'

'Do I need to remind you that we're not together anymore? You can fuck whoever you want. That's not a betrayal.'

'Zara was one of the maniacs who held you prisoner.'

Thistle goes very still. I immediately regret bringing this up. The event was traumatic for both of us—but I've been abducted, beaten, starved and chained up more times than I can count, especially now that I only have four fingers left to count with. It only happened once to Thistle, and it was probably the worst experience of her life.

'She was at Space City,' Thistle says slowly. 'I didn't recognise her.'

'I know you'll never forgive me for that,' I say. 'But I told you anyway. Because I don't lie to you. Not anymore.'

Thistle looks at me for a long time. Then she takes a folder out of her bag and slides it across the table.

'Explain this, then,' she says.

I open the folder. There's a photo printed on cheap copy paper. The image shows a man in the passenger seat of a car. He's unshaven, with dirty skin, a beanie stretched across his skull.

'That's the only photo we have of the Reaper,' Thistle says.

I stare down at the page. The man is unquestionably me.

The room spins, then disappears. Nothing exists except that photo. Incontrovertible proof—but of what?

Thistle's voice floats towards me from somewhere. 'You want to know where that photo was taken?'

I already know. 'Los Angeles.'

'Correct. Right outside the house of one of the Reaper's victims, within the time-of-death window.'

'Not right outside,' I say. 'Around the corner.'

The threads disentangle, separating into parallel lines. I get it. Not just the Reaper case—everything. I know why Sam Garcia confessed to kidnapping a girl he'd never met. I know why Rob Cho was murdered. I know who dragged his body to Mars. I know what the MSS is so desperate to hide.

When I look up from the photo, Thistle is watching me. She can tell I'm thinking hard. She probably believes I'm trying to come up with a plausible lie.

She taps the photograph. 'Why were you at the victim's house, Blake?'

Rob Cho's killer is still out there. If they find out Thistle has talked to me, they might come after her. The only way to keep her safe is to tell her everything.

I start talking, fast. Because it's a long story, and I don't know how much time she'll give me.

'The CIA has been running off-books operations on US soil, spying on American citizens,' I say. 'Zara recruited me to help with some of them. She's a CIA agent—that's why she was at the house, where you were held prisoner.'

'A CIA agent?' Thistle repeats.

I need to skip ahead. Get to the important bit. 'Right. She sent me to the Johnson Space Center to investigate reports of a Chinese astronaut falling out of the sky. The CIA thought there was a secret space station above our heads. But I stole the earlobe from the body, and it didn't taste like it had been frozen or burned, so I figured the dead guy wasn't an astronaut at all.'

Thistle looks horrified. I press on. 'I turned out to be right—he was the head of security at Space City, a guy named Rob Cho. Someone had killed him using a hypobaric chamber, and then dressed him in a flight suit and left him outside to make it look like he'd fallen from space. Or at least, that's what I thought at the time. But now I realise two people were involved. One killed Cho, the other disguised him as an astronaut. And those two people weren't working together. They have very different agendas, and each one is trying to identify the other.'

Thistle's eyes are growing wider and wider. 'Blake . . .' she begins.

'Rob Cho knew something that got him killed,' I say. My voice is getting louder. I can't help it. 'I thought he might have told his sister, Harmony. She's one of the other patients here. I admitted myself to the hospital so I could find out what Rob told her. I thought it might have been the identity of the Chinese asset at the Space Center. But now I realise it was the other way around. Rob didn't tell Harmony anything. *She* told *him* something. About the space station. Don't you see?'

I'm telling the story wrong. The pieces are all out of order.

'Let me start again,' I say. 'Zara has an asset in Shanghai, someone well placed in the Chinese Communist Party—'

Thistle reaches across the table and squeezes my hand. Tears well up in the corners of her eyes.

337

'What?' I ask, alarmed.

'I'm glad you're getting help,' she says.

No, no, no. 'I'm not crazy,' I say. 'Not that kind of crazy.'

But Thistle lets go of me and stands up. Her voice breaks. 'Everything's going to be okay.'

'But it's all true! You have to believe me.' I try to stand up, but Kelly has snuck up behind me. His strong hands wrestle me back down into the chair.

'Let go of me!' I shout.

Thistle is backing away, her eyes sad, her hands covering her mouth.

I keep babbling. 'The Chinese government had a faulty spy plane. They dumped it in the path of a fishing vessel, just to fool us. They'll do anything to keep this a secret. You're in danger. The MSS spy could come after you! You can't trust anybody!'

'Keep still, and this won't hurt,' Kelly says.

I barely feel the sting as the needle goes into the side of my neck.

'No!' I shout. 'Thistle, you have to believe me . . . you're not safe . . . you're . . .' But soon I can't talk anymore. The world is swimming around me. Thistle's face is stony, but the tears are tumbling down her cheeks.

Kelly lied to me. I'm keeping still, but it hurts. My last thought before I black out is: *if only she didn't care about me.*

•

I wake up in my room, strapped to a gurney. This is what Kelly does when a patient has had some kind of freak-out. Straps like seatbelts hold you down, so tight you can't even pick your nose. I can hardly breathe.

Then again, maybe that's not because of the straps. Maybe it's because Thistle is in danger. I thought telling her the truth would keep her safe, but it didn't work. She just thinks I'm crazy.

She's right—I am. That doesn't mean I'm wrong, though. Right now the MSS spy could be planning to kill her, to keep China's secret.

And I can't do anything about it. I can't do anything about anything from in here. I can't even pick my goddamn nose.

I lie on the gurney for hours, my thoughts prowling in circles like caged tigers.

Finally, Kelly comes in. I've never hated anyone so much.

'Are you going to be good?' he asks.

I meet his gaze, keeping my face neutral. 'Sure.'

He starts undoing the straps.

'I'd like to volunteer for kitchen duty,' I say.

'Is that so?'

'I miss cooking. It always helped me calm down.'

Kelly looks suspicious.

'I don't need a knife.' I try to look innocent. 'I'd be happy stirring beans with a wooden spoon.'

'I'll see what I can do,' he says.

Eventually I'm free. He stands aside but doesn't leave. I hobble past him, out the door and down the corridor towards Harmony's room, rubbing my sore chest. The straps have aggravated the puncture wounds from the taser.

I knock on Harmony's door. I don't look back, in case Kelly is watching me.

'Come in,' she says.

It's the first time I've been in Harmony's room. I expected photographs and newspaper clippings to be all over the walls, connected by a web of frayed twine. But instead, her decorations are unremarkable. A painting of a sailboat. A photo of her and Rob—the same one I saw at his house. A poster with a quote—*You have two ears and one mouth. Repeat only half of what you hear.*

I point at the boat. 'Your painting is upside down.'

Harmony is on her bed, reading *Frankenstein*. 'No one ever notices.'

I'm not surprised. The reflection on the water looks a lot like the boat itself.

'Your eyes still work, then,' she says.

I nod. 'Thanks for saving me.'

She waves this off. 'Any idea who Eli was working for?'

It takes me a second to figure out what she means. 'No one,' I say. 'He just wanted a new eyeball, I think.'

She squints at her book. 'Nothing's ever that simple.'

I disagree but don't say so. 'Has he come after you?'

'No. You're the target, not me. And he's a professional.'

It's exhausting, operating on Harmony's level of reality. But I think she's right. Eli's not going to come after her. And since my conversation with Diaz, the staff have been watching him much more closely. Several times over the last few days he's been strapped to a gurney after violent episodes. Hopefully my problems with him are over.

Like mine, Harmony's room doesn't have any chairs. I sit cross-legged on the floor.

I'm surprised to see Harmony with a novel. I assumed she only read manifestos and declassified documents. Maybe there's a crazy person pamphlet tucked between the pages.

'I never read that book,' I say, testing her.

'*Frankenstein*?'

'Yeah. I was supposed to, in high school. But I worked a fast-food job at night, so I didn't get much time for reading. I cribbed my essay from someone else. Is it good?'

Harmony turns a page. 'In 1816, Mary Shelley goes to Geneva with her husband, her stepsister, her stepsister's lover, and her stepsister's lover's doctor . . .'

'I'm out,' I say, raising my hands.

'And the weather sucks, so they have a competition to see who can write the scariest story,' Harmony continues. 'Shelley's husband—who's secretly banging her stepsister— writes a story about a man who's undressing a woman and then finds out she has eyes where her nipples should be. Shelley, meanwhile, writes *Frankenstein*.'

'Did she win?' I ask. 'Because the nipple thing sounds pretty scary.'

'*Frankenstein* is scarier. So Mary defeats her cheating husband and invents the sci-fi genre at the same time. And then she bangs her stepsister's lover. Allegedly.'

I force a smile. 'She sounds badass.'

'She was.' Harmony turns another page.

'The monster—he's stitched together out of human corpses, right?'

'Uh-huh.'

'I met someone like that, once. But it was a woman.'

Harmony glances up.

'Actually, all the pieces were male,' I say. 'But it was woman-shaped. And it wasn't alive, obviously.'

Harmony looks at me like I'm the crazy one. It's good to know where her line is.

She carefully steers the conversation back onto safe ground: 'You can read the book when I'm done.'

'No thanks. I plan to be gone by then.'

Her breath catches. I have her full attention.

'Gone?' she asks, casually.

'Yeah,' I say, equally casually. I can't do this without her, but she won't help if she feels railroaded. 'I'm busting out of here. Care to join me?'

CHAPTER 37

I have many useful buttons, but I'm
a long way from civilisation.
What am I?

It's not the first time a patient has tried to escape from the Behavioural Health Unit of the George Clark Red Memorial Hospital. The nurses never talk about it, but I've heard all sorts of stories from the patients. Two years ago a woman named Delia (depression, anxiety) knocked out a doctor with a heavy book, dressed in the doctor's clothes and tried to walk out. But she didn't know the code for the front door, and the staff at the desk recognised her and called security while she was trying to open the door.

The year before that, a guy named Pedro (paraphrenia) tried to get over the wall that surrounds the gardens, using one of the garden rakes as a pole vault. Unbelievably, he did manage to get up onto the top of the wall, but quickly got tangled in the razor wire. He was found hours later, screaming for help and bleeding everywhere.

The person who made it the furthest was Joni (schizophrenia). She vanished during kitchen duty. The whole building was searched. There was no sign of her. Staff concluded that she'd somehow slipped out the front door, and they spent a few hours watching security recordings hoping to confirm this. Meanwhile, a cleaner was taking trash out from the kitchens to the dumpster behind the hospital and noticed that one of the trash cans was heavier than it should have been. He found Joni hiding inside, covered with crumbs and oil. Less schizo, more schnitzel.

Paranoid as they were, all these patients attempted to escape alone. I'm hoping, with Harmony's help, to do better.

'Do you have the code for the front door?' she asks.

'No.'

'Do you have a way to get over the wall?'

'No.'

'Do you have outside help?'

'I was supposed to. But as it stands, no.'

The sticker has been on my window for a week. Zara isn't coming for me. There are two possible explanations for that, but right now, neither of them really matter.

'Well, don't keep me in suspense,' Harmony says. 'How are we going to get out of here?'

'We're going to need a few things,' I say.

•

To make a letter bomb, you'll need an envelope, some stamps, adhesive tape, a battery, two wires, some paper, aluminium foil and something that explodes when you stick electricity into it. I learned the process at the FBI.

At the Behavioural Health Unit, most of these ingredients aren't hard to find. I volunteer for kitchen duty and swipe some almonds while I'm supposed to be crushing them with a rolling pin. I also take two sheets of aluminium foil.

Bennett, the sad-eyed patient with the dead daughter, sees me do it.

'What's the foil for?' he asks.

'I'm gonna make a hat,' I say, and leave it to him to decide if I'm kidding. He shrugs it off and doesn't turn me in.

I steal the battery from the TV remote in the common room. When the theft is discovered, the patients are horrified—much more than they were by Eli assaulting me. What kind of monster sabotages a communal TV remote? Dasha quickly claims she saw Casey fiddling with the remote, and that she also heard Casey complaining that her vibrator was out of batteries. The whole thing quickly escalates into a screaming match, which the nurses break up. No one suspects me.

I volunteer for gardening duty next. The equipment is kept in a locked shed. Gloves, shovels, mallets, plastic sacks of fertiliser, a leaf-blower. The only thing with a sharp edge is the lawnmower. You'd have to be pretty crazy to commit suicide by lawnmower.

I spend some time cutting the grass, blades shredding blades, letting the staff see I'm working meticulously. Once they've relaxed, I let the motor stall. Under the guise of investigating the problem, I unscrew the cap on the gas tank and dip a tissue into the hole. The tissue comes out soaked with fuel. I pocket it, close the cap and start the motor again. I push the mower around the lawns, whistling.

Once the lawns are done, I put the mower back in the shed, then take a rake and a shovel. I use the shovel to dig an irrigation trench in the vegetable patch—or I try, but with one arm, I can't really lift the dirt out of the hole, just scrape it aside. It takes a long time. Long enough that everyone loses interest in me. When Kelly goes away for a bathroom break and none of the other patients are looking in my direction, I lay the rake down in the trench, then quickly push the dirt onto it.

When we put our equipment back in the shed, no one notices that the rake is missing. Kelly pats us down on our way back into the building. The tissue is just a soft ball in my pocket. He doesn't feel it.

To get the envelope and the stamps, I have an elaborate plan involving breaking into Diaz's office and going through her desk, but Harmony points out that patients are allowed to send letters. Testing her theory, I ask Diaz if I can have an envelope and some stamps during our next session. She just hands them to me, without even asking who I'd like to write to.

'You seem to be embracing life at the hospital,' she says.

I shrug. 'May as well make the best of it, right?'

'I've always thought that volunteering is one of the most selfish things you can do.'

'Really?'

'Yes.' She smiles. 'After all, *you're* the one who feels good.'

'That's a very psychiatrist joke,' I say, after a pause.

'You take my meaning, though?'

'Yeah, I get it. Helping others helps me.'

'I don't want you to get too comfortable here, though.' She squeezes the cushion on the seat next to her, plumping it up. 'Or else you won't want to leave.'

I blink. 'You think I'm almost ready to be released?'

She shakes her head. 'But you won't be here forever.'

'How long, then?'

'I'm reluctant to put a timeline on it.'

'I'm not. Give me a ballpark.'

'At your current rate of progress?' Diaz chews her pen. 'We're talking months rather than years.'

Thistle doesn't have months to wait. Even now, the spy could be closing in.

Diaz can see I'm disappointed. 'I have another joke,' she says. 'How many psychiatrists does it take to change a light bulb?'

'Pretty sure I've heard this one, doc.'

'One,' she says, undeterred. 'But the light bulb has to *want* to change.'

I leave her office with an envelope and stamps. I suspect this place works like a prison—any mail I send will be opened, read and resealed. Fortunately, my letter bomb isn't leaving the building.

I have no idea how to make the explosive itself. My FBI training was about spotting letter bombs, not building them. So I steal all the Blu-Tack from the posters in Dasha's room while she's at lunch and roll it into a ball. I stick the wires into the ball and put it in the package.

Harmony's job delivering mail gives her access to the doctors' offices. I give her the package and instructions about where to leave it.

'You really think this will work?' she asks.

'I have no idea,' I say.

The following morning, Dr Kobald enters his office with his cappuccino. He leaves the door ajar. I watch through the gap as he rests his hat on a filing cabinet and spots a package on his desk. When he picks it up, the batteries rattle inside. The package is addressed to him and marked

CONFIDENTIAL. It's dotted with too many stamps and sealed with way too much tape. It smells faintly of almonds and gasoline. The sender's name is *Ben Franklin* and the address is *123 Main Street, New York, New York, 90210.*

Kobald isn't an idiot. He puts the package back down, very, very carefully. Then he sounds the fire alarm.

•

Whenever there was a bomb threat at the Houston Field Office of the FBI, it used to take us between eight and eleven minutes to evacuate the building. The lower-level employees would come out first, then the higher-ups would earn their salaries for once and check that no one had been left behind. As they left, the bomb squad would charge in, bulked-up like football players, visors muffling their voices. They'd scan the suspicious package with a few different machines—one that detected particles in the air, another that bounced electrons off the package, and another that was basically a portable X-ray machine. If they couldn't prove there was no bomb, they'd put the package in a cube that was more or less indestructible, not unlike the box that contains the flight recorder on a plane. They'd put their own explosive device in the same cube and seal it shut. Then they'd take it out to a field and trigger their bomb from a safe distance. We'd all shuffle back inside, having missed half an hour of work at the most. After my fifth or sixth time, my heart rate didn't even go up.

The hospital's response is more chaotic. People react uncertainly to the alarm, everyone waiting for someone else to take charge. Someone goes looking for a procedures manual, while the nurses try to keep the patients calm. I can hear a doctor on the phone, arguing about whether we're supposed to evacuate the whole hospital or just the Behavioural Health Unit. Eventually it's determined that the package is too small to blow up anything more than Kobald's office, so getting everyone out of the psych wing will do. I don't know who decided this, or how much experience they have with explosives, but it suits me just fine.

Kobald unlocks the front door with his code, and everyone shuffles out into the sunshine, headed for the emergency assembly area around the side. The hospital is at the top of a large, grassy hill, various buildings scattered around. Some of the patients huddle together like sheep, uneasy about being confronted by the outside world. Others bounce up and down on the grass, elated. Freedom is intoxicating.

A couple of patients make a run for it, but hospital security has already set up a perimeter around the campus. They chase the fleeing patients, who duck and dodge and finally get tackled to the ground, some screaming, some laughing.

Nurse Kelly is doing a head count. Given how much everyone's moving around, I figure it'll take him at least five minutes to realise we're not there.

I turn away from the window just as Harmony runs into Kobald's office, holding the rake. Clumps of dirt fall off the tines onto the carpet.

'Are we good?' she asks.

'We're good,' I say. 'You get the keys, I'll get the plant.'

We run back out into the corridor. Harmony turns right, towards reception. I head left. When I look back over my shoulder, Harmony is already feeding the rake through the hole in the glass over the reception counter. The rusty spikes get closer and closer to the pegboard, where all the keys dangle from hooks. Harmony's concentrating, her tongue poking out the side of her mouth. She's lined up the rake with the keys for the ambulances. It's like watching someone operate a claw machine in an arcade.

At the entrance to the bedroom corridor, I grab one of the wheelchairs and approach the potted fern. I was worried the ceramic pot might be too heavy to lift without Harmony's help, but when I wrap my arm around it and heave, it comes up easily. It's only fifty pounds or so.

That's a problem. I need it to be heavy or this won't work.

Thinking quickly, I dump the plant into the seat of the chair and wheel it over to the drinking fountain. I twist the faucet around and push the button. Water shoots out onto the dirt. I keep the heel of my palm on the button, waiting for the pot to be full.

A distant scream. Maybe someone outside, excited to see the bomb squad turn up. We don't have much time.

Soon the dirt is saturated. Mud trickles down the sides of the pot, soaking the seat of the wheelchair. I do some quick calculations—the diameter of the pot is about a foot, so it holds about twenty gallons. Twenty gallons of water would weigh two hundred pounds, but the dirt has displaced a lot of it. Either way, the tubes used by SWAT teams to break down doors weigh only thirty-five pounds. This should do.

The wheelchair has two handles. I ignore them, grabbing the rim of the heavy pot and using it to push the wheelchair up the corridor, towards the back door.

It's heavy. Hard to get going at first. But the longer I push, the more momentum the chair has. It's like charging a battery. I'm putting more and more energy into it, and it's storing that energy. The wheels hum on the linoleum, spinning faster and faster. Soon I have to run just to keep up with it. The big leaves tickle my face as I sprint up the corridor, gritting my teeth.

When the wheelchair is almost at the door, I let go. The chair rockets along the last few feet without me and slams into the door. The energy I put in all comes out at once, the pot flying forwards off the chair, a wrecking ball made of ceramic and wet dirt. It works better than I could possibly have hoped, smashing a hole through the wood and flying out into the sunshine in a cloud of matchsticks. The pot doesn't even break, landing on the grass with a rich bass *thunk*.

I stand in the doorway for a second. Freedom is just beyond. There's no sign of the other patients—we're facing the other side of the hospital, the ER and Maternity buildings ahead. But I won't get far on foot. I need those keys.

As I turn back to help Harmony, there's another scream. Closer this time.

'What's going on?' a voice cries. 'Someone help me!'

It's coming from one of the bedrooms. Someone else has been left behind in the evacuation.

I push the door open. There's Eli, strapped to his bed, extra tight, the way Kelly does it. Whatever sedatives he's been given have worn off. He's struggling like a cocooned moth but can't break free.

'Timothy,' he says, seeing me. 'Thank God.'

The fire alarm keeps wailing as I approach the bed. The straps are as neat as ribbon around a Christmas gift.

'Get me out of this, will you?' Eli says.

I've never seen his bare feet before. The toes are plump and pink. I squeeze one.

'What the hell, man? Untie me!'

I run my fingers up his leg, feeling the muscles under his clothes. He's warm. His taut belly, his soft pectorals, his neck, bulging with veins. His sweat is cloying. Soon my hand reaches his face. The cheek is one of the silkiest parts of the human body. I pinch it gently, watching it blush.

His eye—his real eye—is wide with terror. 'Jesus,' he says. 'Please, don't.' Don't *what*, he doesn't say. Doesn't know.

I can hear Harmony coming, her shoes slapping the floor.

I lean down and open wide. Letting him feel my hot breath on his face.

Then I clamp my jaws shut.

Not on him. Just on the air.

Because I feel nothing. I know what I *would* have wanted to do to him in the past. But I don't think I want that anymore. I can choose not to.

Eli stares, uncomprehending.

'You know what?' I say. 'I think I'm cured.'

I walk out into the corridor to meet Harmony. My smile fades as I see her.

Because it's not Harmony. It's Ariel Wilcox, the CIA agent.

She's pointing a gun at me.

CHAPTER 38

My life begins
above the ground.
What am I?

I raise my hands. But because I only have one, it just looks like I'm asking a question.

Ariel's clothes are so nondescript that she might have typed *plain-clothes agent* into a search bar and bought whatever came up. Dark green slacks, a grey jacket, a black baseball cap. She's wearing the kind of glasses you see in drugstores, and they don't distort her eyes at all. Not corrective lenses, just a disguise.

'Ariel,' I say. 'Thank God you're here.'

Her lip twitches. She doesn't lower the gun. 'Glad I found you. Come with me.'

Kobald discovered the fake letter bomb less than half an hour ago. Wilcox must already have been waiting outside when the alarms went off. No time to wonder why.

I think through my list of options. It doesn't take long. I can run, and she'll shoot me in the back. I can throw a marker pen at her—it's the only thing in my pocket— and I might just get it airborne before she shoots me in the front. Or I can go with her, and get shot in the privacy of an unmarked van. No version of events ends with me alive, which is the point. The CIA has finally decided that I'm a liability.

'Your colleague already debriefed me,' I say, stalling.

'What colleague?'

If she thinks I've talked, she'll need to keep me alive so she can find out who else she needs to kill. 'Big guy,' I say. 'White, thirties, stubble, one eye.'

These are just the first details that come to mind. I'm not deliberately describing Eli. But he must *think* I am, must be listening, because he shouts, 'Hey! Who's out there?'

Wilcox's head snaps towards the door. I take advantage of the momentary distraction to throw the pen at her face. She ducks and shoots at the same time, but I'm already running, at an angle, towards a spot three feet to her right. The bullet misses me, cracking against the doorway behind. I change direction, back towards her, and before she can pull the trigger again, I kick her in the groin. She grunts and crumples, loosing another shot at the same time. This time the bullet would have hit my arm, if I still had an arm to hit, but instead the muzzle flash just burns the side of my chest through my clothes. I swing a punch at her head, but she's faster, lurching forward under the blow, and karate-chopping the side of my knee with her free hand. My leg folds, and I'm down.

Wilcox scrambles up and backs away, raising the gun. As she lines it up with my face, I go through my options again, which now takes no time at all.

She pulls the trigger—

But only depresses it halfway before Harmony slams a fistful of keys into the back of her neck.

The agent's skull jerks so hard that her glasses pop off, and she hits the floor. Harmony wrenches her fist back, tugging the keys free. There's blood on the blades, and a row of holes in the back of Wilcox's neck. The agent squirms slowly, like she's trying to get up but is glued to the floor.

Harmony is breathing heavily.

'You okay?' I ask, though it feels like she should be the one asking that question.

'Yeah,' she says, not taking her eyes off the fallen agent. 'I found the keys.'

'I see that.'

'Who's this?'

'CIA agent. I guess I've been . . .' I try to remember the term.

'Burned,' Harmony says.

'Right. Burned.'

'We should finish her off.' Harmony reaches for the agent's gun.

'Don't.' I kick it out of reach.

'Why not?' Harmony is bug-eyed, quaking from the adrenaline.

I'm not going to stick around and treat Wilcox's wounds, but I'm not going to bear witness to an execution either. I'm not even going to nibble on the body. That part of my life is over.

'No time to explain,' I say. 'Come on.'

•

We sprint downhill across the grass. The ER is just ahead. There's a parking garage beyond it. I know the ambulances are kept there, but I don't know how well guarded they'll be. Hopefully everyone will be distracted by the bomb threat.

'I'll drive,' I say, as we run.

Harmony keeps hold of the keys, still slick with Wilcox's blood. 'Why?'

'The Company has my face on file.' It's hard to lie while I'm so out of breath. 'Any time a photo of me is wirelessly transmitted, they send out interference to block the signal. But you'll need to stay out of sight in the footwell on the passenger side.'

'Haven't you been burned?'

I spit on the ground, panting. 'Takes weeks to update the database.'

Harmony buys this. We slow down as we approach the hospital's emergency entrance, and she tosses me the keys. I catch them. Not even tempted to lick the blades. Diaz deserves the Nobel Prize for Medicine.

We're only fifty feet away when an ambulance pulls up in front of the ER. Two paramedics climb out, hurry around to the back and open it up. They pull out a gurney, the legs unfolding as it emerges, a wheezing patient tied to it with a mask covering her face. Bad luck for her. Good luck for us.

I rifle through the keys until I find the one with a sticker that matches the licence plate of the ambulance. As the paramedics push the gurney into the hospital I start running again, trying to get to the ambulance before Harmony does. I push the button on the key as I run. The lights flash and the doors click. I wrench open the door, climb up into the driver's seat and close the door again. Then I hit the other button on the keys, locking the vehicle.

Harmony hurries around to the passenger side. I hear her pulling uselessly at the handle. 'Timothy!' she calls. 'My door is locked!'

I put the key into the ignition and turn it. The engine grumbles to life, but I can't move the shifter out of park. I remember from my FBI days that some police vehicles are fitted with an anti-theft device—the stick won't move unless you touch a hidden lever near the brake. I feel around, and the ambulance has the same one. I release it, and shift into drive.

'Timothy!' Harmony is jumping up and down. I can only see the top of her head, bouncing in and out of view. 'Open the door!'

The guilt twists in my guts.

'Timothy!' she shouts.

'Sorry, Harmony,' I say. 'You're not coming.'

'What?!'

'You have to stay here.'

'Son of a *bitch*!' she screams. Her fist slams against the glass. 'You're one of *them*!'

'The doctors can help you. I can't. Step back so I can drive.'

Plus, there's a good chance that I'll be dead by sunset. If she comes with me, she's likely to die, too.

'Open this door!' She kicks it so hard that the ambulance rocks on its suspension.

'Hey! You!' One of the paramedics is back, sprinting towards the ambulance, gripping his own set of keys.

I release the park brake. The ambulance starts rolling. Harmony steps back just in time—I see her in the side mirror, staring after me with betrayal in her eyes. The paramedic runs down the hill after me, but the ambulance is gaining speed and he has no hope of catching up. Soon he realises it and slows to a jog, then a walk, as he shouts into the radio on his lapel.

I zoom down the hill, circling the hospital campus. The crowd of psych patients is visible, fifty yards away. I bow my head, even though they're unlikely to notice that the driver is me at that distance.

The security perimeter from the bomb threat is up ahead. Someone has blocked the road with two-by-fours on steel stands, painted yellow and black, with the words *ROAD CLOSED*. There's no other way through—trees have been planted on either side of the road. Two security guards stand on the blacktop, guns or maybe tasers on their hips. I can see more in the distance, blocking off other parts of the hospital. The police will be on their way, too.

I slow down, taking my hand off the wheel and stabbing at the buttons on the dash until I find the siren. The wail is deafening—I don't know how paramedics can think clearly enough to drive. The light bar is going, too. I can see it reflected in the sunglasses of the security guards on either side of the blockade.

I hold my breath. I'm hoping they'll instinctively move the barrier for an emergency vehicle. If they don't, I'll have to ram it, and I don't know what kind of damage that will do to the ambulance. I won't get far with a busted tyre.

One of the security guards moves towards the barrier, but the other blocks him. There's an animated discussion. I stop the ambulance about twenty feet away, not sure what to do.

I see something move from the corner of my eye and turn to look at the crowd of patients gathered near the Behavioural Health Unit. Most of them are looking at the ambulance with the screaming siren. But three people aren't. Dr Diaz, and two men I don't recognise.

Grey jackets. Black baseball caps. More plain-clothes agents. I should have guessed that Wilcox didn't come alone.

The agents are gesturing, asking Diaz questions, pointing at the group of patients and then at the psych ward. I can't see their faces well enough to read their lips, but I can imagine what they're saying. *Timothy Blake. National security.* Diaz's face gets more and more alarmed as she listens.

The guards are still deciding whether to move the barrier. 'Come on,' I mutter and give them a quick blast from the horn.

The noise draws the attention of Diaz and the two agents. They all look at me.

As Diaz recognises me in the driver's seat of the ambulance, I can see the moment she realises everything I told her was true. That I really was recruited by the CIA. That I really did come here undercover. That she's had a cannibal in her office this whole time.

The look of horror transforms her normally calm face. It's the same expression you see in photos of people stumbling away from the wreckage of the Twin Towers, people whose whole world had just turned inside out. The look of someone realising their safe, comfortable life was just an illusion—that they've been in hell alongside the devil this whole time.

The two CIA agents produce handguns from their jackets and sprint towards me. One of the patients screams.

The security guards are finally dragging the barrier aside, but too slowly. I floor the accelerator. The ambulance lurches forwards. There's a *thunk, thunk* noise from behind me as two bullets hit the rear doors. Low. The agents are aiming for the tyres.

The security guards both leap aside and take cover as the ambulance clips the edge of the barrier, sending it flying. I hear a headlight crunch. Then I'm out, zooming onto the main road, hurtling towards the Loop.

I thought I'd be able to do seventy the whole way, but it doesn't work like that. Even with the siren screaming, I have to slow down at every intersection, making sure I don't get T-boned by some driver with their stereo way up. No signs of pursuit yet, but I'm sure the ambulance is LoJacked. The police will be able to track it via cell towers and GPS.

Soon I'm on a long, straight road, away from any heavy traffic. I let go of the wheel and push more buttons at random. Eventually I find the emergency radio frequency. Amid the usual chatter about fires, domestic disturbances and robberies, I hear a report about shots fired at the George Clark Red Memorial Hospital. A suspect fled the scene in a stolen ambulance. It's implied but not stated that I was the one shooting.

There are reports of the stolen ambulance hurtling east on the I-9, towards Louisiana—but I'm actually going west. The CIA must be keeping the police off my trail, so they can dispose of me without any witnesses. I don't have long. I take the wheel again and concentrate on driving.

Forty minutes later I screech into a driveway not far from the safe house. I jump out of the ambulance and run the rest of the way. Soon I'm pounding on the front door. 'Zara! It's me.'

This is a risk. If she's still loyal to the CIA, she might open fire when I walk in. But I'm pretty sure she's been burned, like I have. That's why Wilcox was at the hospital, tying up loose ends.

No answer. I try the door. Locked.

I circle around the back and break in through the kitchen window. Everything is just as I left it. Sawdust around the front door to show prints. The mugs positioned just so on the kitchen counter. Power tools scattered around—drills, a nail gun, a saw. The builders could come back at any moment.

'Zara?' I call.

The house suffocates my voice, burying it. It's the kind of silence that can only mean absence or death.

I check the bedrooms. The bathroom. All the cupboards. My stuff is still here, but Zara's isn't. She's gone—in the wind, in CIA parlance.

I change my clothes and grab what I can fit in my pockets. My wallet, my key to this house, my watch, and the wig and the moustache, though I don't have time to put them on right now. The CIA rushed the operation at the hospital, so the possibility that they've planted trackers in any of my belongings is vanishingly small. My phone is easy to track, so I drop it into the toilet.

The auto-injector full of fake blood isn't hidden in my clothes anymore. It's lying on the bed, in the open. Zara must have found it, and left it behind for me to take. Why?

Not to track—if she'd planted a microdot on it, she would have left the auto-injector in its hiding place. Is it a gift? An apology?

I drop it into my pocket.

As I walk out the front door, I hesitate in the doorway. Even with Zara's stuff gone, her presence lingers. A perfume in the air, so faint that I might be imagining it. I shake it off and leave, locking the door behind me.

I run back to the ambulance, get in, and drive it to the nearest strip mall. Once I'm there, I put on the wig and moustache before I climb out. Leave the ambulance parked behind a grocery store, the key still in the door. Sooner or later someone will take it for a joyride, assuming they find the hidden lever. The Company can chase them instead of me for a while.

I hail a cab. It takes a few attempts, because I still look poor. I keep my lips shut to hide my chipped teeth, but there's nothing I can do about the sun-damaged skin. Eventually someone stops, and I tell him to take me to the nearest Greyhound station. He does. I pay cash and let him see me walk inside before he drives off.

It's not exactly bustling. A man is sleeping on a bench, two young women chat in hushed voices, and a cashier reads a magazine behind the pay window. I walk into the bathroom, which smells of piss and tobacco. No one's in there. I pull off the wig and moustache and rearrange my clothes so I'm wearing my shirt over the top of my jacket, which gives me a bulkier silhouette. I walk out looking homeless.

Despite this, it's easier to hail a cab the second time. Plenty of them are hanging around the bus station. I tell the new driver to take me to the Johnson Space Center.

It's a big fare, so he demands payment upfront. I give him the last of my cash. Looking pleased, he zooms out into traffic.

I look out the window. The sun hasn't set yet. Hopefully Sam Garcia will still be at the complex. If he's gone home already, I don't know what I'll do. It seems unlikely that I'll live to see another sunrise.

'You work here?' the cab driver asks me, when we approach the security gate, angling to make this a regular arrangement.

'Not for much longer,' I say, and leave it at that.

At the gate, the guard with the blue eyes and the crow's-feet approaches us. Spence.

I buzz down the window.

'Haven't seen you in a while,' she says.

'Yeah.' I realise I don't even know what day it is. Hopefully not Saturday, or Garcia won't be here. I won't last until Monday.

'Well, I'm sorry,' Spence says. 'But you got taken off the after hours visitors list.'

I take a gamble. 'I have an appointment with Sam Garcia. You can call him to confirm.'

Spence chews her lip for a moment, then backs away, so she can use her radio without me overhearing.

The cab driver is looking increasingly uneasy.

'You might get another fare out of me,' I tell him. 'It's a long way back to my hotel.'

He perks up a bit.

Spence comes back. 'Open the trunk, sir.'

The driver pushes the button. Spence examines the inside, then sweeps her stick mirror around, checking the undercarriage. 'All right,' she says finally, and hauls the gate open.

As we drive towards the Atmospheric Research Unit, the cab driver says hopefully, 'Perhaps you'll need a ride home later?'

I'd like to think so, but I'd be kidding myself. 'The odds are against that,' I tell him.

•

The receptionist with all the piercings isn't there. I don't sign the register, but I take one of the free pens. It's not much of a weapon, but it worked on Wilcox. And it's free.

Sam Garcia's door is open. He looks worse than when I saw him last. Bags under his eyes, his head bowed over the desk. He's lost a little weight, though he's still a big guy. Big enough to leave those footprints I saw in the field the first time I came here. I should have guessed it was him immediately. This could all have been over on day one. But I was thrown, because the video alibied him for Rob Cho's death, and because he seemed to genuinely believe in the Chinese space station. The one I thought was an obvious lie.

He looks up. Sees me. His eyes are sad.

'Shut the door,' he says.

I do.

'You're CIA, aren't you?'

'I was,' I say. 'Now, not so much.'

He harrumphs, not believing me. For some reason people only seem to doubt me when I tell the truth. It's like an ironic curse from a Greek myth.

'I'm not the guy you're looking for,' Garcia says.

'I know.'

'You have to believe me. I swear I didn't . . .' He trails off, catching up with what I said. 'You know?'

'Most of it,' I say. 'I'm hoping you can tell me the rest.'

He scratches his head with one huge paw, like an anxious dog.

'You may as well,' I say. 'How much worse could things get?'

Actually, they could get a lot worse. But Garcia must be hurting, hiding the truth all this time. There's a pressure difference, like in the hypobaric chamber. A gap between the weight of his knowledge and the vacuum of the world's ignorance.

'I didn't kill Rob Cho,' he says.

'Right,' I said. 'But you killed Harold Broughton.'

His mouth contorts. His hands twitch on his desk.

'I kept wondering why a man would confess to kidnapping a girl he'd never met,' I continue. 'Now I know—it was because you'd committed a worse crime that you didn't want us to know about. If you'd told us where you really were, you would have gotten a lot more than seven years.'

Garcia is trembling in his chair. Angry? Scared?

'You realised your wife was having an affair.' I rub my shoulder. It's still sore from the fight with Wilcox. 'You were furious. You went to the mall to buy some rope, a ski mask and a gun. Then you go find the guy—I don't care how—get him drunk, and take him to the river. You make him put on a bathing suit at gunpoint. Then you tie him up and toss him in the water. Hold him under the water until the bubbles stop coming. After that, you stuff his body into the mangroves. You needed him to be found, or

Esmerelda would spend the rest of her life wondering what had happened to him. Pining, maybe. You can stop me at any time.'

Garcia is looking at my jacket, maybe wondering if I'm recording this conversation.

'Okay, fine. You bought the gun on the same day you killed him,' I say. 'That tells me this was a crime of passion. You didn't really think it through. Didn't even check which way the river ran. But, incredibly, it worked. I can imagine how lucky you felt, when the cops believed the drowning was an accident. When no one suspected you, not even your wife. And then, I can imagine how *unlucky* you felt, when you discovered that a twelve-year-old girl had gone missing from the mall at the same time you were there. That you were one of only three suspects. That your alibi was this: you were at the river, drowning a guy. So . . .' I wave my silicone hand. 'You confess and go to prison, but not for long, because the girl you supposedly kidnapped puts in a good word for you with the judge. Of course she does—you saved her life. If her father had found out she'd tried to run away, he would have killed her.'

I can see by the look on his face that Garcia hadn't known this. It must have been a mystery, all this time, why Lilah had lied.

'All this explains why you didn't call the cops when you found Cho's body in the hypobaric chamber,' I say. 'Because they wouldn't have looked at anyone but you. And then you would have ended up imprisoned for a crime you didn't commit, again. Right?'

Garcia gives the slightest of nods.

'But it doesn't explain why you stole a Chinese spacesuit,

put Cho in it, and then put him on Mars,' I go on. 'You must have known people would see through the ruse right away. There are a million better ways to make a death look like an accident. For all you knew, the death *was* an accident. Except he told you something, didn't he? Before he died. Something that made you realise it was murder, and who was responsible.' I lick my lips. 'I thought I had it figured out. I thought there was a Chinese spy here at the Space Center, and Rob found out about it, and he told his crazy sister. Then the spy killed him, and used his body to make it seem like there was a space station overhead. But I had the whole thing ass backwards, didn't I?'

Garcia finally speaks. 'The space station exists. Or something does. A satellite. I haven't seen it, but it's there.'

'I know,' I say.

Outside the window, thunder rumbles. A haze of rain creeps out from the darkening horizon.

'I grew up with this kid named Ritchie,' I say. 'Every time someone new came to live at the group home, he'd do a magic trick where he'd tell them to think of a card, any card. Then he'd show them that the only card in the box he was holding was the ace of spades. Most of the time he was wrong. But he did it with so many kids that eventually he was right with one of them. They thought it was magic, not just luck.

'Rob's sister has hundreds of conspiracy theories. I suppose it makes statistical sense that eventually one of them would turn out to be true. Like you said: on a long enough timescale, unlikely things become inevitable. The last time Rob went to visit Harmony, she told him her latest theory—that there was a secret Chinese space station over our heads, messing with the news. For once, this was a story Rob was in a position to check. He thought he could help her get better by proving her wrong. He knew that for a space station to be watching the USA day and night, it would have to be in geostationary orbit above the equator, probably right over Ecuador. So he asks you some casual questions about how to send signals to and from the telescope, then when no one's around, he scans a certain patch of sky—and holy shit. There *is* something up there.

'Rob was smart guy, and he understood cybersecurity. He knew that if no one had spotted this before, that meant there was malware in the network, periodically deleting any record of the space station from the automatic scans. And because the Space City network is air-gapped, that malware must have been installed in person, possibly by one of his colleagues. He wasn't sure who to trust. He took some time to think about it, because he didn't know that the malware had already sent a notification to the spy, warning them that he had done a manual scan and spotted the spacecraft.'

Garcia looks haunted now. His face crumples.

'Cho trusted you, though,' I say. 'You'd gone to college together. He was the only person you'd told about what really happened on the night of Lilah's kidnapping. You owed him for helping you get this job. But when he told you what he'd seen, you didn't believe him. Right?'

There are tears in Garcia's eyes. He opens his mouth, and the seal breaks. The pressure equalises. The whole story comes rushing out.

CHAPTER 39

*I surround you but keep my distance, with
no beginning and no end. What am I?*

Garcia tells me a lot of things I'd already worked out, and
a few things I hadn't.

Cho invited Garcia for beers on the rooftop after work.
Garcia accepted, even though it was a Monday. Cho was
a good friend. He knew Garcia was a murderer, but had
visited him in prison, watched his remorse grow, and
forgiven him.

Yet, when Cho told him there was a Chinese space
station circling the Earth, and a spy in Space City who had
installed malware to periodically erase it from the records,
and that his crazy sister had somehow known this, Garcia
hadn't believed a word. Not until the following night,
when he found Cho in the hypobaric chamber, bloated and
purple.

Garcia tried to give him CPR, but the body was already
cold and his oesophagus was packed with his own shredded
lungs. Cho had been murdered, horribly, by a Chinese
spy—but no one else would ever accept that. Garcia was
an ex-con, not to be trusted. His friend's death would be

written up as a bizarre accident, or Garcia himself would get the blame.

Maybe he was mad with grief. His plan, in retrospect, wasn't a sane one. But if China had done this, then Garcia was determined to make it backfire on them. He stole a Chinese spacesuit from the museum and dressed Cho in it. Garcia carried him halfway to Mars, and then, when the dead man became too heavy, he dragged him by the wrists. Then he left Cho on the dirt, staring up at the billions of stars that made up the night sky.

Garcia takes a deep breath. 'And that's pretty much it.'

'Really?'

He avoids my eye. 'Yeah. The next morning, the first person to arrive was Anders. When I saw him go into the parking lot, I went to my office, checked the sat feeds, saw what I knew I would see, and then told him to check it out.'

'Then you told the media.'

'Right. I wanted the story about the Chinese astronaut to be everywhere, so the whole thing would blow up in their faces.'

'Only a few dozen people were in the complex at the time of Cho's death,' I say. 'You seem like a guy who pays close attention to his team. You must have noticed one of those people behaving strangely.'

'*Everyone's* been behaving strangely,' Garcia says. 'A dead body in the field, Rob missing, cops and FBI and CIA everywhere, sabotage in Laurie's lab—it's been a madhouse here.'

I don't tell him that, in my experience, actual madhouses are much less chaotic than what he's describing.

'I thought it might be Laurie,' Garcia says. 'She vanished for a little while. But now she's back—apparently it was just an illness. If she was the spy, she wouldn't be back, right?'

Laurie's plan to hold her own research for ransom seems to have succeeded.

'The Chinese government went to a lot of trouble to hide whatever's up there,' I say. 'They told their asset to kill Rob Cho. When you called the media, they dumped a stealth plane into the ocean to make it look like it was a fighter pilot who fell out of the sky rather than an astronaut. They installed malware on the Space City network—and presumably on some other networks, right? Otherwise someone would have found the space station before now. This isn't the only place with a powerful telescope.'

Garcia nods.

'So whoever's behind this is highly capable. Is there anyone you work with who *hasn't* been acting oddly?'

Garcia thinks about this, then shrugs helplessly.

I close my eyes for a second, imagining I'm the killer. I sabotage the alarm in the hypobaric chamber. I trick Cho into going into the chamber. (How? Don't know. He's the cybersecurity chief—maybe I tell him it's been vandalised.) I trap him in there by blocking the door, and then hang a sign over the window. I steal Laurie's swipe card while she's in the pool. Then I go to an access terminal and use Laurie's card to activate the chamber. Zara said there was no video footage of the killer at the terminal, so I must have used one a fair way away. I return Laurie's card while she's still swimming. Then I go back to the hypobaric chamber, check that Cho is dead, and remove the sign and the blockage so no one realises he was trapped. Then I go home. Maybe I spend a sleepless night, wondering if I've forgotten something, or if I left a clue behind . . .

I open my eyes. 'Did anyone seem unusually tired the following day?'

Garcia frowns. 'Not that I remember.'

'Did anyone arrive at work earlier than usual?' Like they were anxious to check that the ruse had worked?

Garcia thinks about this. But I realise he's already given me the answer.

I think of the first time I saw the body. The anxious scientist hovering nearby, saying that a real astronaut would have burned up on re-entry, and trying to convince me that the writing on the flight suit was Japanese.

'I need to borrow your car,' I say. 'And your phone.'

•

Ten minutes later I'm wandering around the parking lot, looking for Garcia's brown Hyundai. It's dark now. No moon. The rain hasn't reached me yet but I can hear it, hissing in the distance. Thunder rumbles.

As I circle around, I dial Thistle's cell number from memory. The phone rings and rings in my ear.

'You've called Agent Reese Thistle. Leave your name and number.'

She's changed her voicemail message, by just a couple of words. She's always looking for ways to do things slightly better.

'Hey. I escaped from the mental hospital.' I laugh nervously. 'That's not a great start, is it? Not if I want you to believe me. But now I can't take it back. Story of my life. Anyway.' I clear my throat. 'I figured the whole thing out. Rob Cho was murdered by a NASA scientist named Franklin Anders, who's secretly working for Beijing. Cho had seen a Chinese spacecraft on a scan, and Anders killed him to cover it up. If he finds out that we know about it, he might come after us, too.'

I finally spot Garcia's car, parked all the way over on the far side of the lot. I break into a jog towards it.

'Garcia gave me Anders' address. I'm on my way there so I can . . .' Actually, I'm not sure what I'll do when I get there. Hopefully I'll find some way to prove his guilt. But if it comes down to hand-to-hand combat, I'm in real trouble.

'The point is,' I say, 'you should take some steps to protect yourself, in case I screw this up. Remember, he's not just one guy—he's got the Chinese Ministry of State Security behind him. Sweep your car for bugs and then go to a different field office, somewhere they won't think to look for you. Take a gun, and keep your phone switched off. Look . . .' I unlock Garcia's car as I approach. 'I'm really sorry I dragged you into this. I didn't mean to. I thought—' My throat closes up. 'I thought you were done with me, so it didn't matter if I threw my life away. I should have guessed my problems would end up being your problems.' I take a breath. 'I know you think I'm crazy. Can't say I blame you. But please, please—'

There's a beep. I check the screen. The call has ended. There must be a limit on how long a voicemail can be. Probably for the best. I delete the record of the call, just like Garcia did when he was pretending he hadn't contacted the media.

I unlock Garcia's car, climb in, and throw the phone onto the passenger seat. It's a fancier car than I'm used to.

When I start the engine, a warm, bassy stereo comes to life. The speed—currently 0 mp/h—is projected onto a little glass square that unfolds between me and the windshield. There's a warning beep, and a seatbelt symbol flashes. I buckle up and wait for the noise to stop.

Garcia has told me he'll stay in his office. He's safest there, for now. If the MSS comes after him, they'll want to get him somewhere private, like his home.

That damn beeping is still going. I squint at the message under the seatbelt symbol: *Fasten passenger seatbelt.*

I sit perfectly still. Acting natural. Wondering what to do.

Too late. Strong hands shoot out from behind me. A forearm locks across my throat, cutting off my air. A palm clamps down on my forehead, crushing me backwards against the seat. My heart hammers my ribs. I claw at the arm crushing my throat, but my attacker has anticipated this. He's wearing gloves, and a leather jacket.

I scrabble around like an upturned beetle for a while, and then manage to get my foot on the gas. I floor it. The engine screams, and the car moves forwards—but slowly. I haven't released the park brake. I flail around trying to reach it, but my real arm is on the wrong side, and releasing a park brake without a thumb is hard at the best of times. Instead, the car just screeches slowly towards the far side of the lot, smoke pouring from the engine.

My lungs are crying out for air. My vision tunnels. I swing the steering wheel sideways, trying to dislodge the killer.

The car swerves, and there's a thud from behind me as a human skull hits the window. But the killer hangs on, and worse than that, he adjusts his grip. Now he's got my artery clamped, not just my windpipe. I'll be unconscious in five seconds. Four.

I blast the horn, hoping to get the attention of someone, anyone. The response is a swift punch to my right ear. Three. It feels like I'm sinking, down through the seat cushions, through the undercarriage, into the tar beneath the vehicle.

Two. *Stay awake!* I tell myself.

One. *Fight it . . . Don't let . . . Don't . . .*

Zero.

CHAPTER 40

Which sport involves ladling soup?

I wake up on a hard floor under harsh lights. When I go to sit up, I try to put weight on my missing arm, and collapse again. My head is pounding and my throat is raw. I try to sit up again, and succeed this time. I blink until my eyes adjust, and find myself looking at a bowling ball and a feather, suspended from mechanical claws.

I'm in the hypobaric chamber.

I clamber to my feet, stagger over to the door, and try the handle. It turns, but the door won't budge. It's blocked from the outside, something heavy dragged in front of it. I ram the door with my shoulder, but it's like hitting a brick wall. The impact jars my neck and leaves my head spinning.

I get out Garcia's phone. No signal.

'Help!' I shout, because I can't think of anything else to do. I'm in exactly the same position Rob Cho was in, and he ended up as a bloated corpse. If a guy from NASA couldn't think of a way out of this, what hope do I have?

'Good,' a voice says. 'You're awake.'

The sound is coming from a hole in the wall, next to the door. Metal shavings are coiled on the floor beneath it.

This hole has been drilled recently. When I touch the edge, it's still hot.

I peer through it, and see a fragment of a mouth. A gold-capped tooth.

'Franklin Anders,' I say.

Silence for a moment. Then he says, 'I'm really sorry about this.'

'Is that what you told Rob Cho?'

Another pause, then he says, 'They said I'd only have to put a flash drive into my computer. They offered to pay for Emily's treatment. She was dying. What sort of father would say no?'

I remember what he said in the hospital: *There's nothing I wouldn't do for my daughter.*

'Then they told me to put Rob in this chamber and make it seem like an accident. I refused. So they . . .' He chokes. 'Someone at the hospital was working for them. Emily got the wrong medication. She stopped breathing for seven and a half minutes. They said if I didn't kill Rob, it would happen again, and this time there'd be no bringing her back.'

He wants me to forgive him for my own murder. I'm not going to.

'The CIA can protect you,' I say. 'And Emily.' Hopefully he doesn't realise I've been burned.

'There's no way to hide from these people.' His voice hardens. 'Tell me what you know.'

Anders has compromised the seal of the hypobaric chamber to have this conversation. There's no speaker in here, and no signal, so I guess he didn't have a choice. Being an atmospheric composition analyst, he probably knows what he's doing. He could plug the hole at any time, perhaps by putting a steel plate over it. Then he could flick the switch to depressurise the chamber, and the negative pressure would hold the plate in place while I suffocate.

'You really got the drop on me in that parking lot,' I say. Running my mouth, while my brain works on the problem. 'Pretty embarrassing. I won't tell anyone if you don't?'

Anders refuses to be distracted. 'Tell me what you know.'

'And then you'll let me out of here, right?'

'No,' he says. 'But I won't depressurise the chamber. I'll just leave you here. Someone will find you and let you out tomorrow morning. I'll be long gone by then.'

He's lying. I'm a dead man. There's no way out of this. But I can save Thistle, if I'm smart.

'No offence,' I say, 'but what assurances do I have that—'

'None. You'll just have to trust me.'

'You play hardball, huh?' My throat feels like it's stuffed with sandpaper. 'Okay. Can you fit a permanent marker through that hole?'

'Why?'

The free pens in my pocket aren't permanent. 'So I can write your name on my skin,' I say. 'That way, if anything were to happen to me, the police wouldn't have any trouble identifying my killer. You understand.'

There's another pause, just long enough for Anders to think he's outsmarted me. The police will never see my body—I'll be buried in a deep grave or sunk to the bottom of Galveston Bay. It won't matter what's written on my skin.

'Deal,' he says.

A minute later, a thin marker pen emerges through the hole. I remove the cap. I write Anders' name on my belly in big, obvious writing. Then I write a message to Thistle on my right shin, and roll down the cuff of my pants to cover it. The message says, *Call Reese Thistle at FBI. Tell her there's an MSS asset at JSC: Franklin Anders.*

I already told Thistle this in my voicemail, but Anders doesn't know that. After he kills me, he'll read what I've written on my leg, and assume I never got the chance to share the information. He won't see Thistle as a threat. He'll dump my body, and leave her alone.

It's too late to save myself. But hopefully this message will save her.

'Okay.' I put the cap on the marker and drop it into my pocket. 'You want to know what I know?'

'That's correct.'

'Okay.' I take a deep breath, and get ready to lie my ass off. 'Rob Cho discovered you were working for the Chinese government. Maybe he heard you on the phone to your handler, or something—I don't know that part. So you trapped him in this chamber, and stole Laurie's card so you could activate it remotely without getting caught. You wanted the death to look like an accident. But then Garcia found the body.' There's a chance Anders already knows this, and even if he doesn't, I'm willing to sacrifice Garcia, if that's what it takes to save Thistle. 'Garcia must have already suspected there was an MSS asset here, because he did everything he could to implicate China in Cho's death. He stole a Chinese spacesuit from the museum, put it on the body, and dumped it somewhere public, hoping to expose the asset in the resulting chaos. You recognised Cho but pretended not to, because your masters decided to pretend he was a fighter pilot.' I shrug, even though he can't see me. 'Have I missed anything?'

Like the best lies, this story is ninety per cent true, but missing a few key details. Anders has noticed the most important omission: 'How did Cho find out about the spy satellite?'

So it's a satellite, not a space station. 'What spy satellite?'

I can't read the silence from the other side of the hole. I have to convince him of this. The MSS has ordered Anders to kill me either way, but if they think I know about their secret spacecraft, they'll also kill anyone I might have told. A long list of people that includes Thistle.

Anders still hasn't said anything.

'Garcia dumped the body,' I say. 'He only made it *look* like it fell from space. There's nothing up there. You get that, right?'

'Stop bullshitting me,' Anders says. 'I know you know about the satellite.'

He's bluffing. 'There is no satellite,' I say. 'I talked to Garcia—it's impossible. OPIR would pick it up.'

'I'm going to push the button,' he warns.

'Don't!' I try to sound panicked. It's not hard. 'I'm telling you the truth!'

There's another long silence. Then a clack. I peer through the hole again, but this time I see only darkness. He's covered it with a steel plate.

I've convinced him I don't know anything important. Now he's going to kill me.

'I'm telling the truth!' I scream, because that's what he'd expect. It's what I would do if I really had told him everything. I need to keep the act going, right up until I'm dead.

There's a hissing sound, like a snake. A breeze tickles my arm hairs as the air is sucked from the chamber. My ears pop. There's a pressure in my sinuses, getting more and more painful. I pinch my nose between my knuckles, trying to equalise.

Stumbling towards the window, I pound on the glass. Anders is over by one of the computer terminals, not looking in my direction. He doesn't want to watch me die.

'Let me out!' I shout. He shows no sign that he can hear me. Even in here the words sound muffled, either because my ears are already damaged, or because there's not enough air in the chamber to carry the sound.

Steam rises from my flesh like I'm being cooked, though there's no heat. Every instinct screams at me to hold my breath, but when Cho did that, his lungs exploded. I force myself to exhale, letting the chamber take the air. Feeling the terrifying emptiness in my chest. The saliva boils off my tongue. I'm already getting dizzy.

Cho's decompression happened so quickly that his blood bubbled. Mine seems to be taking longer, perhaps because of the damage Anders did to the wall. This will be a slow, agonising death.

I wish I was the kind of person who could go peacefully to his grave. Who could accept that he did his best, even though it wasn't enough.

But that's not me. Even as I get too dizzy to stand, and collapse, my brain is still churning through ideas. There has to be a way out of this. Has to be.

I reach into my pocket—and find something better than a pen.

The auto-injector. The fucking auto-injector is still there!

I dig it out and hold it up to the light with a shaking hand. It's still full, Laurie's lifesaving formula sloshing back and forth inside. I use my teeth to roll up my sleeve.

I've never injected myself with anything before, but I've seen plenty of executions. I know where to put the needle. My veins are already bulging, maybe because of the reduced pressure—but it's going to be hard to do this one-handed, especially when I'm so woozy. I could pass out at any moment.

I bend my wrist forwards, like I'm making a shadow puppet of a swan, so the tip of the needle is against my forearm and the plunger is against my fingertips. Then I push. There's a sharp sting as the needle enters the vein. Laurie's formula floods into my bloodstream.

Like magic, the dizziness starts to fade. My head clears. I heard somewhere that it takes less than a minute for blood to travel the whole way around the body, but I never believed it before now.

Laurie said her formula would keep an astronaut conscious for sixteen minutes. It's hard to think—the pain from my eardrums is agonising. With nothing in my lungs, I still can't equalise. I chew the tip off one of my silicone fingers and stuff it into my right ear. I plug the left with a human fingertip. It helps, a little.

There seems to be no air at all, now. My skin feels like it's being pinched all over. Looking down, I see my body reddening, roasted by the negative pressure. I look delicious. But my vision is blurring. I squeeze my eyelids shut. My lips seem puffy, like I'm allergic to the vacuum.

My lungs burn. I'm still trying to keep them deflated. It's nauseating and surreal, being unable to breathe but somehow staying conscious.

Anders has no hope of disguising my death as an accident. Unlike Rob Cho, I have no reason to be in the chamber, with messages scrawled on my skin. Anders won't leave me overnight to be found by someone else—he'll open the door to collect my body as soon as he's sure I'm dead.

I lie on my side and curl into a ball, heart thudding, the syringe clenched in my fist. The needle is tiny, but it's the only weapon available.

Or is it?

Through half-closed eyelids, I look up at the bowling ball. The only sport you can play with three fingers. I stand up, wrap my arm around it, and wrench it free of the dangling claw. The metal tines snap shut. I lie back down, facing away from the window, hugging the ball to my chest. Then I wait, eyes squeezed shut. My heart is thudding like a panicked animal in a cage.

My ears hurt. My lungs hurt. Everything hurts. I'd be sobbing with pain, except that I can't breathe. Instead I lie frozen on the floor.

I assume I've only got a few more minutes before the life-saving chemicals in my blood run out. What if Anders decides to leave me here for an hour, just to be on the safe side?

I can't take this. I find myself *wishing* the oxygen in my brain would run dry, so I'd lose consciousness. I'm in hell, unable to breathe but unable to die. I lie there for a horrifying minute. Then two. Then three. And then—

A hissing sound. It's probably very loud, but to my damaged ears, it's faint. I would assume I was imagining it, except the pain from my sinuses has begun to retreat. The chamber is repressurising.

I'm desperate to breathe, but I don't move a muscle. Anders is probably watching through the window. If I even twitch, he'll just hit the button again, and suffocate me some more. I just lie there, playing the role of a corpse. Giving the performance of a lifetime.

I don't hear the door open, but I feel it—the air rushing in, ruffling my hair. I still don't move.

The floor vibrates. *Thrum, thrum.* Footsteps coming towards me.

A shadow falls across my closed eyelids.

I uncoil like a spring, and swing the bowling ball at Anders as hard as I can. My vision is still blurry, so I don't see his expression—just the flash of movement as he leaps back, startled.

He doesn't get far enough. The bowling ball hits his ankle with a satisfying *crack*, hard enough to take the whole leg out from under him. He cries out, falls, hits the ground next to me.

I drop the ball, scramble to my feet and head for the open door. Something grabs my leg. I shake it off and keep running. Anders' ankle must not be broken, because a second later he's right behind me—I only realise that when his arm snakes around my throat, like he's planning to choke me out again. But he's taken off the jacket, so I dip my chin and take a bite out of his forearm. He shrieks and lets go. I flee through the door, finally out of the chamber and into the museum.

I swerve right, towards the main exit, but only make it a couple of steps before Anders trips me. I sprawl across the shiny floor, spitting blood and flesh. I roll over in time to see him raising a leg to stomp my lights out.

Listen to me, I shout, without a clear idea of what I want him to listen to, just hoping some more convincing bullshit will come out of my mouth. *Just listen!* I can't even hear myself. One of my eardrums feels ruined.

Anders doesn't listen. He drives his shoe down at my face. I grab it and shove him backwards. As he stumbles away, I stand up again—but a second later he's back in my face, a wild-eyed madman, swinging punches. For the third time tonight his fist crashes into my ear. The world spins and I stagger sideways. I hit the door frame of the hypobaric chamber, ending up half-in, half-out of it.

Seeing this, Anders quickly slams his palm down on the depressurise button. Suddenly air is rushing past my skin, and the massive door is swinging closed, about to crush me, or cut me in half.

I leap aside and snatch my arm out of the gap just in time. The door slams shut, and I don't lose even a fingernail. By my standards, this fight is going well.

Anders swings another wild punch. I dodge aside, and his fist bangs against the steel outer shell of the chamber. He snarls and spins towards me again. I go to kick him inside the knee, but he's faster—he drives a knee into my balls, and I feel the shock all the way up to my stomach. I find myself falling into him. I grab part of his body for support, and it turns out to be his face. We fall together, me forwards, him backwards, and I shove his head against the steel outer shell—right over the drill hole.

I don't hear his skull crack against the metal, but I can feel it. Something gives way, and his whole body goes rigid like a bow that just loosed an arrow, but the back of his head stays against the wall, glued by the negative pressure. His face twists against my palm, a scream making my whole arm vibrate, but then he goes suddenly limp.

After a moment, I let go. His body stays in place, his skull fixed to the wall. I tap the side of his head. His cranium feels as hollow as a gourd.

I peer in the window. The walls of the hypobaric chamber are pink and grey, sprayed with Anders' brilliant brain. Hard to know what the police will make of this. I plan to be gone before they get here.

I look back at Anders. His face is slack now. His eyes are sad. Air whistles quietly through his nose, an endless inward breath, like he's preparing to shout at me. Actually, the whistling probably isn't quiet. I'm still ninety-nine per cent deaf.

He sold out his country, and killed Rob Cho, and tried to kill me. But he did it because he loved his child, and didn't want to let her go. I know what that's like.

'Sorry,' I mutter.

Then I take the cash out of his wallet, because I'm like that.

CHAPTER 41

Who murdered the Cheerios?

Zara looks different when she walks in the door of the safe house. Her hair is shorter, and dyed grey. She's wearing a baggy dress, rather than the flesh-hugging clothes she usually favours. She might even have a new name now.

She's startled when she sees me sitting on the floor in the corner. But she hides it quickly.

'Blake,' she says. 'You're okay!'

She sounds like she's underwater. But my eyesight has recovered well enough to read her lips.

'I knew you'd be back,' I say. 'You left my things behind.'

'When I heard about what happened at the hospital, I was so worried . . .' As she talks, she rummages through her handbag. She takes out her wallet, her keys, her phone— and something else that I don't get a good look at before it disappears into the folds of her dress.

Fine. She's not the only one hiding a weapon.

'Oh my God.' She's noticed the purple stain all over my body. 'What happened?'

'Wilcox said the CIA had accidentally recruited a serial killer,' I say. 'I was offended, because sure, I've killed people, but only in self-defence. But she wasn't talking about me, was she?'

Zara falls silent.

'The stranglings corresponded with places I had been. But of course, they were places you had been, too. Once I realised that, I wondered if you were trying to frame me. But you weren't, were you? It's just something you need to do. You've always enjoyed risks. You like to go right up to the edge of the cliff, and imagine yourself stepping off. When that got boring, you started pushing other people over the edge.'

'I've never pushed anyone off a cliff.' Zara sounds both confused and wistful.

'Your work sends you all over the world,' I say. 'It gives you access to petabytes of personal data. You use it to find people who are vulnerable. Women who won't be able to overpower you, who live alone, who won't be missed for a couple of days. People with cancer—you tell yourself they're dying anyway. Then you go to their homes and strangle them. You like to watch the lights go out in their eyes. To imagine what it must be like for them, crossing that boundary.'

Some people would find this hard to imagine. I don't. I would have seen it far earlier, if not for the distraction of the mess at Space City.

'Blake,' she says warily. 'I don't know who you've been talking to, but they're lying.'

'Imagine you're a branch chief at the CIA,' I say. 'You realise one of your agents is murdering people—the wrong people. Unauthorised people. She'll get caught sooner or later, and you can't let her go to jail, because she has too much classified intel in her brain. So you send her on a recon mission to LA—and assign one of your other agents to poison her drink.'

'It's not what you think.' She's approaching me. Slowly.

'But the plan went wrong,' I say. 'I saved your life at the last minute, so the branch chief put your assassination on the back burner. When a body showed up at Space City, one that seemed connected to China, he sent you, hoping that would help him identify your asset in Shanghai. He wanted to keep running that asset after you were dead.

'Forget all that for a second, though. When we realised someone had stolen Laurie's swipe card and used it to kill Rob Cho, I asked you which terminal they used. You checked it out, and discovered that it was the terminal in Anders' office. We'd both seen the footage of him using the computer in there at the time of Cho's death. So you passed that along to your superiors, who presumably started surveilling Anders to try to work out who his handler was. Case closed.

'You didn't need me to talk to Harmony Cho at all. You already knew Anders was the killer. But you told me there was no video of the terminal he'd used. You convinced me that you needed my help. You dumped me in that mental hospital to get me out of the way—because the branch chief had already ordered you to kill me, hadn't he?'

'Blake,' Zara begins. 'I—'

'It makes sense,' I say. 'I knew too much, I was too unpredictable, and if the branch chief had their way, you weren't going to be around for much longer to keep me on the leash. But you choked. You couldn't bring your-self to kill me. Instead, you put me in a hospital, where the CIA would be unlikely to notice me. Where I could live out the rest of my days in peace, *thinking* I was on a top-secret mission.'

'I did that because I—'

'Because you love me.'

Zara falls silent.

'That's why you're here,' I continue. 'You've been visiting the safe house every day since I escaped, hoping I'd come back. You even left me a present—Laurie's formula, which you should have handed over to the brass. You love me. And it's driving you crazy, isn't it? You *hate* loving me. It makes you feel powerless.'

Zara's eyes are glossed with tears. This whole time I thought she was acting, but I don't think she is. She genuinely believes I'm a 'like-minded individual'. Someone who can save her, the way Thistle saved me.

'I didn't want things to turn out like this,' she says.

'Which part?' I ask. 'All those murdered women? Ruciani? The CIA trying to kill us both?'

'You and me.' Her voice cracks. 'I didn't want to be separated from you. But it was the only way to keep you safe.'

I think of the hospital. Diaz poisoning me with drugs. Eli trying to cut my eye out. Wilcox trying to shoot me.

'Safe,' I repeat.

'But now you're out,' Zara says. 'And I'm not with the Company anymore. I have passports and bank accounts they don't know about. There's a beautiful village called Gondal, forty miles out of Islamabad—just wait until you see the mountains. We can be together there.'

'Until you get bored with me,' I say.

She smiles through the tears. 'Don't you get it? *I'm never bored with you.*'

'Neither of us is going anywhere, Zara. I called 911 as soon as you walked in the door.' I reach behind my back and take out Garcia's phone. Hold it up so she can see that the call is still connected. The dispatcher is listening to all of this.

I put the phone on the floor. 'The Houston PD will be here any minute.'

Zara's smile slips, but only a little. She's coming closer. 'They'll never catch us. Not if we leave now.'

'I'm not coming with you.' I reach behind my back again.

'I wasn't asking.' She extends her left hand and strokes my cheek. Her fingers are soft, cool, kind. Her right hand dips into the folds of her dress.

I twist my head aside. Her right hand comes out holding a taser, the needles already crackling. But her left has slipped off my cheek. As she braces herself against the wall, palm flat, I slam the nail gun against her hand and pull the trigger.

Zara screeches as the steel spike pierces her hand and thunks deep into the wall. I drop the gun and scramble out of the way just in time to avoid a swing of the taser. She swipes at me again, but I'm beyond her reach.

'Goddamn it,' she snarls through gritted teeth. She gives her hand a tug, and then squeals—it's firmly fixed. I watch her squirm for a moment, a pinned butterfly.

'Don't you get it?' she snaps. 'We're the same, you and me!'

I look at her, half-crucified in the half-built living room.

'We could be so happy together!' she sobs.

'Goodbye, Zara,' I say.

'Timothy! Wait!'

I walk out the door. The sirens are coming from some-where to my left, or maybe they just seem to be because that's my good ear. I turn right, and slip away into the dark.

CHAPTER 42

Lay your fingers on me to make a word,
a tune, or an entrance. What am I?

The manager of the motel looks at my bruised skin and
my missing arm, and says nothing for a minute. Maybe
they have a policy against admitting one-armed purple
people eaters.

Finally she says something. With my busted ear, I can
only make out the word 'deposit'. I push all of Anders' cash
under the grimy glass panel, sign a form, and accept a light-
weight key with a heavy fob.

When I unlock room eleven, it's not unlike the room
Zara and I stayed in, back when the police were after us.
After her, I now realise. Not me. Part of me had worried
that I would miss her, but I don't. At least, not yet.

There are two single beds. I wouldn't want to shine a
blacklight on either one. I collapse onto the bed furthest
from the door without even taking my shoes off.

I sleep for ten hours, and wake up when someone knocks
on the door. I croak, 'Go away,' and they do. Daylight
streams through the cheap curtains. I ignore it. I drink
some water, and use the bathroom. There's blood in my

urine. It's possible that being trapped in a vacuum wasn't great for my organs.

I go back to bed, and sleep for another ten hours.

It's two days before I'm hungry enough to leave the motel room. There's a diner on the corner. I buy a cheeseburger, and then look at it for a while. The pink-flecked grey patty looks like Anders' brain. I eat the fries and the bun, leaving the meat untouched. When I get back to the motel, the pillow is encrusted with blood from my ear. I flip it and sleep some more.

I dream that I'm conducting repairs on the lens of a camera on a secret space station. Then I lose my grip and fall down, down, down towards the Earth, trying and failing to swim upwards through the void.

After a couple of days my ears start to itch, like termites are burrowing into them. I guess that means my eardrums are healing, but soon the itching is so bad that I can't sleep. I switch on the TV instead, and see the president yelling with practised anger about the secret Chinese spy satellite. Apparently, it's not so secret anymore. Everyone in the whole world is talking about it, except China's own citizens, who are kept in the dark by the state-run media.

Despite what Harmony believed, the satellite has no crew. It's just a device the size of an oil drum floating over Ecuador, with cameras pointed at the USA. *Wired* is running pieces about how the satellite was engineered, and how it remained undetected for so long. Fox News is warning viewers to expect a Chinese invasion any day now. *CNN* is focused only on how the president's response will play with voters. John Oliver says he should have known something was up—he points at the sky—when the Chinese companies in his spam folder started trying to sell him Rogaine. The studio audience guffaws.

The Chinese president says there's no satellite. The US president insists there is. After a bit of *is-not, is-too*, things appear to settle down. Apparently the threat of a war is great for getting re-elected, but an actual war is bad for business.

I find a local channel, where 'shocking details have emerged' about the murders at Space City. The whole story seems to have come out—Rob Cho is dead, Franklin Anders killed him, Anders himself was then killed by the CIA. A woman named Huang Jie who appears to have been his MSS handler is holed up in the Chinese embassy. The media have been trying to interview Anders' daughter, but the mom is sensibly keeping her hidden. Even the stuff about Laurie's illegal animal testing has been made public, which is fuelling a debate entirely separate from the satellite stuff.

I expected the CIA to sweep this whole thing under the rug. Soon I discover that they tried, but were prevented. Apparently an FBI investigation has exposed widespread corruption at the CIA, including the torture and murder of US citizens on US soil. It's those last six words—*of US citizens, on US soil*—that seem to be upsetting people. The CIA director is in front of a congressional hearing, getting interrogated by smug assholes. He's widely expected to lose his job, but probably nothing else will change.

I'm just wondering who led this FBI investigation when Reese Thistle appears on the screen, bowing her head to accept a medal from the FBI director.

Her uniform is pressed. Her hair is perfect under her cap. She's not smiling. But I can tell she's proud.

The director says she went above and beyond what was expected of her, which is code for either *She was generally ignored,* or *She was told to stop investigating and she didn't.* Knowing Thistle, probably both are true.

I frantically stab the pause button on the remote, but apparently this isn't the kind of TV that can pause a live feed. Soon Thistle is gone, to be replaced by stock prices.

I lie back on the bed, thinking. There's no reason for the CIA to come after me. Everything I know is now in the public domain, and now they're under much more scrutiny. I'm probably not in any danger from the MSS, either. Their asset at the space centre is dead, and their satellite is exposed. I'm free.

So, what am I going to do with that freedom?

In the past, I've always gone looking for a new boss. Some bigger, scarier monster, who will feed me scraps under the table. It wouldn't be hard to find someone like that in Texas.

But maybe I don't have to live that way. Diaz thought I didn't. She thought I could simply choose to be a better man. It would be as easy, and as difficult, as that.

Then again, I'm pretty sure she changed her mind. I think of the way Diaz looked at me, when she realised that I was really a cannibal. *A purple people eater.*

I stare at the motionless ceiling fan for a while, thinking. Then I go into the bathroom and take a shower. I unwrap a disposable razor and shave—carefully, because the skin is tender. I wash the blood out of my clothes in the sink, then roll them up in a towel and stand on it to dry them out. When that doesn't work, I use a hair dryer, and then press them on an ironing board I found in the closet. I put them back on and comb my hair.

In the harsh glow from above the mirror, I still don't look great. But I look like I'm trying.

I turn out the light as I leave.

CHAPTER 43

In what kind of box would you keep a skull?

Reese Thistle doesn't answer her doorbell. I try knocking, and calling out, but there's no response. I stand on the doorstep of her apartment for a while, holding a bunch of flowers that I stole from other people's front yards and wrapped in foil. It's not a big bunch, but I chose them carefully, only picking the ones with colours and smells I was certain she'd like.

I probably look a bit pathetic. Maybe it's for the best that she's not here to see me. This might not even be her home. Just because she broke up with her husband, that doesn't mean she went back to her old place.

I decide to leave the flowers, and a note. I still have the permanent marker from Anders. I'm just looking for something to write on when a Toyota Corolla pulls into the driveway.

The engine dies and the headlights click off. Thistle gets out of the car, carrying a grocery bag with one hand and her keys with the other. For once, I'm dressed better than her—she's in sweatpants and a hoodie, her hair tied back in a messy ponytail. She's clearly thinking about other things, and doesn't notice me until she's walked halfway to the door.

She freezes mid-step. But doesn't reach for her gun, this time. Progress.

I smile awkwardly. 'Hero cops gotta buy their own groceries?'

She looks at me for a long time, and then says, 'We don't even get a discount.'

I've missed her voice. I find myself savouring every syllable, in case this is our last conversation. 'Congratulations, by the way.'

'I didn't do much.' She comes up onto the porch and puts her bags down. 'Between your voicemail and what you told me at the hospital, you basically solved the case for me.'

I shake my head. 'It's one thing to know what happened. Proving it is much harder. And proving it to the point where the CIA director is forced to explain himself to Congress— that's amazing.'

She looks down, taking in my pressed clothes, and the flowers.

'I'm sorry I thought you were crazy,' she says.

'It's okay.' I smile awkwardly. 'I think I was a bit crazy.'

Thistle rests her butt against the rail surrounding the porch. 'I've never seen a corpse with a missing brain before. Thanks for that.'

'Sorry. It was mostly an accident.'

'I noticed that none of his other body parts were missing.'

'Didn't even occur to me,' I say, honestly. 'Have you ever tried therapy? Turns out it's pretty good.'

'There was a bite on his forearm, though.'

I'd forgotten that. 'Self-defence. I didn't swallow.'

Thistle lets out a snort, and takes out her keys. She approaches the door, which brings her closer to me. I can smell her shampoo.

She sticks her key into the lock, but doesn't turn it. She just looks at me.

I thought about not coming here. She's better off without me. But spending the rest of my days longing for her, and never doing anything about it would feel like throwing my life away. And the last time I tried that, she got dragged into my world anyhow.

So I'm trying something different. I hold out the flowers. She doesn't take them.

'You're probably thinking you can do better,' I say.

Her smile is so slight I might be imagining it. 'That might have occurred to me.'

'Well, you're right,' I say. 'You deserve the best, and I've got some pretty obvious drawbacks. One arm, four fingers and a criminal history.'

Thistle squints at me. 'You also seem to be purple.'

'But I was hoping I could convince you to consider some of my strengths. The less obvious ones.'

She looks amused. 'Go on.'

'One: you already know the worst thing about me. That means no nasty surprises, down the road.'

'Feels like you're just reframing another drawback.'

'Two: I'll never lie to you.'

'Again.'

'Again,' I concede. 'But I've admitted some things that other men would hide. You know about the C-word because I told you, remember.'

Thistle doesn't seem convinced. 'There's that same draw-back again.'

'Three: I'd die for you.'

Her eyebrows go up. 'That's a bit dramatic.'

'Yeah,' I say. 'It's true, though.'

In the past, I thought I was a danger to her. I thought I might lose control and hurt her. So I tried to stay away. And yet, in that chamber, I let Anders suffocate me, rather than risk him coming after Thistle. I'm not a threat to her. I would do anything to keep her safe.

'You don't owe me anything,' I say. 'The opposite, in fact. But if you're willing to give me a chance—'

'Timothy,' she says. It's maybe the only time she's ever used my first name.

I exhale, stick my hand in my pocket. 'Reese.'

'I love you,' she says, and for a second my heart soars. 'God knows why, but I do. The thing is . . . you *eat* people.'

'I'm working on that,' I say, though it's clear I've already lost.

'You get why that's a problem for me?'

I nod sadly. 'It's okay. I understand.'

She gives me a last look. 'Goodbye, Blake.' She turns the key, opens the door, and goes inside.

At least I tried. It would have been much easier to accept that I was a monster, and stay in that hotel room, hating myself. Instead, I gave myself a shot. Diaz would be proud of me.

I look out at the setting sun, wondering where I'll go now, and what I'll do.

Then I realise Thistle hasn't closed the door. When I turn, she's just standing in the hallway, looking at the wall.

'I'm such a headcase,' she mutters. Then she turns back to me. 'Do you want to come in?'

When they arrived at the unfinished house, the Houston PD found it empty. Protruding from one wall was a bloody nail.

ACKNOWLEDGEMENTS

Thanks to Jane Palfreyman, Angela Handley, the marketing, sales and publicity teams, and everyone else at Allen & Unwin for their incredible support of this series. Thanks also to editor-extraordinaire Elizabeth Cowell, whose wide-ranging knowledge made a huge difference, to proof-reader Katri Hilden for the final spit and polish, and to Luke Causby for another delightfully ominous cover.

Thanks to my friends at Curtis Brown Australia, especially Clare Forster and Ben Stevenson. You are old-school literary agents, not just selling manuscripts but also working tirelessly to make them the best that they can be.

Thanks to Dr Deane-Peter Baker, Professor David Kilcullen and Professor Clinton Fernandes of the Future Operations Research Group at UNSW, for a chat about satellites and geopolitics. Thanks to Dr Richard Harris for inventing Dr Laurie's (hypothetical) formula and annotating the chapter in the hypobaric chamber, and to the optometrist I met in a shuttle bus in Tamworth who answered all my questions about ocular prostheses. Mistakes are my own. Thanks to all the other health workers I spoke to, past and present, especially those who treat mental illnesses. I'm more grateful to you than I can say, and not just because of this book. Thanks to my own personal Dr Diaz—you know who you are.

For help with all the spy stuff, thanks to ██████.

Thanks to story wizards Alyssa Sego, Sam McGregor and Venetia Major, who suffered through clunky early drafts and added authenticity to even the most preposterous scenes.

Thanks to all the wonderful booksellers, librarians and reviewers who helped Blake find his audience, and to all the amazing authors who provided cover quotes for this series. It's an honour to have your support.

Thank you to my family, especially Mum, Dad and Venetia (again), for cheering me on while I'm racing deadlines. I couldn't do this without you.

Apologies to the staff at the Johnson Space Center—and occupants of Houston more broadly—for all the times I altered your surroundings to benefit the story. Hope y'all don't mind.

Lastly, thanks to the Hangman fans who've been waiting for this book for two years. Your enthusiasm kept me going. To those who shared their own mental health journeys with me: none of you are as crazy as Blake. If he can heal, we all can. Hang in there.